Praise

JO FURNISS

'A brilliant cop, a highly entertaining story and a smart new take on the "locked room" mystery make for a winning combination. I loved it!'
T.M. LOGAN, AUTHOR OF *THE HOLIDAY*

'Spellbindingly original and utterly compelling. Strap yourselves in . . .
Dead Mile is one hell of a ride!'
JACK JORDAN, AUTHOR OF *DO NO HARM*

'An inventive, gripping take on a locked room mystery'
HARRIET TYCE, AUTHOR OF *BLOOD ORANGE*

'The action is brisk, the characters are vividly drawn, and the plot snakes around the throat. A tense and ingenious "locked-traffic" thriller'
VASEEM KHAN, AUTHOR OF THE MALABAR HOUSE SERIES

'An ingenious, high-octane page-turner with twists and turns worthy of a Formula 1 course. Utterly brilliant'
KATE SIMANTS, AUTHOR OF *FREEZE*

'A gripping, grid-locked masterclass in how to how to ratchet up the tension! I devoured it in one sitting!'
ROBERT RUTHERFORD, AUTHOR OF *SEVEN DAYS*

'A pacy page turner with a twisty plot and a sense of tension that doesn't let up until the final page. Loved it'
NIKKI SMITH, AUTHOR OF *LOOK WHAT YOU MADE ME DO*

'Tense, thrilling and brilliantly written . . . A unique modern murder mystery'
S R MASTERS, AUTHOR OF *THE TRIAL*

'A fabulously pulse-pounding crime thriller, an adrenaline rush and a literary joyride like no other'
CAMERON WARD, AUTHOR OF *A STRANGER ON BOARD*

'A super-smart 21st century reinvention of the classic locked room mystery'
FRANCES QUINN, AUTHOR OF *THE SMALLEST MAN*

'A smart, funny, scorching summer thriller . . . blisteringly original'
EMMA STYLES, AUTHOR OF *NO COUNTRY FOR GIRLS*

'A tightly fitted jigsaw of character, tension, murder and road rage . . . it's full throttle'
RACHAEL BLOK, AUTHOR OF *UNDER THE ICE*

'A brilliant concept . . . a gripping race against time'
JAMES DELARGY, AUTHOR OF *55*

'A total page-turner'
LESLEY THOMSON, AUTHOR OF THE DETECTIVE'S DAUGHTER SERIES

'Smart, original and packed with pace'
LAUREN NORTH, AUTHOR OF *THE PERFECT BETRAYAL*

'Absolutely gripping . . . a fresh take on the classic locked room mystery'
FLISS CHESTER, AUTHOR OF THE CRESSIDA FAWCETT MYSTERIES

Jo Furniss is originally from the UK, but spent much of her adult life overseas, living in Cameroon, Switzerland and Singapore. She's now back home, beside the seaside in England. Her novels include the survival thriller, *All the Little Children*, which was an Amazon Chart bestseller in the UK and US. Jo has contributed short stories to the *Afraid of the Light* anthology series, which was nominated for the CWA Dagger Awards in 2021/22, and raised thousands of pounds for British charities. A former BBC broadcast journalist, Jo also writes for the award-winning *Short History Of* podcast from Noiser Productions. Visit her at JoFurniss.com or follow her on Instagram and Twitter @jofurnissauthor.

Also by Jo Furniss

Dead Mile

GUILT TRIP

JO FURNISS

ZAFFRE

First published in the UK in 2025 by
ZAFFRE
An imprint of Bonnier Books UK
5th Floor, HYLO, 105 Bunhill Row,
London, EC1Y 8LZ

A CIP catalogue record for this book is
available from the British Library.

ISBN: 978-1-80418-390-8

Also available as an ebook and an audiobook

1 3 5 7 9 10 8 6 4 2

Typeset by IDSUK (Data Connection) Ltd
Printed and bound in Great Britain by Clays Ltd, Elcograf S.p.A.

The authorised representative in the EEA is
Bonnier Books UK (Ireland) Limited.
Registered office address: Floor 3, Block 3, Miesian Plaza,
Dublin 2, D02 Y754, Ireland
compliance@bonnierbooks.ie
www.bonnierbooks.co.uk

To Mum and Dad

That Morning

The wheels on the bus went round and round, high in the air, until a weighty crust of mud brought the momentum to an abrupt halt. Above was a flock of leaves. Around was a wake of silence. Below was an earthly reminder of the gravity that had been put to the test. It won. The minibus lay on its side on the forest floor.

The girl too. She rolled her head. The fingers of a yew snagged her hair. She startled awake. Beyond the massive tree, the bus blurred into focus.

Why is it there? Why am I out here? Why is my arm bent that way? Why—

The bus. The money. The man.

Her mind threw open its shutters to a winter morning. The stark return of everything that had happened already that day, everything that'd changed, everything that was still to be decided. She needed to get up, move, find the others, right now, because they needed her help. She inched one foot through the mulch until her leg was straight. Other foot. The left arm, judging by the firework shooting into her shoulder, was going to be a problem.

There was a creak and crash inside the bus.

Someone else moving.

As quickly as the pain flared, it faded. It could still send her into shock. Couldn't afford that, needed to think. *Adrenaline numbs pain, aids survival, fight or flight*, she knew this from her studies. She was going to get the grades to get into medicine to get the life she wanted. *And to get through this day.* But she didn't know how long she had until the pyrotechnics returned. She rolled onto her knees and up onto her feet, cupping the arm across her chest.

The minibus was at the bottom of a deeply gouged bank. She staggered around the vehicle, its underneath slick and complex and filthy, as obscenely fascinating as entrails. A few feet beyond, the windscreen had popped out and lay in one piece. Except it had been shattered by a body that must have followed it out of the vehicle and landed in the centre of the glass. Blood pooled around the figure. It looked unreal . . . it looked dead.

'We need to make sure.' A quiet voice from behind jolted her.

'Can you make sure?' She tapped his arm to encourage him forward. 'Please?'

He ventured onto the glass, slip-sliding on foal legs, but managed to keep his balance in the mess. He took stock, levelled himself, then slammed his right boot into the figure's chin. When the body settled, facing the other way now, he stepped back off the windscreen. He wiped his right boot on the fallen leaves. When that was done, his eyes roamed her face.

'You're pale.'

'My arm hurts.'

Slushy footsteps as another person arrived.

'Where's—?' The voice hitched an octave. 'Oh. My. God.'

Pain radiated from her shoulder up her neck to form a hot halo inside her skull.

The newcomer pointed at the windscreen. 'Are we sure they're—?'

'Oh, yeah,' said the boy. 'We're sure now.'

Chapter One

3.00 p.m.

The signage outside Saints College is scarlet and gold. The colours of royalty, danger, theatre curtains. It says 'Welcome to England's Most Aspirational School™'.

A note on the gate says the car park is full, but I manage to find a space in a narrow side street and trot back up the hill to the college. Its façade is red brick with scales of ivy. Two hundred years old and in better nick than me, it was washed clean by this morning's rain, while my trainers are mucky from a HIIT class in the park where my mascara dissolved in the downpour alongside my third client. I've thrown on a pale overcoat that's supposed to pull any ensemble together with Nordic style. The stark winter light reveals bobbles that have grown under its armpits like woolly skin tags. I have my gear in a tote that Olivia calls my Mary Poppins bag. Magically bottomless. I find myself humming the tune to 'Head, Shoulders, Knees and Toes', except in my head I hear 'Mace, Glasses, Keys and Phone'. (Keys and Phone.) A habit from the baby years, when I thought it would stop me losing my mind. Or at least my keys.

I wait for a bus to hiss past and cross the road towards the gatehouse. I'm late. Three missed calls, two from school and one from my friend Mariah, and a text saying there's an urgent meeting in the Great Hall. It's just gone three o'clock on a Monday afternoon. Don't they understand that parents have jobs and can't come in at the drop of a hat? I press the bell and a porter peers through the diamonds of a leaded window.

My sweaty hair is hidden under a beanie with the school crest embroidered on the front. I should get brownie points for that. Or be dismissed as a try-hard. It's difficult to know with the Saints crowd. The hat cost twenty quid, Olivia turned her nose up at it, so now I wear the thing for work.

The gate buzzes and I enter another world. Every time I come to the school, literally every single time, I think of Charlie Bucket entering the chocolate factory.

It's eerily quiet as I set off towards the Great Hall. Everyone is in lessons, no skivers or smokers in secluded corners, not like my old school. Here, there's a highbrow hush.

Olivia won a Golden Ticket to Saints when she was thirteen by passing the entrance test with the highest score. She earned her place. Then she proved herself by getting some of the best GCSE results in the country and now has a shot at getting the A-levels required to study medicine. But I bet any staff peeping out of these mullioned windows wish they could set exams to select parents too. I'm a mess. The gravel sticks to my muddy trainers and I etch a jagged line along their flagstone path.

I scratch my way past Mariah's Tesla. The parents who responded more quickly to the text from school got visitors' parking spaces inside the college walls. How do they do it, these people? Is it natural selection; they've evolved to the demands of this unique environment? Or does privilege buy you extra hours in the day?

I pass a school minibus.

The Saints fleet is painted up to advertise the school everywhere it goes with a gleaming scarlet and gold livery, which displays a nostalgia for the traditional days when boys were boys and Saints was all theirs. Now girls like Olivia are admitted to push up the grade average. The minibus reminds me that I haven't checked online for her results in the swim trial. She was hoping for a personal best today.

The Great Hall is the size of a provincial cathedral. Studded wooden doors under a stone arch. It's as chilly as a church inside too. And as hallowed. I resist running my fingers along the keys of a grand piano that stands in prime position inside the door. There are a few parents scattered over chairs pressed up against the walls. Why is there only a handful of us here? No one can quite keep still. Knees are jigging. No eye contact. Like an AA meeting.

For the first time, my stomach squirms.

Saints is infamous for chucking out their undesirables; pupils who flunk exams or do something embarrassing on social media or display their failure to cope with intense academic pressure by developing a habit that might reflect badly on the school – vaping, cutting, starving. Drugs, of course, loads of drugs. Anyone rocking the yacht gets thrown overboard. I've heard anxious mums describe this school as the 'Squid Game' of education. They live in fear of a tap on the shoulder. The one that says the headmaster no longer requires the services of your underperforming kid.

But surely they don't do 'the tap' like this?

And surely not Olivia? She keeps her grades up and her head down—

'Emily, my days!' It's Mariah Haven, my closest friend in this place. She crosses the hall like a bowling ball. The parquet thrums beneath her. Her lime-green designer sportswear freshens up the stuffy atmosphere even though she rarely moves fast enough to break a sweat. Mariah is way taller than me with the magnificent rump of a racehorse, fake tan the colour of a two-pence piece, Brazilian blow-out and makeup that gives her the air of a drag queen. She envelops me in a hug, which I need right now, and her perfume tickles my nose like a feather boa. She pulls back and pouts. 'I got new lips.'

'They're gorgeous!'

They're awful. And look so painful.

'What the eff is going on?' she says. 'Why are we here?'

'The messages didn't say. Have you heard from Dixie?'

'Not since drop-off.'

'Nothing from Olivia either.'

Our girls are best friends.

'Have you seen? *She's* over there.' Mariah bobs her head at a tidy woman wrapped around her phone in the corner. Heeled court shoes, pencil skirt and a roll-neck jumper in plum cashmere. Sleeveless to show off lightly muscled arms. She turns her back to us, revealing that she does squats. Wherever does she find the time? She's our local MP. A junior minister. Ayesha Reid.

'And who's he?' Mariah nods the other way. Standing off to one side, a big guy in a chic navy coat buttoned to his throat, the collar up to show a flash of vibrant silk lining.

'That's Akin Abiola,' I say. 'Temi's dad?'

'What's he do, then? Looks expensive.'

'Doctor. Consultant. Him and his wife are both anaesthetists. She's in London most of the time, only does private practice. Harley Street.'

'You know all the goss.' Mariah tucks her arm in mine.

I do. It's my capital.

'She's the Botswana one.'

'Oh, her!' says Mariah. Then after a moment's contemplation. 'Fuck her.'

A reasonable response. Right before Christmas, Shona Abiola posted a picture on Facebook of herself on the red carpet at a charity fundraising dinner at Soho House. She'd just bought a safari in Botswana at the silent auction. I looked it up afterwards, the trip costs £25,000. Before flights. A salary. And her humble brag caption: Oops, tipsy late-night purchase! Looks like we're going to Botswana, then!! *Laugh-until-you-cry-emoji.*

Envy is ugly. But so is being a massive show-off. So . . .

Mariah and I took against her.

Akin looks our way as though he knows we're talking about his wife. I hold his eye and give him a sympathetic smile, which he returns and looks away.

I think we got away with it.

Then I realise something; everyone's kids are on the swim team. There are too many parents here for it to be 'the tap', but not enough for it to be nothing. It must be to do with the trip. When were they due back? My stomach stops squirming and starts doing a hollow falling thing.

'Ladies!' A good-looking blond with a neck like Popeye inserts himself between us and I step aside to make room for him. He plants his hand on the small of Mariah's back and kisses her bronzed cheek.

'New lips!' he says.

'They'll go down in a bit,' she says but seems pleased.

'Any idea why we're here?' He turns to me and holds out a hand. 'I'm Jack Kent.'

I smile, reacting to social cues on autopilot.

'Good to meet you,' he says as his eyes drift over my shoulder.

Maybe it's the tension in the room but a flare of irritation takes me by surprise. I don't need to be compliant. Don't have to people please. I've driven his son to and from parties, swim meets, fairs, back and forth to his McMansion on the seafront. And I'm old, not invisible. I've often said I should've been a spy, I'm that unremarkable. Being forgettable is my superpower, but that doesn't mean I like it.

'We've met. Quite a few times.' My voice stays light. 'I'm Olivia's mum, Emily. Alix has been to my house?'

'That's what I meant.' He waves the slight away. 'You look so well, Em!'

No one calls me Em. And I don't look well, I look like a cat dunked in a puddle. He's pointedly paying attention to me now, hand on the small of *my* back, but I turn away. A door at the side of the hall opens and the headmaster comes in.

He looks troubled. He has a clipboard.

Dr Sam Maunder.

'Thanks for coming at short notice,' he says to the clipboard.

The kids call him Salamander.

Because his eyes are too wide and too wet.

The kids say he can swivel them independently.

I try to focus, but my stomach keeps dropping and I don't know where it's going to stop.

It's like being back at school. I never could concentrate.

'As you know,' says Maunder, 'your children attended a swim meet this morning.'

He grips the clipboard with his hands at ten and two like it's a steering wheel. He's always been decent to me. Pushed through a 110 per cent bursary so we could afford books and uniforms and what have you. Now, though, he takes too long to get to the point and I find myself cursing him.

'What's going on, Sammy?' Jack cuts to the chase.

'Is my son okay?' Ayesha the MP is off the phone.

'Oh my God, has there been an accident?' Mariah. I grab her hand and she squeezes.

'Which hospital?' Akin's hand hovers over the phone in his pocket like a gunslinger.

'There's not been an accident.' Maunder holds up a palm. 'As far as we know.'

'What does that mean?' says Ayesha.

'We don't know where they are at the moment. They're unaccounted for.'

Silence.

'We're working on the assumption that the minibus has gone somewhere,' he says.

'Of course it's gone somewhere,' says Ayesha with a quiet menace that reminds me that she must discuss matters of state with the prime minister. 'It's a minibus.'

'I mean it's gone somewhere unauthorised.'

Where?

Is it lost?

What do you mean?

Everyone talks at once.

When Salamander finally gets a word in edgeways, and confirms what it is that he knows, my stomach goes into free fall.

Chapter Two

That morning, 7.45 a.m.

Olivia spooned the white jellyfish bell off the top of her boiled egg. She dabbed it into a pile of salt and popped it in her mouth, while thinking, *swimming kit, homework, banking app*.

Her mum came in holding aloft a drawstring bag. 'Forget something?'

Olivia had left the swimming kit in the hallway precisely so that she didn't forget it.

'Got your homework?' Emily nagged. 'You're going to be late for Mariah.'

Her mother projected her own chaos onto others. Didn't notice that her daughter was together. She said she was proud of her but acted . . . *not proud*. In Emily-world the sky was always falling. Chicken Little. Olivia took her dirty plate to the sink, then filled her water bottle, considering an opening gambit to an awkward conversation.

'Mum?'

'Yes, love?' said Emily. 'Can you get me some water too?'

Under Olivia's stockinged feet, the plywood was raw and pockmarked by lumps of dried plaster. She reached for another bottle. Kitchen cupboards with no doors made it easy to access the contents. That was the positive side. On the negative side, bare bulbs lolled from tangles of cable falling from the ceiling.

'Do you think we could tidy up before my birthday party?' Olivia asked.

Emily looked around the kitchen with her mouth open.

'But this is the latest style. Bombsite chic. It's in all the magazines.'

'Mum. It's been a year since—'

'I know. I keep meaning to find the time.'

That meant she needed to find the money. Olivia had peeped at her account via their shared banking app. A year earlier, Emily received an invoice from their builder late one night and made a transfer for the final instalment of the kitchen renovation. It had been a scam. The address had one letter different to the real builder's email. Her savings disappeared into an untraceable account. The bank and the police couldn't help – she'd made the transfer of her own free will. The builder was sorry, but said it wasn't his fault (it actually wasn't) and without further payment for materials, his blokes downed tools. Since then, Olivia and her mum had lived in this world of plywood. At least the heating and electrics worked.

Emily came up behind Olivia and cinched her waist.

'I'm sorry,' her mum said.

A spark of guilt ignited anger.

'That's too tight, I feel sick.' Olivia wriggled free to brush her teeth in the tannin-stained sink, as she'd done since she was in Reception to speed up their morning routine, while her mum asked loads of questions about how long she'd been feeling sick, and she had to say she'd felt bad all night to cover up the fact she just hadn't wanted her mum to cling on to her.

'The girls won't judge, you know,' Mum said. 'It's good for them to see real life.'

Olivia spoke through toothpaste. 'Maybe I don't want to be their pet povvo.'

'Oh, please!' said Emily. Now she felt guilty and annoyed. 'We have more than most.'

Olivia spat into the plughole.

'Have you seen their houses? Dixie has a shed bigger than our entire downstairs.'

'Dixie's dad is a property developer and owns half the town. Plus he's never home.'

I guess the positive side of not having a dad is that I don't feel bad that he's never home . . .

Her mum bent to tie her trainers. It was January and she'd spend most of the day in the park, squatting alongside clients in rain that was right now defying gravity to run horizontally across the window. Even the cat was balled on top of the fridge, having none of it.

Olivia rinsed her mouth and swallowed minty water.

'What if we decorate?' her mum said. 'Put up fairy lights?'

She resisted an eye roll. 'It's just a bit embarrassing because it looked like this last year as well.'

Her mother said nothing, but flipped her torso upright in a gymnastic movement, taut with control. Her hair needed a wash. Olivia felt like a bitch. More guilt. More anger.

'You put me in that school,' she said.

'And?' her mum fired back. 'You're outrunning the lot of them. You get A-stars, you're through to the regional swim trials, and the final of that science fair. This school claims to be the best of the best, and you're the best there, so you're the best of the best of the best. The others pay to go, but you're so good they pay you—'

'Mum—'

'You're like an influencer who gets freebies, only for you it's a place at the Aspirational School of the Year, School of the Millennium, School of Forever and Ever Amen, whatever they call it now—'

'Take a breather, Mum . . .' But the anger drained away like the rain gurgling down the gutter. The school *was* lucky to have her. She worked hard and didn't get into trouble. Didn't even vape. She was killing it right now.

'I need a pound for the swimming locker,' she said.

Emily went into a flap, hammering upstairs two at a time.

'Maybe we should go out for my birthday instead?' Olivia called after her.

'Pizza Express?'

For Dixie's birthday, they'd gone to the Ivy.

Olivia grabbed her phone and opened their shared banking app.

There was a new sushi place. Cheaper than the Ivy, but definitely more than pizza.

She held up the screen to let it recognise her face. Then navigated to her personal account called Olivia Smith Piggy Bank. Checked her balance – got a tingle in her tum at the sight of all those noughts – and hit the 'payment' button. She tapped in £250, selected transfer to Emily Smith Family Pot, and hesitated over the reference . . .

Where could she say this money came from?

Her mum started down the stairs. Olivia typed 'Bursary Honorarium' and hit 'send'. Her phone buzzed a confirmation. On the counter, her mum's phone buzzed too, but Olivia hit the screen and swiped the notification away.

Emily came in brandishing a euro. Triumphant. She assured Olivia it would pass for a pound coin in a locker. Her mum looked girlish when her cheeks flushed. The impression was fleeting and oddly melancholy, like the moving photos of old, dead people in *Harry Potter*. There but not there. She wondered if our younger selves are trapped inside us like Russian dolls. Or hostages. Olivia pocketed the euro and then, casually, showed her mum the account balance of the Family Pot. Emily glanced at the screen and nodded at the headline figure.

'In credit at the end of the month. That's new.'

She didn't even notice the Bursary Honorarium transfer.

'What about that new sushi place for my birthday?' Olivia asked.

So it was decided.

A car horn beeped in the street outside.

Olivia grabbed her backpack and swimming bag, hunched up her shoulders when her mum hugged her too tight. Outside, rain shot down her neck until she ducked under the gull-wing door of Mariah's Tesla. In the hug of heated seats, she planned with Dixie what to wear for her birthday party.

Chapter Three

3.15 p.m.

In the Great Hall, parents stagger around on sea legs. A few minutes ago, the headmaster realised he'd forgotten his phone and ran to get it. His exit leaves us adrift. Everyone immediately calls their children's mobiles, but with no joy. No answers. Mariah mutters darkly about the 'no-phones-in-school' policy that she hates even at the best of times. For once, I agree. I keep trying Olivia's number, hoping that maybe for once in her life she's rebelled and kept her phone in her bag. The ringtone echoes through my insides. Again and again, I hear Olivia's answerphone message – unfamiliar because we always use WhatsApp. We only call if it's urgent. We always pick up.

You know what to do after the beep, she says.

But I don't, so I hang up. Stress caffeinates my veins. I want to run, but where to? Outside, a weak sun appears, too bright and too late, throwing light into the hall through the massive arched windows. It reminds me of the brave smiles Olivia used to summon up after crying. The stained glass projects a pearlescent angel onto the wall. I hold my hand in the rainbow and do this trick I know, making and releasing a fist, until my energy settles into something more useful than panic. Slowly, I tune back to my surroundings.

Five parents of five missing children. We should be in this together.

But it rarely goes that way.

'How long have they been missing?' Akin Abiola is saying. He hasn't taken off his wool coat. His hand cups his throat, long fingers stroking the silk of his collar; it's yellow, the colour of sunshine, butter, cowardice. 'They were due back for lunch, so it's a couple of hours already?' His eyes slide over mine and around the group.

'Two hours isn't so long,' says Jack Kent. 'They're not babies. When I was a boy, I'd stay out all day and my mother didn't have the foggiest what I was up to. Could've been on the railway line.'

Akin winces but I don't know if it's the thought of kids on the railway line or the fact that Jack allegedly doesn't know what his kid gets up to now any more than his mother did back then – that's according to the leisurely mums who gather for breakfast in Dough, the world's most expensive café, just down the road. Some of them come straight from there to my late-morning HIIT class. Gossip on their coffee breath.

I want to discuss the situation with Mariah but she's across the hall by the window where the signal is stronger. Mariah normally speaks into her phone with it held flat in front of her mouth like a taser, her conversation blasting out for all to hear. But now she's got it pressed to her ear, clamped around the device with her back to the room. She's on the phone to her husband, Kash. He goes by a nickname from their school days; Kash is short for Keith Ashworth. They've been together since they were sixteen. Mariah's husband does not look like a 'Keith'. And he has a lot of cash, so . . .

She calls Kash her 'does-band' because he does everything, not just the bins. He's a significant presence. But right now it would be better if she talked to me instead. I'm here and he isn't. The sign of a good friend isn't whether you can lean on them, but whether they lean on you. But, of course, at times of stress, everyone focuses on their own. Today might turn into a 'blood is thicker' situation. I look at Akin, to see if he's calling his wife, but he's staring at the door.

'Where is Sam Maunder?' he says to no one in particular.

Jack doesn't reply even though he's standing right there. He doesn't seem to have called his wife either. I know there is one, flitting about in the background with fairy-blonde hair and eccentric clothes cut to be as least flattering as possible. Starchy trousers with the crotch by her knees, dresses with geometric folds, straitjacket-style canvas shirts. I imagine they're extremely expensive as only rich people buy clothes that actively make them look worse. It's a power play, I think. *I don't have to try hard.* What is her name? Something Shakespearean, like Cordelia, but not that. I've seen it on the year group WhatsApp. Thinking about it, I can't recall ever speaking to her in real life.

It's not Cecilia . . . not Cornelia. It'll come if I stop thinking about it.

Ayesha marches across the hall and joins the men. 'Google Maps says it's thirty-two minutes door to door,' she says. 'The traffic is fine so they should be here.' She goes into a prima donna rant about how she should have been alerted in a timely fashion about this incident. I suspect that the wrong juice on the breakfast table would be an incident for Ayesha.

Her self-importance is grating but she's not wrong. A lot can go wrong in a couple of hours.

Calpurnia. Jack's wife. What a name.

I think she goes by Cally, but it comes up as Calpurnia Kent on my phone.

I wonder why she's not here. Is that significant?

Ayesha Reid is very much present. She holds the room, which is no surprise. She's a chameleon. Imperious on Radio 4, relatable on *Woman's Hour*, witty on *Have I Got News for You*. Barely forty and tipped for PM, if she gets through this election cycle unscathed.

My phone pings with a WhatsApp message.

Think she gets police protection?

I catch her eye across the room and do a little head shake. Mariah frowns like, why not?

She's only a junior minister

So would she have security?

Not senior enough

and she would have said

Mariah nods and speaks into her phone for a bit.

Akin and Jack launch into a debate about whether phones should be allowed in school. I zone out. It's an important topic but stale as Brexit and I just can't discuss it again. Plus, my head is jostling with random thoughts, I barely finish one before another arrives. I don't usually spend this long cooped up indoors—

My phone pings, a welcome distraction from myself.

What party is she?

        She's your local MP

And?

           Labour!

Across the room, I see her shrug.

Got a face like a Tory

Mariah texts the joke with a deadpan expression and then stares unblinkingly at the MP. I can't work out if it's her new Botox or if she's trying not to cry. She's compulsively fiddling with a lime-green fluffy keyring that she tugs through her fist like she's wringing its neck. I've never seen her rattled. She presents as so confident that other people don't see her vulnerability. Like me, she wasn't born to all this. Just because you've earned it, doesn't mean you feel worth it. I cross the hall to reach her, passing Ayesha, Akin and Jack, knotted together into a clique.

'How you holding up?' I ask Mariah.

'Even if she doesn't have close protection, surely the security services will pull out the stops for her boy? Bloody Rees-Mogg.'

Despite my tension – or perhaps because of it – I give a cough of gallows humour. Rees-Mogg is what she calls Ayesha Reid's son. The boy is uncommonly tall, thin and chinless. Like an alpaca in a suit. To add to his nerdy reputation, he's excused by his mother from any sports where her precious darling might get injured. They say he's only on the swim squad because he can spend most of the time underwater.

Mariah zones out again. She looks bleakly into the middle distance. I squeeze her shoulder and she comes round and shoots me a half-smile.

I recognise her reaction: cynicism, snarkiness, shutdown. It's a coping mechanism.

We all jerk round as the headmaster re-enters the hall. Everyone takes half a step towards him, shoulders snap back. We're ready. He looks more amphibian than ever, as though his skin would be wet to the touch.

Maunder apologises for the delay but he had to take a call while he was in his office. The school governors required an update.

Before us, the parents? I don't say this aloud, but I can see other people thinking it too.

Of course, it is Ayesha who rounds on him.

'What have you been doing while this bus has been missing?' she asks.

Jack chips in, 'Can't you call the driver, Sammy?'

'That was the first thing I did, *Jack*,' he says. 'Both phones go to voicemail.'

There's tension between them. This 'Sammy and Jack' business. I know they both went to Saints as boys. Must have been around the same age. But I'm guessing they weren't best mates.

Mariah asks, 'Couldn't they be running late? Broken down . . .'

'The driver would have called by now—'

Jack: 'Not if his phone was out of battery.'

'There's a charger on every bus. We know they left the venue on time, but we've heard nothing since. Maybe you could keep trying your children's phones? As you know, we collect devices and lock them in a box for the duration of the trip, but sometimes kids hand over a dummy phone in order to keep their real mobile. For once, I'd be willing to forego a detention if one of them answers and lets us know where they are . . .' His attempt at lightheartedness lands like a cowpat.

Mariah says, 'I've never understood why you can't let them use their bloody phones on the bus. It's what phones are for.'

Ayesha: 'I'm not sure now's the time to debate policy—'

Mariah turns on her. 'Is your security onto it?'

Maunder says, 'I don't know that it is necessary to report it just yet.'

A beat.

Ayesha: 'Are you telling me you haven't called the police?'

All the parents react.

They could be trapped in wreckage.

They could be in the back of a van.

They could have run out of petrol.

Some pervert could be halfway to his basement.

Doesn't the bus have a radio?

Doesn't the bus have a tracker?

Doesn't the school have a responsibility—?

'I'm calling the police,' says Akin. 'Tell me the number plate of the minibus.'

He seems very competent and this settles everyone.

'I'll do it,' says the headmaster. 'I was going to do it as soon as you'd been informed.'

'Right,' says Jack with leaden sarcasm.

Maunder turns to go but Ayesha holds out a hand to stop him. 'I have a tracker in Kiran's backpack.'

Of course she does.

'I can log onto it . . .' She taps her phone. 'Oh, the app needs an update.'

Every other human being on the planet would jab the screen in a vain attempt to hurry it up, but her face is impassive as she waits, robotic.

'Hang on,' says Mariah, 'weren't there two buses going to the swim meet? I saw them when I dropped the girls off.'

Maunder nods. 'The bus with the younger ones got back to school safe and sound. Those kids have gone home.'

'But they're our only witnesses,' I say.

All heads snap round, as though they've spotted a mouse. It's the first thing I've said to the group so far.

'They've got exams tomorrow, Mrs Smith,' says Maunder.

And that's more important?

I say, 'It's Ms Smith.'

Ayesha narrows her eyes. 'What did the other driver say?'

'Everything was normal when they left. He doesn't know any more than we do.'

Her phone beeps. 'The tracker shows the bag here, on site? Maybe they just got back?'

There's a ripple of relief.

But the headmaster marches across the hall: 'Some bags ended up on the second bus. And the box with the students' confiscated mobiles . . .' He opens a door to reveal the corridor outside. A pile of backpacks is slumped in the hallway. 'Is it one of these?'

Ayesha makes a beeline for a grey rucksack that doesn't appear to have pockets, zips or handles. It looks fit for a Scandinavian astronaut. She rifles through its folds. Then sits heavily onto a chair and holds out her palm to show a black button. 'The tracker.' She holds up the other palm to show a white cigar-shaped object. 'And Kiran's EpiPen. I will sue this school to kingdom come if he has an allergic reaction now.'

Chapter Four

7.59 a.m.

Olivia hunkered down in the back seat of Dixie's mum's Tesla as they idled at the gate to the school. It took an age to open. She tried to look in the wing mirror but it was at the wrong angle. The rain on the glass only pixelated her face.

'What you doing?' asked Dixie. 'What you looking at?'

Olivia grimaced to shut her up. Didn't want Dixie's mum to overhear. Although Mariah was staring from her window, lost in thought, or rapt by the rain-silvered street where kids hunched under backpacks scootered along the pavement like so many snails.

On the far side of the road, a skinny lad in a white Stüssy hoodie had his hands deep in his pockets, shoulders about his ears, stock-still, soaked and staring.

'Is that him?' Dixie spun the pearls on her Vivienne Westwood necklace. 'He's quite fit.'

A city bus stopped in the traffic, blocking their view.

'I wasn't looking,' Olivia said. She licked her lips.

The bus moved on and the lad in the hoodie was gone.

The gate finally clanked against the wall and the Tesla whirred into the school.

Mariah dropped them at the front door of their House to save them from the rain.

Then she whirred away to do whatever she did with her day.

'Olivia! Dixie!' They turned in response to the distinctive Kiwi accent of their sports master, Mr Sadler. 'We're going straight to the swim gala now, the traffic is bad in this weather and it's going to take longer. You don't need to go to registration, just get on the bus.'

'Can I go to the loo, sir?' asked Dixie.

'Quickly, then!' He bustled off.

Dixie ran into the House, but Olivia scuttled over to the mini-buses that were parked in the shelter of an overhang. Younger kids were tramping onto the first one, so she bundled her two bags through the door of the second bus then stepped back to shake the rain out of her hair before getting on board.

Annoyingly, Kiran Reid had already occupied the back seat so his lanky legs could stretch down the aisle. His space-age backpack claimed the seat in front. It yawned open with folders. He'd taken off his suit jacket and hung it from a hook by the window. Only Kiran would find the coat hook on a school minibus. Busy flicking through index cards, he didn't look up.

Alix Kent loped across the quad. Even in sports kit, he carried himself like a man in a tuxedo, with languid bow-tie loosened, top-button popped, end-of-the-night energy. He saluted Olivia and the bus creaked as he leapt aboard. 'Move,' Alix barked at Kiran. The rucksack was hastily lifted out of Alix's favoured seat. He was in the rugby first XV, which gave him the authority of a teacher. More, probably.

Olivia lingered outside even though the wind sharpened the rain into needles. She watched a pigeon flap from gable to gable to gable. She pulled out her phone—

'Devices in the lock-box, please,' said Mr Sadler as he clambered on board the back of the minibus holding the metal security box that they used to lock up phones on any trip.

'Can I send my mum a text to say we're leaving early?' Olivia wheedled.

'Quickly, then,' said Sadler and moved down the aisle to gather the boys' devices.

Olivia went to her banking app. Something niggled. She clicked the balance of her Olivia Smith Piggy Bank account. Her stomach swooped. Her balance was 49p. She refreshed the page. The same. But how? She checked the amount she had transferred to her mum's account earlier – £250, as she thought – not enough to drain her account.

Not a thousand pounds.

'Phone, please.' The teacher emerged and the lock-box clanked as he jumped down from the bus. 'We need to get going.'

'Dixie isn't even here yet,' Olivia snapped.

'Olivia . . .' he warned in a new tone of voice.

'Sorry, sir.'

Dixie appeared and bounced up to them. 'You okay, Liv? You look like you received a dick pic from someone's grandad.'

'Dixie,' Mr Sadler said. 'Bad taste!'

'She does, though, sir. Look, she's stone grey.'

Olivia managed to say that she didn't feel well, she felt nauseous.

Mr Sadler looked up to the heavens and let rain spit in his face for a second, then placed his hands together in a prayer prose. 'Olivia, it's the regionals . . .'

'I might vomit,' she said.

'I'm not going on a bus with someone who might blow,' called out Alix.

'Shut up, Kent,' said Dixie. 'She was fine a minute ago.'

The teacher dithered.

'Let me take a walk,' Olivia said. 'Get some fresh air.'

She set off across the quad, hearing Mr Sadler moan that they were already in the fresh air. She drew level with the gateway from where she could see onto the street. A bus passed. There was no one there, no one waiting or watching. No lad in a Stüssy hoodie.

Olivia leant over a flower bed. Her whole body spiked hot, and her mouth filled with saliva. She opened it wide but nothing came, no vomit, no words, no scream.

A hand tapped her briskly between the shoulder blades.

'You alright, mate?' Temi Abiola, Saints' butterfly champion and rugby captain. Neither of which was for the faint-hearted. Olivia stood up. Temi looked like he'd swallowed a light bulb. Universally liked, although not close to anyone in particular, he'd probably grow up to be a diplomat. Or archbishop. Or a medic like both of his parents. He had a Yoda air, like he'd already seen what was going to happen.

'D'you want my water bottle?' Temi held it out to Olivia. 'Or I can take you to the infirmary?'

She had no doubt that he'd throw her over his shoulder and carry her there, if need be. But she shook her head.

'I feel a bit better now. I need to get on the bus.'

'You don't have to if you're sick—'

'She bloody does.' Mr Sadler joined them. 'It's the regionals. It's what we've been training for all year.'

'But, sir . . .' said Temi.

Olivia patted his arm to say *it's okay*. Mr Sadler was decent, one of the cooler teachers, which wasn't saying much . . . He was ultra fit, an almost-Olympic swimmer in his youth, but remarkably un-bitter about an injury that had ended his career. Olivia wondered if it came as a relief to stop having to live up to all that potential. He swam the English Channel every year for charity and that seemed to be enough.

'I have sick bags,' he said. 'If you sit in the front with the cold blower in your face, you'll feel better.'

Maybe he did want a little glory. She was his best chance to reach the nationals today.

Dixie ran across the quad, high-stepping onto the crackly grass as though that would make a difference to how wet her shoes got. 'What Mr Sadler is *saying* is that we need you in that pool or we're going to crash out of a competition which he's worked his tits off for.'

'I'm not saying that at all,' said Mr Sadler. 'Don't make me give you a demerit, Dixie, because then I'll have to deal with your terrifying mother phoning up to complain. But also, yeah, can we get on the bus? If you want to throw up, I'll stop, I promise. But look, your colour is back, you look fine.'

Olivia was already swimming. Inside her own head.

A thousand pounds.

She floated over to the bus.

Mr Sadler added her phone to the metal box and locked it with a key that hung on the minibus fob.

Dixie thumped on board.

Temi sat on the opposite side from her.

Mr Sadler scampered around the bonnet, giving it a triumphant double tap.

Olivia hung in the doorway.

She couldn't do it, couldn't make her legs move—

'Get your butt on the bus,' Dixie bellowed.

Olivia did as she was told.

Chapter Five

3.25 p.m.

Olivia needn't have been on that bus. She felt sick this morning; I should have kept her home. Of course I didn't, I couldn't. I have work, she has work. *Stupid work.*

I wonder if any parent thinks about the important things before it's too late.

Although some of these parents actually do important things. Akin removes his coat to reveal green surgical scrubs with a V-necked cashmere jumper over the top. There is a spatter of blood in the shape of prayer beads on his thigh. Straight from the hospital.

Someone has cranked up the heating in the Great Hall because there's a burning smell of radiator dust. Do they think we're going to be here for a while? That's concerning. Perhaps Akin is wearing the jumper because there's even more blood on his top.

He takes the lead on contacting local hospitals between here and the venue. He has a Rolodex memory of hospital registrars and A&E contacts who can cut through red tape.

Ayesha is on the phone too, getting legal advice by the sounds of it, probably about the EpiPen. But then her device rings and she jabs the screen to answer the incoming call. She murmurs the name of the prime minister. I look at Mariah to see if she clocked it too; the MP's under-her-breath, intimate tone. But

Mariah is miles away, pulling her pillowy bottom lip with her talons. I'm worried she's going to pop it.

Ayesha turns her back on us and I can't hear her conversation until she raises her voice to say, 'This is my son we're talking about!' and darts a glance over her shoulder to check who's listening.

Her outburst stills the room.

Then everyone carries on as though it never happened.

Ayesha's rise and fall of emotion reflects how we're all feeling. And yet no one makes a move to console her. We're trapped together but alone with our fears. It's every man – or parent – for themselves.

They all have wealth or privilege or influence to throw at this problem. Powerful people disempowered. That's dangerous. They'll do whatever it takes to protect their own. But so will I. I just have to be cleverer. That's what Olivia does every day in this place.

The others have hung their coats on a line of hooks by the door but I take off my overcoat, fold it inside out so it doesn't get dirty, and lay it over a chair to claim a little territory. Off to the side where I can survey the hall.

It bothers me that I haven't worked out yet who is our leader.

One always emerges. It should be the headmaster, Dr Maunder, but he's pissed everyone off by not raising the alarm sooner. It won't be me. Ayesha is an obvious candidate, but she's in her own world right now. Mariah wouldn't want it; her lime-green outfit is a plea not to be taken seriously. Akin might step up but his job as anaesthetist suggests he's not motivated by glory, otherwise he'd be a surgeon. And God help us if it's Jack bloody Kent.

He acts like he owns the place because he went to Saints himself, but the man is a bona fide tit. Even now, with his kid missing, he's taken off to the far side of the room and seems to be filming himself on his phone. He's an influencer. Turned a fast buck in the dot-com era, retired at thirty, and now posts videos of himself doing survival challenges to get the attention he craves. Must have been handsome once and can't let it go. In harsh lighting, you can see scars behind his ears like silver slug trails.

The mums who meet in the Dough café refer to him as Daddy Cool because at the end of last term he let the kids have a party that got out of hand and left one girl with more lasting effects than a hangover . . . The Dough mums don't fight tooth and nail to clear every obstacle out of their kids' paths to glory, only to have them go off-piste and snort God-knows-what in some idiot's kitchen. Rumour has it one of the mums reported Daddy Cool to the school and they alerted social services to the shenanigans at the McMansion.

Apart from that, Jack Kent is great.

I want to ask Mariah if she thinks Daddy Cool could have anything to do with the minibus, but she's gone. So I text her.

Where you?

. . . then comes her instant reply

I need a fucking Earl Grey

I set off in search of tea. Out through the side door that Maunder used and into the guts of the school. They're big on bold, uplifting colours, like a fairground fun house. I'm sure there's a waiting room with a machine around here somewhere. I follow a corridor lined with self-portraits by a younger year. A class of Mr Potato Heads. Olivia always loved art, but had to drop it to focus on the subjects for medicine. When she was tiny, she drew a picture of a skinny house with a roof and door, but also eyes and arms. Scribbly things swarming all around. Bats, she explained. And, *It's not a house, Mummy, it's you.* But why so many bats? What did they want with us? Did the bats mean she was scared? Or was I protecting her from these bats? So many unanswered questions.

Mariah steps out of a bathroom and I almost walk into her arms.

'Sometimes I think I've done it all wrong,' I say.

Mariah hears tears in my voice and fixes me with a look. 'You silly moo, they're going to be fine.'

'I don't just mean today. This school . . . She's only seventeen and she's always working. When does she lie on the grass and look at the clouds? Hang out at the beach ogling life-guards? Or sing pop songs while reading the lyrics off the album cover?'

'Don't have album covers no more,' Mariah says. 'And anyway, do you want her to have the same choices you had?'

'No, I want her to have all the options in the world—'

'And that's why we got our kids in here. We're giving them opportunities we never had. If you get dealt a trump card, don't waste it, you gotta play it. Me and Kash came into money, you got a bursary, so now our kids are in the game. That's democracy. And our girls are going to be alright.' She gives me a hard hug. 'I can feel it in my bones.'

We approach the imposing door of the headmaster's office. It's open and Maunder is inside. I take a glimpse – he's kneeling in front of a low cupboard – and we keep moving past.

'What was he doing?' Mariah whispers. 'Shoving stuff inside a cupboard?'

'Maybe that's where he keeps the bodies,' I say, and immediately regret it. Why do I think these things?

'Too dark,' mutters Mariah.

We find the waiting room. There's coffee and Earl Grey.

'Shall we make a round for everyone?' I ask.

'They won't respect you if you start waiting on them.' Mariah folds her arms.

'Really?'

'I'm not staff. Not anymore. I never serve anyone a drink. Except champagne. And then I prefer Kash to do it, that's just manners.'

'I didn't realise you were so traditional.'

'For etiquette, I am. It's better when everyone knows how to behave.'

I wonder why anyone would find it so hard.

'I'm going to take some cups of hot water and a selection of tea bags. Then they can make their own.'

'That's why I like you.' Mariah taps her temple. 'Always thinking.'

'So has Kash had any bright ideas?'

'Never had an idea in his life, it's all me.' Her smile is weak.

'I mean about the bus? Is there anyone he . . . knows?'

She arches her back to stretch it out. Her clothing crackles as it rubs together. Imbalance of positive and negative charges. I remember that from Olivia's GCSE revision.

33

'He knows a copper, quite high up, and he reckons they'll find them. Can't have gone far.'

I reckon they could have gone very far in the time they've been missing, but it sounds reassuring.

'All set?' she says.

I pick up the tray and she pockets some sugar. She's willing to be subservient enough to open the door for me. As we pass the headmaster's office again, Maunder is closing the cupboard door. Mariah stops.

'Tea?' she says.

'Trying to find my Ordnance Survey map,' he explains, though we didn't ask. He reaches up to a shelf and plucks it out from between two books. 'Here it is.'

I wonder why he didn't check the bookshelf before pulling everything out of that cupboard. He leads us back into the hall. Only Akin takes a herbal tea. He must have finished calling round the hospitals because he says there've been no accidents involving a minibus.

Maunder nods distractedly at that news as he opens up the map and goes over to spread it on top of the grand piano. Then he takes a red pen from his inside pocket and starts marking the driving route of the second minibus that already arrived back.

'Are the police on their way?' Ayesha asks him.

'They took all the details – make, model, registration number – and they're going to look at logistics first. They'll check the cameras on the motorway, there's a system—' He stalls over the details.

It's called ANPR. Automatic number plate recognition. Don't these people watch TV? Maybe that's why they have so much time.

'The officer said they should pick up a trail in minutes,' Maunder says. 'But it won't be so easy if they've gone cross country to avoid traffic . . .' He trails off as he considers the map, the veins of B-roads and lanes that wind through the hills from there to here.

Akin brings over a piece of paper. It's covered with bullet points, chicken scratch writing like a secret code. 'While I was ringing round, I made a list of reasons someone might take a minibus with children on board,' he says.

'What?' says Ayesha.

'Seriously?' Mariah. 'You trying to frighten us?'

'If we think about *why* it might tell us *who*.' Akin's eyes are wide with worry.

The women look aghast, but it occurs to me that he's a doctor trying to diagnose a problem. It's instinct. Training. We're all running on adrenaline right now.

'Why do you think they've been taken?' I ask.

'We don't know they've been taken,' says the headmaster.

'Then where are they?' asks Akin.

No one responds, so he flattens his list on the piano lid.

'Someone could have taken them for ransom.'

A few sharp statements of *No!*

He goes on. 'We drive our kids around in buses branded with a school logo, advertising the fact that the children of high-net-worth individuals are on board—'

'I'm not a high-net-worth individual,' I say.

'You've got your kid in private school,' says Ayesha.

'On a bursary,' I say.

'Apologies,' says Ayesha.

'Don't feel sorry for me.'

'I didn't mean it like that.' She grips my wrist and makes eye contact for the first time today. 'I apologise for mis-speaking . . .'

She seems genuine but the slight burns. I relax my facial muscles, show no reaction. I can feel bird-like bones inside the soft fabric of her skin.

'Come on,' says Mariah. 'We're on the same team.'

Ayesha gives my wrist a last squeeze and lets go.

Akin continues. 'A ransom could mean someone wants money, yes, but that's not the only reason for a demand. They could want something more complicated. Leverage, data, the release of a prisoner.' He looks directly at Ayesha. 'Political influence.'

She says nothing.

'That sounds a bit James Bond,' says Mariah. 'What else is on your list?'

He frowns at his own writing. 'Express kidnapping. Common in South America. They grab someone and drive them around ATMs to withdraw cash, then let them go. They could be doing that. We should tell the police their card numbers so they can check cash machines for withdrawals.'

It's almost the end of the month. Olivia would only have access to a tenner. Tell a lie, there was £250 on our balance this morning – would that be enough to buy them off?

'The good news about express kidnappings is that as long as they get some money, they'll let them go.' Akin ticks off that theory. 'Or someone might take kids for sexual—'

'Don't go there,' says Mariah. 'That's my daughter you're talking about. It's different for you—'

'Why is it different?'

'You've got a son!'

'This is why we have to move fast,' says Jack, who's sensed intrigue and joined us. 'In the world of survival we talk about the *rule of threes*. Three minutes without air. Three days without water. And in a harsh environment like a winter's day—'

Everyone follows his gaze to the window and back.

'—in cold weather, you've got about three hours.'

Chapter Six

10.05 a.m.

Inside the tropical swelter of the swimming hall, a hundred teenagers made the din of a battlefield. The cannon-boom of bodies hitting water, shrieks from the viewing gallery, a choking tannoy. Olivia stood on the starting block. Closed her eyes to find her focus. Toes exploring the edge.

A piercing scream. Olivia looked up to try to identify who was putting her off—

And there was the lad in the white Stüssy hoodie.

Sitting in the back row, far corner, alone.

The only one not clapping.

Looking right at her.

A whistle blast shot through Olivia's veins like adrenaline.

The marshal called, 'Get set!'

She raised her arms, crouched and, on the second whistle, launched.

Muscle memory kicked in. The cold rush of the dive, the rhythm of the stroke, the demand for breath. The approaching turn.

Why is he here?

She tucked, she rolled, she kicked—

There was no wall.

She'd gone too soon.

The other swimmers streamed ahead of her.

She clawed water aside to chase their shadows but seconds later, when she slammed the timer, she bobbed up to see the seal-like heads of the winners already above water.

'What happened, Liv?' said a girl in the next lane. 'You sick?'

Eyes on her all down the line.

It was her race to lose. And she'd lost it.

She looked over their heads to the viewing gallery.

No Stüssy hoodie.

Olivia hauled herself out of the deep end. Dried her face on her towel, a chewed fingernail catching on the hooks of the fabric and dragging a thread. Mr Sadler had no words. He sat with one knee bouncing, while Kiran got settled on the starting block.

'Come on,' muttered Dixie. 'Our hopes and dreams rest on your scrawny shoulders.'

The whistle blew. He dived, too deep. Mr Sadler buried his head in his hands.

'Fluffed it,' said Dixie.

Mr Sadler stormed off and heel-slammed an emergency exit door out of his way.

Dixie went to get changed.

Alone, Olivia shivered in the cold that Sadler had let in.

The far corner of the viewing area was empty. She'd blown the race for the sake of a ghost. Kiran came in fourth. Wouldn't qualify. His loss made Olivia's guilt heavier. Dixie and Temi swam below their PBs. Alix was never a serious contender. He'd got into the squad by maturing early, growing a head taller than everyone else. But his rivals were catching up in size and now his lack of technique was showing because he'd grown lazy on superior strength. Kiran slapped his wet arse onto the bench and threw a towel over his head, arms hanging limp.

Olivia left him to rollercoaster through emotions and went to shower. Fifteen minutes later, she exited the building with her hair in a turban. The rain had settled into what her mum called mizzle so she kept the towel on. Mr Sadler was already at the minibus, where he wrenched open the back to fling a kit bag into the luggage area, then slammed the doors so hard that one bounced open again and he had to slam it a second time. He stomped along the side of the vehicle and the whole bus rocked when he got in behind the steering wheel. He slapped over his eyes a pair of wraparound sunglasses that didn't seem necessary in the murky light.

Dixie came up behind Olivia. 'Is he sulking?'

Olivia flinched. He might be able to hear. 'He's put a lot of work into this team.'

'Get over it, man-baby.'

The sag of Mr Sadler's shoulders made Olivia's stomach twist. Mr Sadler was upset because she'd fluffed the race and she'd fluffed the race because she'd been thinking about the money. *Has it really gone? It might have been a glitch?* She could check the app . . .

'Sir?' Olivia leant in through the door. 'Can I have my phone to text my mum?'

'Not possible,' said Mr Sadler.

End of.

Olivia glanced at Dixie, who made a *wow* face.

'Sir, I really need to message her because she'll be worried about my result—'

'The phones went on the other bus.' He pointed to where the minibus with the younger kids on board was already in the line of traffic leaving the car park.

Kiran arrived. In suit and tie.

He stopped a few metres short of them.

'This is the wrong bus,' he said.

It was true – they'd swapped. They came on the other bus.

'They're both going back to school,' muttered Mr Sadler.

Kiran threw his swimming bag onto the steps, its drawstrings ready to trip anyone who tried to board, but stood his ground outside.

'My rucksack is on the other bus. With my index cards. I need to do my maths. We have a test.'

Mr Sadler didn't budge. 'You'll have them in half an hour.'

'That's not fair. You only let us take our swimming bags inside. We had to leave our school bags on board and now our bus has gone and I don't have my revision.'

'Have a nap, it'll do you good.'

'But, sir—'

'GET ON THE EFFING BUS!'

Mr Sadler's outburst was so sudden and shrill and abrupt, and it was delivered without the teacher moving a single unnecessary muscle, so that even after the words scattered into the sky like a flock of disturbed pigeons, Olivia couldn't believe it had really happened. It was only Kiran's stunned face that confirmed it. His robotic plod over his swimming bag and onto the bus. Even Dixie had no comeback and got on board.

Alix and Temi arrived and – picking up on the mood – got on without a word. Temi caught Olivia's eye and raised an eyebrow, but she gave a tight shake of the head, like *don't even . . .* He didn't. He swung into his seat, watching the back of Sadler's head with that placid air he had, like he was watching a film for the second time to appreciate its nuances. Alix started eating a tube of Pringles.

41

In a voice that sounded like it was being held tightly under control, Mr Sadler said, 'It's nearly eleven o'clock. We need to go. Now.'

Olivia stepped on board. As she did, a white figure across the car park caught her eye. A lad in a Stüssy hoodie. She hesitated a moment, her mouth filling with saliva.

'Are you feeling sick again?' Temi asked.

She swallowed and said, 'I just want to get back.' She kicked Kiran's swimming bag and got on board. The door slid shut behind her.

'My EpiPen is in my school bag,' Kiran whispered as she sat down.

'Have you ever needed it before?' asked Temi.

Kiran hadn't.

'Sadler's going to blow if you say anything,' said Olivia. 'Just . . . don't eat.'

'I'm allergic to wasps.'

'So don't eat a wasp,' said Alix.

The bus juddered as the engine fired up. No one spoke as they accelerated across the car park and onto the main road. No one dared ask for the radio to be switched on. But minutes later the bus stopped again. Traffic had backed up from the motorway. Sadler fiddled with the sat nav, which showed a thick red line ahead. He slammed the heel of his hand three times against the steering wheel.

'He's losing his shit,' whispered Dixie.

'And that's because' – said Mr Sadler, prompting them all to exchange looks at his bat-like hearing – 'I'm supposed to be back in time for the lunchtime swim club, for which I get paid extra. Some of us have to think about where money comes from, you know.' By the end of this speech, he sounded almost tearful.

'Sorry,' muttered Olivia.

'Sorry,' echoed Temi.

Think about where money comes from.

A thousand pounds.

Gone.

Olivia let her hair down from the towel and wrenched apart tangles. She rolled a few loose hairs into a knot on the palm of one hand then didn't know where to dispose of it so held it in a fist. She laid her cheek against the cold window, watching in the wing mirror the cars in their wake. Then she lifted her head again. In the passenger seat of a red BMW behind was a lad with a Nike-swoosh fringe of hair and a white Stüssy hoodie.

Chapter Seven

3.35 p.m.

Akin taps his BuzzFeed-style list of 'Ten ways your children could be suffering while you stand there and talk' and says, 'White slavery.'

Ayesha scoffs.

'We do live by the coast,' says Jack. 'You could get out of the country in a small boat. Enough of them get in that way. Our kids could be down a dock and gone.'

'Human traffickers ship people in, not out,' says Ayesha.

'Or it could be revenge,' says Akin. 'Payback for a parent.'

Awkward silence. No one wants to unpack that one.

'What about revenge against the school?' Jack looks down at the headmaster. 'It could be one of these kids you've expelled, Sammy.'

'What kids?' he asks, his lips moist.

A disbelieving silence follows. We all know someone whose child has been excluded one way or another. Akin adds it to the list.

'What about a stalker?' the headmaster suggests. 'People with large followings on social media attract trouble.'

Jack rubs his eyebrows but doesn't rise to the bait.

'We should check the kids' social media accounts,' says Mariah. 'One of them could have been groomed.'

'It could be love,' Akin jumps in.

What?

'Obsessive love,' he clarifies.

'That's what I said, a stalker,' says Maunder.

'No, not a stalker. I mean a parent or grandparent, someone estranged, trying to get access to their child—'

'If we're going for wild theories, what about someone trying to cover up a crime?' says Jack. 'Perhaps one of the kids saw something they shouldn't have?'

'This isn't *Line of Duty*,' says Ayesha.

But Akin nods and adds it to the list. 'To stop someone testifying in court.'

Everyone looks at everyone else. None of us is testifying in court.

When no one reacts, Mariah shrugs. 'Or it could be that the driver got sick and the bus had to stop. He might have had a heart attack and the kids don't have the password for his phone. Or they've had an accident somewhere remote and haven't been found yet. Or they got hungry and stopped for a bite to eat . . .' She runs out of ideas.

'The Nokias that belong to the buses don't have passwords,' says Maunder quietly. 'So they could have called any time on the bus phone.'

Akin dots a full stop on the paper.

'Or . . .' he says. He presses his lips together.

What?

'One of the kids might have turned on the others. Like a school shooting.'

Mariah walks away.

Jack raises a hand in Akin's direction, almost like he's toasting him. 'True that. The pressure they're under. Exams coming up. One of them could have flipped—'

'And done what?' Ayesha.

'Hurt the others.'

'Our kids don't have guns. It's not Sandy Hook.'

'I mean with a knife or a taser.'

'Where would they get a taser?' says Maunder, not unreasonably.

'I don't know but one of them could have hijacked that bus.'

It goes on the list. And we're left to mull the multitudes of ways our children could be in danger from each other.

'What about the driver?' I ask.

Akin nods sagely and writes *driver* on his scrap of paper.

'The minibus was driven by the swim coach, Mr Sadler,' says the headmaster.

'What do you mean *was*?' says Ayesha. 'Why the past tense?'

'I don't know, I just mean—' Maunder stalls. 'He was driving it earlier when they left the campus. The bus is being driven by Mr Sadler. James.'

'And you've called his number?' asks Akin.

He seems to be emerging as our leader after all.

'I've called his personal number and the bus Nokia. He isn't answering but we know he left the swim meet just after the other bus. The venue had CCTV in the car park.'

The swim meet. Perhaps one of the other parents went to watch their child compete? I get my phone and scroll through my WhatsApp groups. A few months ago, I did a charity abseil with a load of school mums from various year groups. I open that old chat window and post a message:

Hi was anyone at the swimming this morning? X

I press 'send'.

'A driver would have plenty of opportunity to hijack a mini-bus,' Jack muses.

'But why would he want to?' asks Maunder.

There's silence.

'Well . . .' says Mariah, pulling at her lip like the answer is obvious.

'Money.' Akin says it.

'Obviously,' says Jack with a shrug.

My phone pings with a DMed response from the mums' abseiling group:

I was at the meet. Absolute scenes!!
No qualifiers. Coach stormed out! X

I fire one back to ask who stormed out.

Three dots show she's typing.

Jack is talking about Mr Sadler: 'He has to drive rich kids around all day without a word of thanks and maybe today was the last straw.'

My phone pings:

The hot Kiwi. Sadler. I almost went to console him ;)

'Didn't he get injured right before he was due to compete at the Olympics?' asks Jack. 'Dragged up by his boot straps, almost made it to the top, now has to watch these kids choose between a smorgasbord of opportunities—'

'It's not James Sadler,' says Maunder. For the first time, he sounds steely.

'What do we know about him?' asks Ayesha.

'I know he's a friend,' says the headmaster.

Voices outside in the quad make us startle. You can hear the jabber of radios, so I say: 'Police.' Two officers appear in the entrance to the Great Hall, pause to take in their surroundings, then come inside.

The older one is called DS Chantale Slocombe. She's my age and looks like she stays fit. Navy blue suit with two fitted T-shirts layered underneath. I bet she keeps clean ones in her desk for long days. Chunky brogues. Practical cornrows. No makeup and slightly puffy bags under her eyes. They fix on me for a moment, their honey colour bright in the dull light of the hall.

She introduces a younger sidekick as DC Gill Singh. A cocky gait gives him the air of an action hero. He's got himself a Luther-style overcoat to drive home the point. Fine by me; I want someone who's keen to get on with it. There are also two uniforms in a patrol car outside. Four officers in all. The police are not messing about.

DS Slocombe shakes every hand in turn and asks a few questions as she goes. When she gets to me, last in the circle, she says, 'So you're Olivia's mother?' I smile to acknowledge the time she's taking to establish a personal touch. She asks for our full names. My daughter is Olivia Ruby Smith. I'm Emily Grace Smith. Singh takes notes.

Slocombe reassures us that this is being treated as a major incident, a fast-time inquiry. There are two forces involved in a search, traffic police driving the obvious routes the bus might have taken. A helicopter already airborne. Obviously, that will cover a much wider area in a short time. As soon as they narrow down the search area, they'll put up drones that detect infra-red heat signals and send out dogs that track human scents.

'Helicopter,' says Mariah.

The word seems to settle our nerves. There's a sense that the big guns have arrived.

But no one asks the key question.

What if they're not on the obvious routes?

What if they can't narrow down the search area?

What if they're already out of the reach of these two police forces?

They could be a hundred miles away, easily, if someone needed to get away from the area fast—

'Have there been any other crimes reported in the area this morning?' I ask.

'We're checking for unconnected incidents,' says DS Slocombe.

The other parents frown at me.

Slocombe explains. 'In case someone leaving the scene of a separate crime has used the minibus as a getaway vehicle. Long shot, but it does happen.' She turns to Maunder. 'Any kids who should have taken the bus, but didn't get on?'

He shakes his head. 'All present and correct.'

Which is more than they are now.

Akin jumps in with a question; the driver, Mr Sadler – has he been DBS checked?

'Obviously,' says Maunder. 'He's been a teacher here for five years. He passed the highest level of DBS check when he got the job.'

'Except—' I say.

As a pack, everyone looks at me. The scrutiny is intense when they turn on you.

'Is it true, DS Slocombe, that a DBS check is only reported to the school as a pass or fail? It doesn't reveal specific details of the person's background? I had to do one once to teach after-school fitness classes and I remember someone saying that . . .'

'That's right,' she says with a question in her voice.

'So someone might have a conviction for a lesser offence and still pass a DBS check?'

This prompts a shuffle as several parents adjust their stance.

'What sort of lesser offence?' says Mariah.

Slocombe nods to her DC, who hurries off.

The detective scratches her lip. 'With certain summary offences, for example motoring charges or low-level fraud, a person could still pass a DBS check. My colleague will request the file on Mr Sadler and see what's what.'

'How long will that take?' asks the headmaster.

'Minutes,' says Slocombe with a side-eye that silences him. She turns to Ayesha and asks for a private word. They retreat across the hall.

'What's that about?' Jack watches them go.

'Our Majesty's government minister is the most obvious target,' I say.

'Don't see why she gets special treatment,' Mariah huffs.

'It's not special treatment.' Akin smacks his lips with irritation. 'Think about recent events. Attacks on MPs – murders, even.'

'If she is the target, it might even be considered an act of terrorism,' I say.

'Terrorism,' Mariah scoffs. 'Come on.'

'Might explain why they got this helicopter up so fast,' I add. 'I bet DS Slocombe is under pressure to find a minister's son. Home secretary on the phone demanding results.'

We all watch as Slocombe comes back. Her stony face backs up my point. Ayesha remains at a distance, on her phone again. What a weight to carry, a job that endangers your family.

Jack accosts Slocombe immediately. 'Maybe the driver, Mr Sadler, flipped? The kids have money—'

'It's a leap to assume a teacher would steal from his own students,' says Maunder. His amphibian features remain unblinking.

My phone pings.

If looks could kill . . .

True. Maunder does not like this line of questioning.

Wants to protect his friend

Or the school rep

Akin tries to show Slocombe his list of theories, but she finds a polite way to say *leave it to the experts*. He steps back but his eyes flit side to side like he's trapped. Not happy, not happy at all.

Are you comfortable with this?

What?

Police might make it worse?

How could it be worse? Well, it could, obviously. God forbid. But I don't want to do this without the police.

Mariah is texting again. But nothing arrives, so she must be messaging Kash. I remember him saying that it's not about building properties, it's about building relationships. And Mariah sprawling across the marble island in their bespoke kitchen, flicking the fingerpads of one hand across the palm of the other. Doling out invisible money.

I took it to mean backhanders.

Kash knows people. And right now I don't mind. Not if it means more pressure on the police to look for my girl.

Slocombe receives a text and scans it in a second.

'There's nothing conclusive on ANPR,' she says. 'But the southbound carriageway of the motorway was closed for a short time following a collision, so maybe they diverted. They can't be in town or we'd have seen them on the cameras. It'll take longer to search CCTV on minor roads, but we're on it.'

'And Mr Sadler?' Jack says.

'We're looking at that too.'

I pipe up. 'One of the mums who was at the swimming pool messaged me to say that Mr Sadler seemed upset this morning. She said he' – I made speech marks with my fingers – '"stormed out".'

Slocombe purses her lips. 'Alright. If this teacher was erratic, I'll make him a priority, while we wait for news from the patrols. And other lines of enquiry.'

Which presumably means Ayesha Reid.

'But—' says the headmaster.

Slocombe cuts him off. 'CCTV could provide us with an answer. Assuming Mr Sadler hasn't gone off-piste.'

Chapter Eight

10.45 a.m.

The minibus tilted as Mr Sadler changed route on the motorway. They'd been heading down the slip-lane towards the services, but now the minibus crossed the dotted line to return to the main carriageway.

'What's happening, sir?' asked Kiran.

Through the spray, Olivia saw the red BMW behind them. The sky was lightening and turning the wet road to pewter. The lad in the Stüssy hoodie had his sun visor down.

Mr Sadler swore under his breath and jabbed the sat nav. The bus wobbled a little. Olivia wished he'd keep his eyes on the road.

'Listen up, guys,' he said.

They listened up.

'We need to forego our usual pitstop—'

'Sir!' Dixie and Alix exclaimed.

'But it's tradition,' said Kiran. 'We always stop here.'

Olivia said nothing. There was nothing to celebrate.

Mr Sadler gave a harrumph that suggested he was thinking the same thing.

'It's not fair,' said Kiran. 'I want Nobby's Nuts.'

Everyone burst out laughing. Only Kiran stayed straight-faced.

'Kiran Reid, you are never normal,' said Dixie. 'I like that about you.'

'This service station is the only one that stocks Nobby's Nuts,' he said in his defence. 'And Worcestershire Sauce French Fries.'

'Ew,' said Temi.

'As much I respect your discerning choice of snacks, Kiran,' said Mr Sadler, whose sense of humour had returned a little since the traffic got moving and he realised he could make it back to school for his lunchtime whatever-it-was, 'we don't have time to stop now. The traffic is so bad – look at this screen, it's all red, an accident, I think, because of the rain – so we should push on and I'll stop nearer home if we make up some time.'

'But we've already made up time, look.' Kiran made a gesture like he was lobbing a ball of paper into a faraway bin. He was pointing into the traffic ahead. 'There's the other bus.'

He was right. The first Saints bus was in the slip-lane up ahead, signalling left as it approached the roundabout. They were making the traditional pitstop.

'Well ...' Mr Sadler chewed on the word. Then his indicator tick-tocked as the bus lurched onto the slip-road at the last moment, earning a horn-blast from a driver behind. 'You folks have five minutes. Not even five, three minutes, tops.'

'Yas!' Kiran celebrated and Alix fist-bumped him.

Olivia slumped in her seat, picking threads of skin off her chlorinated lips. Then she reached a decision and planted her hands on the leather to spin herself around.

'Kiran, pass my swimming bag? I need my lip balm.'

Kiran reached over to where Olivia's bag was on top of the rest of their luggage—He gave a loud cry, almost a shriek, that made Mr Sadler swerve again.

'My jammers!' He stammered out an explanation about his jammers, brand-new compression swimming trunks that cost

£300, which were in his bag, which was missing. They checked all the seats and the floor, but the bus wasn't big, the bag wasn't there. Olivia remembered it lying on the steps, its looping string liable to trip someone up.

'You left it on the steps, Kiran,' she said. 'It must've fallen out. It'll be in the car park.'

'Mr Sadler, Coach, sir, we have to get the jammers. Please. My mother—' Kiran clamped a fist in his own hair.

'Sir,' said Temi. 'I think we need to go back for Kiran's jammers. He's not okay.'

'Of course I'm not okay.' Kiran's voice was shrill. 'My mother said I'd lose them and now I have!'

Maybe it was the threat of Kiran's mother – Ayesha Reid, who wasn't only a very important person but also a very scary person – but instead of heading into the services, their vehicle veered around the roundabout and back onto the motorway in the opposite direction. Kiran simmered down, slumped in his seat, gnawing on his thumb.

Mr Sadler slapped his wraparound sunglasses back on, once again fuming.

Alix gave an exaggerated sigh. 'And we never got our hands on Nobby's Nuts.'

Chapter Nine

3.45 p.m.

'Insurance scam,' says DS Slocombe.

'Bloody knew it,' says Jack. 'Mr Sadler; Mr Swindler, more like. Bet he didn't get anywhere near the Olympics. No wonder he left New Zealand—'

'Mr Sadler's credentials are good,' says Maunder. 'We have original certificates for his teaching qualifications and official references for his sporting achievements. It's all online, he only retired from swimming ten years ago. The conviction is a surprise, I must say, but I don't think it should divert us from the issue at hand.'

'The key question,' says Ayesha and, as usual, everyone snaps to attention, even the headmaster, 'is what Mr Sadler might want with our children?'

'He wants to bring them back to school safely,' says Maunder, petulantly.

But Akin nods in agreement with Ayesha. 'If he owes money, then we give him money. Pay off his debts, get the kids back safe. It's the best way.'

'This is speculation and probably slander,' insists the headmaster. 'So he was convicted of a minor crime a decade ago—'

'Insurance fraud, 2016, in New Zealand,' confirms Slocombe.

'It's irrelevant, I'm telling you that now,' says Maunder. His skin has taken on a greenish hue.

'What about this helicopter?' asks Mariah.

DS Slocombe nods. I like the way she stands, her phone grasped in one hand and a police radio in the other. Up on her toes a little. Poised. 'We'll know more soon. We know the bus wasn't involved in an accident because patrols have driven the whole route.'

I exchange a look with Akin because he's already established this by phoning his medical contacts, but he doesn't say anything.

'And now patrols are following main roads through the South Downs, driving all the likely routes—'

'What if he's taken them down a deserted country lane? They could be miles away – what time did they leave the swimming pool?'

'Just before eleven,' says Maunder.

'So it's—Wait, it's *five hours* since they left the pool?' says Akin.

In five hours, they could be anywhere.

The headmaster swipes his eye. 'They should have got back to school by midday, in time for lunch. That's when the first bus arrived, delayed by traffic. I was told at 12.30 that the second bus wasn't back and I asked the office to contact Mr Sadler. There was no reply and they decided to keep trying. We gave it until one o'clock. When that deadline passed, I called the swimming pool and they confirmed that the meet finished on time. I contacted the other driver, Mr Pimlico, who'd already left school again to take the Year 8 cricketers to the county ground for nets. He thought he saw the second bus behind him at the services—'

'It's a tradition to stop there for snacks,' I say. 'Have we checked CCTV at the services?'

Slocombe nods.

Maunder doesn't break stride. 'Mr Pimlico didn't see them inside the services. After I spoke to him, I tried every mobile number available – Mr Sadler's personal phone, the bus phone, all five students.'

'Any answer?' Slocombe.

'No answer.'

'Then I called two other schools who were at the meet and their teams were back home, no problem. I called the pool again and they checked CCTV in the car park – it showed the bus leaving on time, just before eleven.'

Slocombe interrupts. 'We know from ANPR that the bus returned to the swimming pool around fifteen minutes later. It stayed for just over ten minutes and then we have it heading back towards the motorway, but it must have diverted because it doesn't join the motorway. We don't have it on ANPR after that.'

There's a solemn moment, then Maunder picks up again.

'At 2.30, I started to call you, the parents, one by one. You started to arrive around three and we've been here for an hour already, so . . . Yes, that's five hours. Time flies.'

Slocombe slowly nods.

'Five hours,' mutters Ayesha. 'Why didn't you call it in sooner?'

No one responds. Because she's not asking the right question.

'If we think they might have been taken,' I ask instead, 'how come we haven't had a ransom demand?'

No one replies.

'Have we?' I look around the group.

Jack and Mariah look confused. Ayesha is fiddling with her phone. Akin avoids my eye.

Slocombe picks up on my meaning. 'If anyone receives a private message about their child, then it's vital we know, okay?'

Everyone agrees that this is okay. But Ayesha and Akin don't offer anything up.

The detective says she's going to speak to each of us in private. She'll start with the headmaster? It's not really a question, but everyone agrees. They leave us behind in the hall.

Akin clears his throat. He looks around and sees DC Singh speaking into his phone over beside a fireplace that rises over his head. Akin tilts forward to speak confidentially. 'I've been thinking . . . I had a text from my brother. He recommended a private security firm. He uses them from time to time, professionally, and they can have a consultant available within the hour.'

No one else in the room seems surprised by a brother who requires private security not just once but from 'time to time'. Is that normal?

As though he's read my mind, Akin says, 'My brother runs businesses in Nigeria. Kidnapping is not uncommon there. This company can negotiate with terrorists—'

'Terrorists again!' huffs Jack. 'We don't need a bunch of mercenary thugs wading into a situation involving children.'

'They're professionals, experts in hostage negotiation. Not thugs. Their aim is to de-escalate the situation. Most of them are ex-military or former police officers.' Akin points to the door through which the detective went with the headmaster and lifts his chin towards Singh. 'These local cops are doing their best, but what do they know about kidnapping or terrorism? They're more experienced in knife crime, cars, drugs. They're here to babysit us.'

'I'm in favour of anyone who can get to the kids quick,' mutters Mariah. 'Detective Slocombe . . . Slow Coach, more like.'

Ayesha says nothing. But a politician can't really slag off her local constabulary, I suppose. It'll hinge on her decision. With Akin and Ayesha behind the plan, it'll take hold.

'Well,' she says. Then she marches off towards the main doors. For a second, I think she's leaving, but she makes for the light switches. The room has turned gloomy, the winter sun on its way down outside. Ayesha flicks on two huge chandeliers. Spotlights beam up the stone columns and across the timbered ceiling. A beautiful room put to an ugly purpose.

'That's better,' she says.

Ayesha returns.

'A junior minister,' she says, 'should have full confidence in British policing. Our officers are the finest in the world – very best modern training and all that.'

Akin folds his arms. 'Is that a no?'

'Is what a no?' she asks.

'To the private security?' says Akin.

'What private security?' says Ayesha.

Akin blinks. 'Okay,' he says.

'Hold on a minute.' Jack's stance is getting wider as the conversation goes on. 'That's my son out there, I don't want wallies with AK-47s running around.'

'They won't be armed,' says Akin. 'And they won't be out there, they'll be in an office on the telephone.'

'It's a moot point,' I say. 'Until we know what's happened to them.'

'That's right.' Jack stares at the chandelier as though noticing it for the first time. 'First job is to find them. And we're not going to do that by sitting here.' He marches out the door.

Ayesha watches him leave, shaking her head. 'The irony of Jack Kent talking about macho wallies.'

Akin types something into his phone and then switches it off. I'm not sure if he's just given the go-ahead to his brother. Obviously, Ayesha isn't going to ask. She goes over to the piano and stares down at the map that the headmaster left behind. I follow and Mariah joins us too. The map is covered with shaky red lines, roads twisting like arteries.

'Do you remember those young people whose car crashed off the road down an embankment and it took two days to find them?' Ayesha whispers. 'I sent the parents a sympathy card. Now I can't remember their names.' The woman has feelings buried somewhere under the cashmere. Maybe they'll come to the surface as the afternoon wears on.

I trace a line along main roads, the route that Olivia and her friends should have taken. I wish I could drop myself down to her, like that little man on Google Maps who hangs precariously by one arm until you find the right place. I'm stuck like that, dangling.

The contours of this map could be waves on an ocean – a wilderness. My finger lingers on rivers, lakes, bridges, railway lines, inland cliffs, a reservoir, the treacherous drop of the Devil's Dyke. Endless places where a bus might have gone off the road and Olivia could be lying cold and hurt and hidden, waiting for help from a mother who is comfortable and warm inside a school hall.

Chapter Ten

11.30 a.m.

The bus raced along the country lane between knotty strings of hedgerows that made Olivia feel more hemmed in than city streets. A blue road sign whipped past too quickly for her to read. *Something* Reservoir. She could only recognise the familiar word, not the name, so she still didn't know where they were. The road narrowed and water replaced the hedges. The reservoir. A mouldy-looking wooden fence was the only barrier between the tarmac and the icy shallows. Or maybe icy depths? This was a reservoir, after all, and weren't they dangerous, too unpredictable even for wild swimming?

Mr Sadler didn't slow down despite the glassy tarmac. Black ice. A few miles back, Kiran had said he felt queasy. It was the twisting roads. But Kiran was on Sadler's shit list for forgetting his jammers. By the time he'd found them at the pool where his whole bag had been taken into lost property, the motorway was closed because of a massive crash, and Sadler diverted onto a cross-country route. No one dared ask if they were lost.

'This dude's going to cause an accident,' said Alix from the back seat.

'Stop eyeballing him, man,' said Temi.

Olivia stretched her seatbelt so she could turn around and see what they were talking about. Alix had his arm slung along the seat, looking out of the window in the back doors. A red BMW was right up their exhaust pipe, as Olivia's mum might say. Weaving, looking to overtake, even though the road was hardly wide enough for a cat to sneak past. Olivia faced the front. The belt zipped itself up and slapped her chest.

'Liv!' hissed Dixie from across the aisle.

Olivia pretended not to hear. Her heart was pounding faster than engine pistons.

Dixie tried again. 'Alix, can you see the one in the passenger seat?'

'Good-looking bastard. Why?'

Dixie didn't answer but unclicked her belt and staggered one seat forward to sit beside Olivia. She clipped herself back in again.

'What's going on with you?' Dixie asked.

Olivia shrugged. 'It's just a guy in a car—'

'That BMW is everywhere. It was behind us on the motorway. And here it is again.'

'Probably came this way to avoid the traffic, same as us.'

Dixie craned over her shoulder to see if it was still following.

'We should tell Sadler,' she said.

'Don't,' hissed Olivia. 'He's already in a mood. Ignore the car, it's fine.'

Dixie opened her mouth to say more, but Olivia shifted in her seat to look out of the side window, took the lid off her lip balm and scooped a fingernail of salve that took all of her attention to work into the dry corners of her mouth. In a reflection in the glass, she saw Dixie pout her lips in an expression she'd picked up from her mother.

The minibus bounced over a causeway with water held back on both sides by mysterious forces of nature or feats of engineering. Then they were across the reservoir and the road entered woodland. Mr Sadler went down a gear with a great lurch.

'What is with this *bogan*?' said Mr Sadler, looking in his wing mirror. 'Right up my jacksie.'

'We should let him pass,' said Alix.

'It's too narrow,' said Olivia.

The woodland was dense enough for trees to arch the road and form a tunnel. Undergrowth and gnarled stumps came down to fringe the tarmac. One mistake and they'd be in the forest.

'Why's he flashing his lights now?' Kiran piped up too. 'Sir—?'

'He's an idiot,' said Mr Sadler. 'Ignore him.'

Olivia turned. 'Do what he says. Sit down and stop winding them up.'

The bus lurched as it suddenly slowed, and Olivia heard the fast tick of hazard lights. Right ahead, the road widened for a short distance, enough for the BMW to pass. Sadler kept left and buzzed down his window to stick out one hand, waving the car to come by.

'Maybe he can't see your hand?' said Kiran.

'He can bloody see my hand!' muttered Mr Sadler, staring into his wing mirror. 'Come on, dipstick, come past.'

'He's not coming past,' said Alix. 'He's just, like, flashing and yelling.'

'Come by,' said Mr Sadler. 'Come by!'

Olivia gave an involuntary snort of laughter. Dixie snapped her head round in response, her face scrunched up, like, *what the actual—?*

'Sorry, sorry,' said Olivia. She waved one hand to signal that she was okay. But she couldn't stifle the laughter, it seemed to bubble up from inside. She felt light-headed. 'Mr Sadler is so funny, *come by*, like he's herding sheep.'

Dixie frowned but said nothing.

'If he doesn't come by soon, it's going to be too late,' said Sadler.

A few seconds later, the road narrowed again.

'Well, he had his chance,' said Sadler and his window slid up. He clicked the radio on and the cabin filled with soft rock. Olivia felt the steady pressure of the seat against her spine as the bus accelerated. A few moments later, the road curved out of the wood into open farmland. The longer view made it less claustrophobic. Temi reported that the BMW had dropped back.

Dixie got a compact out of her bag, opened it and held the mirror up to check her face. She lifted it higher. High enough to see behind.

'What're you doing?' Olivia asked.

'Looking for the red car.'

Dixie snapped the compact shut and pushed it inside her bag. Then she unclipped her belt and staggered forward to sit in the first row of seats.

'Belt on, Dixie!' Sadler threw over his shoulder.

'I need to stop, sir,' Dixie said.

'What?'

'It's been coming on for a while. It's the winding road—'

'I've got a sick bag.' He indicated the glove box.

'No, sir. I need to stop. I really do.'

Up ahead, the road once again sank into woodland.

'Here's good. I can go behind a tree. It's not sick, sir, it's—' Dixie stopped and lowered her voice. 'Maybe the water was bad.'

'Using the toilet is a basic human right,' said Kiran. 'Holding in urine or faeces can lead to bladder or digestive infection.'

'TMI,' said Alix. 'Or more like UTI.'

'Hush now,' said Temi.

Alix made a long and wet raspberry.

Sadler raised his voice. 'Alix Kent, I'm giving you a demerit card—'

'Oh, sir,' protested Alix. 'I was only messing.'

'It's not funny,' said Dixie. 'I really need to stop.'

Kiran handed over a packet of wet wipes without a word.

The indicator tick-tocked and the bus pulled up into a flat clearing under the trees. The moment it stopped, Dixie bolted out of the side door. There was a funny wooden building in the trees, a tiny shed. Dixie ran behind it for privacy. Olivia got up to follow her—

'Everyone stay on board,' said Mr Sadler. 'I'll give her a minute then check if she's—'

Olivia turned in response to the sound of a powerful engine approaching on the road. The red BMW swerved onto the hard-packed earth of the clearing, sending up a spray of dead leaves. It ground to a halt about twenty metres behind them. Its engine fell silent. Music pumped for a few seconds, then that fell silent too. Mr Sadler clicked off their radio. In the shade of the trees, the interior of the BMW was dark. Olivia could make out two figures. Both hooded.

'Oh, shit,' said Alix.

'Stay on the bus,' said Mr Sadler, opening his door. He scooped a Nokia phone off the dashboard. 'In case of emergencies, there are hockey sticks in the luggage rack.'

first. An arrow strike in the heart. Before I can protect myself, I'm overwhelmed, moving upstream against a barrage of young bodies, none of which is my daughter, who assault me with laughter and too-sweet odours and soft jostling. Their faces are taut and tired and impatient for freedom even though they're safe and on their way home to parents who don't know how lucky they are, and some cruel part of me wants it to be one of them instead of Olivia. And then I feel such instant guilt and shame that I want to grab one of them and hug her to my shoulder in apology. Or just know what it would feel like to hold a child again. But I don't. I keep moving. I pass the headmaster's office. I make no eye contact with any kids. I enter a small room behind the detective and focus my mind on details. Two fuchsia-coloured sofas, facing each other. Coffee table with brochures of the school. Tiny bottles of water lined up obediently. The walls are decorated with blown-up photos of Saints pupils being dynamic; rugby, sailing, drama. I slow my breathing and feel my pulse regulate.

The detective sits down and opens a bottle of water. She glances over the photos.

'All very impressive,' she says.

I point at the young sailor. The photo must have been taken a couple of years ago. 'That boy got expelled at the end of last term for writing a girl's coursework in exchange for a photo of her bra. She got an A-star, but he got expelled.'

Slocombe raises her eyebrows.

'I don't know if the girl got to keep the A-star,' I say, then regret my caustic humour.

She doesn't smile.

'Emily Smith, was it? Should I call you Emily?'

'Please do call me Emily.'

She's looking at the photos on the wall. 'This school has a certain reputation . . .'

'For ruthless marketing verging on propaganda?'

'And for expelling kids. I have two teens so I know how common it is to send or receive nudes nowadays. A picture of a bra doesn't seem egregious, all things considered.'

Hark at you, I think, *egregious*.

'I'm not saying it's acceptable,' she clarifies, 'but they all do it. Most schools don't expel a pupil for that, not a first offence anyway.'

I agree, it was heavy-handed. But that's what it's like at Saints. I like the detective's bedside manner. She's not dawdling – despite Mariah calling her DS Slow Coach – but not rushing either. She's pulling at threads to see what unravels.

'This school is a business; reputation is everything,' I explain. 'We've only been here a couple of years and we don't have any problems so I keep my head down for Olivia's sake, but I see that it's dog-eat-dog out there. Mess up once and you're out. We've been to a few schools, some nice and some not, and this place is by far the most ruthless. They call it a hothouse, but I'd say it's more like a tinderbox.'

Slocombe writes something down, but I can't see what.

'And Olivia is on a bursary?'

'Is that relevant?'

She raises her eyebrows. 'I'm not going to lie to you, Emily, I don't know. This is an unusual case. A mass missing persons . . . It's complex. Anything could be relevant.'

I reach for a bottle of water but manage to hit one that takes the others down like skittles.

'Sorry,' I say, although they're not hers, it's not her room.

She stands them all back up, opens another bottle and hands it to me.

We go through some logistical questions about our daily routine. Then more personal stuff about behaviour, arguments, acquaintances.

'There really aren't any problems. Olivia is the adult in our house sometimes. I'm more—'

Slocombe makes a note.

'I'm a bit more chaotic.'

I tell her that I lost a lot of money a year ago in an email scam.

'Do you think that's relevant?' I ask.

'Do you?' she says.

We agree that it doesn't feel relevant. They owe me, not the other way around. Then she asks if there's anything she should know about the other parents.

My brain lights up like a pinball machine.

Jack 'Daddy Cool' Kent and his irresponsible parties.

Dr Akin Abiola and the private security.

Ayesha Reid and her whispered conversations with – perhaps – the prime minister.

Mariah Haven and whoever she knows through Kash.

But I'm sure we've all got baggage that would seem suspicious to a stranger.

I take a sip from my tiny bottle. Return it carefully to the table. My hands are fluttering.

'I suppose I am concerned that all these parents have the means – financial, influential – to take matters into their own hands. And that may make the situation volatile,' I say.

'You know why I called you in first?' she says.

Her index finger drums her notepad, right where she's written my full name.

'To stop them feeling like they're in control?' I say. 'I'm the weakest link, least likely to be a target—'

'Are you?' she asks.

'As far as I know,' I say. 'Unless you're telling me otherwise?'

She shakes her head.

'Money would seem like the obvious motive,' I say.

She nods.

'And I don't have any. You chose me first to confound their expectations. Show them who's in charge.'

She smiles. It's an unreserved smile, a bit goofy. She has a gap between her front teeth that looks girlish. I wonder who her friends are, how they let their hair down of an evening, what she's like to go drinking with.

'No, it's because you're the quiet one,' she says. 'You've been doing all the listening. Can you keep listening for me?'

'Are you asking me to spy on the other parents?'

She writes something then glances up at the photos of the kids.

'This school really is impressive,' she says. 'Such a *reputation* to uphold.'

She wants me to spy on the parents *and* the headmaster.

'Okay,' I say.

I slip the tiny bottle of water into my pocket before we leave the room.

Back in the Great Hall, a great debate is underway.

Jack has a finger pointed at Ayesha, and he's talking about Saudis.

'Is this because I'm mixed race?' she says. 'You assume I'm in league with anyone with brown skin?'

'I'm not racist, but we all know government ministers are in the pocket of anyone with money—'

'Oh, listen to the class crusader with his kids in private school—'

'Saudis, Iranians, Israelis, Russians—'

'Israelis, too?' Ayesha scoffs. 'Throw a bit of anti-Semitism in for good measure, why don't you?'

'That's not my point and you know it—'

They finally notice DS Slocombe and I have returned, and fizzle out.

'Ms Reid,' says Slocombe.

Ayesha nods, rather gratefully, I think, and follows her out.

Jack slumps down on his seat again.

'All I was *saying* is that she's the most likely to have brought unwanted attention our way. She's a government fucking minister! God knows what she's involved in. The police are all over her, special treatment, so it's obvious they think so too—'

'She's a junior minister in charge of farms and fisheries,' says Mariah. 'Who do you think has taken our children? Captain Birds Eye?'

No one responds.

'What do you think?' Jack prods. He's talking to Akin now. 'Was I out of order, mentioning the Saudis and that?'

'I don't know enough to comment.'

'Politician's answer. You've been withholding too. You're not just a surgeon—'

'I'm an anaesthetist.'

'—you're an heir to a multi-million-dollar communications fortune.'

'My father and uncle own the largest mobile phone network in Nigeria.'

'So, there's a motive for your kid to be taken,' says Jack.

'Which is why I suggested private security. In Nigeria, the children of high-net-worth individuals are considered targets. I thought we were safer here where no one knows us, but maybe not. Maybe someone bribed this Mr Sadler, who has a criminal conviction, and paid him to deliver the kids to a remote location. I don't care what it costs, I'm going to get my son back. And your children, too, if I can.'

'What do you mean, *if I can*?' Jack says. 'Is your kid worth more than mine?'

It kicks off again. Jack Kent would fight his own shadow, the mood he's in.

Mariah signals that we should get more tea, leave them to it. I shake my head. I need to hear this. Jack is a blunt tool, but he seems to be digging up dirt.

But the side door flies open. Slocombe strides in, followed by Ayesha. The MP looks deflated, physically smaller. The sight of her makes my stomach tight.

'I have an update,' Slocombe says in a *you might want to sit down* tone of voice. 'I'm now confident this case is an abduction or kidnapping. I'm going to alert the Major Crime Unit.'

'Has there been an escalation?' I ask.

DS Slocombe presses her lips together.

But I can't let it go.

'Tell us!' My anger surprises me as well as the others. The mouse roars.

Slocombe sighs and shakes her head. But she answers.

'One of the patrols has found a body. In woodland off the motorway.'

Chapter Twelve

11.45 a.m.

Aggression drifted through the trees like fox musk.

'Something's wrong,' Olivia said.

Mr Sadler had left them in the minibus to go out there, into the woods, after Dixie.

'Get the hockey sticks,' said Alix. 'I'm going too.'

'Sadler said to stay on the bus,' said Temi. But he sat on his knees on the back seat, frowning through the rear windows, Alix beside him. Kiran was sitting one row in front of them, turned halfway round so his legs were in the aisle, muttering about jammers. Olivia shushed him. Her window only opened a hand-width. The trees were pattering after the rain. Sadler was too far away to hear.

'If he didn't want us to go, why did he tell us about the hockey sticks?' Alix asked.

Temi glanced at Olivia and she rolled her eyes.

Everyone at school had shipped Dixie and Temi until they finally started dating. It didn't last long. She'd been thrown by his lack of drama. It wasn't anything like dating on the TV. Temi wasn't jealous or unfaithful. They never fell out and so they never *made up* either. She dumped him at a party, crying on Olivia because 'he won't let me in'. Temi was baffled but Dixie was adamant that he must be hiding something. 'No one is that perfect, it freaks me out.' Now, Olivia pressed her ear to the window, listening for her friend who had perhaps got more drama than she craved.

It had happened so fast. Dixie ran from the minibus, crossed the clearing and disappeared behind the wooden shed set back in the trees. The BMW then pulled up. The two lads got out. But instead of approaching the minibus for whatever reason they'd stopped, they looked towards the shed, hesitated a moment and went in that direction. After Dixie. That made Sadler go running after them. No good reason for two men to follow a girl into the woods. So now, Sadler was standing in the clearing near the BMW, facing the shed with hands on hips. Listening and shaking his head. But was he talking to the lads or Dixie?

If she was having an emergency poo beyond the shed, then she was doing it with three blokes nearby, which was *so embarrassing*. Perhaps Olivia should go out there? Female solidarity?

'Maybe she collapsed?' said Temi.

'Wouldn't Sadler be with her, if that was the case? Not just standing there . . .'

Dixie hadn't seemed that ill . . .

Maybe the lads had stopped to get something from the shed, and this was nothing to do with Dixie at all, she was further away behind a tree. Just a coincidence that both vehicles had stopped in this clearing. Now, Sadler was having a chat while waiting for her to come back? But his body looked tense. The hands on his hips were bunched into fists.

No, there was definitely something wrong.

'Look—' said Olivia, pointing out of the back window.

Mr Sadler walked forward and out of sight behind the shed.

'Maybe we should get those hockey sticks,' said Temi.

From outside, a shout. Sadler? Too abrupt to tell. Then he reappeared, staggering backwards into the clearing, mid-fall, as though he'd been shoved in the chest. He lost balance and sprawled onto the ground. One of the lads was on him in a moment, straddling his chest in a chimp-like posture, arm pumping up and down—

Olivia screamed and looked away.

Temi barged past and grappled with a hockey bag wedged in the luggage rack.

'Help me!' he shouted.

Alix froze. Kiran goldfished. Olivia stood up and grabbed one end of the bag—

They both stopped and spun round as the driver's door opened. The lad in the Stüssy hoodie clambered into the seat. Before they could pull the bag from the rack, the minibus shuddered to life. Olivia was thrown sideways onto a seat as it lurched forward. The driver's door slammed itself. The engine roared and the vehicle bumped over the clearing and onto the road. Olivia took a last glance back at the wood.

No sign of Dixie. Or the other man from the BMW. He'd left Mr Sadler alone in the clearing. Mr Sadler looked like a pile of fly-tipped bin bags.

'Sit down, belt up.' The driver's voice sounded young. Nasal and nervous. But he worked smoothly through the gears to get the bus up to speed. Alix and Kiran were already sitting. They clicked their belts. Temi staggered to the back seat. Olivia moved to be one row in front of him, across the aisle from Kiran. She belted up too.

'What happened to Dixie?' called out Temi. 'And Mr Sadler, our teacher?'

The driver's hand went up and moved the rear-view ɪ
they couldn't see his eyes.

'Was Mr Sadler moving?' Olivia whispered to Temi. 'Was he okay?'

'I didn't see.' Temi shook his head.

'What about Dixie?'

'What's he doing to her?' Temi shouted to the driver. 'Your mate? What's he want with her?'

The driver ignored them.

'Is he a rapist? Is he raping her?'

The driver adjusted the mirror to see them.

'Don't be saying that,' he said. 'He's no rapist.'

'What, then?' asked Olivia. 'This isn't right!' Even to herself, she sounded prim.

The driver glared at her via the mirror and then tilted it to the ceiling.

'This is my fault,' said Kiran, barely audible over the drumroll of tyres.

'It really isn't,' said Olivia.

It actually was, but there was no point getting into that now.

'We had to go back for my jammers. We'd be at school by now if I hadn't forgotten my bag—'

'It's not always about you, Mummy's boy,' said Alix.

Olivia watched Kiran for a reaction. He blinked rapidly but said nothing. This distraction meant she missed a blue sign that flashed past outside. She craned her head to look after it and swore in frustration. How were they going to find their way back to Dixie if she didn't even know where they were?

'I'm missing maths.' Kiran's voice had gravel in it. 'We've got a test tomorrow. Top set does anyway.'

'I'm off the hook, then,' said Alix.

'They'd better not cancel it,' muttered Kiran.

'Result if they do.' Alix fist-pumped the air.

'Give it a rest, mate,' said Temi. 'Kiran, man, your maths test will be fine, you got this—'

'I'll fall behind—'

'You will not fall behind because you're way, way ahead already. You've got this under control. Yeah? Yeah, Kiran? You are in control.' Temi crouched low in his seat to look across the aisle into Kiran's face. He sat up straighter but said nothing. Temi went on in a low voice. 'Right now, we have to think about Dixie and Mr Sadler.'

'We can rush the driver,' hissed Alix. 'Take him out. Then drive back to the woods. I can drive, I've had lessons . . . a lesson.'

Temi sucked his lips into his mouth while Alix went on about his plan. Olivia took the time to check their surroundings. They'd driven out of the woods into open countryside. They were putting distance between themselves and the clearing where their teacher lay on the ground and God-knows-what was happening to Dixie. They must have travelled a mile already, two. They had to act fast.

'Do you know where we are?' she asked Temi. The way he craned his head to look for signs told her he didn't. Alix started talking about a survival course he'd taken near here. His father had been filming. Which meant they didn't travel very far. They'd gone round and round the camp, over the same terrain. Alix thought it wasn't far from the reservoir they'd passed earlier . . .

'Where exactly?' Olivia pushed him.

'Let me get my bearings,' he said.

She tutted and left him to it.

'Maybe we should sneak a hockey stick out of the bag?' she whispered.

'We need the bus to slow down before we try anything,' said Temi. 'A crash at this speed could kill us.'

Hedges blurred past. Up ahead, a new patch of woodland. Lots of trees to potentially hit, head-on.

Olivia whispered, 'I'll distract him. You slide a hockey stick out of the bag. Then the next time we slow down for a junction, maybe I can jump into the front and grab the wheel . . .'

'I don't know . . .' said Temi. 'You're going to go through the windscreen if we get this wrong.'

Alix sat forward and placed his hands on their knees. 'Just get him to slow down and I'll take care of the rest.'

Olivia ignored his attempt at a *main character* moment.

'Oi, you!' the driver called out. His mirror was back in place. Olivia could see pale blue eyes. But he wasn't looking at her. He was looking at Temi. 'Come here, you, come forward into the front seats.'

Temi stayed where he was.

'Move forward, bruh!' The driver waved something over his shoulder. He was holding it inside a plastic carrier bag.

'He wants you,' said Alix.

Temi unbuckled his belt and moved down the bus, steadying himself hand over hand on the seat backs. He crouched over the driver. Olivia couldn't hear their conversation, but it had something to do with the plastic bag. Temi was looking inside at whatever the driver was holding. He glanced back at her and made a significant nod at Kiran.

What did that mean?

Then he clambered over the seats into the front alongside the driver.

'He's left us,' said Alix.

Temi looked back miserably as he did up his seatbelt.

'The driver wants to split us up so we can't rush him,' he called out. 'Do what he says. He's got a gun.'

A gun.

It hit Olivia like a punch.

A gun hidden in that bag.

Now she was alone, with Kiran on a slippery slope to a panic attack and Alix on a mission to be a hero. But she was better off than Dixie.

Dixie had no one.

Chapter Thirteen

4.10 p.m.

'Dixie's okay.' Mariah has both fists clenched under her chin as though she's fighting off an invisible strangler. 'I can feel her.'

Everyone regards her with hard faces. Akin wears the unreadable expression of a medical practitioner, but Ayesha shows open disdain for such woo-woo sentiment. Jack resumes fussing with his phone, disinterested or distracted or distressed, I can't tell.

Mariah's reaction has taken me by surprise too. I guess you never know someone until they're under pressure. I grab her elbow and lead her to a seat. We drop in unison. The chairs creak melodramatically. She's shivering. Normally, she's steel covered in warpaint. I've often wondered if she wants people to underestimate her in order to get the upper hand. Dixie is the same. Fathomless eyes. When she turns them on you and stands there with the body language of a doe staring down headlights, it's unworldly, as though she can see in the dark.

Like mother, like daughter.

I hope Dixie is holding up better than her mum. I hold her wrist and feel her pulse pattering. DS Slocombe is on her phone in the corner. She's trying to get more information on this body. Major Crimes will go straight to the scene. Slocombe ends the call and comes to us.

We're panting for news.

'It's an adult,' she says. The group sags with relief. 'A male. We assume, the teacher.'

The headmaster's hand flies to his forehead. If there's any sympathy for Maunder – or indeed the games master, Mr Sadler – it's not apparent in this room. We're myopic with fear.

'If the teacher is dead,' says Akin, 'then who is looking after our kids?'

That comment takes a moment to sink into the silence.

'There's some confusion,' says Slocombe. 'It seems he's alive.'

Mariah groans like she's winded. It speaks for us all; a ripple passes round the group.

'So what happened?' asks Ayesha. 'What can he tell us?'

'Is he conscious?' asks Akin.

'I'm afraid not. He was found in a ditch. Which is why the report came in of a fatality. A driver saw a body and reported it as a hit and run. He's badly injured.'

'What kind of injuries?' asks Akin. 'I might be able to tell you what happened.'

'I can't reveal that information right now,' says Slocombe.

'So he can't tell us where the children are? Or the bus?' This is Ayesha. 'Can't we bring him round? Question him?'

Akin frowns at her.

'It narrows the search,' says Slocombe. 'He must have been on foot when he went into the ditch. Presumably, he collapsed due to his injuries. It means they can put up drones now, look for heat signals—'

'Or his body was dumped there,' says Akin.

Beside me, Mariah gulps down a breath. I lift my hand from her wrist, but she turns her arm to catch my fingers.

'So let's go there,' Jack jostles forward. 'Tell us where the body was found and we'll get out there to join the search—'

Slocombe holds up one palm. 'We have patrols, a helicopter, drones and dogs. It's a tightly coordinated—'

'You can't expect us to sit here and do nothing!'

The detective holds her ground. 'I know it's hard—'

'Do you?' Kent is up in her face.

Akin puts himself between them.

'So the bus must have crashed,' Ayesha says in a perfectly modulated voice. All the male energy washes right off her duck's back. A skill acquired from her career in politics, perhaps. 'The teacher crawled out and went for help—'

'Maybe,' says Slocombe.

'Why haven't they found the bus, then?' I ask.

The group goes quiet.

'If it's not a crash . . .' I continue. 'What?'

'It's too early to—'

'Don't "too early" me, DS Slocombe,' I snap. 'If the teacher wasn't hurt in a crash, then what? He's been attacked?'

Slocombe gives me a significant look. 'It really is too early to say.'

Akin turns his back on the officer to address the group.

'It seems clear there's criminal activity. Like I said before, there is another solution . . .'

Jack shakes his head. Ayesha's face is blank. I glance at Slocombe and her eyebrows betray curiosity.

'What kind of solution?' she asks.

No one answers. I don't know how I feel about this private security option. My gut says no, but I wonder if Akin Abiola might go ahead and organise it whatever we say, so

I'd rather stay in the loop – and that won't happen if I oppose him publicly.

Slocombe addresses everyone but stares at Akin. 'We are best placed to find the bus, much more quickly than any of you can reach the scene. And Major Crimes will be there soon. We need you to stay here and, as best you can in challenging circumstances, help us with background information that might prove crucial.' Slocombe turns to Ayesha. 'Ms Reid? Can we resume our conversation, please?'

The minister and the detective leave the room.

Jack looks after them.

'To be a fly on that wall,' he says.

'I need a wee,' announces Mariah and launches herself off the chair.

I offer to go with her and we leave the hall, retracing our steps past the headmaster's imposing door. The toilet is along to the right and Mariah rushes ahead as though she's about to vomit or something. In case it's 'something', I wait outside the bathroom.

After a moment, I drift along to the closed door of the office where I spoke to DS Slocombe.

I wonder what she'll get from each of us? How much our stories may differ. The truth will be in the gaps or overlaps.

As Jack said, to be a fly on the wall.

The door next to the office has a lock. What they call a wafer lock. Must be a cupboard. The lock is nothing more than a deterrent, presumably to keep naughty fingers out of the stationery supply.

I look over my shoulder. The door to the hall swung shut behind us. There's no one else in the corridor. I delve into my bag. There's a bunch of rubbish in the bottom, but it only takes a moment to find a key ring with a set of stubby picks. A weird thing to carry, I know, but I lost the key to our bike shed and a set of jiggler keys from Amazon cost a fraction of the price of a locksmith.

I pull them out, select one and slide it into the lock. Jiggle and turn, jiggle and turn, and – voilà – the lock springs apart. There's no sound of the flush or hand dryer from the bathroom, so I doubt Mariah is about to come out. I open the door and close myself inside the cupboard before anyone can see what I'm up to.

I discover that I'm correct: it's a storage cupboard. Long and thin. The Victorian origins of the building are more obvious in here; unlike the Farrow-and-Balled public spaces, this room is bare. Dust and cobwebs. Shelves up to the high ceiling. A small window with a grill. And air vents. Between rooms. Which is what I was hoping for.

The vent between the cupboard and the neighbouring office is high on the wall. I could touch it with my fingertips, if I stretched, but I need to get closer to hear what's being said. There are boxes of printing paper stacked on the bottom shelf. I build myself a podium and clamber up. It's still too short and I get down, place one more box on top, and step up again. Wobbly now. If I fall, they'll hear the crash. But the shelving is bolted to the wall and it steadies me. I strain closer to the vent and I hear Slocombe murmuring. Dust catches my throat but I stifle a cough. Can't see down into the office, but that's okay, I don't need to. Ayesha has a monotone voice and that tone is 'everyone listen to me' so I have no trouble hearing her.

'I think it was perfectly justified,' she's saying. 'Nothing happened so I took matters into my own hands.'

'But something did happen.' The detective's voice is lower in tone and volume. 'The school informed social services right after you reported Mr Kent.'

'Did Maunder tell you that?' Ayesha sounds more curious than cross. 'Should be confidential, surely?'

'In the circumstances, he thought it best to share the information with me.'

'And in the circumstances, I thought it best to hire a private investigator. A retired detective from Sussex Police. Not a gumshoe.'

'What do you expect him to find?'

'Mr Kent isn't who he says he is. Maunder refused to share his old school records with me—'

'Because Mr Kent attended Saints?'

'Until he got thrown out. Back when it was all boys.' Ayesha gave a bitter laugh. 'Maybe that's why Maunder won't reveal his record, the old boys' club. But they say he was expelled.'

'That was over twenty years ago.' Slocombe sounds curious. 'So what relevance—'

Ayesha made a dismissive sound. 'He presents himself as a guru, but he destroys lives.'

'He's a survivalist, more Bear Grylls than Andrew Tate?' says Slocombe.

'It's one thing to bring up your own child without boundaries, but when it affects other children . . . It's not right.'

A beat passes. The conversation has forked. Ayesha avoided a question but offered a new line of enquiry. Olivia imagines Slocombe rapidly deciding which path to follow.

'Why do you believe Mr Kent isn't who he says he is?' She stays on course.

A chair creaks as though someone has shifted. I imagine Ayesha leaning forward. 'Social media whatever-he-does can't pay for all this. What about his wife? Why is she never seen? Where is she today?'

'This is . . .' Slocombe pauses and I assume she's checking her notes. 'Calpurnia, is that right?'

'Wouldn't you be here, if your child was missing?'

Slocombe says nothing, which is in itself a tacit agreement.

'Did your private investigator find anything pertinent?' the detective asks.

'He agrees that Kent has . . . let's say "reinvented himself". But we can't prove anything. Kent got expelled from Saints but ended up working in Silicon Valley. It was the dot-com era. But, again, that ended abruptly. Some say he made a fortune and retired, others say he came home with his tail between his legs.'

'He went to private school, so maybe there was family money to fall back on . . .?'

'No sign of that. His parents scrimped and saved to send him here; he had a bursary. Wasted it, getting expelled. More recently, he turned to this survivalist guru stuff. Utter rubbish, of course, he treks around fields not a mile from the nearest car park. We've got enough photos of his crew faking it to get him cancelled.'

'But you haven't?'

Ayesha's chair creaks again. 'You misunderstand me, Sergeant. I'm not out to ruin anyone. I have a genuine concern and I want to understand him. These parties he throws. The impact on our children. They're at such a vulnerable age.'

'I was going to parties at seventeen,' says Slocombe mildly.

'Not these kinds of parties, I'll bet.'

'Can you elaborate?'

'You don't know about the girl? Didn't Maunder mention that? Well, well . . . what a surprise.'

I'm distracted momentarily by footsteps outside in the corridor, hard heels on the parquet floor. Not Mariah, she's in trainers. The ones she buys in Flannels. Maybe Major Crimes are here? Or another teacher?

I tune into Ayesha again. She's explaining about the girl at the party. Thank God, we had tickets for a show that night so Olivia didn't go to the infamous party.

It was at Alix's house, the McMansion. Jack said it would be fine, he'd be on site. But the address was posted on Snapchat and fifty randoms turned up. Amid the chaos, a foreign student in their year, called Li Na, got injured. Badly. Almost severed her thumb on a broken windowpane. Never regained full use of it. She was a sporting champion – fencing, I think – an Olympic hopeful. The injury ended her career. She flew back to Singapore for treatment, never returned to Saints.

The school was tight-lipped about the incident and so the rumour mill was left to turn. You never quite know if it's blowing out chaff, but Ayesha's story echoes the version I've heard so it's probably close to the truth.

'That's horrible for the girl,' says Slocombe. 'But it doesn't sound like Kent's fault—'

'There's more.'

My legs are starting to tremble under the effort of keeping my balance on the boxes. But I strain closer because this is new to me, I never realised there was more.

'Go on.' Slocombe is curious too.

'Bear in mind that Kent was present at this party, right? He was there in the house.'

'Okay . . .'

'The kids were off their heads. Drink and drugs. Kids taking cocaine. Snorting it, rubbing it on their gums. Where did they get hold of Class A drugs, I ask you?'

Slocombe says nothing.

'Kiran was there. He witnessed it and was offered drugs, but he's a little, ah, shall we say *anxious* about academic performance. They do random drug testing at school, hair samples and what have you. At least they say they do. Maybe it's only a deterrent, but it's enough to scare him into submission. So he didn't take anything. He was the only sober one there, I think, including Daddy Cool.'

'Daddy Cool?'

'Jack Kent. It's what the mums call him.' She stops for long enough that I wonder if I should try to climb up and see them. But then she clears her throat. When she resumes, her voice is an octave lower. 'I've never told anyone about Kiran being present at a party where there were drugs and I'd rather it stays in this room.'

'Understood.'

'Kiran said that a group of boys started hassling this girl, Li Na. You know how it is, starts as banter, gets out of hand. She went to the loo and someone followed her. She was struggling to get away when a windowpane in a door broke and she cut herself on the glass. It wouldn't have happened if they hadn't been trying to force her to—Well, I don't know what they were trying to do, but I can imagine. So can you, I'm sure.'

Slocombe hummed in agreement.

'There is a significant amount of evidence to show that cocaine makes some people both violent and libidinous.' Ayesha sounds petulant. She wants more of a reaction from the detective. She's used to being in the middle of the Punch and Judy show that is modern politics.

'Who were the boys involved?' Slocombe still doesn't rise to it.

'Kiran took a photo. No one knows it was him and I'd rather it stayed that way. There were three or four, egging each other on. Some were unidentified – they might have been the kids who gatecrashed, no one knows their names – but another boy was quite easily identifiable.'

'Okay?'

'One of their friends. Temi Abiola.'

'He's on the bus today?'

'He is.'

'Kiran and Temi on the same bus? After Kiran shared this photo that got Temi in trouble?'

'As I said, no one knows Kiran took the photo.'

But what would happen if someone found out?

Chapter Fourteen

11.55 a.m.

Olivia was thrown forward as the minibus braked hard and darted into the open gateway of a field. It rattled over a few metres of rutted ground before stopping. The frozen earth shook the vehicle so violently that the hockey bag came free from the luggage rack and crashed into the aisle in front of her. Presenting her with an opportunity. But did she dare, now that she knew the driver could shoot her? The driver left the engine running, switched the radio on and turned the volume up, then got out. He didn't go far, staying in the doorway. Chilly air swept inside. Music covered his conversation on a phone that was pressed to his ear inside the raised hoodie. Olivia could only see the curve of his cheek and nose. Would she be able to describe him later? If there was a later.

A voice on the radio babbled through the bus. It sounded artificial, manic, like a fairground caller. Olivia had always been afraid of fairgrounds, ever since she heard about a girl who disappeared when the fair left town. Probably an urban legend. Now, the hectic voice invited them to *call in, take part in a quiz, Join the Chain Gang!* Answer a question correctly and you can invite a friend to take part the next day and if they answer a question correctly then another friend joins in and so on until Friday when the whole team faces a music round to win the money. *You're in it together on the Chain Gang!*

Then he played a song called 'Back on the Chain Gang'.

'Where are our phones?' Alix asked. 'Where's the lock-box?'

'In the other bus, with my EpiPen,' said Kiran.

'We could take the driver out,' said Alix. 'We could do it now.'

'He's got a gun,' said Olivia.

'He can't shoot all of us,' said Alix.

'Shooting one of us is enough.'

'Shooting is harder than people think,' Alix said. 'He'd probably miss.'

Olivia ignored him but heard Kiran mutter, 'Probably.'

'How do we even know he's really got a gun?' asked Alix.

'Temi said,' she answered.

'I didn't see it,' said Alix.

'You weren't close enough.'

Alix shrugged.

'Temi,' Olivia hissed. 'Temi!'

He didn't respond. The driver leant inside the bus and said something to Temi. Then he looked from under his hoodie straight at Olivia. The plastic bag with the gun was on the dashboard. It looked solid. Heavy enough to be a gun. But if it was a gun, wouldn't the driver keep hold of it?

Maybe Alix was right. Maybe Temi had been tricked. Maybe the driver was lying.

'Oh, fuck,' said Kiran. He launched a string of fucks. Over and over until the word lost its meaning. Temi usually stepped in to ease Kiran's panics, but he was stuck up front. Alix caught Olivia's eye and made a face. She made one back that told him to *shut it*. For once, he did. Kiran pushed his back against the window and pulled his knees to his chest, hands balled tight. His knees pressed together, pigeon-toed, back hunched.

'What's happening, Kiran?' Olivia tried. She said a few platitudes that came to mind, but it seemed like he couldn't hear.

Fuck, fuck, fuck.

'Pack it in, mate,' muttered Alix.

Olivia shot him a glare.

'Kiran, can you look at me? You're having a panic attack. It's not real, it's just thoughts—'

Kiran locked into her eye contact. His were grass green. Watery.

'Can you breathe?'

Kiran gulped down some air.

Then he said, 'I'm going to miss my tutor.'

Alix snorted.

'Your *tutor*?' said Olivia.

'For English. That's my weak subject. I need her,' said Kiran. 'She's expensive. The best. Comes to the house. I won't be there. I can't call her. She'll be angry. She'll dump me—'

'Your mum will call her, man,' said Alix.

Olivia's mouth felt dry. His mum. She hadn't thought once about her mum. She didn't even know Olivia was in danger. She'd be so scared.

'My mother won't be home,' said Kiran. 'My tutor will come and no one will be there—'

'Shut up, man,' said Alix. 'You're top set in everything, even English. Why'd you need a tutor?'

The music stopped. Silence struck them like a slap to the head. The driver was back in his seat. His door slammed. The bus lurched into gear and rocked over the icy ground. Back through the gateway, its chassis creaked and groaned as it accelerated onto the road again.

They should have been looking out for passing cars. Olivia cursed herself. Someone might have passed by the field. She could have flagged them down. But they'd been too caught up with Kiran and stupid Alix making it worse. And Temi doing nothing, just sitting there in the front. They were doing this all wrong.

'Has it occurred to you,' Alix said in a low voice, 'that it might not be Dixie they want?'

'What do you mean?'

Kiran was scrunched up like a ball of paper.

'Could be him.' Alix nodded at Kiran.

'Don't,' Olivia said, her voice flat with warning. 'You'll set him off again.'

Alix shrugged. 'His mother is a government minister. She knows people. Bad people. Like Russians—'

'What do Russians want with us?'

'Someone might be trying to get the nuclear codes?'

'Wouldn't they have taken the prime minister's son?'

'Harder to get to. Or' – Alix snapped his fingers in Olivia's face – 'Kiran hasn't got a father, has he? No one knows who his dad is.'

Olivia side-eyed Kiran. He was staring into the middle distance. Blinking too much.

'Maybe the prime minister is his father. That's what people say. And these fuckers know. Now they *have* got the prime minister's son. And—'

Olivia had to brace herself in her seat as the driver swung into a narrow lane.

'That's why his mother keeps his father a secret. Because it's the prime minister. So he isn't freaking out about his jammers and the exams and this tutor, it's because he knows this is all his fault.'

'Alix—'

She didn't have a chance to tell him to back off. The bus shuddered ferociously. Olivia tasted blood and realised she'd bitten her tongue. They'd gone too fast over a cattle grid. The bus jerked as it hit tarmac again and slowed as the driver struggled to find the right gear.

Temi turned, looking to see if they were alright. Olivia made eye contact and tried to read his expression. Maybe there was a gun after all. He looked terrified—

Something hit Olivia from behind. She found herself on the floor in the aisle. Kiran had blundered past, shoulder-barging her aside. He stood at the front, right behind the driver, one hand on the ceiling to brace himself. She clambered away from him, finding the back seat, dragging herself into place as though fighting G-forces. In reality, it was the swaying of the bus on the rough road.

'Sit down,' yelled the driver to Kiran. 'Back in your seat!'

Olivia may have shouted too. Or she may have frozen. She had no awareness of anything except Kiran raising a hockey stick. The driver reaching for his plastic bag. Kiran swinging the hooked end with all his force towards the driver's ear.

Chapter Fifteen

4.25 p.m.

Ayesha's ears must be burning. I slip out of the cupboard just before she storms from the next-door room, barely noticing me in the corridor. I head the other way. Mariah isn't in the bathroom or the meeting room with the drinks machine. In the doorway, I turn and bump into Jack.

'Didn't hear you coming,' I say.

'Sorry, Emily.' After his previous faux pas, he keeps shoehorning my name into sentences. 'I've learnt to tread quietly in the wilderness.'

Survival is his *entire personality*, as Olivia might say.

Compulsively, I check my phone for a message from her, but there's nothing.

I linger in the doorway.

'This the coffee machine, is it?' Jack says, pointing at a machine with COFFEE printed on the side in massive black letters.

Weaponised incompetence. *Make your own coffee, Jack.* I fold my arms.

'It's hard being in here, knowing the kids are out there,' I say.

He shakes his head. Smooshes his lips together.

'I could be tracking them,' he huffs.

'Yeah, they have sniffer dogs. And it'll be dark soon. The helicopter has heat-seeking equipment . . .' I glance outside as though it's coming overhead. But it's not; it's miles away, as is Olivia.

'I would have gone out earlier, if they'd chosen to share that information. I'd be there by now if they'd told us when we first arrived.'

'You just want to help, right?' I ask.

'I want what's best for the kids. Don't we all?' He looks to me for confirmation that doesn't seem necessary, but I nod anyway.

'Except Maunder,' he says. 'He only cares about reputation. He'd sell his grandpa for this place. You don't drink his Kool-Aid, do you?'

I murmur something noncommittal. Jack drops both hands to his side, capsule in one, tiny cup in the other. 'Don't think I should drink any more coffee actually, I'm kind of wired. Can I make you a cup, though?' He actually makes eye contact.

'Sure, that'd be great. Black, please.'

He jams the capsule into the slot on the machine.

'Surely Dr Maunder wants to get the kids back safe and sound?' I ask. 'Even if it's only for the school's reputation? Maybe we have different motives but the same goal?'

'We both went to Saints, you know. In the same year, actually—'

'I heard that.'

'His nickname was Salamander. Do you know why?'

'I guess because if you say his name quickly, Sam Maunder, it sounds like—'

'That's where it started. But you know what's special about a salamander?'

I don't.

'They regrow limbs and even internal organs. Never mind cockroaches, salamanders are the ultimate survivors.'

Jack jabs a button and the machine starts grinding.

'The kids hang out at yours sometimes, right?' I ask over the groan. 'What's the group dynamic? How will they cope on their own? Are they working together right now?'

He side-eyes me. 'They're good kids.'

'The best.'

The machine burps and he passes me a cup with what looks like tar in the bottom.

He twists open a bottle of water and downs half in one gulp. Wipes his mouth with the back of his hand. Then locks his gaze onto mine like he's looking down a camera lens. 'Alix is a survivor. He's accompanied me on expeditions before. Knows how to find water, stay warm, stay safe. Temi's a great kid. Old soul, that one.'

I nod. That is actually the perfect description of Temi. An old soul.

I've never seen a hint of nastiness in him so I can hardly believe these allegations about him and the young woman who got hurt. But I don't want to disregard the claim of a traumatised girl either. It's a classic he-said-she-said nightmare. I suppose raging hormones and hard drugs could bring out the worst, even in a fundamentally good kid like Temi?

I let Jack go on.

'Dixie's a live wire. And Kiran ... Well, we all know about Kiran.'

I scrunch up my eyebrows in bewilderment.

'No?' he asks. He steps closer and shrinks about six inches into conspiratorial mode. 'I'd be curious to know who's the father of that boy because the man might be out of the picture but his influence must be strong. That lad is nothing like his mother.'

I sip my coffee. Thick as cough syrup. I'm not sure what he means. Kiran is exactly like his mother – they even look alike – except he's about a foot taller, as though someone's made a freaky voodoo doll of her.

'I know they look similar,' Jack goes on, must have heard my thoughts, 'but think about it . . . She's smart, competent, hard as nails, impeccable, *charming* – that's why she's prime minister material, am I right?'

I shrug my agreement.

'And he . . . is a wimp.' He downs the water and slam-dunks the bottle into the bin. Not the recycling. I guess his interest in survival doesn't extend to the environment. 'Right, I'm heading back into the fray.'

I follow him.

Smart, competent, hard as nails, impeccable, charming . . .

Get a room . . .

I wonder if he'd find Ayesha quite so alluring if he knew she'd reported him to social services.

'Is it strange being back at Saints?' I ask his back.

He glances over his shoulder but doesn't break his stride. 'It seems small.'

We pass the headmaster's office. Sam Maunder. Salamander. The ultimate survivor.

'His dad was headmaster,' Jack says. 'And now he is too.'

My trainers screech as I push to keep up with Jack's long stride. We're almost at the hall. He's well over six feet, conventionally handsome, fit and healthy. I'm puzzled why I've never found him remotely attractive. There would be no harm in window shopping, but I just don't fancy him. I watch his steely profile as he walks half a pace ahead of me. Everything is in the right place. So what is it about Jack Kent that leaves me cold?

It's the manner. Online, he connects and invites you into his world. But in person he's empty. An avatar of himself. That gossiping session was the most engaged I've ever seen him.

We stop outside the hall and he steps aside to let me go ahead. Instead, I fall back. I'm trying to formulate another question about the party where Temi was accused of God-knows-what.

And yet Jack just described him as an 'old soul' . . .

It doesn't fit.

This might be my only chance to hear Daddy Cool's version of events.

'Jack,' I start. He hums in response. Attention snared by the phone in his hand. 'I've been thinking about why someone might want to take the kids, hurt them, get revenge . . .'

'Uh-hm.' His phone gives a flurry of pings.

If he isn't going to pay attention, I'll hit him with it.

'I'm wondering about that girl whose thumb got severed at your house.'

Jack still doesn't look up. 'Nasty cut.'

'It ended her sports career. She left the country. Those parents must be distraught.'

'They made it sound worse for the lawyers. Dropped the case, though, of course.'

This is new. The parents tried to sue? Who, him? Wonder if Ayesha knows that? If her private investigator found out? She didn't mention it to Slocombe, at least not in my hearing.

Another thought strikes. 'When did they drop the case?'

'Last month.' Jack looks up now, open irritation on his face. 'How is this relevant?'

'Could they have dropped the case because they decided to take action another way? An eye for an eye, a child for a child?'

'A thumb for a thumb?' Jack scoffs. 'You think Li Na's parents flew over from Singapore and kidnapped a load of Saints kids because their daughter cut her finger at a party?'

'Maybe they haven't kidnapped a load of kids. Maybe they've kidnapped one particular child.'

'You think someone is targeting Alix because they blame him?'

'No, because they blame you.'

He stares at me.

'Or maybe they blame Temi and he's the target,' I say. 'Because he took the flak for your party getting out of control, didn't he?'

He smooshes his lips together but says nothing.

The door to the headmaster's office whips open.

Slocombe exits, followed by Maunder and Ayesha in mid-conversation. She says in her clear-as-a-bell voice:

'What sort of person would see this as an opportunity to raise their profile—?'

It must be bad if a politician is asking that question.

She stops as they see us in the corridor.

There's a moment. It's unclear who's going to take charge. Then Slocombe approaches.

'Mr Kent,' she says. 'We need you to take down this TikTok post. We've imposed a media blackout while we search for the bus and your post has revealed operational details—'

'If I can't go out there myself,' Jack hits back, 'then you can't blame me for using my network to help the search.'

'Help?' Ayesha is every inch the lady-boss. Fists on hips. Hair flicked back. 'How is this helping?'

'I've got a million followers.' He speaks to Ayesha as though no one else is here. 'Most of them survivalists. We need people out there, scouring the countryside, and they're the right kind of people. I'm doing my bit.'

'You need to take it down,' repeats Slocombe.

'Do what the detective says, Jack,' adds Maunder.

Jack looks at Maunder like he's got nits. He backs into the Great Hall, maintaining eye contact with the headmaster all the way, and only turns as the door swings shut.

Maunder smooths his hair and discovers there isn't much left. I suspect he was a late developer. All the more cruel that he's an early balder too.

'What's been posted on TikTok?' I have an account from when I used to keep an eye on Olivia – ages ago – but I don't feel the need to stalk her any more. So my account is dormant. In any case, I'd prefer to know what they all think about Jack's post.

DS Slocombe sighs. 'He recorded a video standing beside a Saints minibus in the quad, asking people to look out for the red and gold vehicles on the roads. Inciting them to flag one down if they see it.'

That must have been what Kent was doing when he went outside. Filming himself.

'We have at least twenty buses still out,' adds Maunder. 'Late matches and the tail end of the school run. Buses all over the city. What if they get set upon by idiots thinking they're foiling a crime? Vigilantes?'

He appeals to me as though I'm on Jack's side. I was just standing with him. I shrug and flatten my palms to show that I agree.

Placated, he jabs his phone and holds it up for me to see.

I can barely see Jack on the screen, but I recognise the quad and his voice fills the corridor.

Hi, guys, Jack here . . . your man, Jack Kent.

He has the phone close to his face so we only see him in increments, his mouth, his cheek, his eyes. It makes him look like he's in action, rather than standing in the safety of a nineteenth-century quadrangle. Or like he's too much to handle in one go. His face close enough to punch. Or kiss, I suppose, for his fangirls.

You know me best as a survivalist, an explorer, but I'm also a father and a husband, yeah? So I come to you today as a family man, yeah? I need your help, guys, it's an emergency, so I'm turning the tables. Whatever you're doing, stop and listen. This really is a matter of survival. Life and death. I need you warriors up and out there, to help find our son, Alix, who you know. He's missing, gone, we need to find him. And his schoolmates.

Jack goes on to show the kind of bus Alix is in. Jack describes where they were coming from in the first place – the pool – and the approximate route. Jack details the other kids who were on board, giving their names and ages. He's put it all out there.

If you're with Alix now, let me know, yeah, and we can talk. Consider this a call to arms, yeah? Keep 'em peeled for a bus like this – he flourishes an arm at the scarlet and gold bus behind him, so very distinctive – *Jack Kent, signing off. Remember, we don't just survive, we thrive.*

The screen goes dark with an arrow in the centre.

Ayesha does a sigh large enough for all of us.

'"We don't just survive, we thrive,"' she mimics under her breath so that only I can hear.

'And he has how many followers?' I ask.

'Over a million. Probably incels,' says Ayesha.

I ask DS Slocombe how much of a problem this post has caused.

'Major Crimes are pissed off,' she mutters. 'I'm pissed off.'

'It's had a massive response.' Maunder shakes his head in disbelief.

'What are they saying?' Ayesha asks.

Maunder scrolls.

'On TikTok it's mostly conspiracy theorists, nutters, misogynists. One literally blames' – he makes air quotes with one hand – '"a girl who must've got her claws into Alix".' He swipes again. 'Someone shared it to Twitter and everyone there thinks it's our fault for painting the school name on the side of the bus.' He looks up at us in bewilderment.

The buses aren't exactly low profile . . . They advertise the fact there are rich kids inside. I think of Akin talking about kidnapping in Nigeria; I bet their schools know better than to draw attention to themselves, make themselves a target.

'Have we still not received a ransom demand?' I ask Slocombe. She shakes her head.

'Do we think that's strange?' I push.

Ayesha jumps in. She's still scrolling. 'The optics are awful. All the crazies are out. The ranters and ravers. Class warriors. Look what they're saying; this would never happen in a state school. How is that relevant?'

'I can't believe' – Maunder glares at the door to the hall, as though it was Jack Kent himself – 'that he'd use the disappearance of his own son to get followers. What sort of man does this for attention? Like it's a publicity stunt?'

The detective's look slides over all of us. She's computing something. The likelihood of Jack Kent staging this thing, perhaps.

Then the DS visibly shrugs it away. Another door opens into the corridor and Singh comes in. Spot of colour high in his cheeks.

'Boss?' he says and they disappear into the office.

I'm left alone with Maunder and Ayesha, head boy and head girl.

Awkward silence.

'What do you do?' she asks me, as though we're juggling canapés and a glass of warm wine at some event.

'I'm a PT.'

She looks confused.

'Personal trainer.'

'Oh, I have one of those.' She still looks confused, although I assume now it's because she's trying to work out how someone who earns £30 an hour to make women do squats could have the audacity to aspire to a place like this. 'And Dad?' she says, searching for a quick solution to this conundrum.

'Not applicable,' I say.

Her eyes narrow slightly, but I know it can't be moral judgement. She's never publicly identified Kiran's dad. Not just an absent father, but a secret father. It caused her problems in the past. Political rivals bring it up constantly, revealing an archaic but surprisingly enduring value system that doesn't like single mothers, especially single mothers who're doing just fine on their own, thanks. The optics, as Ayesha might say, are awful.

At least I don't have to explain my choices on *Question Time*.

But even though we have common ground, Ayesha and I, she shows no mercy. Doesn't hide her incredulity that she and I, as two Saints parents, are equals.

Maunder's door opens and Slocombe comes out.

'What's happening?' Ayesha asks.

'We should go to the hall,' he says.

My heart is a stopped clock.

I drift behind them.

In the hall, DS Slocombe calls for attention. Checks that all the parents are here.

'We've located the bus,' she says.

Silence.

We're beyond the naiveté of thinking this will end so simply.

'The children were not there.'

Mariah slams her palm on her forehead. A gesture I recognise from Dixie.

'Where is this bus?' says Akin.

'Yeah, can we go there?' says Jack.

'I'm afraid I'm not at liberty to tell you the exact location—'

Everyone reacts.

DS Slocombe raises her voice. 'It's a crime scene. There are forensic officers on site.'

'Crime scene?' I ask. 'Why?'

She kisses her teeth. 'They've found another body.'

'And, this time, has anyone thought to check for a pulse?' mutters Akin.

Slocombe slides cool eyes over him. 'I'm afraid the individual is deceased.'

'Who?' I ask. 'I know you won't have a formal identification yet, but you must have a description. You must know if it's one of ours.'

She looks at me, exasperated, like I should zip it. But it's my daughter out there.

'Is it an adult?' Ayesha presses. 'A boy . . . or a girl?'

'It would be better to wait—'

'We're not children!' Akin's voice scatters to the rafters like pigeons.

Slocombe tilts her head as though dodging one of them. Her eyes flick to mine. I wonder why and my heart falters.

'I'm waiting for confirmation from officers at the scene. You will be the first to know as soon as there's anything definite. All I do know is, the body was wrapped in a Saints flag.'

Chapter Sixteen

12.05 p.m.

Hockey stick met driver's ear with a sound like a dropped egg. Kiran staggered as the vehicle jerked and decelerated. His arm fell to his side. His head tipped back to look at the ceiling where blood spread in tendrils as the bus slewed over the road. Kiran fell onto his backside on the nearest seat, the hockey stick clattering under a chair.

Olivia undid her belt and tried to get up, but it was like being at sea. She was tossed back down.

In the front, Temi pressed his back against the passenger door with his hands held up in a pantomime pose of shock. Only feet away, the driver's hood had fallen back to reveal the remains of his ear.

'You should have finished him off,' said Alix.

He was speaking to Kiran.

The driver didn't react or turn, just hunched over the wheel. Like an old lady peering very hard over the top of their glasses. Stunned. If he passed out, they'd crash. At least their speed had dropped a bit.

'Stop the bus.' Temi came back to life. He appealed to the driver. 'Stop the bus, man, you're hurt. You need help. You can't drive.'

If anything, they seemed to speed up again.

Temi looked helplessly at Olivia.

She noticed the driver wasn't reaching for the gun. Surely he should grab the gun?

If Olivia had a gun, and a boy had just smashed her ear with a hockey stick, she'd grab hold of that gun. Even as a deterrent. Why hadn't the driver done that?

Unless he couldn't think straight. He was concussed. Brain damaged. They had to make him stop the bus.

'Kiran?' Alix hissed. 'Kiran!'

Kiran got unsteadily to his feet.

'Sit down,' Olivia shouted. 'Don't!'

Kiran found the hockey stick under the seat. When he lifted it again, the end was already bloody.

'In for a penny, in for a pound,' Alix called out encouragingly.

Olivia didn't have her belt on. The strap had slipped between the seats. She pulled it free, found the metal end, fumbled the latch into the socket, but it wouldn't click. She pressed again and again. Again and again, it came free—

Another dropped egg.

Olivia felt a pop as her head bounced off the window. She put a hand to her temple and felt it burn from the impact. She jolted the other way so hard her neck twinged. The bus was swerving from side to side. Olivia saw it in her mind like the tail of a shark. As if she'd detached and could watch from above. Time moved too slowly. The injured driver fought, perhaps through sheer instinct, to keep the bus pointing forward. Temi had his hands planted on the dash. Kiran fought with his belt. Alix went into a brace position. The air darkened as the road swept under a tunnel of trees.

Another pop. Her head on the window again. She blinked, slightly stunned. A rushing noise made her turn— The back doors had burst open and she realised the rear end of the bus must have glanced off a roadside tree.

A sudden deceleration tipped her forward. As though his foot had slipped off the accelerator. The driver was losing it.

'Don't!' Temi was shouting. 'You'll kill him!'

Kiran had the curved end of the hockey stick hooked around the driver's throat. He was pulling with all his might. The bus was slowing more and more, but how long would they stay on the road?

Up ahead, the lane cut into the side of a hill. The road continued straight but the woodland fell away sharply to the left. And the nose of the bus was drifting that way.

'Grab the wheel!' Olivia shouted. 'Temi, lean over and grab the wheel!'

But he seemed to have frozen.

There was no fence, no barrier, nothing to stop them veering down the bank.

And Olivia had no belt.

The back doors slammed against the side of the bus as its left-hand wheels bumped onto the rutted verge. They drifted towards the drop. They were going to crash. Olivia launched herself over the back seat into the luggage compartment, tangling up in the Saints kit. Instinct drove her. She knew how to roll from swimming. She tucked into a ball and went out through the back doors as the bus plummeted off the road.

Chapter Seventeen

4.45 p.m.

A body. Wrapped in a Saints flag. Whose body?

Mariah is beside me. And beside herself. One leg jiggling like she's in the electric chair.

'Are you alright?' I lay one hand on her knee to settle it.

'No,' she snaps.

'Physically, I mean. You rushed to the loo—'

'I said I'm fine.' She whips her leg from under my hand. My chair crunches as I sit back and fold my arms. She's worried, I get it. But so are we all. Why does she get to be more stressed out than me? Unless she knows something I don't. I shift again to place both feet firmly on the floor. I can't push her to speak, she is not a woman whose castle can be stormed, but I can wait her out. I unfold my arms and busy myself pushing back the cuticles of my fingernails. I only get as far as the index fingers before she cracks.

'If Slow Coach doesn't tell us more, I'm gonna place my hands around her throat and squeeze her blue.'

'Where's Kash?' I know her husband is out of town but it's been ages.

'It's rush hour.'

I don't know why she's being so tight-lipped.

Maybe he's looking for the bus. Which I could understand. Or getting his contacts to look for the bus. Which I could not.

Maybe someone snatched Dixie to get at him? It makes me think again about the rumours that his property developments sit on a dodgy foundation; some say illegal foreign money, others mention high-interest loans, the wildest say it's all built on Masonic connections, although I think the conspiracy theorists have read too much Dan Brown and confuse the local planning department with the Illuminati. I can't help but hear all the stories even if I take some with a pinch of salt.

Mariah got jittery after we heard about the bus crash. The news is terrifying, of course it is, and I can't think directly about the ID of this body. I'm holding that thought at bay, looking at it askance, as though it's a dangerous dog. So I get it: Mariah is scared, but she was all woo-woo before, *in tune with Dixie's spirit*, now she's a cat on a hot plate. Does she know more than she's letting on? More than she's telling the police? If Kash has taken matters into his own hands and our kids got hurt as a result, I'll have him thrown away and will personally swallow the key.

'When will Kash get here?' I press Mariah.

She stands up and tugs her lime-green bottoms. 'These leggings are so far up my arse, they're flossing my teeth.'

She does that. Acts crass when she doesn't want to talk.

Well, if she's going to disengage, I can do the same.

I get up and grab my bag.

'Where you going?' she asks.

'Loo,' I say. 'Tea while I'm up?'

'I've had so much tannin I'm developing a Trump tan.'

I take a look round the hall as I leave. Jack Kent is having his turn in the office with DS Slocombe. Maunder is off somewhere in the building. The students have gone, but there are a couple of staff, I think, keeping out of the way to give us privacy at a difficult time. Ayesha has taken a seat in the opposite corner from me and Mariah. On her phone, as ever. And Akin is now missing.

I wander up the corridor, past the loos and the headmaster's office. I consider ducking inside the storage cupboard again to hear what Jack has to say, but I'm more curious about Akin and his private security. He stopped mentioning it. Does that mean he abandoned the idea? Or has he disappeared to go and organise it?

There's a cubby opposite Maunder's office and I stick my head inside. Three chairs tucked out of the way. This must be where pupils sit before facing the headmaster. I spent a lot of time in chairs like these, awaiting my fate while classmates snickered past. I was the kid who got the blame. You get done once, you get done every time. Lesson for life, right there.

A dingy set of stairs disappears into the gloom.

I leave the alcove and decide to stretch my legs by walking to the end of the corridor. It turns a corner and the classrooms begin. Modern languages. Noticeboards flutter with flags. I was good at languages, French and German, wish I'd kept them up. Geography. Walls decorated with photos from a field trip. Iceland, by the looks of it. Science. Blueprints—

Hands grab my arm and drag me sideways through an open door.

I spin round.

Lungs up in my throat.

It's a chemistry lab.

I steady myself on the end of a high wooden bench.

Akin Abiola checks up and down the corridor outside, then silently presses the door into its frame. There's a little blind which he pulls down too. He faces me.

I regain my breath as I move down the laboratory so that I'm standing at the end of a high bench at the back of the class.

'I'm glad it's you,' he says.

He follows me down the room.

'Shouldn't you check before you drag someone off their feet?'

'I need to talk to you.'

He stops beside the next bench. Safe distance. Picks up a short length of orange hose, which I know is from a Bunsen burner, and puts it down again.

'Great facilities,' he says in a monotone.

I'd be more impressed by the ovens and chillers and fumigation tanks and centrifuges and other bits of kit on shelves along the side of the room, most of which look like they cost more than my car, and according to Olivia are high enough spec for a pharmaceutical company or university research department rather than a secondary school. But he's impressed by Bunsen burners. Perhaps I should be grateful that he's so easily pleased.

He moves closer, lifts a high wooden stool and places it in front of him. Between us. I have my back to the bench, both hands hip-height, holding the edge of the wood. Casual. He tries to lean on the stool, but it looks awkward.

'How are you holding up?' I ask. It sounds inadequate. Crass, even.

'Shona is home with Abi,' he replies. His wife and daughter.

'Good to know they're safe.'

He nods. The stool has a gap in the centre of the seat and he runs his index finger around it.

'When something like this happens, it makes you think about what's important.'

'Family,' I say.

He nods again.

He lifts the stool aside.

One step and he's on me. Barely a hand span between our bellies.

He says my name.

His voice rumbles through his chest like an oncoming train.

Up close, he's massive. Blocks my view of the door.

He reaches forward and covers my hands with his. I arch my back, the wooden bench a hard line across my spine. The movement only lifts my chest towards him. His eyes flit but he doesn't close the gap between us any further. Instead, he purses his lips and places a soft kiss in the small space between my eyebrow and my hairline. I turn my hands under his palms until our fingers interlock.

This is the invitation he's waiting for. He closes the gap and our bodies jigsaw, his thigh tucking between mine. His hands sweep up to surround my throat. He doesn't kiss me. His hands run over the back of my skull and knock off my beanie, skim my nape to press the wings of my shoulder blades and finally settle in the dip of my back. He pulls me away from the bench so I'm fully in his arms and we come to rest nose to nose.

'That was a bit like a medical.' I try to sound wry but my short breath gives me away. He gave me a similar forensic examination in the shower once and I'm still not entirely over it.

'I needed to know you're alright,' he says. 'You feel so familiar.'

'This is pretty familiar—'

He kisses me. I hesitate for all of a second and then tip my head and slide my hands over his shoulders to pull him onto me. I'm against the wooden bench, crushed by his weight, which is what I need, to feel enclosed, overwhelmed, limited to simple sensations instead of roiling feelings. He sets about my clothing like a man looking for something he's lost—

'Akin.'

He groans and doubles over to rest his cheek awkwardly against my chest.

'Akin.'

'Don't make it stop,' he mumbles.

'Stop,' I say.

He lifts his head. Stands up straight. Takes hold of my running jacket and reels up the arms, bringing the two sides together over my torso. 'I'm sorry. I just . . .' He tries to zip me up but fails and steps away, flapping his hands in a way that tells me to cover myself.

'You need comfort,' I say.

'This is driving me mad.'

He means our missing kids. Not the decision we made to end our relationship, which was sordid and beautiful and had to end before it got sordid and ugly.

I zip up my running jacket. Fully insulated against him.

'I've missed you,' he says. 'Every day.'

I close my eyes and shake my head. When I open them, he's taken a step further away.

'Does my hair look mad?' I ask, gathering up the hat he knocked off.

'You might want to put your beanie on.'

I scrape my hair to one side, then pull the hat down to my eyebrows.

Modest now.

'Do you think anyone knows?' I ask.

'About us? We've hardly spoken to each other today. Does Mariah know?'

It wasn't Mariah I was worried about. Maybe I should tell Akin about Ayesha and her private investigator. Maybe her ex-cop is only looking into Jack's doings. But what if Ayesha is interested in other parents too? She might also be investigating Akin – after all, Temi was the one accused of misbehaving at the party. But how can I tell Akin about the PI without revealing that I eavesdropped on a police interview? That vantage point in the cupboard might come in useful again, I don't want to share it with anyone yet . . .

'I never told Mariah about us. I've never told anyone.'

He rubs his lips. 'Same here.'

'It's been hard.'

'Like grieving for a ghost,' he nods.

I want to hold him again, but I grip the wooden bench behind me instead.

'Do you think we should drive out to where they found the bus?' I ask. 'Instead of sitting here and waiting?'

'We don't know where to go,' he says gently.

'We could just drive around. I think maybe Mariah's husband is doing that?'

'Then let him. He'll call if he finds them.'

He rubs his fingertips from the corners of his mouth to the centre of his lips, manually puckering them up. His thoughtful tic.

My mouth tastes of him. It reminds me of when we ate oysters from a shack on the beach. Shucking as we went, tossing shells to torment the seagulls. Whatever were we thinking? The risks we took . . .

'I phoned the private security firm,' he says.

I wait for him to say more but he only rubs his lips.

'And? What are they doing? I'm worried they'll make things worse.'

'How could it be any worse?' he asks.

'We could aggravate whoever has taken them.'

'We don't know they've been taken. That's what the guy said. They're starting background checks, but without a ransom demand . . .' He shrugs.

Background checks on who? Us?

'It's weird there's no ransom,' I say.

'It's been five hours. More now. And they've found the bus, so it's not some freak accident, the bus under water in the reservoir or something.'

'Were you thinking about that too?'

'When I saw the rivers and reservoir on that map— Doesn't help that I see too much every day . . .'

An imagination full of A&E horrors. I reach out and brush his fingertips with mine, but don't hold onto his hand.

'It could be anything,' I say. 'That list you made . . . You said yourself it could be targeted against one of us. Or one of the kids?'

'They're children, how could they be involved in anything—'

'They're not babies. The things they do have serious consequences.'

His gaze hardens.

'What are you getting at?' An edge to his voice now.

'We shouldn't stay here long. If someone sees us—' I say.

'We're just talking. What do you mean by "serious consequences"?'

I realise I'm rubbing my lips, too, parroting his gesture. I stop myself. He must know about Temi. That he was accused of harassing that girl at a party. Temi was the only one identified from the photo. Of course, I know why. He was identified because he was the only child of colour. The others were nondescript white lads. All the more reason for Akin to have said something to me – share the anger and shock with a sympathetic ear, the unfairness of it – we were still seeing each other at the time of that party. But he didn't tell me. Didn't trust me.

He was convinced I would let slip our 'situationship', as Olivia might call it. Didn't matter that I fervently didn't want my daughter to know. Akin was my cross to bear, and if there's one thing he should have learnt about me, it's that I carry my own weight.

'DS Slocombe knows about the party. About Temi.' I'm not giving him any space to interrupt and ask how I know. 'So this situation with the bus could be connected to that. The parents of that injured girl threatened to sue, they're angry, and Temi didn't get expelled or even suspended—'

'Of course not. There was no basis to any of it. I dealt with it.'

What does that mean?

'Did the school tell DS Slocombe?' Akin asks.

'That's what she said. But there's more – the parents threatened to sue Jack Kent. Then dropped the case. Don't you think that's strange?'

He glances at his watch.

'Are you so sure this isn't to do with that party?' I press.

He flips my question aside with his hand. It's an arrogant gesture and I see him for a moment, the doctor, consultant, dismissing underlings with their boring questions.

It piques my anger.

'I'm warning you, Ayesha Reid is a dog with a bone. She's got it in for Jack Kent, but she'll take down anyone who gets in the way.'

'What do you mean?'

'She reported him to social services and now she's got a private investigator onto him.'

'Seriously?'

'Seriously.'

Akin looks ashen.

For the first time I wonder about Temi. Model student. Bright, handsome, sporty, hard-working, polite, funny. He's fucking perfect. Except no one is perfect.

Not me.

Not his dad.

And maybe not Temi.

Chapter Eighteen

12.10 p.m.

The chill of the earth seeped into Olivia's bones like rising water. A flock of leaves stirred overhead. In the wake of silence, she opened her eyes.

A vast yew tree, its trunk as wide as the bus, gnarled like something out of a fairy tale. Perhaps some kind of magic had saved her because the bus blurred into focus and it was on its side a few metres beyond the tree. Must have missed it by a whisker. The bus had taken a deep gouge out of the embankment as though clawing the ground to stop itself. Then she learnt that there was no fairy-tale magic, only gravity and pain, because an incandescent flame fired into her shoulder. It burnt like magnesium in the chemistry lab. Gathering up her white-hot arm, she staggered around the bus to find the others.

Temi had been sitting up front on the side that was now in the air. She had to help him—

She stopped walking.

There was a body on a shattered piece of glass. The windscreen had popped out whole. Someone had followed it.

It was slumped like Mr Sadler in that clearing. A heap. Except this one was bloody. But she recognised the white Stüssy hoodie even if it was pinky-red now. The driver.

He looked dead. She only realised she had said that aloud when a voice behind her replied:

'We need to make sure.'

Temi.

Silvery flecks of glass in his hair as though he'd prematurely aged.

Olivia had seen her first dead body a month previously. She'd done work experience in a drug rehab unit, assisting a nurse whose advice covered everything from signs that a patient had relapsed to the best place to find snacks on a nightshift to shoes that didn't make your feet grow bunions. So she'd seen a dead person. But Olivia didn't want to approach this one. A death in the sterility of the clinic was one thing. It was expected. Death in a wood beside a country lane was not.

Maybe she should force herself? She'd have to get used to death if she wanted to be a doctor. But something held her back. A kind of dread seeping through her like the cold earth rising again. What if they got in trouble over this dead man? What if no one believed that he was a kidnapper, that it was self-defence, that it was Kiran who swung the hockey stick? Was it even self-defence? Was it only Kiran who was to blame? Were they all responsible? Would she be accused? Convicted? Wasn't there something like *aiding a crime*? Aiding and abetting, that was it. Would a conviction prevent her from becoming a medic? Was her dream over before it began? The treetops swam and she wasn't sure if it was the wind, or her vision, or dizziness caused by all these questions. She realised she'd stopped breathing. She dragged air inside herself. Waited for oxygen to flow. Waited for the panic to pass. Told herself it's just adrenaline. Hormones. A physical process. She could control it. She controlled it.

First things first. Is the man definitely dead?

'Can you make sure?' She reached out and tapped Temi's arm. 'Please?'

People said Temi was a machine. The sportiest, the brightest, the coolest. Now was his chance to prove it. Sure enough, he did exactly what was expected of him, robotically stepping forward onto the bloody windscreen. Got his balance.

Kicked the guy in the face.

That wasn't what she'd meant. She meant take his pulse or something. But it was done now. The driver must be dead. No one's neck should be in that position. At least he couldn't tell anyone about the hockey stick. The injury to his ear might be explained by him going through the windscreen. They should dispose of the hockey stick.

Alix arrived. Stared at the dead guy. OMGing until Olivia found a cloth that had flown out of the back of the bus with her – a red and gold Saints flag – and wrapped it around the body so they didn't have to see it.

Olivia checked everyone for concussion. Temi said he'd been knocked out loads of times on the rugby field and this didn't feel the same, he didn't feel nauseous or anything, but Olivia wasn't sure if that made it better or worse – accumulative concussion was even more dangerous, wasn't it?

'If we don't get out of here soon,' said Alix, 'concussion won't be the thing that kills us. If this guy had a gun then his mate must have one too.'

The gun. They should get it.

'Where's Kiran?' Olivia asked.

She turned to see him sitting on his bum in the mulch a little way off.

'You okay, tough guy?' asked Alix.

'Don't call me that.' Kiran's voice had dropped an octave. 'Or I'll take a hockey stick to you too.'

Alix raised his eyebrows at Olivia and laughed.

'I like this new Kiran,' he said.

Olivia didn't laugh. This kind of male energy was tedious. A joke long gone stale.

'We've got to go back,' Olivia said. 'For Dixie.'

'Hard agree,' said Temi.

'Let's find the gun,' she said.

Alix darted around the front of the bus. The plastic bag was in the undergrowth. He snatched it up and fished out the gun— Except it wasn't a gun. It was an electronic device. A smartphone in a brick-sized leather wallet-case.

'What's this?' Alix held it up to show to Temi. The cover flapped open to reveal a bright yellow sticker on the inside – Homer Simpson pointing at his bare bum.

Temi shrugged. 'It's a phone.'

'Where's the gun?' Olivia asked. 'The gun must be somewhere here?'

Alix kicked his feet through the mulch around the windscreen.

'It might be near the body—' he said.

'You won't find a gun,' said Temi.

All around them, naked branches shivered.

'There wasn't a gun. It was the phone in the plastic bag. I made up the gun because he had a photo of Abi on the phone.'

His sister.

'And?' pressed Alix.

Temi frowned at him. 'He said he'd snatch her from school if I didn't do what he said. I only had to sit in the front, that's all he wanted. Said he needed to split us up. I guess he thought I was the biggest threat—'

'Well, that's bollocks,' said Alix.

'—and he wanted me where he could see me. He said he'd let us go, but someone is waiting outside school to get Abi if we play up. He had her photo, he knew what she looked like, he knew her name. She walks home, so it wouldn't be hard to get hold of her. People—' He choked and swallowed it. 'People have targeted my family before.'

Temi looked at the bus. Then looked back at Olivia.

'This is my fault. If there's someone outside the school, waiting for Abi, and this guy doesn't call him, won't they grab her? They want money. They'll hurt her—'

'He could have got her name and photo off the internet,' said Olivia.

'How did he know my name?' Temi asked. 'I didn't speak to him before he got in the bus?'

All three boys frowned at Olivia.

'I saw him at the swim meet. He was in the viewing gallery. I noticed him because he was alone and staring at me.' When Alix looked dubious, she added, 'Girls have a radar for pervs, okay? We grow up with this shit. You don't. And I recognise his hoodie. Stüssy, right?' Temi nodded. 'So if he was at the pool, then he could have seen our names on the team sheets, googled you, found your sister.' Olivia shrugged. 'Used it to frighten you into doing what he wanted.'

Temi stared down at the dead driver as though waiting for him to apologise. For all his physical presence and academic brilliance, there was still a naive boy inside Temi who thought the world should play fair.

'So there was no gun?' asked Kiran. He was sitting away from them. The hockey stick on the ground next to him.

'No, no gun,' said Temi. 'I said that so you'd sit down and shut up and not get hurt. I needed to protect my sister.'

'So why did I hit him?'

'Because you're fucking mental,' muttered Alix under his breath.

'What?' Kiran got to his feet. 'What did you say?'

'I said,' Alix spoke loud enough for Kiran to hear, 'you hit him because you thought there was a gun. It's not your fault you overreacted.'

'Right,' said Kiran, nodding hard. 'That's right. I had to do it. To stop the bus.'

'And because you're fucking mental,' muttered Alix behind his hand.

'How do we know you're telling the truth now?' Kiran fired at Temi.

'He is,' said Olivia.

Kiran ignored her.

'Show us the phone. Show us the picture of your sister.'

'Sure,' said Temi, his voice hitched. He gestured for Alix to hand over the device. 'If we can get into the phone. It might be locked—'

Alix ignored Temi, opened the leather wallet and tapped the screen.

'Doesn't matter if there's a passcode or not,' said Kiran. 'We can use the driver's face recognition.'

'Not sure it'll recognise him after your hockey stick and Temi's boot,' said Alix.

'Wait—' Olivia waved her hands to silence the boys. 'If we've got a phone then we can call for help. They'll find us. We can lead them to Dixie. You have to call the police, Alix, now.'

But Alix held up the blank screen. 'Phone's dead.'

'But it was working,' said Temi. 'It was working a few minutes ago.'

'Convenient,' said Kiran.

'It's not convenient.' Olivia lost her temper with him. 'We need to call the police!'

'I mean,' Kiran came closer with the hockey stick in his hand, 'it's convenient for Temi that the phone was *apparently* working a few minutes ago, but now it's dead. Out of battery just in time so that he can't prove there was a photo of his sister.'

Temi let his hands flop against his sides.

Alix shrugged. 'Calm down, Kiran, phones run out of battery. We'll take it with us and find a charger. Then Temi can prove it. Right, Temi?'

'Sure,' he agreed. 'But where are we going?'

'A place I know,' said Alix. 'Near the reservoir. I went there with my dad when he was filming. There'll be shelter and a phone.'

'Why don't we split up into pairs and find a house?' Kiran said.

'We must be in the national park,' Alix said. 'It covers this whole area. So there're no houses.'

'There must be . . .' muttered Temi. 'We just have to walk a bit.'

'We should go back to the wood,' Olivia said. 'For Dixie.'

'It'll be quicker if we go cross country,' said Alix. 'We're fit, we'll move fast as we've got no packs. I'll make a sling for your arm. This is my forte, remember, it's in my blood.'

His dad, the 'survivalist', who the mums called Daddy Cool because he's a twit. Olivia had assumed he filmed in places like the Arctic, not a national park an hour from home. But what choice did they have? Sit in the forest and freeze to death? Leave Dixie to her fate? No, they had to move. Let Alix do his heroics, at least he knew the way.

He made a sling with a bib from the hockey bag. It eased the pain in her shoulder, so maybe he did have some skills.

They got in line as they moved off from the crash site. Alix in front. Kiran swinging his hockey stick in sullen silence. Temi in disgrace. As they pulled themselves up the mossy embankment onto the lane, Olivia took one last look at the Saints bus, its dirty underside revealed to the clouds.

Chapter Nineteen

5.00 p.m.

Akin leaves the chemistry lab first and I wait five minutes before following. I shouldn't have told him about Ayesha's private investigator. That was my information to hold back for the opportune moment, not to fritter away as ammunition to hurt him. I'm tired and emotional. Need to reset. On the way back down the corridor, I dive into the bathroom. There are three cubicles. One occupied.

The room stays silent as I enter a cubicle, lower the seat and sit on it. I fold forward and look under the stalls. As I do, I catch sight of the other person's hands lifting off the floor. Was she looking underneath too? Checking my shoes, just as I'm checking hers?

Interesting.

In any case, it's Ayesha. Heeled court shoes. Smart, sensible and pointed enough to be a tiny bit sexy. Like her.

'Did you hear about the body they found with the bus?' Her voice echoes between stalls. 'It's not one of our kids. It was a young man, not wearing a Saints uniform, but wrapped in the flag – they don't know why, maybe to cover the body. This is off the record, unconfirmed, not to be repeated, but they wouldn't have said anything if they weren't pretty sure. I think they're trying to stop us going absolutely fucking nuclear.'

Relief sucks the air out of my lungs. It's a second before I can reply.

'Thank you for telling me.'

She doesn't say any more. I hear the tug-tug-tug of toilet paper being pulled from its cat's-arse dispenser. I WhatsApp Mariah just as she WhatsApps me with the same news. Jinx. Then I message Akin and he replies, *Thank God!* Then I google Ayesha Reid. She has a Wikipedia page. State grammar school, then Oxford, then postgrad at Stanford. She worked in public policy before being elected as an MP at her second attempt, aged thirty. Sped through the ranks. Varied interests, she's worked on campaigns relating to childcare, tax on alcohol, asylum, workplace productivity. Then became junior minister in farms and fisheries.

Nothing controversial. Hard to imagine any of those issues making her a target.

But then I see she was in a delegation to Ukraine to support sanctions on Russia. She lobbied the Chinese ambassador on the same issue. Opposition to Russia could certainly have repercussions . . .

And her first parliamentary vote was in favour of bombing Islamic targets in Syria. She's been outspoken on Israel and Palestine.

More red flags . . .

My eye is drawn down to the word 'scandal'. It's only a brief paragraph about how Ayesha gave evidence in an espionage trial against a parliamentary researcher called Jerry Ladbroke. The paragraph below is more interesting: the controversy about her son. Ayesha had Kiran shortly after graduating from Oxford and steadfastly refused to name the father. It's not even on the birth certificate. Her secrecy fans the flames of controversy. So what if the boy was the result of a one-night stand? If she just said that, no one would care. Instead, her silence creates space for conspiracy theories. I skim the most popular ones: it's the prime minister's son, it's her university tutor's son and that's how she got a First, she's a closet lesbian and paid the father for his donation (which is illegal, apparently – who knew?), she used a surrogate because she didn't want to ruin her career and/or figure. It's judgemental at best, sexist at worst.

And I don't see how it's relevant to today.

Unless the father took the minibus to get hold of Kiran. But why not just grab the boy and leave the others? And surely, if it was the father, Ayesha would be making a song and dance about it? But it does strike me as rich that someone who fiercely protects the secret of her son's paternity would take it upon herself to employ a private investigator to dig up another parent's private life. A hypocritical politician? Shocker.

I shut off my phone to save the battery.

No movement from the other cubicle.

I go out and wash my hands. Then I fill a sink and hold my breath, splashing my face several times. The water is icy enough to sting the inside of my nose. I stand up, letting it run into my eyes. My body responds, sending blood to protect my internal organs from a cold threat. Stupid body, easily tricked. Lingering by the sinks, I take off the beanie, but Akin was right about my hair, so I put it on again.

Eventually, the occupied cubicle opens and Ayesha exits.

She acknowledges me with a glance before studying herself in the mirror. She uses the heel of her right hand to pummel out a palmful of soap, then lets the water run as she washes. She's very thorough, uses a paper towel rather than the dryer. Once she's satisfied that she's clean, she turns to me.

'I'm curious about you, Emily Smith.'

Okay.

I make a surprised face.

'Your daughter is Olivia, right?'

I agree.

'Kiran likes her. Not *likes* likes her. He doesn't seem interested in anyone that way, girls or boys, or at least he doesn't tell me. But he respects her. She's bright. Is she Oxbridge stream?'

She is. I don't say that I'm not sure I want Olivia to go there even if she gets a place. It sounds like Saints only *more so*. Like they make you feel you owe them. When, in fact, they should feel lucky to have you – the brightest and best. One of the many little ways that life is arranged back to front.

'So what have you found out so far?' Ayesha asks.

'Found out?'

'You're out of the hall more than you're in it. If I didn't know better, I'd say you were sneaking about, up to something.'

Okay.

'Why our kids? Why today? Why no ransom demand? DS Slocombe is more like DS Slow Coach.' I help myself to Mariah's joke.

Ayesha doesn't smile. Maybe she's already heard it.

I feel like throwing the private investigator back in her face – *and why are you nosing into people's lives?* – but refrain.

'It seems to me,' I say, 'that everyone has a reason why someone might want to punish them by taking their child.'

'What's yours, then?' Ayesha says.

Good question. And it stumps me.

'Olivia's dad?' Ayesha asks.

I shake my head. 'Long gone.'

I hesitate a moment and then think, *Fuck it*.

'What about Kiran's dad?' I ask.

She gives a mirthless smile.

'Also long gone. But that's an interesting thought. An estranged parent grabbing their child ... That could be it. At least they wouldn't hurt them.'

Obsessive love, that's what Akin called it on his list earlier.

Who could Ayesha mean? I run the Rolodex in my mind. Temi and Dixie have married parents. Olivia and Kiran have long-gone fathers – neither likely to come after them, if what Ayesha says is true. So that only leaves Alix. Jack Kent. Ayesha's fixation. Except Jack is married – to Alix's mum, Cally, Calpurnia, so . . .

'The Kents aren't estranged, are they?'

Ayesha's eyebrows shoot up to her hairline.

'Where is she, then?' she whispers.

Jack hasn't mentioned that.

'Calpurnia was the wife of Julius Caesar,' Ayesha murmurs. 'We did the play at Oxford. She has a vision of his murder and tries to warn him, but he won't fucking listen.'

I don't know what to say to that so I don't say anything.

'You know Jack Kent was expelled from Saints for bullying,' she says.

'That was a long time ago.'

'His wife is in and out of mental health care. Sectioned.'

'How do you know all this?' I ask. See if she'll admit to the PI.

But she just gives a tiny shrug as though it's a natural state of being. *I know things you don't*.

I decide to take a risk. 'Jack seems paranoid. The survival skills. And he said someone has been following him . . .' He said no such thing, but Ayesha is hardly likely to get into a huddle with Jack Kent and tell him what I said.

Ayesha rolls her eyes. 'Can't get the staff these days.'

I frown.

She drops her voice. 'I hired a private investigator. Obviously not the surveillance genius he claimed to be, if a bonehead like Jack Kent has spotted that he's being followed. My guy is only supposed to focus on paperwork, contacts, skeletons in closets . . .'

'So how boney is Jack Kent?'

Ayesha gives a single laugh. 'I was suspecting something financial, but now I'm not so sure. If he's trying to sideline the wife . . .'

'Isn't it a bit Victorian to suggest he's had her sectioned?'

'He's an established bully . . .' She raises her hands to indicate the school around us. A school that expelled Jack Kent decades ago. A direct line between then and now feels stretched to breaking point.

Ayesha seems to respect my frankness, so I keep firing questions.

'Has your PI looked into anyone else?'

'Anyone you have in mind?'

'I'm asking you,' I stall.

That shark smile again.

'Do you think anyone here earns their money virtuously?' she asks.

This is a dogleg.

'I don't know. We don't have any money, so . . .'

She frowns at me, disappointed by my coyness.

'I guess you can't make an omelette, and all that . . .' I say. 'Wealth often comes at a cost.'

'Some people break more eggs than others.' She gathers her bag and wraps the leather strap around her hand.

'What about Akin Abiola?' I offer. 'Anaesthetists earn good money. He's a consultant and so's his wife. That's virtuous?'

'He's got family money. And that comes from what?'

'Telecoms?' I hold her eye. 'My point stands: he must be decent to work in the NHS when he doesn't need the money.'

Ayesha acknowledges this with a hum.

'And your friend Mariah?' she says. 'She's not as fluorescent-lime-coloured as she makes out.'

'She's not daft. Don't let the lashes and lips fool you.'

'I don't judge a book by its cover.' She gives me a top-to-toe sweep and I wonder what aspect of my cover she's not judging.

A slam of a door outside is followed by raised voices in the corridor. Another slam. Maunder's office. Ayesha is out of the bathroom like a moth to the moon. The disturbance is behind the closed door. I recognise Akin's voice right away although I don't think I've ever heard him shout.

'So what am I paying you for?'

The response is too quiet to hear.

Ayesha glances at me, frustrated, and presses close to the door.

I join her.

'Akin Abiola and Sam Maunder,' she whispers. 'Man's a weasel.'

'A lizard,' I whisper back. 'The kids call him Salamander.'

'That fits,' she says.

Akin shouts again. 'Off the record means off the record. It means nothing on file. It means no snitching. I could make things very bloody difficult for you.'

Ayesha raises her eyebrows at me.

'How virtuous now?' she whispers.

Good question. What did Akin mean by *what am I paying you for*?

'We should go,' I say.

She shakes her head.

I will Akin to shut up, but he's not done.

'Whatever happens next, this is on you, Maunder!'

There's something final in his statement. Ayesha hauls me back into the bathroom. She has good instincts. The door hasn't even closed behind us when Akin slams out of Maunder's office and strides down the corridor in the direction of the chemistry lab.

Chapter Twenty

1.00 p.m.

Olivia crouched in a ditch between Temi and Kiran. They watched Alix creep on his belly along the road towards a wooden gate. The lane they were on now was little more than a farm track made of concrete slabs with grass in the cracks. Alix thought they should be getting close to the place where Dixie was taken and Sadler was attacked. He seemed confident. But then a crash of branches had sent them ducking for cover. The other kidnapper might be nearby. Dangerous.

Crouching hurt Olivia's shoulder, her injured arm crushed into her knees. She wished Alix would get up and walk, it would be quicker. His theatrics made her think of the boys at school who did military training on Tuesday lunchtime. Marching about the quad in soldier hats. The drill acted like steroids to their teenage egos so they were pumped-up all afternoon, overinflated and officious in the corridors.

She put her good hand on Temi's back and pushed herself out of the ditch.

'Olivia . . .' he whispered.

She waved at him to stay quiet.

Bending so she was lower than the boney hedgerow, she skipped past Alix to the gate, supporting her sling with her right hand. There was a stand of trees beyond the thicket. In the copse, a herd of horses who must have made the crashing noise. They scattered, tossing their heads as they cantered away.

'Wild ponies,' she called to the boys. In any other circumstances, she'd be delighted to see them.

Temi and Kiran got out of the ditch.

Alix stood up too.

'It could have been anyone,' he huffed. 'It could have been *him*.'

They'd been hiking cross country for half an hour. Her arm throbbed. She was parched. And she knew they weren't in the same place they'd left Dixie. It would have been slower to go by road but at least they'd have found the way. Now, they could be anywhere. They'd not passed a single home. Only an industrial site with piles of pallets and old tyres, then a barn with farming stuff inside, a massive piece of equipment that they decided must be a plough. It was January. Not a lot of farming happening. All these sites were deserted.

'If it *had* been him,' she said, 'I would've asked what the bloody hell he thinks he's doing.'

She carried on down the lane, the way they'd been going before they got startled.

The boys followed. Alix sped up and overtook so he was in front again.

'I didn't know there was this much wilderness in England,' Kiran moaned.

'Never been to Yorkshire?' Alix asked. 'Dartmoor?'

'This isn't wilderness,' Olivia said. 'We're just lost. We've only covered a couple of miles. We might have been going round in circles for all we know. The police would find us in minutes if we had a phone.'

'We're not lost,' said Alix. 'We're heading to the reservoir.'

They rounded a corner and the view opened up to reveal water in the valley below.

Alix put his fists smugly on his hips.

There were patches of woodland dotted all over the mottled landscape. It was like looking at a giant painting. Which daub contained Dixie?

The wind rushed to greet them. Another reminder that it was January. Walking had kept Olivia's core temperature up, but her right hand – the good arm that wasn't in a sling – was pink and tingling. Her head throbbed without a hat to cover her thick hair that was still damp in the winter air. Her mum went in the sea year-round with her Friday Dippers. She knew all about hypothermia. How it tricked you into feeling warm. That was the first sign, her mum said, as soon as you feel comfortable, get out of the water. Could they get hypothermia? How embarrassing if they managed to die in a national park. But it was hard to know what to believe when you couldn't believe your own body.

Talking of not knowing who to trust . . . Alix started yomping downhill towards the reservoir.

Now she saw why. He'd spotted a place beside the water. Buildings that looked like big metal sheds. Barns. They were in the middle of nowhere, but offered shelter, at least, maybe someone who could help, a phone. A sound bounced up and over the land. *Slap*. Followed by another *slap*.

Temi looked at her.

'Car doors?' he said. The vehicle must be hidden behind the sheds.

'Look,' Olivia said.

Way down below, there was movement. Two figures that flitted between buildings.

A flash of scarlet and gold.

'Did you see that?' she asked.

'Looked like a Saints uniform,' Temi said.

'Dixie.'

Crouched further down the field, Alix raised one fist. It meant stop and wait. She knew because she'd seen it in films.

She strode past him.

'Let's go get her,' she said.

Chapter Twenty-One

5.15 p.m.

When did it get dark? I didn't notice. Through the arched windows of the Great Hall, I can just make out the pollarded stumps of plane trees outside, their limbs raised like clubs.

'I wish I'd never come to this school,' I whisper to Mariah. 'We don't belong here.'

She plucks her swollen lips with pointed fingernails.

'Olivia does.'

'This wouldn't have happened in a normal school,' I insist.

'Stuff happens all the time.'

Ayesha glances over from where she's taken a seat at the piano. She's poised like she's going to play but the cover is over the keys. Jack returns from his interview with DS Slocombe. He looks reduced. Across the expanse of the hall, they keep each other in their peripheral vision like bull and matador. Don't know which one's which, though.

I haven't seen Akin since he stormed off from Maunder's office.

My phone pings.

Mariah has WhatsApped me a Twitter link. I click it. Someone has tweeted a screenshot of Jack's TikTok appeal asking his followers to look out for Saints buses. Even if he took his original post down, it's too late, the retweet has half a million likes and a thousand comments.

#FindKentsKid is trending.

Over in the corner of the hall, Jack sits with his phone limp in his hand. He has the posture of a post-party balloon. So much for bushcraft, he lit a fire and it's burning out of control.

I tap #FindKentsKid and hundreds of messages pop up.

A bland statement from the police press office confirms that an investigation is underway. Below that, someone posted a photo from 'the scene'. A police car in a lane. I enlarge it and scour the image for any sign of our kids, or the bus, or the location, then chide myself for getting taken in. This could be anywhere. It could be a stock photo. How would some dickhead on Twitter know the real location when we don't?

More posts dribble down the page like a stupid lolling tongue.

Legacy media peddling #fakenews to slur #policeheroes

How long until we learn this is another foney #asylum lunatic? Stop the #openborders liberal agenda. Stop #migrants

I hope these little angels RIP in a better place *prayer hands*

What are they on about? Fake news and migrants and RIP? What is wrong with these people? Why does everyone have an opinion? It reminds me why I hate social media. I would usually switch off as people use serious events to peddle their own, offensive agendas. But Mariah nudges me to search #SaintsCollege instead.

I do as she says. Fewer posts, but more threads. Conversations rather than idiots bellowing into the void.

Shocked about missing #SaintsCollege bus. Someone got a grudge?? Makes you think!

In reply:

ikr. You should see threads about #SaintsCollege on #MumsNet. I'd never send a kid to that school even if I could afford it

What are you implying?

The school is ruthless. Dozens of kids kicked out. Wouldn't be surprised if one of them has gone on a gun spree?? #SaintsCollege

Gun?? No one said anything about a gun. We don't know if it has anything to do with the school, it could be an accident or kidnapper

Oh, it has everything to do with that school.

Archaic system of private education. Schools like #SaintsCollege should go!

#SaintsCollege uses dodgy tactics to block criticism. Mumsnet threads forced down by threats of legal action. It happened to a friend! Make no mistake this is someone getting back at the school

Hard agree. And I think I know who you mean? DM me!!

School won't admit it publicly bc they'd have to admit the amount of complaints from parents! Hothouse schooling destroys young minds! Never mind #FindKentsKid what about #SaveSaintsKids??

That's enough.

'I'm going to find DS Slocombe,' I tell Mariah.

I head outside the Great Hall into the quad. It's bitterly cold now the sun has gone down, and I remember what Jack said about the rule of threes – you've got three hours in the cold. It's due to drop below freezing overnight. I can't think about the possibility of Olivia, out there somewhere, alone, shivering, afraid.

DC Gill Singh intercepts me. He captures me by the upper arms and I realise I've got tears running down my face. The warmth of his grip is too welcome. I shift away for fear of letting my guard down any more than I already have done.

'I need DS Slocombe. Where is she?'

'Can I help—?'

I grab the lapels of his Luther coat. 'You need to push Maunder for information. He's not being honest with you.'

Singh gently removes my hands.

'Look online,' I say. 'There are so many complaints about this school. What if this is targeted against the school, not us or the kids? Someone on Twitter thinks they know who might hold a grudge. Maunder must have access to official complaints or parents who've complained to the school governors. There could be someone who stands out as a risk, someone who's made threats—'

'Emily.'

I turn to see Slocombe. I show her the Twitter thread but stop when I see a tinge of pity in her eyes. I seem desperate. I *am* desperate. This is a case for her, but for me it's my whole life.

'I'll ask him myself.' I march back inside the Great Hall.

I can hear and feel the detectives following in my wake. I have a long stride. And I'm fit. Slocombe is struggling to keep up. Good. I'll make her work harder.

I'm through the hall in a few paces and up the corridor to Maunder's office. I stop outside his door, which is open an inch. It's so tall, designed to be imposing. How many children have stood here in fear? How many adults too? Well, not me, not now.

I push the door open and enter, aware that everyone has followed, responding to my burst of action. Akin appears too, exiting the men's bathroom and joining the group.

Maunder sits behind his desk, looking startled by us gate-crashing his wood-panelled privacy.

'We need to see your record of complaints. Someone might hold a grudge against the school.' I walk right up to the desk and lean on my hands. 'Now.'

Maunder hesitates. Off to the side of his desk stands a bank of TV screens showing live surveillance footage from around the school. The Great Hall stands empty. Only coats hanging on hooks like a line of grey ghosts. Outside the front gate, a cleaner is sweeping the pavement and I'm disoriented by the idea that life continues as normal for everyone but us.

Maunder jerks into action. He goes to open the cupboard where Mariah and I saw him rooting around earlier. He has to squat down to reach far into the back, but comes out with a memory stick. Returning to his desk, without making eye contact with anyone, he spins his laptop round and jams the flash drive in the side. On the screen, he taps a folder, then a file. A media player opens.

It's a film, looks like CCTV. I recognise the west playground. This is where we collect our children. Maunder hits 'play' and the footage starts, but there's nothing except swaying leaves for a few seconds.

The other parents say nothing, just watch, frowns on faces.

I walk into shot.

Okay, that's unexpected.

I rest my bum against a picnic table. I'm the only person there.

I lean forward to check the date stamp on the CCTV. It was recorded in October last year. My stomach sinks towards my trainers.

Twilight. Must be a late pick-up. Extra training session, maybe. My wool coat hangs open so it can't be too cold. I put my little finger in my ear and give it a good waggle.

Hot blood bursts through my cheeks. I can't look at the other parents. It's humiliating to see myself unselfconscious and unchecked, an invasion of privacy, but I have the sinking feeling it's going to get worse.

Akin walks into shot. We greet each other. He looks over both shoulders. Then he scoops me against the table and we snog like teenagers.

I glance away from the screen to see Mariah staring at it open-jawed. When she shifts her look to me, I avoid her eye. Maunder helps me by choosing that moment to stop the recording. He looks satisfied, like a pastor identifying a sin.

'What is this?' says Akin. 'Why were you filming us?'

'It's CCTV. You were on school property,' says Maunder.

'But this happened months ago, why keep it?' asks Akin.

'And why share it?' I add. 'I asked for the names of parents who've filed legal cases against the school, lodged official complaints, made threats—'

'So I'm giving you what you want; anything I know about our parents that might have a bearing on this case—'

Akin launches a flat-handed swipe across the desk at Maunder's face. Slocombe lunges and blocks him with a forearm. Akin raises his palms in apology to the police officer he just struck. She tilts her chin and gives him a warning look. When it's clear he has settled, she turns to the headmaster instead.

'Is there a specific reason for showing this footage?'

'Or are you just trying to discredit us?' Akin huffs.

'He's trying to divert our attention away from my question,' I say. 'About complaints.'

Akin lunges again but grabs the laptop this time. Drags it to his end of the desk. Maunder protests but Akin closes down the window with our shameful footage on it. He clicks the tab for the memory stick. It reveals folders marked with names. Pupil names.

'What is this?' demands Ayesha.

She points at one folder titled KIRAN REID.

Akin double-clicks and it opens. There are photos and more CCTV clips. Akin clicks 'back'. Ayesha protests that she wants to see the images of her son but Akin waves her away and keeps searching. The headmaster blusters, but can't reach his laptop.

Slocombe is on the radio, calling for backup.

Akin types 'Temi' into the search box and it comes up with a folder. There are far more photos and clips, plus some documents. Akin double-clicks a CCTV clip and it plays.

East playground. Break time. Younger children play football in the foreground. Behind, Temi and Dixie stroll into shot. He's not looking at her. She's half turned to him, entreating with her hands. Whatever is happening, it looks fraught. Suddenly, he grabs her by the waist and swings her into an alcove out of sight of the playground. The screen flicks to another angle, a different camera. This footage has been edited. Now Temi is pressing Dixie against the wall with the length of his body. Her hands grip his biceps. The film stops.

'What is that?' Akin turns on Maunder.

'That is your son sexually assaulting a girl.'

Silence in the room.

'They were kissing,' says Akin.

'He did not ask her consent.'

'How do you know? And she was his girlfriend.'

'That doesn't make sexual assault okay,' says Maunder piously.

'I didn't hear anything about this,' Akin says.

Maunder shrugs.

Akin steps back. He looks like he's been punched. The laptop screen goes black.

'We can't tell if that was consensual or not,' I say to Maunder. 'We can't hear it. Did Dixie make a complaint?'

I look to Mariah, who shakes her head.

'If this was a sexual assault on my daughter, why wasn't I informed?'

'Privacy,' says Maunder. 'And safe-guarding guidance advises that we don't wait for a complaint before taking proactive steps to protect children.' Maunder is as smug as an inquisitor, confident that all the powers that be are on his side in his kingdom.

'You can't just *decide* it's a sexual assault,' I say.

'You're gathering evidence to use against my son,' says Akin.

Ayesha pushes Akin aside.

'You've got a folder on Kiran too. I want to know what's on his record.'

Maunder stays behind the desk. Outside the door, Singh arrives. Two uniformed officers flank him. Slocombe shows a palm to make them wait.

'Dr Maunder,' she says, 'do you hold images of all the children who have gone missing on the bus?'

'This is nothing to do with them going missing. And these images are well within the limits of the GDPR,' he blusters.

'I'm not here about data protection,' she says. 'I want to know what information you hold on these children. Show me.'

Maunder slinks between us parents to reach his laptop. He must be able to feel our hot breath on his neck as he passes under our noses.

He is not the man I thought he was. He's not on my side.

And I suspect he's not on the kids' sides either.

Chapter Twenty-Two

1.20 p.m.

Olivia could hardly hear her own thoughts over a clattering heart. She pressed down on the back tyre of the BMW – the same car that had followed them and then stopped in the wood – and pushed herself up with her good arm to look through the vehicle towards the barn. Corrugated iron with massive double doors to let lorries inside. Padlocked. But a regular-sized door that was cut into the bigger door stood ajar. There was a strong smell of ammonia hanging over the place. And something sulphurous, like her own hair being singed by straighteners.

It must have been Dixie they'd seen flitting between the buildings that lay beyond this barn. That flash of scarlet and gold. But now there was no sign of anyone. Alix hunkered beside the front tyre. Temi and Kiran hid at the back.

'What do we do now?' Olivia whispered.

Alix pursed his lips. 'Let's—' He stopped. A man stepped out of the door. The guy from the wood. The one who had beaten Mr Sadler. He was older than the one in the Stüssy hoodie, maybe twenty-five, with dirty-blond hair cut in a hard line too high on his forehead. A roadman uniform of sportswear and a puffer gilet. An expensive one, too; she recognised the logo on the chest. He held his arms out wide from his body, making himself look bigger, and stared stonily at them. He was holding a crowbar with a vicious claw on one end. Judging by his treatment of Mr Sadler, it probably wasn't just for busting padlocks.

Alix swallowed so loudly that Olivia heard his throat close and open again.

'She's through here,' the man with the crowbar called out, and turned back inside the barn.

Olivia stood up.

'What you doing?' Alix hissed.

Temi stood up too.

'We're not fooling anyone,' he said. 'They know we're here.'

Kiran pushed himself to his feet by pressing down on the hockey stick he was still carrying. They needed to get rid of it. It would have traces of the kidnapper's blood on it. Plus, it reminded Kiran of what he'd done. He'd hardly spoken a word since they left behind the body of the man he'd whacked.

'Do we just go after him?' Olivia asked. 'The one with the crowbar?'

'You follow Crowbar. I'll scout outside,' said Alix.

'Stop trying to be the main character,' said Kiran. 'You're not your dad. And he's no hero anyway, just a social media fake.'

Harsh, but true.

From the look Alix gave him, the appeal of 'new Kiran' was wearing off.

'Did you see the size of that crowbar?' said Temi.

'Means he probably doesn't have a gun,' mused Kiran.

'I know there's no gun,' Temi sounded testy.

'I just mean it's good news,' said Kiran mildly.

'There's only one of him,' said Olivia. 'And four of us.'

The boys looked at her.

She shrugged. 'Just saying.'

Together they walked out from behind the BMW and approached the metal door into the barn. Inside, it was clear where the smell came from. There were lines and lines of cages. The floor was clean, but the metal racks were covered in excrement and worse. Olivia jammed her fingers under her nose to block the smell.

'Battery farm,' said Kiran.

'Where are all the chickens?' Temi asked.

Olivia pointed to a notice pinned on the end of one row of cages. Bright yellow, it warned of avian flu.

Alix was already across the barn and leaning out of another door on the opposite side. They followed him, stepping out into the cold again.

Off to one side, a sticky-looking mound told Olivia where the sulphur smell came from. Not singed hair but burnt feathers.

'Must have destroyed the whole flock,' said Temi.

'Poor chickens,' said Kiran.

There was another building ahead, a smaller wooden structure, a Portakabin that reminded Olivia of a mobile classroom at her old school.

'There might be a phone,' she whispered.

They moved towards it two-by-two. Kiran and Olivia in front. Alix and Temi behind.

'I should go in first,' said Temi.

'Aren't they less likely to hit a woman?' Olivia asked.

Alix pulled a face but said nothing.

Olivia pushed the wooden door and it swung open.

It was shadowy inside. No lights. Dark in contrast to the brightness of the winter-white sky outside. Olivia blinked to adjust her eyes. There was someone sitting against the back wall.

A knot of a person, knees drawn to chest with arms wrapped around for good measure.

'Dixie!' Olivia ran straight to her.

Dixie looked up. She had a perfectly round black eye.

'You need ice!' Olivia said before she realised how stupid it was to think about bruising at a time like this.

'It's fine.' Dixie's voice was flat as mud.

'What happ—' Olivia started.

There was a thump behind her. Alix hitting the floor. He'd come last through the door and must have been shoved from behind so hard that he fell. Crowbar entered too, making Alix scramble forward on all fours to get out of his way.

'All of youse, sit down next to your mate, up against the wall.' He gestured with his weapon.

Olivia hesitated then folded down next to Dixie.

Temi and Kiran sat on the other side of her.

Alix picked himself up and moved beside Olivia, where he sat down, rubbing his right knee.

Crowbar went out and closed the door behind him, then they heard a padlock.

Cold seeped up like it had from the forest floor. It was no warmer in here than outside. The place obviously hadn't been heated in a while.

Very gently, as though putting herself to sleep, Dixie laid her cheek against the platform made by her arms wrapped around her knees and closed her eyes.

Her silence shocked Olivia more than the black eye. Dixie always had a retort. She was not the shrug-it-off type. Temi made wide eyes at Olivia.

Alix shuffled forward to see Dixie.

'What did they do to you, mate?' he said. 'If they raped—'

'Alix!' Olivia warned.

'No, but seriously,' he went on, 'we'll back you up, Dix. We all saw what happened. If he touched you, did stuff to you, hurt you—'

'Shut up, Alix.' Olivia's tone silenced him.

'What?'

'She doesn't need you pushing her around as well!'

'I'm supporting her, you're doing nothing.' He got up and went over to a desk on one side of the room. There wasn't much on it. No phone. Just a dented old Anglepoise lamp. He clicked its switch a couple of times, but nothing happened. No electricity. There was a filing cabinet. He opened and closed a couple of drawers, then dropped onto the spinning office chair and swung his knees from side to side. He pushed his hands between his thighs for warmth.

Olivia turned her attention to Dixie. She still had her eyes closed. Should she put an arm around her? Or was it wrong to touch her? Her hair was mussed up, but then Dixie struggled with frizz. Her clothes looked intact. Hands clean, no blood or mud. Wouldn't she have fought an attacker? Is that where the black eye came from? What are the tell-tale signs? This wasn't the sort of thing they taught in school.

'Dix,' she said. 'I don't know what to do.'

Dixie still didn't open her eyes. But she murmured, 'Do whatever he says.'

There was a clunk as the door unlocked and cracked open.

A dart of wind reminded Olivia that it could – and would – get colder the longer they sat here. Alix scuttled off the chair to sit beside her. Dixie pulled herself into a tighter knot.

Crowbar was silhouetted against the harsh sky. The weapon hung by his side like a third limb. Olivia heard a distant crunch and roar. A vehicle approaching.

'Who's coming?' she asked.

Crowbar checked his pockets. He seemed . . . nervous.

'Is it the police?' she asked.

He bent his mouth into a sarky smile. 'I thought you lot were brainy.'

A Range Rover appeared around the metal barn and rolled across the broken concrete of the yard towards the office. It had tinted windows, even the windscreen, so they had no idea how many people were inside. It passed the open door and stopped a short distance beyond, out of sight. The engine cut. Nothing else, no car doors opened, no one moved.

Crowbar smoothed his hair. Tugged his gilet. Put the crowbar on the desk, then picked it up again. He bounded out of the door and turned out of sight.

Kiran whispered, 'You know that bit in *Jurassic Park* where the velociraptors suddenly run away, and for a second the kids think they're saved, but then they realise it's because the T-Rex has arrived, so now they're in even more shit?'

Outside, a car door opened. Slammed. Footsteps. A bark of anger, an indistinct shout. And then the very distinct sound of a punch that landed with dull finality.

'I think the T-Rex just arrived,' said Temi.

A moment later, Crowbar came in, wiping his face with the scrunched fingers of one fist. He spread an arc of blood from his mouth to his left ear. His nostrils flared with fear or anger, Olivia couldn't tell which. He told them to get up and they obeyed like they were on strings, standing with their backs pressed against the wall. Even Dixie.

A man stepped into the space framed by the open door. Older white guy. Black hair with grey creeping up from behind the ears like lichen. Average height and slender figure. He wore all black, giving him the air of a mercenary. Well-cut jeans and a thin knit with a utility jacket over the top. Lace-up boots. He massaged his right fist with his left, then shook it out.

His eyes ranged over the five of them. He clocked Dixie's bruise and gave Crowbar a dirty look. The boys got short shrift. His gaze stopped on Olivia. She met it. A dose of guilt about what happened to Dixie out in that wood spread through Olivia's veins, turning into a shard of anger. She was damned if she'd back down. She held his eye until his mouth puckered into something she read as amused respect. But her arm throbbed in its sling. It made her feel weak, vulnerable. She wished this man wasn't looking at her quite so thoroughly.

Chapter Twenty-Three

5.25 p.m.

Open mutiny in the Great Hall. Even Ayesha and Jack forget their animosity and join in plotting the downfall of Maunder and his CIA-style witch-hunt against our children.

'I will ruin him!' Akin is the most mild-mannered person I've ever met, but everyone has a limit and he passed it hours ago. 'After that irresponsible party at your McMansion—' He points a finger at Jack, who starts to bluster, but Akin shuts him down with a dismissive gesture. 'After that damn party, Maunder picked my boy out of a photograph because of the colour of his skin. He was the only one to take any blame for what happened to that girl. And I let it go to keep the peace. I agreed that Temi should face punishment *if there was any evidence.* Of course, in the end there wasn't any evidence because he did nothing wrong—'

'Was this before or after you donated to the school's theatre renovation fund?' asks Ayesha.

Akin's eyes go headlight-wide.

'Your name is on the list of donors that went to the board of governors,' she says.

'Coincidence.' Akin makes that gesture with his hand again, sweeping away an inconvenient question. 'Maunder said he wouldn't act on rumours, but all this time, he's been collecting evidence so that he can oust Temi if he wants to. In fact, he's doing that to all of our children. If they embarrass his school in any way, he can have them out like that.' He snaps his fingers.

It reminds me what Jack said about a salamander doing anything to survive. Even cut off its own damaged limbs.

Maunder stood by Temi because the boy is a star pupil and a brilliant rugby player in a school that relies on grades and silverware. But if that injured girl's family were to sue the school – and Temi's continued presence threatened its reputation – then Salamander wanted to be able to get rid of him. Cut off the injured limb. That CCTV footage of Temi grabbing Dixie – Maunder didn't care if it was consensual or not, didn't care about the girl's feelings – it would count as a second strike against the boy.

But also I didn't know Akin had 'donated' to the school. We've laughed at parents who sponsor buildings to get their names on brass plaques. Brass-Necks, we called them. I wonder if Akin is remembering that as he avoids my eye. Hands in fists by his side like a petulant boy. My first thought is: *I can't believe you'd pay off the headmaster*. My second thought is: *Yes, I can*. Life has shown me never to underestimate the basic human instinct for survival. Social shame is a powerful motivator.

'I'll talk to the chairman of the board of governors,' Ayesha is saying. 'I'm going to have a serious conversation about Dr Sam Maunder's leadership.'

There's finality in her tone. Like it's done already. But Maunder is still in his office, with his cameras and his recordings, taking 'donation' bribes and making decisions that mar children's lives, covering his arse and the school's precious reputation. He'll get away with it too. His sort always do. Dodgy clergy, corrupt coppers, board members, all the ones who feast on the buttered side of the bread. School governors will cover it up to protect themselves—

A clatter of doors interrupts my silent rant. Two uniformed officers come in from outside. They bring a vicious chill and an air of purpose.

Singh has his notebook out. He makes a beeline for us.

'Would any of you recognise a vehicle of interest? Red BMW Mark 3.' He reels off a number plate. There's a lull. Around the group, heads shake and shoulders shrug.

'Why?' I ask.

Singh ignores me.

'The vehicle is registered to a Cole Beattie?'

Nothing.

'The registration was transferred three months ago from someone with the surname Kershaw?'

Blood rushes into my cheeks like I've been slapped round the face.

That name.

One I never thought I'd hear again.

My mind goes murky as my memory kicks up sediment. I don't dare speak. Just focus on keeping the breath moving in and out of my body. Let the blood drain from my face. I keep my eyes on Singh. His look ticks around the group like the second hand of a clock. Taking in our responses. I release my jaw. No clenching, not now.

'No?' he prompts.

I glance around, too, and my eye meets the detective's.

She knows.

She knows that I know.

And she's waiting to see if I'll let anyone else know.

My legs feel restless in that way they do before bedtime. I need to move. Walk. Out of this hall, through the wrought iron gates, down the hill to the seafront where the salty wind never fails to blow away cobwebs of memories, and over the pebbles into water that will hit me like a stiff gin and tonic.

'What's the significance of this vehicle?' Ayesha asks.

'That's operational—'

'It might help us place the car, if we know the context,' she says.

Singh glances at his senior colleague and receives a tight nod. Of course, Ayesha gets what she wants.

'Our colleagues have been tracing the minibus on the ANPR, establishing its movements before it disappeared. All along the route, we've picked up a red BMW as well. This vehicle seems to have followed them towards the services, turned back when they turned back, then tailed them again when they got on their way the second time.'

I can't keep my legs still much longer.

I manage to contain myself until Singh is satisfied that no one knows this vehicle. Then I go straight to the bathroom and make for the sink. Cold water on the face settles the dregs of my mind. I study my dripping face in the mirror. My unremarkable face. Pretty enough when I'm gussied up, but right now I look like an NPC, as Olivia might say. Non-player character. A face in a crowd. Non-entity. Just another middle-aged woman.

Unthreatening. Unassuming. Unmemorable.

When you're this much of a nobody, you can be anybody. My single greatest skill—

Bam

The bathroom door interrupts me feeling sorry for myself.

Chantale Slocombe.

'Can we talk?' she asks. 'Not here.'

I follow her out. She heads up the corridor and we end up in the chemistry lab, the same one I was in with Akin. She shuts the door. The blind is still down. Once again, I back up to a bench and steady myself on the wooden top.

'Detective,' I say.

She was a police constable last time I saw her. Over twenty years ago. She's done well. Detective sergeant now. Better than me, anyway.

'Emma—' she says.

'Emily. Has been for a long time—'

'What do I need to know, Emily?'

What does she need to know? All of it, but I don't have the time or the inclination.

'This needs to be quick or they're going to twig . . .' I say.

'If you're compromised,' she says, 'you need to bail.'

I shake my head. Not compromised and not bailing. Not after two years of work on a case. It's a stark choice but I've done it before. I've spent a lifetime hiding, officially and unofficially. I can help to find Olivia without exposing myself. I just need to work all the angles. Bottom line is, I'm not leaving this place without my baby.

But now I know.

A cameo appearance by Kershaw changes everything.

It means someone could have taken that bus to get my daughter.

Because of me.

I'm not who these parents think I am.

And I need it to stay that way.

Chapter Twenty-Four

1.40 p.m.

'I'm not who you think I am,' said the man in black. 'Do what I say and we'll be friends.' He spoke with a countryside accent that Olivia couldn't place, chewing words like a grazing animal. It made him sound friendly, but maybe that's what he meant by *not who you think I am*. He wasn't friendly. He turned up and seconds later, punched Crowbar. To be fair, Crowbar deserved it, but still . . . It made an impression, which was probably what it was designed to do. A bit like a teacher giving out a detention on the first day, letting it be known they weren't bluffing. They'd thought Crowbar was a bad guy. The man in black was an even worse guy.

Man in Black. Made her think of *Men in Black*. One of her mum's *back in the day* films. It was pretty funny. Mr Smith and Mr Jones. She was Smith, so Man in Black would have to be Jones. Giving him a name made him seem more human, less scary.

'Where's the bus?' Jones asked.

The kids looked at each other.

He pointed to Olivia. 'In my day, girls were the first to put their hands up.'

'That's because girls were raised to be people pleasers,' she said.

Jones snorted through his nose, then smiled enough to show teeth. He seemed to like the fact that she stood up to him. Jones would almost be okay-looking, if he wasn't holding them hostage in a Portakabin in a field. Okay for an old bloke. Must be her mum's age.

Alix nudged her with his knee, a warning to be quiet. But she'd read a book about hostages. You should build rapport. Let them get to know you. Make the captor like you.

'Seriously, though,' Jones said. 'We need the bus. And Cole. Where's Cole?'

He meant the one in the Stüssy hoodie.

'He drove too fast and crashed,' Olivia said. 'He went through the windscreen. We're pretty sure he was dead. So we came looking for help.'

'Did you call the police?' he asked.

'We don't have phones.'

He pulled a face. 'Teenagers without phones, what is this, my childhood?'

Temi spoke up. 'They take our devices off us. No phones policy. They're back at school.'

'How d'you get here?' Jones asked.

'I tracked our route across country,' Alix began. 'My dad is Jack Kent.'

'Who?' said Jones.

'The survival guru?' said Alix in a *duh-huh* tone.

Jones stepped closer. Olivia immediately revised her assessment; he respected a bit of sass, but not that much. Alix shrank backwards but Jones kept coming until the boy smeared himself against the wall. Jones stopped when they were nose to nose. He was a few inches shorter, but Alix disappeared into his shadow. Jones lifted a fist, Alix flinched, but the hand slapped down onto his shoulder. That brought the boy down to the man's height. He whispered into his ear, loud enough for them all to hear.

'And how long do you reckon your dad would *survive* in my line of work?'

He released Alix and sauntered back to the doorway.

'Cold,' whispered Kiran.

'Look, I guess finding Dixie was dumb luck,' Olivia said. 'We set off to find a phone. All we got was dead chickens. Then we got locked in by your . . . henchman—'

Jones scoffed at the word 'henchman' and that made Olivia stop in her tracks. She wanted him to respect her, not laugh at her. Jones seemed to realise that he'd hurt her feelings as he made a placatory gesture with one hand.

'I just need to find Cole,' he said. 'Where's his phone?'

'Dead,' said Olivia. Out of the corner of her eye, she saw Kiran flinch at the word.

'Broken in the crash?' Jones asked.

'Out of battery.'

'Useless little . . .' He shook his head. 'Corner boy can't even keep a phone on charge.'

Corner boy. She knew the phrase from another *back in the day* show, *The Wire*. *Corner boy*s were the street-level drug dealers, the lowest of the low.

Jones jerked his head at the open door. 'Show us the way to this bus.'

Olivia's feet felt like they were stapled to the floor.

'We cut over the fields, got lost, walked for half an hour—'

'We didn't get lost,' Alix cut in. 'We headed west, saw the reservoir, turned south. I knew where I was going.'

'Then you can both come and help me find him.'

Dixie darted to her side as if to prevent her friend from being taken, but Jones told her to 'stop being such a drama queen' and the kind of patronising words that might have come from one of their teachers took the wind out of her sails. Olivia whispered, 'I'll be fine,' and Jones rolled his eyes as he went out the door. She moved to follow, but realised Alix wasn't behind her. She gestured for him to come and he pushed off the wall, gangly and unsteady, to totter after Jones.

Olivia's mum got on her nerves sometimes, sighing over her daughter's plump skin, thick hair, boundless energy. As though youth was the lost love of her life. But, looking at Alix walking behind Jones, Olivia recognised what her mum saw in her – a fawn-like newness beside an older person's world-weary poise. She felt bad for Alix, he couldn't help fucking up, he had no experience of this.

A few months ago, she'd walked into the chemistry lab at school one break time when two teaching assistants were cleaning up. She overheard one say, 'They're spoon-fed, these kids, they barely think for themselves.' Olivia had grabbed her test paper and left. But the comment followed her. Was she spoon-fed? Did it make her results less of an achievement? Now, she realised it was true. Alix was the same, all of them; they had no clue. They'd made every wrong decision. Because there was no one to spoon-feed them.

'Why are you doing this?' she blurted out to Jones. 'Why are we here?'

He turned back. Scarred eyebrow, break on the nose, abandoned ear piercing. The silvery light flattened his face to harsh edges. Like a profile on a coin that's been tarnished by too many hands.

'Believe it or not,' Jones said, 'I want to help. Can you trust me on that?'

He left behind a question to which no one had a ready answer. So Olivia followed him out of the cabin. And Alix followed her. Crowbar locked the door behind them.

'Come on, *henchman*, we're taking both cars,' Jones said to Crowbar, who got in the BMW. Olivia scooted across the back seat of the Range Rover to let Alix come in after her. The engine started with authority. Tinted windows dulled the too-white daylight. When the doors slammed, the outside world receded. It was a little like sinking into the deep end of a pool, suspended in a liminal space that wasn't safety or danger but contained the possibility of both.

They rumbled over the broken concrete and swept past the barn. It was a bumpy ride along a farm track that skirted the field before they reached the road. Due to the high trees, the buildings wouldn't be visible from the lane. Olivia wondered if this place was even marked on a map. Would anyone come looking for them? Probably not. That was why these guys had chosen it.

The BMW tailed them like it had when they were on the bus. Olivia's eyes were sharp with tears. Should have said something at the pool. When she saw the lad in the Stüssy hoodie in the viewing gallery. But she hadn't been sure what was happening. Didn't want to look silly. Maybe Mr Sadler wouldn't have believed her, but at least he'd have been forewarned, he wouldn't have walked straight into the trap in the woods. Their kidnapper wouldn't be dead. They wouldn't be in this car with Jones, whoever he was.

'Who are you?' Olivia asked.

'Ever seen a film called *Pulp Fiction*?'

Alix said no, but Olivia nodded. Another one her mum had made her watch. Again, surprisingly good considering it came out literally last century. But violent. So she didn't like where this conversation was going.

'I'm basically Harvey Keitel,' Jones said.

'I don't know who that is.'

'He's the one who cleans up other people's mess.' He nudged the rear-view mirror to see her. 'What time're they expecting you back at school?'

'Midday. They'll have reported us missing.'

'Maybe. Maybe not. Bit embarrassing for a school to lose their kids. I reckon we've got a while before they hit the panic button. What time is it now, two o'clock? They'll still be busy covering their arses.'

'Turn right,' said Alix.

The vehicle slowed to take the corner. Alix shifted and there was a dull clunk from his side. The car stopped so sharply that the belt snapped tight across Olivia's chest.

'The door is child locked,' said Jones. 'Don't be a silly bugger, Jack-Kent's-son. Just relax and you'll live to tell your old man all about how you survived.'

Olivia thumped back in her seat as the vehicle accelerated again.

'I saw a TV show once,' Jones said, 'a true crime thing, about these little kids who were kidnapped on a bus and buried underground.'

'They were buried?' Olivia said.

'They buried a whole shipping container – somewhere in America or Australia, can't remember which – with the kids and their teacher inside.'

No one said a word.

'The kids dug themselves out.' He shook his head. 'Bloody stupid plan, could have gone horribly wrong.'

'Sounds like it did go wrong,' said Olivia quietly, 'for the kids.'

Jones gave her a long look in the rear-view mirror.

'Could have been worse,' he said.

She looked out the window. Too-close hedgerows rushed past.

'Bear right,' said Alix and the car took a fork. In fairness, he had navigated back to the forest where the bus crashed. Soon, the road went up an incline and the trees fell away to the left.

'Here,' said Alix.

'I see it.'

The Range Rover slowed and halted. The scene was exactly as it had been when she'd taken a last look over her shoulder an hour or so ago. Saints bus on its side. Audience of trees. Windscreen. Body. Crumpled and small. Like Mr Sadler. He didn't deserve any of this—

'How did you lot get out of that bus alive?' Jones asked.

'The power of seatbelts,' Olivia snapped. Sardonic side-eye from the driver's seat. She had to control her emotions. She gabbled on, hoping to wash clean the atmosphere with a fresh deluge of chat, as she did when she accidentally pissed off her mother with a snarky comment that came out wrong. 'The bus wasn't going all that fast actually. And speed of impact reduces trauma to the body. I'm going to do medicine and I love TV shows set in hospitals. But also, I jumped out the back and banged my shoulder so I did get hurt, yeah, but we were lucky actually.' His look was steady. Maybe even a hint of a smile. He said nothing and then got out of the car.

'What are you doing?' Alix whispered.

'Trying to get him to like us.'

'Don't go all Stockholm syndrome. He's not our friend.'

She shushed him. Jones went behind the Range Rover to talk to Crowbar. But the vehicle was too well insulated to hear their conversation. Within minutes, he was back and Olivia's door flew open.

'Get in the other car, we need to deal with this mess.'

They moved into the BMW, sat together in the back seat.

Jones leant through the open door.

'Do not try to get out. The alarm will go off and we'll come after you. We'll hurt you and we'll hurt your friends. Understood?'

Olivia nodded. Alix kept his eyes down.

Jones stood up and slammed the door. The locks thunked.

At the Range Rover, he pulled out a duffel bag and slid down the embankment into the trees with Crowbar close behind. For a few seconds, she watched the treetops jostle one another like fidgeting children.

'What now?' said Olivia.

'Nobby's Nuts,' Alix replied. He nodded to the centre console. An open packet was wedged in a cup holder. He reached forward and plunged his fingers inside, offered one to Olivia and, when she declined, threw both into his mouth.

'Maybe we should take them back for Kiran,' said Olivia.

'He totally lost the plot before.' Alix shook his head in disbelief.

'Kiran gets stressed,' she said. 'Grades.'

'He's top set in everything. What's he got to be stressed about?'

'Just the A-stars he needs for Cambridge.'

'Who cares enough to make themselves that miserable?'

'He does. His mum does.'

Alix snorted. 'I know he gets wound up about work, but I've never seen him go the full Piglet.'

That made Olivia smile. 'What does that make you, then, Tigger?'

'Probably. You're Owl, obviously.'

'Fuck off, Owl can't even spell.'

Alix laughed and let it go. Olivia was glad to have steered the conversation away from Kiran. She knew things about Kiran. She held her counsel for his sake and for Temi who'd blabbed the gossip.

'Which character is Temi?' Alix mused.

Olivia thought about it for a second. 'He's none of them. He's Christopher Robin.'

Alix hummed in agreement. 'They're probably far enough away, we could make a run for it?' He started to climb between the front seats.

Olivia caught sight of movement in her wing mirror.

'Stop!'

Alix darted back. Jones was coming along the road from behind. They must have walked through the woods and back up the road. He had a white paper boiler suit on, the ones forensics people wear, but he was peeling it off his arms. It had a smear of blood on the front. He passed her window to the Range Rover, where he trod the white suit off his feet. He bundled it up and shoved it inside a bin bag. Without closing the boot, he got in the Range Rover, performed a tricky three-point turn on the narrow lane, carefully inching back towards the edge of the embankment, then roared back the way they had come.

'Are they leaving the body, then?' Alix asked.

'I guess. Maybe they removed anything that might identify him.'

'Like teeth and fingers?' Alix said.

'Wow . . . Okay. I feel like Jones would have more blood on him if they'd just severed a man's hands?'

'Good point.'

'I was thinking they took his wallet, a mobile phone that might link him to them – that kind of thing. If they remove the body from the crash site, then the police would know someone else was involved. This way, it looks like he crashed the bus and went through the windscreen. Which he did. Kinda.'

Crowbar arrived and got into the driver's seat. He said nothing as he performed the same breath-holding three-point turn, then sped up to follow the Range Rover. Crowbar slotted his phone into a holder clipped on the air conditioning vent. As they drove away, it picked up a bar of signal. Olivia wondered if she could grab it and dial 999. But even if she got through, she didn't know what location to tell the operator.

The screen showed Maps.

'Try to see where we are,' she whispered to Alix.

'Shut it,' said Crowbar. 'No talking.'

Alix angled his body forward, looking at the map. It was recalibrating, planning a route. Finally, it scrolled to a destination, before zooming back to their current location. An arrow moving along a blue road that had no place names.

Alix sat back hard in his seat. Now he was chewing his fingers.

'That's weird,' he said.

'What?'

'I said, shut it,' said Crowbar.

It took them a few minutes to drive back, then cross the rutted field to reach the barn. Soon, they rumbled onto the smashed concrete again.

They were ordered back into the Portakabin.

Temi, Dixie and Kiran were huddled along the back wall, their hands raised in front of their eyes, as daylight stormed inside. Jones came in and pointed to a wheeled office chair sprawled on the floor.

'You can't smash a double-glazed window.'

'That's what I told them,' mused Kiran. 'The air trapped in between the panes acts as a shock absorber. You could use a hammer and hit it in one corner. But a diamond would work best. If you placed the point against the glass and hit it, the diamond would focus the pressure into one small point, so the glass would shatter.'

Jones listened patiently to this physics lesson. 'Do you have any diamonds, then?'

Kiran shook his head sadly. 'I do not.'

'Then you're stuck, aren't you?' Jones said.

'How is the minibus driver?' Kiran asked. 'What was his name?'

'Dead, mate. And why don't we leave names out of this, for everyone's sake?'

Kiran nodded as though this was sage advice.

Jones went outside and closed the door.

Olivia slid down next to Dixie, who gave a tight smile.

'What happened?' asked Temi.

'What happened?' Alix stayed standing as he repeated the question. He was speaking too loudly. 'What happened is that I found out we have a traitor.'

Dixie's head snapped up. Temi got to his feet. Kiran too.

'What are you talking about?' Olivia stayed sitting.

'The sat nav in the BMW was programmed to go to the service station. Our service station, where we always stop. They hadn't updated the destination, so it was still trying to take us there.' He spoke to Olivia now. 'You didn't notice?'

She shook her head.

'Why were they going to the same service station as us?' he pressed on.

'Petrol?' said Temi.

'Bit of a coincidence, isn't it? And they had a packet of Nobby's Nuts in the car—'

'That service station is the only one that sells them,' said Kiran.

'Right, so they must have gone there earlier to recce the site. I think they were planning to intercept us there.'

'Intercept?' said Temi.

'Grab us and do . . . whatever it is they want to do. The point is, how did they know we always stop at those services? Who told them?'

Dixie lifted her head and spoke for the first time in ages. 'They could have got the nuts from anywhere, it's a coincidence.'

'Is it? They were following us, and when we turned back for Kiran's jammers, they followed us again. Someone told them. Someone is in on it. Someone' – Alix looked around the group – 'is not who we think they are.'

Chapter Twenty-Five

5.35 p.m.

I'm not who these parents think I am.

I'm not who my parents think I am.

Worst of all, I'm not who my daughter thinks I am.

DS Slocombe asks me to wait in the chemistry lab. She goes outside in response to a call from her colleague. Something about the BMW. Or maybe she wants me to stew. A mind game. She thinks I know more than I do, but she's mistaken. I'm lost.

Olivia has lessons in this lab. There must be traces of her. Fingerprints on glass beakers, hair in the grouting between tiles. A flashbulb memory strikes me of something she once said . . .

Brushing her hair, releasing great long strands and rubbing them between her palms to make hairy spiders, and I was nagging her about dropping them on the carpet, and she said, *At least if I go missing, I'll leave a trail for you to follow.*

Her utter trust makes me sag under its weight. I spin on the high stool and place my cheek on the wooden bench she must have touched. I let my mind go, hoping it will settle or exhaust itself, but instead it pinwheels . . . I've turned into a civilian. Can't hide my emotions. Like all of them out there in the Great Hall. Suspicion so thick I can taste it on the air like fuel in a petrol station. Everyone doubling down, becoming more *themselves*: Akin more haughty, Ayesha more imperious, Jack more craven,

Mariah more *extra*, Maunder more reptilian and me . . . I need to be more hidden.

Slocombe comes back in and mutters an apology.

I snap upright and ask if they've found the car and she says not.

I ask if we can go to the place where the bus crashed and she says not.

She asks if I'm withholding anything that she should know and I say I'm not.

We stare at each other until there's a spaghetti western atmosphere. She looks good but tired. I want to ask if she's married, has kids, owns a dog. Who she calls when she needs to let off steam. If she goes to the pub or the theatre or prefers Netflix. If the job makes her lonely.

But I don't start that conversation because she might turn the tables. And I'd have to admit that Mariah Haven, Dixie's mum, is my only friend, not just in this place but anywhere. It's hard to live a lie *and* make friends. That makes me sound psycho, so maybe I should flip it around. *It's easier to live a lie when you don't have friends.* My work fills a social hole. I hang out with women all day every day; chat, cry, laugh. Gossip is my currency so I'm a wealthy woman. Once people have shown you their belly fat and confessed to midnight binges and TMI-ed about IBS, all the rest of it comes out with the sweat. And I get invited to parties, hen dos, theatre nights. But at the end of the month they pay me. A reset button that makes us not quite friends.

So it's just me and Olivia. And Mariah and Dixie.

Slocombe opens her mouth like she's going to speak, but there's a clatter and a shout outside in the corridor. Her eyelids flicker in irritation. She slides off her high stool, the ball of one foot on the floor. I hear a male voice, unfamiliar, insisting that, 'There are questions that need answers.' Then the hum of DC Singh. He's dealing with it. Slocombe looks torn but pulls herself back up onto the stool.

'Sorry to keep you waiting,' she says.

I shake my head. I know it looks impatient.

'I wanted to touch base, see if you'd heard anything significant from the other parents . . .'

Is that all she wants from me? I doubt it.

DS Slocombe tilts her head to one side.

'Have we met before?' she asks.

I tip my head to the other side.

'It's on the tip of my tongue,' she muses. 'I'm thinking . . . Hendon?'

'The police training college?'

Not what I was expecting.

'I trained in the Met, moved here a couple of years ago. Do I recognise you from Hendon?'

I shake my head. She folds her arms.

When you're swimming in the sea on a choppy day, a set of waves can blow up and force you to make a quick decision: fight the waves to get to shore or save your energy and let them pass overhead. Then get out of trouble later.

I decide to keep my head down. But I have to give Slocombe something.

'Maybe our paths crossed, but not at Hendon . . . I was briefly on the beat in Sussex?'

I pull a sheepish expression.

'I knew it.' DS Slocombe looks relieved. 'Why so brief?'

I blow my cheeks out. 'I did a year and moved on. I feel guilty about it sometimes, all that training and then . . . I don't know, uniform wasn't for me.'

'It happens,' she says.

'It does.'

'So why isn't it in your bio on your website for the personal training? There's a whole page about triathlons, but it doesn't say you were a police officer. I would have thought that would be relevant – good credentials – to show you went through police training and passed?'

What's her angle?

'Like I say, it's embarrassing, isn't it? Dropping out . . .'

She shrugs.

'Makes me look like a quitter. Do you know how much it costs the taxpayer to train a police officer? Over twenty grand. And then only a year in uniform? It's not a good look.'

'No different to all those kids who go to university and never use their degree.'

'I guess, I just . . . I'm not proud of it.'

Slocombe is scrolling on her phone. I recognise the lipstick colours of my website.

'You don't have any photos of yourself on your page . . .?'

'There are some, I think?'

'Blurry . . . Not so I could recognise you.'

'I don't know what you're asking me, DS Slocombe. The website was designed by a friend, it's . . . aspirational. Supposed to look like an Instagram feed. It's basic, I know, but most clients come from word of mouth.'

She scrolls the page fully up, leaves her fingertip on the screen, scrolls it back down.

Then clicks the phone off and puts it in her pocket.

'There's a lot going on in this place, isn't there? Saints College? A lot of intrigue . . .'

'Oh, Detective Sergeant, you would not believe what goes on in this place.'

'How does Ayesha Reid seem?' Slocombe asks.

'You coming under pressure? The powers that be must think this is targeted at her. That would make it an act of terrorism.'

Slocombe does a down-frown, impressed. 'You picked up a lot during your one year on the force. I've had the chief on the phone just now. The Home Office want updates every half hour . . . You know.'

I never spoke to the chief constable once in my whole career.

'Sorry, I barely know Ayesha Reid. She doesn't confide in me. Olivia isn't all that close to her son either, so . . .' I shrug apologetically. Slocombe sucks her bottom lip deep into her mouth.

A door slams in the corridor. A burst of voices, staccato jabs like fists flying.

I won't—

Look—

Stop—

Squealing footsteps reach our door.

They shriek to a stop.

'If Ms Reid won't speak then I'll take matters into my own hands. You can't stop me leaving this building—'

'I can arrest you—' Singh.

'For what? Running in the corridor? Give me a detention, if you like, detective, then I'll be on my way. And tell Ayesha Reid that I go to press in an hour.'

Go to press? Old school.

Slocombe gets heavily to her feet.

'Better deal with this.'

I pretend to stay put but as soon as her back is turned, I'm out the door.

Chapter Twenty-Six

2.25 p.m.

'Someone is in on it?' repeated Temi. 'Anyone could have told them about the services.'

'Who else knows our tradition? Mr Sadler didn't tell them. So who else? One of our parents? A teacher? I don't think so.'

After Alix made his accusation everyone went quiet. So quiet that Olivia became aware of a clock on the wall. Ticking. Hands approaching half two. In school, they'd be on the move to their last period of lessons. Shriek of rubber soles. Clamour of voices. Slam of lockers. That monkey-house atmosphere that marks the end of a day. *Do the students back at school know we're missing?* The big hand lurched forward a minute. *Is it possible to hear the hand moving?* The clock face showed the surface of the moon. They were so far from home, here in this cabin, in this bubble. Only a short distance as the crow flies, probably, like half an hour or something? But it might as well be a million miles. Like a spaceship stranded far from Earth. *Does anyone know we're missing?* Her shoulder throbbed. Dull stabs in time with the passing seconds.

'I'm the one . . .' Kiran broke the silence. He was sitting against the wall, knees wide, head dropped between them.

'You?' spat Alix. 'You told them about the service station?'

'Shut up, no!' Kiran said. 'I mean, I'm the one they want. This pair outside. They want me, don't they?'

Another lurch of the second hand.

'Because of your mum?' Olivia asked.

'Because I whacked whatsisname, him in the Stüssy hoodie. I killed their driver. They're not going to let that go. They must have seen his head? His ear? Did they say anything about me, the hockey stick—?'

'They didn't seem to care about him—' Olivia tried.

'If they realise, they'll come after me.'

'They just left him at the bus, mate,' said Alix. 'It's not that deep.'

Kiran shook his head. Pearls of sweat sprayed from his hair. It was cold, but he was sweating. 'What about the police, then? When they find the body, there'll be forensics – blood, skin, fingerprints, fibres – they can't have cleaned it down, Dextered it or whatever, it'll be covered in DNA, something will connect me to the body. And they'll know—' Kiran got to his feet, unsteady.

'Easy,' said Temi. He grabbed the wheeled office chair and shoved it behind Kiran, collapsing his knees so he fell between its arms. But Kiran pushed himself to the edge of the seat, head in his hands again. 'I feel sick,' he moaned. 'I'm going to chunder.'

Olivia scouted under the office desk and found a plastic bin. She placed it between his feet and rubbed him between the shoulder blades.

'Take a few breaths—'

'I'm dizzy,' moaned Kiran.

Alix groaned. Olivia shot him a *shut it* look. Temi noticed and shoved Alix in the chest.

'You're making him feel worse!'

'How could he feel any worse?'

Olivia ignored them and watched Kiran.

Shaky hands pulling at his own hair.

Nausea. Dizziness. Sweats.

It started to make sense now . . .

It wasn't just a panic attack. This was something she recognised from the drug unit. Withdrawal. She'd seen all the signs of a comedown. And not just in the patients – there were medical students there, a few years her senior, who'd told her about performance-enhancing drugs they used to get through their intense courses. Cocaine, amphetamines, Ritalin, Modafinil prescribed for narcolepsy . . . whatever they could get hold of, really. Not all of them did it, obviously, but enough. And not always the ones you'd expect.

Kiran was an addict. Temi had told Dixie as much, and Dixie had told Olivia. Goody-two-shoes Kiran, on speed so he could work harder and faster. But now he was showing all the signs of withdrawal – separated from his supply, presumably, by the kidnapping. She thought of his space age bag, left on the other bus. Was it the lost EpiPen he was stressed about or did he use the device to smuggle a stash into school? Dosing himself so he could keep up with the workload, the four A-levels he needed to please everyone. His own expectations, his mother, the school – the bloody school! Pitting them against one another, like an academic *Hunger Games*.

Olivia knelt down beside Kiran. Under cover of Temi and Alix butting each other like baby goats, she whispered in his ear.

'What is it you've been taking, Kiran?'

He shrugged her off.

Alix shoved Temi away and they retreated to opposite sides of the room.

Olivia backed off too. She folded down next to Dixie, who tucked her limbs into a tighter knot as a shiver went through her body.

'Do you think our mums know?' Olivia whispered.

'Can't think about Mum or I'll cry.'

'Me too,' said Olivia. She rarely cried. Learned behaviour. Her mum didn't either. Mum dealt with everything, good or bad, by going for a swim. Cold sea numbed the feelings, maybe? Dixie was right, though, it was hard to imagine what their mums must be going through right now. Olivia slid the fingers of her right hand under the sling holding her left. Pressed down. The pyrotechnics in her shoulder felt better than guilt. She stared at the ceiling and let her thoughts scatter while the pain fizzled into a burning ember.

Time passed on the moon-faced clock. Ten ticks. Twenty. More.

She hoped her mum was with Mariah. Who else did she have to call? It had never really occurred to Olivia, but her mother didn't have many friends. Acquaintances, through her work, but few close friends. Any friends, in fact . . . Why was that?

'Here, eat something, for God's sake, it might help.' Alix's voice was level. Olivia looked up to see him holding out the bag of Nobby's Nuts from the BMW to Kiran. A peace offering.

'What are you implying?' Kiran leapt to his feet, the chair spiralling away.

Alix rolled his head. 'I'm not accusing *you* of anything.'

'Who are you accusing, then?' Temi piped up. 'If this is another jibe at me then I've already told you the truth. Yes, I lied about the gun, but only because of my sister. But, you know, maybe you're right. Maybe it would be best if I left, got far away from you all. Because this is to do with my family, isn't it? I'm the target, I should go and then you'll be safe.'

'Why are you the target?' Alix said. 'My dad is a celebrity—'

'D-list,' muttered Kiran.

'It's about fucking money!' Dixie silenced them all. She got to her feet. It seemed to be a huge effort and Olivia wondered if she was injured after all. Or maybe her arse had gone to sleep on the unforgiving floor. Dixie got upright and continued more quietly. 'It's about money. It always is. We just have to work out how to give them what they want—'

'Shush!' Olivia waved at them to shut up. There was someone outside. She crawled across the office until she was under the window. Dixie followed, crouching beside her. Crowbar was talking. He was making a call.

'Cash,' he said, 'it has to be cash. We need to know it won't be traced—'

'See!' said Dixie.

'Shush!'

Crowbar stopped talking. He grunted, agreeing with whoever was on the line.

Olivia hooked her fingers on the metal window frame and inched up.

'Careful!' Dixie hissed.

She managed to peek out. Crowbar was so close, she could see a shiny scar nestled into the short hair on the back of his head. He should've got stitches for whatever left that mess. Guess a – what did Jones call him? – *corner boy* doesn't get to go to hospital for stitches. He turned slightly and she ducked.

'Careful!' Dixie said again.

'Shush, he's right outside.'

Olivia stretched back up. Now she could see the phone against his ear. His hand covered most of it, but the leather case was folded back and she could just make out a bright yellow sticker on the inside. Homer Simpson.

Olivia slumped back down.

'He said "it has to be cash" . . . He's demanding a ransom.' Temi hissed. He was so close she could smell fear sweat under his fragrance.

'Cash,' whispered Alix. 'Who's he talking to? He hasn't asked for any of our parents' numbers, has he, so how . . .?'

Olivia scooted away from the window and pressed her back against the far wall.

She needed to think.

The others followed.

'What?' said Temi, his eyes fixed on hers.

'Liv?' Dixie, too.

'What did you see?' Alix got right up in her face.

She placed her hands one by one on his chest and after a beat shoved him. He sprawled onto his backside.

'You!' She advanced and pointed down at him.

He goldfished in reply.

'You said the driver's phone was dead.'

'Whose?' Alix asked.

'When we crashed. You said we couldn't call for help because the phone was dead. But it's not—' She flung her arm wide to point at the window where Crowbar's voice was still a low murmur. 'Because he's using it right now. It has that Homer Simpson sticker on it. He's using it now, so it wasn't dead.'

Alix licked his lips but stayed on the floor. 'They must've charged it.'

'How?' asked Temi. 'There's no power.'

'It wasn't on charge in the car,' said Olivia. 'In the Range Rover or the BMW. We went in both cars, we would've seen it plugged in, if they'd left it there we would've used it. So they haven't had time to charge it. It wasn't flat. You were lying.'

Alix said nothing.

Temi sent the office chair wheeling across the floor so that Alix had to throw up one hand to block it. 'What the fuck, Alix? Why did you stop us calling for help?'

Olivia raised both palms. It silenced them. She walked over to Alix and offered him one hand, leaning back to drag him to his feet. He towered a full head over her, but she glared into his eyes as she poked his chest. 'Maybe you're the traitor, Alix Kent. Maybe you're the one who's in on it.'

Chapter Twenty-Seven

5.50 p.m.

Outside the chemistry lab, I'm drawn along the corridor by a thread of voices. Coming from the meeting room with the coffee machine. I lighten my tread, slip along the wall on the same side as the half-open door and stop a metre short. It's gone quiet. There's no cover. I'm fully exposed if someone comes out—

'Do not underestimate me.' Mariah. The bounce has gone from her voice. She sounds bleak, flat, dismal. A tinny voice replies, on speakerphone, sounds like Kash. Too distorted to hear clearly but he doesn't get much time to speak anyway.

'You had one job!' Mariah again. 'Do I have to get a man in to do it for you?'

Ouch.

More tinny voice. Kash not happy. Which isn't surprising, Mariah did rather aim for the balls with that comment. I decide to retreat—

The door from the Great Hall crashes against the wall.

Jack Kent moves at pace, elbows pumping, up the corridor towards me. Within a few strides he passes the coffee room. Mariah pops her head out in surprise, clocks Jack, then frowns at me. Hopefully it looks like I'm on my way to the hall, not loitering and listening to her.

Jack sweeps past, barely registering us. He marches up to the headmaster's door and hammers with the heel of his hand.

'Salamander!'

I can't hear the reply, but he enters and slams the door behind him.

I'm still standing there. Mariah is at ten o'clock, mouth akimbo, and the headmaster's door is at two o'clock. Mariah gives a little dog whistle between her front teeth to get my attention. 'What was that about?'

There's only one way to find out. Take a leaf out of Ayesha's book. I wave Mariah over and she darts across the corridor to join me.

'You keep watch,' I whisper. 'I'll listen.'

She backs into the alcove opposite the office and waits. I press my ear to his door, but I can't hear anything. I wish there was a convenient cupboard, like the one next to the meeting room, where I could listen through the air vent, but I'll have to make do—

'How many others?' Jack Kent is shouting.

Maunder replies. Can't hear the detail but it's short.

'Let me tell you, then.' Jack wants to be heard; there is something performative about his volume. I'm surprised he did this behind closed doors. 'I've been down a social media rabbit hole in the last hour—'

'Typical!' Maunder must have moved closer to the door. Perhaps getting near the exit. Jack is riled-up. 'Busy on the *socials* when you could be worrying about your son.'

'We'll get to my son in a moment. How many children have you managed out of this school, Salamander? Like you were doing to Temi?'

'It's a selective school, Jack, you know that better than anyone.'

'That doesn't mean children are guilty until proven innocent. Doesn't mean you can hire and fire them like staff in a fast-food restaurant. They're adolescents. They make mistakes. This is their education, their childhood. Your school's reputation isn't the only thing that matters.'

'You knew what you were signing up for. You were a Saints boy too. Briefly.'

'I've been getting a lot of DMs after my TikTok. There are dozens of parents – hundreds maybe, going back years – with cases of children being managed out of this school. As soon as their face doesn't fit, you get rid. And it's always the same story – some paltry allegation, backed by your favourite toy, the CCTV—'

A thump as though someone, presumably Jack, slams the desk.

'Fist fight?' Mariah is supposed to be keeping watch but she's crept closer to listen.

I shake my head to silence her.

'I've been sent link after link to Mumsnet, thread after thread, where Saints threatens parents with libel action if they publicly criticise the school or mention what's happened to their children.'

'Children have a right to be protected from social media,' says Maunder.

'You don't care about children! You don't care about education. Or well-being. You pick and choose who gets to stay and who gets to go. What you are is a bully who's always been a bully. And what I've realised today is that what you're doing to Temi now is what you did to me two decades ago.'

'What now?' Maunder laughs. I glance at Mariah. She grimaces.

I whisper, 'I don't think Jack Kent likes being laughed at.'

She makes a hanging-from-a-noose motion complete with poking tongue.

'You bullied *me*, Kent.' Maunder speaks very slowly. 'About my father being headmaster.'

'I didn't. And you know it.' Jack matches his tone. 'I was popular, and you were jealous. I didn't want to be friends because we had nothing in common. That's not the same as bullying. And you were *weird*. No one liked you. It was nothing to do with your dad, it was because you were a little . . . winnet, a dingleberry, a hanger-on. Even now, hanging on, doing your father's job. But I only just put two and two together and made four – you used CCTV to get me expelled, didn't you?'

'Don't be ridic—'

'That's what happened that day – you made sure I was in front of the camera. You grabbed my sports bag and ran into the car park. I ran after you and grabbed the bag to get it back, and you fell over. Said you hit your head on the kerb. And that bit was caught on CCTV. But it didn't show what happened before, did it? Didn't show you stealing my kit. It looked like I'd attacked you. So your dad expelled me. I'd never thought about the coincidence of it happening right in front of the camera. It was the only area of the school with CCTV. You knew exactly where it was . . . And your plan worked perfectly. And that's still your MO, isn't it? Only now you've got cameras everywhere—'

'MO?'

'Modus operandi.'

'You've been watching too much telly, Jack.'

'Getting expelled ruined my life—'

'What is it they say? Once you reach thirty, you have to stop blaming your parents? Don't you have to stop blaming your school too?'

There's a pause. The shush of feet on the carpet.

'You know what it did to me?' Jack has moved closer to the door. Closer to Maunder.

'It stopped you walking around like you owned the place . . .'

'It destroyed my trust, in anyone, including myself. I was on a bursary, and I already felt like I didn't belong because my family weren't rich, so when I got chucked out, it proved I wasn't worthy. Never had been. I tried my hardest, got the grades, got on the rugby team, behaved myself, but I got found out. *I just wasn't good enough.* And I've never stopped feeling that.'

'You did alright . . .'

'I got a job without my father's help, which is more than you ever did. But still . . . I never felt worthy. Making millions, but having panic attacks. I worked all the hours to prove I was up to it. Until a deal went tits-up and that was the proof I'd been waiting for – I'd been found out, it was happening all over again. So I walked away—No, I *ran* away. New wife, new baby and I let them down. Cally hasn't looked at me the same way since. It wasn't until I went to a therapist, a decade later, more, that I realised the whole thing was just . . . imposter syndrome. That was all. Pathetic, really. All that torment . . . caused by this place. Caused by you.'

'So why send your son here, then?'

'I've used him, haven't I? Didn't even realise until today. Using my son to prove that I'm worthy of this place.'

Maunder laughs again. A playground snigger.

'Little shit,' whispers Mariah.

I've never been a fan of Jack Kent, but that snigger . . .

'Nasty little shit,' I echo.

Mariah's phone buzzes. The two of us make eye contact. She high-tails it into the coffee room. I scoot into the alcove and duck behind the wall.

The headmaster's door flies open.

Silence. We got away with it.

'This is all very interesting, Jack . . .' Maunder's voice moves away as he returns to his desk. He must have left the door open, wanting Jack out of his office. A trick that probably works on the children. 'I have a school to run. And don't you have a son to worry about, instead of worrying about yourself, and who slighted you twenty years ago?'

'We're onto you, *Sammy*,' says Jack. 'We're not going to let you treat our children the way you treated me.'

'Don't worry, Jack. I have complete confidence that Alix will fuck up all by himself—'

It goes quiet.

For too long.

I peep out of the alcove. The headmaster's door is open but I can only see the wood-panelled cupboards, the rest of the office is hidden. There's a knock of wood, a scuff of shoes, a sack-of-spuds thump.

Jack appears in the doorway. I shrink back, but he's looking over his shoulder into the office. He glances up and down the corridor. Pulls the door closed behind him. Then he runs, away from the hall, further into the school. He disappears around the corner past foreign languages.

I look along to the coffee room. Mariah doesn't appear. I do the front teeth dog-whistle. No response. She's not there. Or she's on the phone. I go to the headmaster's door and listen. It's completely silent.

I pause for a moment, staring in the direction Jack went, not really seeing, but *seeing*. He makes so much more sense now. I've seen extreme imposter syndrome before. It explains the job, the failed marriage, the macho validation of his 'survivalist' schtick. It even explains the reckless parties he holds for Alix at the McMansion – the 'Daddy Cool' act – so that his son can be the oxygen of the Saints social bubble, proving that he *belongs* in a way Jack never did. I almost feel sorry for Jack Kent.

Still no sound from Maunder's office.

Something's wrong.

Why did Jack run?

Tensions were pretty high . . . I should call Slocombe.

But also . . .

Maunder's CCTV feed would have recorded me creeping about earlier, breaking into that cupboard to listen to a police interview. It would be better if that recording didn't exist. It would be better if Maunder's entire CCTV archive didn't exist.

There's no one in the corridor. I put my hand on the brass knob of the headmaster's door.

Chapter Twenty-Eight

4.30 p.m.

You're the best of the best. Olivia remembered her mum's words from that morning. They were supposed to be smart kids. They behaved more like pampered pooches, yapping and whining. Temi was the most mild-mannered boy at school – even on the rugby field he was politely ruthless – but now he opened and closed his fists like he might throw a punch. Kiran was green with nausea. Dixie had folded up into an envelope of her own limbs. Alix swirled his palms together like he might throw a hex.

'I switched off the phone' – he shrugged – 'so what? Doesn't mean I'm in on it. You're missing the big picture.'

'We could've called for help!' Olivia said.

'We couldn't have called for help because there was no signal. We were in the middle of a wood. The phone had no bars.'

'We could've walked and got some signal,' said Temi. 'Why did you tell us it was broken?'

'I knew this farm was here, I knew I could lead us to safety—'

'Safety!' Olivia said.

'Hero complex,' muttered Kiran.

'Yeah, maybe I did want to . . . be the hero.'

'Like your dad,' said Temi in a sing-song tone of contempt. Then he dropped it. 'How dare you risk our lives for the sake of some followers?'

'What about Dixie?' Olivia asked. 'We didn't know if she was alive or dead. Maybe Mr Sadler *is* dead—'

'You're psycho, Kent,' Kiran muttered.

Alix sighed, as though he was too tired for all this.

'I didn't realise these dickheads were here, did I?'

Temi rubbed hard at the top of his head. 'We've got to get out of here.'

'Agreed. Boss man' – Alix jacked his thumb at the door to indicate the guys outside, specifically Jones – 'he mentioned a case in America or somewhere some kids were buried, fucking *buried*, in a shipping container, and they managed to escape. They were just little kids. So there must be a way out if we look hard enough.'

He went over to the window and glanced out. It was greyer than ever, the sun starting to fall. The coast must have been clear because he started pushing and shoving at the door. It didn't budge. Temi got the wheeled chair and stood on it, lifting the polystyrene ceiling tiles to see what was above in the pitch-black roof space. 'Give me a boost.' Alix came over, then Temi put his foot on one shoulder and pivoted into the crawl space.

'Olivia?' Dixie's voice was raspy like she had a cold coming.

Olivia moved to her friend, but her eyes stayed on Alix. He'd always been a chore, but this thing with the phone . . . She didn't realise he was capable of something so pathetic.

'Liv?' Dixie sounded more insistent. 'Did you hear what the guy outside was saying on the phone?'

'He was asking for money.'

Dixie grabbed Olivia's wrist, the most alert she'd seemed since they found her.

'What he said was, "It has to be cash." Did I hear that right?'

'Exactly.'

Temi swung down from the ceiling in an athletic forward roll and brushed himself off.

'Anything?' she asked him.

'There might be a panel in the roof. We need something to use as a lever—'

'Olivia, listen!' Dixie hissed. 'What if he didn't say, "It has to be cash," what if he said, "It has to be Kash," with a K?'

'Kash? Like your dad?'

'Yeah. *It has to be Kash*. Meaning it has to be my dad who brings the money.'

Olivia slid down the wall to sit beside her friend.

Dixie kept on. 'The kidnappers wouldn't want the police to know, would they? They'd go direct to our parents, make demands, get hold of the money before the police find us.'

'If they've asked for a ransom,' Olivia asked, 'will he pay it?'

'My dad? Fuck, yes. He can get his hands on money, untraceable money, just like they asked. Between us' – Dixie turned her back to the boys even though they were occupied with their search for a lever – 'I think he knows bad people. He takes a lot of phone calls outside on the patio. In January.'

'What kind of bad people?' The air felt thinner. 'People who drop litter?'

Dixie ignored the gallows humour. 'Properly bad people. But the thing is' – she chewed her thumb as though masking her words – 'people aren't bad when they're on your side. Right?'

'Every villain thinks they're the hero of the story.'

'Exactly. If they get the money and my dad brings it and we get out of here, then . . .' She ended on a shrug. 'That's a good thing, right?'

'Here!' Alix said in triumph. In the back of one of the filing cabinets, he'd found a letter opener. He held up an old-fashioned thing, just recognisable in the dim light as a thick blade with a blunt handle.

Temi tested it, bending it between two fists.

'It's pretty sturdy, I can have a go.'

'But what then?' Alix said.

'Let me get the panel open, then we'll decide. It's going dark, which is good. Maybe we can cause a diversion and one of us runs for it—'

'Stop!' said Olivia.

The boys froze.

She told them about *cash* and *Kash*.

'They've asked for a ransom?' Temi asked.

'This is great!' Kiran said. 'As soon as they get their money, they'll leave us. Then we can get out or just wait for help. It means we'll go home soon.'

Olivia wondered if Kiran was suffering from the optimism of an addict seeing their next hit on the horizon.

'They don't want to kill five kids,' said Temi.

'He seems pretty ruthless,' Alix said. 'You saw what he did to me.'

'He literally tapped you on the shoulder,' Kiran scoffed. 'I've had worse chafing from my backpack.'

Alix swirled his palms again. 'I don't know . . .'

Kiran sat down pointedly by the wall. 'Enough toy heroes for one day, yeah, Alix?'

It was definitive. They agreed to wait. Help was coming.

Chapter Twenty-Nine

5.55 p.m.

'We can't help them if we don't know where they are.' Mariah's shrill voice carries from the meeting room. I almost run to her, but she has Kash to comfort her, and I have to get into the headmaster's office.

The brass knob of his door is mottled by the patina of centuries'-worth of sweaty little palms. This might be my only chance. But I have to be careful.

Head over heart, Em, not head over heels.

I steady myself with a hand on the wood of the door. The grain swirls like Olivia's hair in the bath when she was little. God, why did I send her into this hothouse? How many kids have quaked in front of this intimidating door? The headmaster relies on it for gravitas. Like the Wizard of Oz behind his curtain.

I turn the handle and the door opens silently on greased hinges.

As greasy as the headmaster.

A shit in wolf's clothing.

I slip inside. The door snicks behind me. The wood panelling presses in. I have a schoolgirl's urge to shrink to the size they want you to be in these institutions. Small, hard and brilliant, a child's nature crushed by intense pressure until they can call you a diamond and sell you to the highest bidder – Oxford, Cambridge, Yale. I correct my posture – *fuck 'em* – and grow an inch.

I stare for a moment past the headmaster's desk. The surveillance screens show the feed from CCTV cameras around the school. I scan corridors and classrooms. Empty. As a kid, I could freak myself out by thinking of my empty bedroom, the toys lying there as though they were dead.

I come back to life and scoot behind the desk. I carefully avoid the legs that dangle over its short side. Give wide berth to Maunder's feet hanging limp in Paul Smith socks.

He's out cold. I test his pulse. Strong and steady. He'll have to wait. Time is ticking.

A phone rings. It's coming from Maunder on the desk. His pocket. I use one finger to edge the phone out, careful not to rouse him. No reaction. Eyelids are still. I nudge the screen and it prompts me for face recognition. I hold it over Maunder. The screen clears and I cruise around. Inbox. WhatsApp. Call history. All deleted. That's weird. I let my hand flop. The surveillance screens show parents waiting in the school hall. Trusting and obedient. We all trusted this school, this man. Until today, when the wizard's curtain was whipped back and it was all revealed to be smoke and mirrors.

I read once that parenting is an act of trust, you must deliver your child to the shore and recede with the tide.

Except we're not fucking turtles, are we?

I'm distracted by movement on the screens.

Parents moving in the hall.

What set them off?

An officer enters from the playground.

Another exits the kitchen.

One on the main stairs.

The screens update second by second. Figures jerk along corridors in zombie-motion.

Closing in on the headmaster's office.

Incoming.

On the phone, I find the app that controls the CCTV and navigate to settings. Deselect 'auto record'. On the screens, the red recording lights blink out. I hit delete on today's recordings. Confirm? *Confirm.*

That was easier than I thought it would be . . .

On the surveillance system, figures jump from screen to screen. Only one corridor remains empty – the one outside.

I slide the phone deep into my bra. Then pluck the flash drive from his laptop and stow that too.

On screen, the leader of the pack is a corner away.

I run to the door and exit. The well-oiled hinges do their bit. I duck into the alcove opposite and catch my breath at the foot of a shadowy set of stairs. Pressed up against the wall, I smell crayon from an art display of pictures, a pride of paper lions stirs under my breath.

Footsteps shriek along the corridor. The pack arrives with enough hullabaloo to cover my tread up the wooden stairs. I recognise the voices of both detectives and Ayesha.

A rap on the headmaster's door. A rattle as the brass knob turns. A scream.

Chapter Thirty

5.00 p.m.

In the time they spent screaming at each other, the sun snuck off. The Portakabin was lit only by a sickly glow from car head-lights outside. Olivia pulled her sleeves over her hands that were stiff from the cold. An urgent thudding drew them all to the window. Outside, Crowbar was sprawled on the ground behind the Range Rover. Jones straddled his chest. He held something to the younger man's face. In the red glare of the vehicle tail lights, Olivia saw a metallic glint. A gun, pushed into Crowbar's mouth. He was choking, hands grasping Jones's wrists, trying to pull the man off, his feet trying to gain purchase on a smooth bumper. This was the frantic noise that had got their attention.

'Haven't you done enough?' Jones's loose country accent was tightened by menace. 'You've got all the brains of a garlic crusher. One of you is dead, isn't that enough to make you think?'

In reply, Crowbar made the ugh-ugh-ugh sound of someone with a gun in their mouth.

'That's the most sense you've made all afternoon,' said Jones. 'How dare you go behind my back? What? What are you saying? Teeth? You're worried about teeth? You're going to have a face like a plum pudding.'

He pulled the gun from Crowbar's mouth and hauled the front of his shirt to move him into a sitting position. Jones was shorter than Crowbar, plus twenty years older, but he manhandled him like a Ken doll. Either that or the younger man knew better than to make it worse by fighting back. Crowbar slumped against the wheel of the Range Rover. Stuffing gone out of him.

'You see,' whispered Alix.

Maybe he was right. Did they want to wait here with this man any longer than necessary?

Jones pushed the gun into the back of his trousers.

Olivia felt Dixie's hand slip over hers. Temi swore under his breath.

Jones said, 'You've been making calls, haven't you?'

Crowbar kicked sullenly at the dirt. It flicked over Jones's black boots.

Olivia sucked a breath through her teeth. Wrong move. Even she knew that and she'd only just met Jones. Crowbar was as thick as biscuits.

Jones was on top of the lad in a flash. Gun back in his hand.

Dixie let out a yelp.

Jones jumped up. Looked over his shoulder at the Portakabin.

Everyone ducked. Except Olivia. Jones seemed to stare right into her. It was dark in the cabin, maybe he couldn't see her . . .?

Jones nudged Crowbar's leg with his foot. 'In the barn.'

Crowbar rolled onto his feet and staggered off towards the chicken shed.

When they were out of sight, Olivia told the others to get up.

'What was all that about?' Alix asked.

'He didn't like Crowbar making that call about the ransom,' Olivia said.

They speculated about what this might mean, weaving strands into a story to tell themselves. Then came footsteps. The padlock rattled. The door flew open.

'Olivia,' Jones demanded.

'What do you want with her?' Temi said.

'She's fine, nobody's threatening the lady's honour, Mr Darcy.'

Olivia followed him and he locked the door after her. Pocketed the key.

'How's your shoulder?' Jones asked as they walked towards the barn. 'I had a broken collarbone once. You're being very stoic. Are your mates ready to escape yet?'

'First chance they get,' Olivia said.

He laughed under his breath.

'I'd be disappointed if you lot didn't have a good go.'

They trudged to the barn. It looked cavernous. It looked like a hole in the world. Jones switched on his phone torch. Olivia had to get up beside him to walk in the spotlight and avoid the broken concrete. His left arm bumped against her right.

'Can we slow down?'

He marched on.

A backcloth of woodland hung to one side. The tree line looked close. Or that could be a trick of the dark. But she could run for it. He had a gun; she could hear a faint metallic rattle swinging in time with his strides. Senses heightened by the dark. She'd just seen him jam the gun into someone's mouth, but he wouldn't shoot her, would he? She listened to his breathing. It was steady, calm. He was in control. Not running on anger. He wouldn't shoot.

They were almost at the barn. She glanced at the trees . . . and stumbled on the uneven ground. Jones grabbed her elbow to steady her.

'Thanks,' she muttered. He let go and walked on.

Now or never. *Go now if you're going.*

'Olivia.' Jones stopped and turned to face her. Too late. Stupid idea anyway. He would have caught her. She would have fallen in the dark. Maybe she was wrong about him and he would have shot her without hesitation. He pointed his phone torch into the doorway. 'Watch your step.'

Inside the barn, the same reek of ammonia and burnt hair. And something fresh. A tang of blood.

The circle of light scuttled round to illuminate Crowbar. He was lying flat on his back inside the door. He groaned, semi-conscious.

'You did make him into a plum pudding,' Olivia said.

The mess around Crowbar's mouth made him look like a mucky toddler. He gagged and blood welled up and ran down his chin.

'You said you're going to be a doctor, right?' Jones asked. 'Can you help him?'

'I'm doing A-levels. I volunteer in a rehab clinic. They don't let me do any actual medicine.'

'I don't know what's wrong with him.'

'Did you shoot him in the face?' Olivia asked. 'Could that be a clue?'

'I didn't shoot him.'

'You had your gun in his mouth before, and now look at him.'

'I shouldn't have done that in front of you kids. I lost my rag.'

'He needs an ambulance.'

'Be realistic.'

'He's choking on his own blood!'

Jones grabbed him under the shoulders.

'Don't! He might have a neck injury. I need light.' She held out a hand for Jones's phone. He hesitated, then placed it in her palm. The torch icon was right under her thumb. Olivia ran through a scenario in her mind. Turn off the light. Run for the door. Run for the trees. Use the phone to call 999—

Jones lifted the mobile from her hand.

'I forgot about your shoulder,' he said. 'I'll hold the light for you.'

She pulled open Crowbar's mouth. He whimpered but didn't regain consciousness.

'What did you do?' she asked.

'Nothing, I—'

Jones stepped away, taking the light with him, turning a full circle on the spot. If Olivia didn't know better, she'd say he felt bad.

She had to do what she could. 'I've done a St John's Ambulance course. And I volunteer at school rugby matches. If someone gets knocked out, we make sure the airway is clear.'

She tilted back his head to open the throat, fished inside with her fingers. Scooped out gunk. Flicked it onto the floor. Vomit, maybe, blood. Lumpy, so more likely vomit. She was glad of the dark.

Jones swore. 'You're determined about this career in medicine, then?'

'It's all I've ever wanted to do.'

'I can imagine you in A&E. You're bossy enough.'

'I'm not bossy, I'm the boss.' Her mum had bought a notebook with that embossed on the front.

She felt him staring at her, even in the dark.

'You're going to be a great doctor,' he said.

She didn't dignify him with an answer. 'If he has a broken jaw, it could be pressing into his larynx. That happened at rugby once. Did you punch him again?'

'No . . . I promise.' He sounded like a little boy. Whiny.

She placed her hands either side of Crowbar's jaw. Not broken. She listened to his breathing. 'I think his tongue is the problem, look. It's hanging off.'

'He fell through the doorway, must have bitten it. I don't need another one of them dead.'

'How inconvenient . . .' Olivia muttered. 'I don't think you can bleed out from a cut tongue. Do you have ice?'

'No.'

'Fabric?' she asked.

'Only what I'm wearing.' He didn't move.

'Well, I'm not taking my clothes off . . .'

'No, I wasn't suggesting . . . alright.' Jones shouldered his way out of his jacket and grabbed the left sleeve of his top, managing with a few tugs to rip it off his arm. Olivia tore the cloth into smaller sections and balled one into Crowbar's cheek so he looked like a bloodthirsty chipmunk. Then she got Jones to shift him into the recovery position so he couldn't choke on his own vomit. She stood up. 'He needs a hospital.'

'I'll deal with him later,' said Jones. 'If he's not going to die.'

'What are you going to do with us?' she asked. 'Why are we here?'

'The *why* is nothing to do with me. I'm a cleaner-upper, a fixer. I do whatever my boss wants me to do.'

'If he said jump off a cliff, would you?'

Jones gave a huff of laughter. 'No, but I'd happily push this plum pudding off.'

Olivia looked down at the bloodied man.

'In fairness,' she said, 'I would too.'

Jones was looking at her again very intently, the same way he had through the window of the office, like he could see into her mind.

'I'm sorry about the gore,' he said.

'He looks like something out of *Reservoir Dogs*.'

'You know that film?'

'Mum makes me watch her old favourites.'

'Nostalgic, is she?'

Olivia wiped her face and felt a splodge that might be blood. She didn't particularly want to share family details with this stranger, but she was supposed to be bonding with him, as per her previous plan. Reminding him that she had a family who would miss her would raise the sympathy quota. He seemed calm now but might 'lose his rag' again any time.

'My mum's been on her own a long time. Doesn't have anyone to share memories, I suppose. Plus, a lot of her films are actually quite good, better than what we get now, all superheroes and reboots.'

'This is true. Is she okay, then, on her own?'

'My mum? She could meet someone if she wanted, she's good-looking enough.'

Jones agreed with a hum.

Olivia scoffed. 'How would you know?'

'I meant she must be good-looking because you are. But that would sound weird coming from an old duffer like me. You can't say shit like that to girls these days.'

'Women,' said Olivia.

'Sorry, I—'

'I'm messing with you.'

He rocked back on his heels. 'We should get you back to your friends. Before they worry.'

'They got worried around midday when we were kidnapped.'

'That was not me.'

Jones led the way out of the barn. They trudged across the smashed ground. It was a still evening and they heard a distant wail. Jones told her it was an owl. And then what type of owl. Olivia concentrated on crossing the broken concrete without stumbling. Maybe she'd overdone the bonding. He stuck close to her right shoulder. But she did want him to like her – at least, more than he liked the others. In case he had to sacrifice one of them and it meant it wouldn't be her. She was dealing with this situation no differently to the way she dealt with school: working harder, working smarter. It wasn't her fault the others felt entitled to get off scot-free. But nothing came for free. She glanced down at Jones's big boots, walking in stride with hers. She wasn't so unlike him after all.

Self-preservation was the name of this game – and every game.

Chapter Thirty-One

6.00 p.m.

Call it ruthlessness, call it self-preservation, but I cannot let up until Olivia is safe. Maybe I should have put the headmaster into the recovery position, but that would have given away that someone else had been in the office. The police are with him now, help is on the way, he's only been unconscious for a few minutes. Jack Kent must have head-butted him or something. That's no worse than the battering Maunder's lads get on the rugby pitch week in, week out, for the glory of his school.

I sneak along the upper corridor between empty classrooms. I pull Maunder's phone out of my bra – its screen kept awake by the press of my flesh – and navigate to iCloud. In his documents, I find a folder containing case files on our children.

Delete.

I can wipe the flash drive later. No one will know what I've done, but everyone would thank me if they did. I return the phone to my cleavage. The others have privilege to rely on. I have street smarts. This school seems to be the dead eye of a storm of secrets and sorrows. I'll make someone pay for putting Olivia through this.

I don't know my way around the school very well, it's spread between interconnecting buildings, and I rarely visit outside of open days and parent–teacher evenings. But I orientate myself with glimpses through the windows. I'm moving along the length of the quad. Another corner and I should reach the gatehouse . . .

It seems extraordinary that a journalist would get into the school and try to confront Ayesha Reid. Even if she is an MP and the journalistic gloves are off, that reporter sounded het-up. I want to know why.

I round a bend and there's a glass lift and I know where I am. I go down and emerge on the far side of the car park. The night air is damp with cold. It tastes of the sea. I slip along the front fence to a pedestrian gate. A green button makes it swing open.

Outside, a knot of journalists huddle together like meerkats. Heads go up amid a pall of vape smoke. One figure stirs up the smog as it breaks away. It's a woman. Not my guy. I set off in the opposite direction. The door of a parked car opens and a tall man steps into my path. In the citric street light, he's got the air of a Victorian baddie, boney and black-clad. More grave-robber than journalist, but his manner is polite as he falls into step beside me. Introduces himself. I recognise his voice at once. The man I heard inside the school. The female reporter is advancing too.

'Get rid of her,' I mutter and speed up into a side street, where there are dumpster-style bins. I tuck in behind them and a minute later he appears, alone. I cough and he finds me.

'Are you a parent?' he asks. 'I'm so sorry for what you're going through . . .'

I don't want sympathy. It'll crack my defences.

'What is it you want to speak to Ayesha Reid about?' I go on the offensive.

'Is her son, Kiran, on the missing bus?' He ignores my question with one of his own.

'There are five children on the bus. Including my daughter. They're all equally important.'

He bows his head. 'Of course they are. But the police must be considering the . . . uh . . . public profile of those involved? Do they know where the bus might be?'

'We don't know any more than you do.'

'Who else is invo—?'

'Tell me what you wanted to speak to Ayesha about. If the kids have been taken to get at a parent for some reason, then she's the most obvious target, she's a government minister.'

'Has there been a ransom demand?'

'If you tell me what you know, I'll speak to her on your behalf. I'll do anything you want, but you have to tell me what you know.'

'Alright, but it's complicated, and I've been silenced for years by an NDA. A non-disclos—'

'I know what it is.'

'It concerns the identity of her son's father.'

'If you say his father is the prime minister—' I could punch him in the plums. I snuck out of school for a fucking conspiracy theory?

'Not the prime minister, no,' he says. 'I have evidence that the boy's father is a *criminal*. Ayesha Reid suppressed this information to protect her career.'

Okay.

'What kind of criminal?'

'A spy. In the House of Commons. There's a lot more to this, but what's relevant to the events of today is an allegation that Ayesha previously paid a ransom to a blackmailer who threatened to expose the truth. So I'm thinking that—'

'Are you saying the father, the spy, has taken our kids? Or the blackmailer she paid off has snatched them to get more money?'

He raises his palms as though my guess is as good as his. 'I've never been able to run the story because of an NDA, but now there are kids' lives at stake so I'll break it if necessary and hang the consequences . . .'

Give the man a halo . . . 'Did you speak to Ayesha today?'

'Ms Reid wouldn't speak to me.'

'Did you tell the police?'

'DC Gill Singh took the details, but . . .' He shrugs. 'Something happened because his radio went and he handed me over to security and ran inside.'

I'm not about to tell him that a minor celebrity KO-ed the headmaster. I don't want this to turn into a tidbit for the *Sidebar of Shame*.

But would the police listen to his half-garbled story of a government minister, a secret father, a spy, a ransom . . . Could I trust Singh to look into this with urgency?

The journalist glances over his shoulder. Concerned another reporter might hear. I see at once that he doesn't care about Olivia, the kids, me. He's focused on his scoop.

I'm done here. If Ayesha wouldn't speak to this journalist – and who can blame her? – then I'll speak to her myself.

Chapter Thirty-Two

5.45 p.m.

Jones stopped with his hand flat on the Portakabin door. Olivia hadn't realised how cold she had got until a shiver ran the full length of her body. The temperature had dropped with the sun. And it wouldn't be any warmer inside. The floor might as well be bare earth.

'Can we go home now? I'm cold.'

'Have you heard of the Brink's-Mat Robbery?'

'What?'

'Happened in the '80s . . . Brink's-Mat was a heist – biggest robbery of all time. They got gold bullion worth millions, almost a billion pounds. Trouble was, it was *too* valuable. They bit off more than they could chew. They couldn't fence that much gold. Fence means to sell stolen goods—'

'I know what it means.'

'They reckon most of it is still buried somewhere.'

'We're not gold bars. You can't just bury us.'

'Well, I could . . .' His smile dropped as the joke fell flat. He put the key in the lock and wrestled the door open, checking no one was there to ambush him. Dixie ran out of the shadows and hugged Olivia around the waist, dragging her away from Jones.

'Ah, sweet,' he said. 'Now behave yourselves.'

He slammed and locked the door again. It plunged them into darkness.

After Olivia explained about the bloodbath in the barn, they slid back into an argument that must have been raging while she'd been away.

'Why've they made a ransom demand to one parent only?' Temi asked. 'Why not all of them? Not being funny, but my family is worth a lot, so why not mine? It happened to my cousins and the family coughed up, no questions asked. If the kidnappers had done their homework, they'd know that.'

'Maybe they hate Dixie's parents?' Alix held up one hand in apology. 'Don't take that personally.'

She pulled a face. 'You're saying "maybe it's personal, but don't take it personally"?'

'This whole thing doesn't feel right.' Temi wasn't backing down. 'I've had hostage training since I could walk—'

'Actually?' asked Alix.

Temi grimaced. 'This nice man and woman – who I always called Aunty and Uncle, but were probably ex-SAS or something – came to the house to run drills with me and my sister and the nanny.'

'Such as?' asked Kiran.

'Such as . . .' Temi waved his hands while he thought of an example. 'If a vehicle starts kerb crawling alongside you, you run back the way you came, in the opposite direction to the way the car is moving, so it has to reverse or turn around in the road. Buys you some time. We used to act out role plays. They made it fun.'

'What a childhood,' muttered Dixie.

'They were trying to keep us safe so we could live a normal life,' Temi huffed.

'Not like your dad, Kent,' said Kiran. 'With his fake danger . . .'

Temi ignored the interruption. 'So this doesn't feel right. It's taking too long. There's not enough of them. How are they supposed to transport us out of here? If this bloke – the one Olivia calls *Jones* – tries to put us in the car, we can run away because it's only him now. The other half has bitten his own tongue off. These guys are not professionals . . . I, personally, am insulted to be kidnapped by these people.'

'Dixie,' Olivia said when there was a lull in Temi's monologue, 'what happened back there in the wood?'

'I thought we weren't supposed to ask her about it,' said Alix.

Olivia shushed him.

'Dixie?' she pressed. 'Did you give them your dad's number?'

She closed her eyes and drops squeezed out of the corners. Olivia watched them fall down her friend's cheeks. Kiran looked away. Alix stared. Temi moved to console her. Interesting to see each of their reactions to emotion. Discomfort. Morbid curiosity. Comfort. Each of their characters right there.

'Dixie?' Olivia nudged.

'I gave them my mum's number.' Dixie's voice clogged with tears. 'But this isn't what I expected, not at all.'

'What do you mean?'

'Back in the woodland . . . I recognised those blokes, I knew what they wanted, so I offered them a deal—'

'Whoa, whoa – what?' Alix jumped in. 'Start at the beginning. You recognised them? Who are they? What do they want?'

'Alix, you think you're so *street* . . . They're drug dealers.'

'What's that got to do with us?' asked Temi.

'We know people with the money to spend on drugs.'

'You've been selling drugs?' Kiran was aghast. 'You would be expelled—'

'Of course I haven't been selling drugs!'

'So what, then?' Temi asked.

Dixie wiped tears away with the heels of both hands.

'I've seen that lad with the Stüssy hoodie outside school. And I've heard about him. So when they followed us I figured they wanted something . . . They stopped behind the minibus and I knew it would be about money, so I called them over into the wood. Spoke as quickly as I could, cos I knew Mr Sadler would come—Mr Sadler!' She bubbled over into tears. They let her weep. She didn't look at any of them when she spoke again.

'I gave them the number. I said if they want real money, then call my mum and say I was a hostage and they'd let me go for five grand—'

'Five thousand pounds?' Temi was incredulous. 'Is that all?'

'They're *corner boys*,' Dixie said. 'They think they're dealing with a few posh kids, not the sons of the next prime minister, off-brand Bear Grylls and fucking Elon Musk. Five grand is a fortune to them, enough to spin their eyeballs like slot machines. They had a quick chat, which got interrupted by Mr Sadler, and they must have decided to go for it because one of them bashed him and the other one ran for the bus. But I didn't expect—'

'What the fuck did you expect, Dixie?' Alix asked. 'You *offered* yourself to them?'

'I offered to sit with him – Crowbar – in the wood for an hour while my parents got five grand out of the safe and met us at the end of the lane. I thought they'd dump the minibus a few miles away in a field with you lot inside, and it would all be over by the time you found your way to the nearest phone. And then they'd leave us alone.'

'Oh right,' said Kiran in a monotone, 'cos after you give people easy money, they always leave you alone. Also, I am not the prime minister's son, just saying.'

'Dixie . . .' Temi's voice was dangerously low. 'Mr Sadler has a family. He might be dead.'

She said nothing, just stood there trembling with the tears rolling.

When no one else moved, Alix went over and stood in front of Dixie with his arms wide. He asked, 'Can I?'

She nodded.

He enclosed her in a hug. After a beat her hands gripped his shoulder blades and she sobbed. Temi went to the window and stood in a power pose, fingers interlaced on the back of his head. Kiran was almost invisible in a dark corner. Olivia put her hand to her face and realised she was crying, too, so much that her neck was wet and cold.

Alix pushed Dixie back so he could see her.

'Those boys didn't have to be violent. It was brave of you to confront them like that—'

'Brave or stupid,' muttered Temi.

'And Sadler might be okay, he might be in hospital right now, getting treatment.'

'I hope so,' Dixie agreed in a snotty splutter.

'What now?' Kiran's voice was reedy. 'We know Crowbar phoned your mum. And he made the demand for money. So does that mean your dad's coming? Or the police?'

'Not the police.' Dixie was barely audible. 'I don't think . . .'

'Isn't that the first thing your dad would do?' Kiran. 'Call the police?'

'Not necessarily.' Temi. 'Your mum, Kiran, would call the secret service. My dad would call his private security. Olivia's mum would kick their arses all by herself.'

Olivia gave him a small smile. Temi and her mum got on great guns. Olivia sometimes thought Emily might have an inappropriate crush on him. Or maybe his dad, which would still be inappropriate because he was married to Temi's mum, but much better.

Olivia cleared her throat.

'What do you think your dad would do, Dixie?'

'He won't call the police. He knows . . . people.'

'Bad people?' Kiran sounded very young.

'Bad enough.'

'Good,' said Kiran decisively.

'Two bads don't make a good.' Temi's face was half-illuminated by light from the window.

'He's only trying to help,' said Alix.

'It's each man for himself with you, isn't it, Kent? "The Kents"' – Temi put speech marks around the name with his fingers – 'It's all about survival. Your own survival.'

'Not now!' said Alix.

'Why not now? Your shit always makes me stink. I'm not carrying the can a second time.'

'You got off scot-free the first time,' muttered Kiran.

Olivia put her face in her hands. They had enough to deal with here and now without dredging up the past.

'Is that what your mummy told you?' Temi sneered. 'Mummy has an opinion about everything because she wants to be *pwime* minister?'

'She was concerned about that girl who got hurt. That mental party. My mum doesn't want me being exposed to alcohol and drugs—'

The irony, Olivia thought.

'I was the one trying to keep everyone clean!' Temi exploded. 'Li Na found a bag of white powder in your bathroom' – he shot one finger at Alix – 'and she was about to call the police. If they came and we got identified, then we'd have random drugs tests at school and maybe some of us' – his eyes flit over Kiran – 'might get caught out.'

'You didn't have to touch the girl!' Dixie huffed. 'I don't know why you liked her so much anyway!'

'I didn't *touch* her. I grabbed her phone and she snatched her hand back and put it through the glass and ran off. I didn't realise how bad it was, none of us did, did we?' Temi looked around for confirmation and they all, except Olivia, nodded. Olivia hadn't been at that party, she'd gone with her mother to the theatre, thankfully. 'Everyone assumed it was some kind of attempted rape. Imagine being accused of that!'

'No one actually accused you . . .' said Alix.

'They all think it. And when that photo from the party turned up, I was the only one who got identified. So that's racist. And now I'm on thin ice at school, working twice as hard to be absolutely bloody perfect, can't drop a grade or miss a rugby match or put a foot wrong, or it could all come tumbling down. And I didn't even do anything! I don't even know how the drugs got to that party.'

'I do,' said Alix.

That shut everyone up.

'Then, please,' said Temi. He had the weary tone of someone twice his age. 'Do tell.'

Alix brushed himself down with a prissy Poirot air. 'I've suspected for a while, but today confirmed it. This is connected. There is only one person who had the cover to bring drugs to that party. And that person is the one who's in on it.'

Alix pointed his finger. Even in the dark, it was clear who he was accusing.

Chapter Thirty-Three

6.15 p.m.

It's never a good idea to accuse someone unless you're armed with weaponry in the form of facts. What the journalist told me was hardly high-caliber ammunition. Potentially, it was a load of old blanks . . . But I go looking for Ayesha.

She's with everyone in the corridor outside Maunder's office. The headmaster is alive. Awake. Agog. He can't believe Jack Kent isn't being arrested.

'You fell.' Jack is cocky. 'I went to get help.'

'Let's see on the CCTV, shall we?' Maunder is smug. 'You used a death grip on my neck.'

'Death grip?' scoffs Ayesha. 'Like *Star Trek*?'

Maunder clutches his neck.

'Looks like a hickey,' Jack says. 'First time for everything.'

'About the CCTV . . .' Singh is behind the headmaster's desk. He points at the surveillance screens. 'Wasn't this recording before?'

Maunder skates round the desk and clicks the mouse. He pats his pockets, looking for his phone. It's wedged under my left boob, my biggest one, so he's not getting it back until I say so.

I catch Slocombe's eye and incline my head towards the women's bathroom. She seems glad of an excuse to leave. Ayesha looks up and I signal for her to come too. We slip across the corridor. As soon as the door closes, I start.

'Has there been a ransom demand?'

Slocombe pushes her fingers into her pockets, purses her lips, shakes her head.

'Have you, Ayesha, received a ransom demand?' I ask.

'Is this about the journalist?' she sighs.

I should have known she'd be well-briefed.

'You tell us. He told me you've been blackmailed before. And you paid them off. So *is this* about the journalist? Has your blackmailer come back for more?'

'No,' she says.

'Has Kiran's Russian-spy father taken him?'

'Russian—?' she splutters. 'Not Russian, no. He's . . . well, he's none of your business!'

I've never seen Ayesha Reid even slightly flustered. Slocombe removes her hands from her pockets. She can also see I've hit a nerve.

'Ms Reid, if there is *anything*—'

'That journalist is the only one blackmailing me!' Ayesha spits the words out. 'He never gives up, he comes back year after year like a fucking verruca. The NDA is supposed to protect Kiran's privacy, as the innocent child of a public figure.'

'The journalist claims that Kiran's father is a convicted spy.'

Slocombe looks dubious but keeps quiet. I don't think she's going to have patience with this conspiracy theory stuff for much longer.

But Ayesha hesitates.

Slocombe's eyes flick between the minister and me. Her lips part.

'Do I need to put DC Singh onto this, Ms Reid? See what he can find out about a previous extortionist?'

'No.' She turns into the stall behind her and closes the door. We hear the crumple of fabric, creak of a toilet seat, splash. Slocombe raises her eyebrows at me. I widen my eyes in reply. There's a flush and the MP reappears.

'If I tell you,' she says, 'it stays in this room. It does not go for further investigation, Detective Sergeant. And it does not reach that journalist, Emily Smith. It dies here and now. Or I will retaliate.'

Dramatic, but okay. I agree. Slocombe, too.

Ayesha hasn't washed her hands, but I won't tell that to the journalist either.

'I'm absolutely confident that what happened in my past has nothing to do with the events of today. Not least because one person involved is no longer in this country, and the other is dead. It happened over fifteen years ago, it's over.'

Ayesha starts a tap running. Still not washing her hands, but to cover her voice. Even so, she speaks so quietly that Slocombe and I step in towards her.

'Kiran's father was a parliamentary researcher in the Commons. Jerry Ladbroke. Knew him since Oxford. It was an on–off relationship, we kept it secret because we were young and ambitious. I fell pregnant unexpectedly. He was Catholic, felt strongly that I should keep it, and I came round to the idea. But right after the – how shall I say? – after the ship had sailed—'

'You were too far gone to terminate?' I clarify.

'Please never repeat this in front of anyone who might tell Kiran, but yes. I was just gone twenty-four weeks when Jerry was arrested and charged with spying. Passing state secrets for money. I honestly didn't believe the allegations. We'd known each other for years. I was called to give evidence in his defence.

But at work I distanced myself from him. No one knew I was pregnant. I was very slim, hardly any bump.' Ayesha stops and looks at the ceiling for a moment. 'And a promotion was coming up so I wanted to get the job before I announced I'd need maternity leave.'

Slocombe and I make noises of solidarity. This is the most human side of Ayesha Reid I've ever seen.

'So you're pregnant. Single. Baby-father accused of spying . . .' Slocombe tries to nudge it along.

'His case eventually goes to court. I have to give evidence that includes dates and times he was working late with me, occasions he was supposed to have met his contact. And some of those dates and times were a little . . . elastic. But I genuinely believed him and . . .' She purses her lips.

'You didn't want the father of your child to be found guilty of espionage?' I say.

'You committed perjury?' Slocombe zeroes in.

'It didn't make any difference. He went to prison. Full tariff, fourteen years.'

'Shit,' I whisper.

'And, yes, a year or so after that I was blackmailed by a former work colleague. He'd dug up evidence to dispute the statement I gave in court.'

'He threatened to expose the fact that you perjured yourself for your boyfriend—'

'Jerry wasn't my boyfriend. We'd been very clandestine. Turns out he was good at that . . .'

'But a charge of perjury would have ruined your career?'

'I should think so, yes.'

'Still would,' I add.

'I paid the blackmailer and he fucked off to Washington, where he's now a lobbyist for the tobacco industry. So an all-round nice guy.'

'And you said that the other person who knows anything is dead?'

'Kiran's father.' Ayesha glances down. 'Jerry didn't last a year. Got *shanked*, I think that's the term, in the shower.'

'Poor Kiran,' I say.

'He knows his father is dead. Not that it happened in prison. The rumour that his father is the prime minister has always been a useful distraction from the real story, so I kind of let it run, maybe encouraged it a little with total silence. People are fucking easy to manipulate.'

Slocombe rubs her eyes.

'I need to go.'

'Please don't get distracted from finding our kids,' Ayesha pleads with the detective. Her eyes well up. 'If I had the slightest bit of information . . .'

Slocombe gives a tight nod and leaves.

Ayesha shoots me a dirty look and follows.

I hold my hands under the still-running tap. The water is ice-cold and after a few seconds my knuckles burn. Ayesha is not the cause of the kidnapping. So that brings me back to the possibility that I am. I turn the water off and get back to work.

I head to the coffee room. I pick up a packet of biscuits and rest a moment on the fuchsia-coloured sofa, eating mechanically, fuelling my body. On any normal day I'd be panicking about dinner, about now. Olivia isn't picky but one day she wants something healthy, the next day something comforting, it's hard to predict. I close my eyes for a moment and make a little promise: I'll never complain about anything domestic ever again.

Mariah comes in.

'Fuck's sake, I thought you'd done a runner,' is how she greets me.

She walks over and wordlessly envelops me in a hug.

'Heard anything new?' I ask her armpit.

'Fuck all,' she tells my hairline.

We break apart and sit down.

'Shitty sofa,' she mutters. 'It's like perching on a hippo.'

'Earl Grey?' I ask.

'Bit beyond that now. It's been three hours.'

'Don't have anything stronger,' I say.

'Is it cold? I saw you outside.'

And there was me thinking I'd been stealthy. 'There was a journalist, long story, turned out to be nothing. But, yeah, it's cold. I really hope . . .' I can't say it.

'The girls can't be outside.' Mariah does the dirty work.

'It's dark. Wherever they are, they'll be scared.' My mind skips away to an early police job, back in the 90s, the most frightened I've been in my life. Before now. I was so naive. I thought I was a townie through and through, living in a dream like an ironic Pulp video where *all the parks were car parks*, or something like that. I found every grimy inch of my city so darkly glamorous . . . until the first night I walked to a dodgy squat to meet a drug dealer, the first time I realised that I lived on the surface. Where it never gets dark. Street lights, headlamps, hope. None of these existed in that squat. I'd never seen darkness like it. Alleyways, doorways, corners. I thought it could suck me in. Of course, that's exactly what it does to some people; no horror movie, that's just drugs for you. Could Olivia be somewhere like that now? Somewhere she can't see the sky, can't see her own hand in front of her face, can't see a way out—

'Don't think about it.' Mariah reads my mind. She knows nothing about my past, but she can see I've gone to a dark place now. She grabs my chin on both sides and wipes my tears away with her thumbs. Her lips buckle. One eyelash has come off at the corner and for some reason that's the thing that makes my stomach heave into a sob right into her outstretched hands. She grips me tighter. 'Stop it, skank, you're all over the place. You can't think like that, you'll go mad.'

I pull back but a mozzarella string of snot joins us. She doesn't even wipe me off her.

'They'll get through it. They're together, I'm sure of it. There's no way Dixie will let anything happen to Olivia, those girls are close as sisters. Closer. I fucking hate my sister.'

I didn't even know she had a sister. I use my sleeve to wipe my face.

'I know,' I say. 'They'll stick together. Look after each other.'

'I'm going to make you an Earl fucking Grey, that's the best we've got right now.'

Strong emotion always turns to anger inside me. I press my lips together to stop myself saying what I'm thinking. I love Dixie, I do, but she's the reckless one, the wild child, bright and dangerous as a firework, not the one you'd expect to do the looking after. That is obviously Olivia. If they're together, she'll be the mother hen . . . the one who won't let anything bad happen.

Mariah plonks tea in front of me. The bag rolls under the surface like something floating in the canal. Again, she grabs my hand so tight her nails are needles. 'Listen to me, Em.

Olivia is okay, she's coming home. She's a grafter, never puts a foot wrong. Believe you me, our girls are chips off the old blocks, they're just like us. They won't let nothing stand in their way.'

Chapter Thirty-Four

6.15 p.m.

Olivia's breath left her body as though the collective gaze of her friends was a weight on her chest. Alix held a finger pointed at her face.

'Me?' she said. 'But I wasn't at your party, Alix. I was in London watching *Hamilton* with my mum.'

'How can it be Liv?' said Temi. 'You can't make wild allegations, Alix.'

'Olivia's too clever for that.' Dixie's raspy voice like a moth scratching in the dark.

'She had an alibi for the party,' said Alix. 'But she came round earlier that day to revise, didn't you? She was in the house then.'

It was true. Olivia had been to his place to work on their Extended Project Qualification about the ethics of a trade in human organs.

Alix nodded rapidly. 'She could have stashed a baggie in the bathroom. The one where Li Na found the powder.'

'Drug dealers don't leave stashes lying around so that users can help themselves,' scoffed Temi.

'She's the mule,' Alix pointed out. 'She doesn't actually deal—'

'Let's ask her,' Kiran said. 'Olivia, are you selling drugs?'

'No!'

A key at the door silenced them. It opened and Jones blocked the doorway.

'Is he alright?' Olivia asked him. 'Your friend?'

'Not my friend,' said Jones. 'But he's still with us.'

It would actually be better if he died. He knew too much.

'Shame,' Olivia muttered.

Jones gave a low chuckle of surprise.

Olivia made a showy shrug. 'Just saying there's a way out of this. He was the one following us on the motorway. His BMW would have been caught on cameras, not your Range Rover. The police won't know about your car. So if Crowbar – that's what we call him – if Crowbar was dead, then he couldn't tell anyone who he worked for. You could drive away and leave everything behind, the police would blame it all on him, and you'd have plenty of time to get away.'

'Unless you told them,' Jones pointed out.

Kiran piped up from his corner. 'But we wouldn't, would we? We don't know your name. We don't know your number plate. It's dark out there, we can't see it. It's just a random Range Rover.'

'What do you want me to do, put a bullet in him?' Jones's eyes crinkled with amusement. He was toying with her, seeing what she was made of, a big dog cuffing an insolent puppy.

Olivia raised one shoulder. 'It's about priorities, right? In hospital they'd call it triage.'

'Actually,' said Kiran, 'triage is designed to enable patients to survive.'

'I know that.' Olivia's voice was hard and she kept her eyes on Jones. 'My point is that medics make difficult choices. It's not always fair, who gets treated first, who gets the expensive medicines, who gets a "do not resuscitate". The needs of the many overwhelm the few. And the needs of the many *now* would be served by Crowbar being dead and left here with his car for the police to find. And you' – she nodded at Jones – 'could leave and never see us again. We'd say we have no idea what happened to Crowbar because we were locked inside here. He must have had a fight with the other bloke, we didn't see.'

Jones ran his tongue over the back of his teeth. But he wasn't laughing at her anymore. 'You're a tough one, Olivia, I'm quite proud of you.'

Dixie gave a little cough. Or a scoff.

'Now what?' said Alix.

'He's going to kill us,' said Kiran.

'Don't be silly,' Olivia said. 'We just need to work with him—'

'Why are you always cosying up to him?' Dixie leapt up, yelling.

'Because' – Olivia kept her voice level; Dixie's intelligence could be a trapeze act with spectacular highs but alarming lows – 'if we can find a way for him to leave us without getting into trouble, then we'll get out of here alive. But if he thinks the police are going to catch up with him later, then none of us get out. See? We can't make knee-jerk reactions like you—'

'Such as?' Dixie.

'Such as ransom attempts?' Olivia said. 'Giving out our parents' phone numbers . . .'

Dixie's mouth went slack. At once, Olivia realised she herself had fumbled the ball. The full truth of Dixie's plan dawned on her like an old-fashioned photo developing. Misty outline clearing to vivid detail. Olivia realised why Dixie had asked for that ransom money.

Dixie turned with her hands on her hips to the rest of the group.

'Would anyone like to know why I really made that ransom demand? So you can see that it wasn't quite as *knee-jerk* as Liv would have you believe . . .'

'I'd bloody love to know,' said Jones. 'Why does a kid black-mail her own parents?'

'Shall I tell them, Olivia, or do you want to?'

'Dixie . . .'

'Me then, okay. Olivia Smith might have the best grades at Saints but she's not as clever as she thinks. That ransom money was for *her*. To pay off her debts. She's the one who's in on it. Olivia works for these drug dealers.'

Chapter Thirty-Five

6.25 p.m.

A hand between my shoulder blades makes me turn. It's Kash. We say nothing, but cling for a moment in an awkward greeting, unsure how to conduct ourselves outside a superficial social setting, my attempted air kiss landing on his neck as he crushes me a little too hard against one shoulder. His whole body trembles. I think he needs comfort more than I do. His hair smells of cold night air. He's wearing his usual uniform of dark, sleek layers in quality fabrics, creases new or dry cleaned, the image of success. He always wears it well, as though Mariah ordered him from a catalogue. He looks the same but the way he carries himself is different, like he's his own twin. As I pull back, I note mud splashed up the ankles of his blue-black chinos. But clean shoes. Must have changed them. Why go to that effort when you're in so much of a panic that you're shaking?

'Where is she?' he asks.

I point him towards Mariah in the coffee room. He goes in and closes the door.

Akin calls my name from along the corridor and beckons me to our chemistry lab.

We slip inside and he presses the door closed with a flat hand.

'I thought you might like an update,' he says. 'From the hospital where Mr Sadler is being treated. I just got a call from a friend there.'

I don't admit that I've hardly thought about the injured teacher, only my child.

'Mr Sadler is out of surgery. But he has intracranial haematoma, pneumothorax, broken ribs—'

'Slow down . . . Is he going to survive?'

'He's critical but stable. He'll pull through.'

'When will he be able to talk?'

'As soon as they think it won't kill him. Detectives are waiting. My friend knows it's time-critical.'

'Can't they wake him?'

'Emily . . .' Akin takes my elbows. 'Believe me, they understand. But he's their patient—'

'He's a teacher, he'd want to help!'

Akin pushes me to arm's length and ignores my questions. 'What have you been doing? You've not been in the hall.'

'I spoke to a journalist—'

'Bastard!' Akin spits. 'Jack and I saw him off. Can't believe that parasite would come round with his bullshit stories.'

I say nothing. I'm sitting on Ayesha's secret. She'll come out squeaky clean. When the plight of our children is turned into the inevitable news story, it will no doubt win her sympathy. She'll be seen as a dedicated mother and tragic figure . . . It might even humanise her enough to win the election. A conspiracy theorist might suspect she'd set the whole thing up . . . But I'm more certain than ever that it's about me, and I'm no closer to working out what to do about it.

'Emily . . .' Akin's voice is loaded with pity. I know what he's going to say. He's decided that our kiss earlier was a mistake and he's going to explain this to me so that he feels better – congratulate himself on *doing the right thing* – and he thinks I'll be upset by this rejection, and maybe I will in time, but what he fails to realise is that I've had the same wake-up call today for different reasons. Life has a sick way of knocking you down and standing your pieces back up where they ought to be. Akin needs a long-term family, I don't need to be a dead-end fling.

'No time now,' I say. 'Thanks for the update from the hospital. Kash just arrived.' I move to the door.

'Dixie's father? Where has he been all this time?'

'That's what I want to know.'

'And Jack Kent's wife – where is she? What's her name again?'

'Calpurnia. Cally. I'm wondering if she's left him? He's not quite what I thought he was.'

'I thought he was a moron and now I think he's pitiful.'

'That's something, I suppose.' I can't help laughing. 'Do you want to do some snooping?'

He shrugs his agreement. We creep down the corridor. I tell him to keep watch, while I get my jiggler keys and open the cupboard again.

'Are we stealing stationery?' Akin asks.

I push him through the door. He resists until I whisper, 'I'm not going to jump you, just get inside.' He capitulates. I point to the air vent. He still frowns and I whisper that Mariah and Kash are in the room next door. I climb onto my podium of paper. He holds my hips so I don't wobble.

Again, I can't see either of them, but I hear clearly enough. My phone is in my back pocket and I draw it out, fumble and almost drop it, but manage to tap the recording app and set it going. I place it on the shelf nearest the vent.

Kash is talking.

'. . . we should have asked ourselves right from the start – five grand? It's not enough. It's not just fishy, it's beyond fishy, it's— And that's another thing, they know better than to call you. Who in their right mind would call—You don't go direct to the top, do you, and make demands? Not if it was really them, they'd know better, they'd go through me.'

'One thing at a time. Did you actually see them?' Mariah's voice has that flat tone again, the one I don't recognise. I look down at Akin and he has a little frown between his eyebrows. I point to my ears like, *Can you hear*? He waggles a flat hand like, *So-so*. I shoo him away to get his own podium. I want his take on this conversation. He reaches behind a rack in the corner and slides out a plastic thing that turns out to be a folding step. Wish I'd noticed that earlier. His movements are slow and careful and quiet, a man used to handling delicate things, like patients' veins. Soon, he's a few inches taller than me again. He nods. Now we can both hear.

'—we need to tell them.' Kash.

'Are you having me on?' Mariah.

'We need help. It's out of our league.'

'You need help if you think we can go to the police.'

'It's our daughter, Mariah, it's Dixie. You haven't been out there. It's dark and cold. It's the woods. You can't see your hand in front of your face. She must be terrified.'

Now Akin's eyes are wide. He's looking hard at me.

I put a finger on my lips. But I knew it, I knew Kash had been out there.

'We know she's not out in the woods.'

'She'll still be frightened!'

'That's why I told you to fucking find her! You had the money. You had the boy's number.'

What money? Akin mouths at me.

I widen my eyes to silence him, but isn't it obvious? It means a ransom.

'The number went dead, disconnected. Must be a burner. He wasn't where he said they'd be, in the wood.'

'What about the teacher? Did he see you? They found him in a ditch. We can only hope he carks it on the operating table, otherwise he knows you were there, and we'll have to get him *offed* in a fucking hospital with all the law and the press looking.'

I know Akin is going to react. I put my hand over his mouth right as it opens.

I silently shush him.

My heart is pumping like a piston, but I'm used to it. Akin is used to constant pressure but not sheer fight-or-flight fear. I let adrenaline flood through me like a shot of alcohol and wait for the buzz to pass. I have to keep thinking straight. The effort leaves me shaking.

Kash sounds close to tears. 'Aren't you supposed to get – what's it called – proof of life? I didn't speak to her. Just took their word for it. Stupid. They said she'd be there, they said drop the money and drive. There's like a little shed—'

'Tell me you went back for the money. It's not still there with your prints all over it?'

'I used gloves, I'm not— It was right where I left it, but they didn't come. I drove down the lane to the shed. No one there. I was calling out to her. Phoning her number, and the other number. Nothing. I walked around the forest. She wasn't there, Mariah, I was thorough. Then I went back to the drop spot.

Retrieved the money and parked a little way off and waited, just to make sure. Nothing. She just *wasn't there*.'

'When did the law arrive?'

'A patrol car passed. About half four, I suppose, bit earlier. Must have found Sadler further up the lane, I don't know how they spotted him in the dark. I must have driven right past without noticing him—'

'You could have finished him off.'

Silence from Kash. Then: 'Do you hear yourself?'

'If he saw your car . . . You've got a personalised fucking number plate, *Keith*.'

'This is not my doing, *Mariah*. Kidnap and ransom . . . Not my wheelhouse. I'm a builder made good. That's all I wanted. You're the one who—You wanted more. You said we could handle it. I didn't sign up for this!'

'I can handle it. What I want to know is why they'd do this? We've done everything they've asked. Dixie is off limits.'

'The trouble with you, Mariah—'

'The trouble with me, Kash, is you!'

'You reckon? You think they respect you? They own you, Mariah.'

There's the sound of a slap.

In the gloom, Akin turns to me with headlight eyes. I shake my head to make him stay quiet.

'Very *mature*,' Kash says. 'Take it out on me if you want to but they do own you, they own us and now they own our daughter. If you won't tell the police, then I—' He stops abruptly and there's a sound of choking.

Akin strains to see through the vent. He gets his fingers hooked on the edge and pulls himself up for a few seconds, long enough to look down into the room. He drops onto his stool and the plastic creaks. The scrabbling in the coffee room stops.

'She's got him by the throat,' Akin whispers.

I put my hand to my neck. I can almost feel her nails.

I should be shocked. In denial. This is my friend. But somehow I'm not. I've always known Mariah is *extra*. She's not like regular people. That suits me. I've very little experience of regular people, I don't fit in with that crowd. Mariah does things differently, makes her own rules, lives by her own code. A woman of extremes and absolutes. We don't always see the world the same way, but where I thought we agreed, where we both knew the difference between black and white, was in regard to our daughters. They come first. They're the best of us. They're everything. But now I can see that she doesn't put Dixie first at all.

I get down off my paper podium and Akin is waiting. He doesn't say a word, but holds me, a heavy weight on my shoulders as I support him even as he supports me.

'I thought it was all Kash,' I whisper.

'What? What was Kash?'

All those rumours . . .

'Sounds like Mariah knew about this ransom demand,' says Akin.

Mariah knew about the ransom. She knew our girls were alive, had a location for them, even. A police helicopter could have focused on that area. Drones too. Sniffer dogs. My face heats up as I remember something from earlier: her woo-woo bullshit about Dixie being okay – *I can feel it in my bones* – did she know then?

She withheld it from the police, she kept it secret from me.

What does that say about our friendship?

What does it say about her?

What does it say about me, if I've never seen what she's really like?

My best frenemy.

Chapter Thirty-Six

6.25 p.m.

Dixie took the floor. She struck Olivia as different, changed, harder – that was it, harder than she thought Dixie capable of being. Her sleepy-lidded eye contact was gone. Her softness that usually absorbed any blows. Now she held herself taut. Even her raspy voice had sharpened to a metallic edge.

'The ransom money was for Olivia, to bail her out. She fell for some roadman at the bus stop outside school. And he has messed her up.'

'How?' Temi.

'Olivia is up to her tiny shuttlecock tits in debt.'

'Wait, wait, I don't understa—' said Kiran.

'County lines,' Olivia interrupted. If this story had to be told, she'd rather tell it herself, without the random insults about her body.

'Drugs?' asked Kiran.

'No, well, not at first. At first, it was just flirting with this lad while I waited for the bus. Hardly anyone from Saints takes the public bus, so it was just the two of us waiting there after school. He seemed cool. One night my bus pass ran out, the driver was being a troll and wanted to chuck me off, so he gave me a quid for a ticket. Wouldn't let me pay him back, he was all like, *What's a pound between friends?* Then he told me he had some headphones he didn't want. Said Amazon delivered two pairs by mistake and no one minds taking from the 'Zon. Turns out they were Beats. I said he should sell them on Vinted, they're worth a mint, but he said he couldn't be bothered with the hassle—'

'So obviously we thought he fancied her,' Dixie cut in. 'I mean, Beats headphones . . .'

'And he looked a bit like Keanu Reeves, so . . .'

'Who's that?' Temi asked.

'*The Matrix*?' Kiran said.

Temi shrugged.

'Anyway, next thing, he told me he did deliveries but he had more work than he could manage. He needed someone he could trust to deliver a parcel to an address not far from school – I could get off the bus two stops down, hand it to this bloke who'd be waiting and get back on the bus. I'd get paid fifty quid and it would take literally two minutes. Of course, I asked what was in the parcel cos it sounded dodgy and he said it was a bit, but only counterfeit stuff. He reckoned it was watches. And I thought, fake Rolexes never hurt anyone, and fifty quid . . . that's two nights' babysitting . . . I don't expect you to understand, you have credit cards with no limit.'

'That's not our fault,' said Kiran.

'To be fair, I'd hand someone a box for fifty quid,' said Alix.

'And that's why you're not in the top set . . .' said Kiran.

'Well, I needed the money and it didn't seem like the end of the world,' Olivia said. 'It turned out to be easy, so I delivered one the next night too.'

'For the one who looked like Keanu Reeves?' Alix.

'Yeah, he dropped fifty quid into my account each time I delivered a parcel and by the end of the month I'd saved nearly five hundred pounds.'

'Didn't you think that was a lot of watches?' asked Temi.

'He said it was all different things – SIM cards, collectible football cards, vapes . . . All counterfeit but not drugs. And my mum was having a mare about money around that time – when isn't she? – it wasn't long after she lost her savings in a scam, so I started dropping extra pennies into her account to pay for things we couldn't afford. I'd mark the transfers as "refund" so she didn't suspect. But she didn't even notice. She avoids anything to do with money cos it stresses her, she just gets to the end of the month like the emoji monkey.' Olivia put her hands over her eyes. 'Last month, I made it look like she'd had a rebate so we could pay for a boiler repair when it packed up because I didn't want to have cold showers for ages while she worked out how to afford it. It's amazing how much these things cost!'

From across the room, Jones groaned under his breath.

'What a pity party,' muttered Dixie.

Olivia ignored her. As did the others. 'And then it all sort of went wrong.'

'I'd say.' Dixie.

'Let her talk!' said Temi.

'One day a grand appeared in my account. A *thousand* pounds. He said I could keep ten per cent of it if I withdrew the rest in cash and took it to the Hope Estate.'

'The Hope Estate?' Alix said. 'You know they call it the Abandon Hope Estate? My dad filmed there once. Got hit by a flying nappy. It was not a clean one.'

'You shouldn't have gone there.' Jones pushed himself away from the doorjamb and folded his arms across his chest. 'Even coppers avoid Hope. I can't believe you walked in with your Saints blazer on. They're like piranha, they'll strip you to the bone.'

'He's all concern now,' said Dixie.

Olivia waved both of them away. 'Someone met me by the bus stop. But after I did it once, they put pressure on me to do it a few more times. By then I'd worked it out. I was their cuckoo.'

'Actually, they're the cuckoos,' said Kiran. 'My mum explained county lines – well, her parliamentary assistant did: drug dealers get people under their control and cuckoo their homes, occupy their home to use as a temporary base. In your case, they cuckooed your bank account to launder money.'

'Thanks, Sherlock, I didn't need a parliamentary researcher to explain that to me. So I told him that I wanted to stop delivering for them, but he said it doesn't work like that. He said I owed him because he'd gone out of his way to look after me. And he started asking questions about school. How much pocket money people have. Where they go to party. Whether they take drugs. Which drugs. I twigged that he wanted to sell into school, that it was a potential new market. Saints kids would buy quality drugs, coke rather than ket. But then he said money had gone missing from my account. I was supposed to be looking after it for them and it had gone. I hadn't spent it, though, I never took any more than I earned from the deliveries, but he said his boss didn't believe me, he wanted me to pay back everything that had ever gone into my account. It was thousands by then. Of course, I didn't have the money so he said I'd have to work it off. I never got anything in writing, a contract or anything, no receipt for the cash I'd handed over at the Hope Estate—'

She glanced up at Jones, expecting him to laugh at her, but he was rubbing his eyeballs with thumb and forefinger.

'—so that's why I took a parcel into Saints.'

'What the hell!' Temi.

'You would get *so* expelled,' said Kiran. 'Not just expelled. They would burn you at the stake on the stage during Friday morning assembly. They would sacrifice you on the altar during chapel.'

'You'd be arrested,' said Temi in a flat tone.

'Well, they didn't find out, did they? They never suspected me, which was kind of the point. I'm so far under the radar I might as well be a mole. And you're right, Alix, I did take an envelope to your house before the party. I didn't deal, I'm just deliveries. There must have been someone else at the party to sell the stuff . . . One of the gatecrashers? I can't believe your dad thinks it's safe to invite strangers into your house. But, anyway, even after I did that, I still never seemed to make any headway in paying them off . . .'

'So you came up with another plan?' Alix.

'Has it got something to do with today?' Temi.

'Yes.'

The three boys reacted like the opposite team had scored a goal.

'But this is not what I planned!' Olivia insisted. 'A ransom – no! It wasn't supposed to be like this, it was just a quick thing – a one-off, painless way to pay them back what I owed, and then I would close my bank account so they couldn't access it anymore, and I'd tell them to leave me alone or I'd go to the police and face the consequences.'

'What painless way?' Dixie asked, her voice rock bottom.

'Just a little . . . highway robbery.'

Silence.

Jones sucked air between his teeth.

'Where?' said Dixie.

'At the service station . . .'

'So you *were* in on it!' Alix was triumphant.

'Not all this!' She waved her arm around the office and at Jones. 'What choice did I have? I owe them hundreds, even before the money that disappeared this morning.'

'What money this morning?' Temi.

'There was a thousand pounds in my account but this morning it disappeared again.'

Kiran frowned. 'You can't withdraw money from someone else's account.'

'Well, he must have found a way. I guess he got my login details. Maybe looked over my shoulder while I used my phone? I wasn't that careful at the start . . .' Olivia said. 'Which means they have access to all my accounts, even my mum's.'

She didn't point out that there wasn't any money in her mum's account, so security had always been more of an in-principle issue.

Temi swore under his breath.

'I owe more than I can possibly earn, so I offered to give it to them in kind.'

'What kind of . . . kind?' Alix.

'They said I could give them valuables. So long as it was quality stuff.'

'You don't have valuables,' he sneered. 'You are strictly high street.'

'No need to be nasty,' Temi said.

'It's true, though. Where were you intending to source these valuables—Oh!'

'From us,' said Dixie.

Alix gave a hollow laugh.

'Like you'd suffer,' Olivia whispered.

'What?' Alix.

'Dixie and her Vivienne Westwood necklaces. Temi's watch, worth more than my entire debt. Alix and your Canada Goose coat. Kiran has limited edition Jordan's on.'

'My mum brought these back from America when she went to the White House!'

'Second-hand they'd sell for hundreds on Vinted,' Olivia said. And then more quietly, 'I checked.'

'And you thought they'd leave you alone after this?' asked Temi.

Olivia side-eyed Jones, wondering how much more to say in front of him. But what did it matter? He knew enough already.

'I compiled a dossier. Their identities and contacts.'

Jones made a low whistle but said nothing.

'What?' Olivia challenged him. 'I planned to pay them off, once and for all, and then threaten to drop the file at the police station unless they leave me alone.'

Jones's shrug suggested this was a very bad idea indeed.

Olivia copied the shrug and turned back to the others. 'Don't worry, Alix, there was nothing about you and your dad's weird parties. It was just the stuff in the Hope Estate.'

'So how was this *highway robbery* going to happen?' asked Temi.

'They were going to find us at the service station where we always park, in the lorry spaces at the back. Mr Sadler always stays with the bus. We always take a shortcut to the side entrance by Pizza Express. We are creatures of habit. So they were going to grab us at the secluded bit behind the recycling bins, get our stuff and go. It would be over in seconds. We'd be shocked, but no lasting damage. Your parents could claim on their insurance, victimless crime. But that much stuff would have cleared my debt.'

'Surely there'd be CCTV?' Alix asked.

'Not round the side by the bins. I told them to go check, which they must have done earlier this morning. You were right, Alix, they did a recce. They weren't supposed to go inside the building because of the cameras, but they must have gone in to buy snacks. The flaw in my plan is that they turned out to be a right pair of Nobby's Nuts.'

Temi winced at Olivia's half-hearted attempt at levity.

Alix marched across the office and kicked a bin.

Temi went to stop him and they ended up grappling, two shadows in the dark.

Kiran stared straight ahead, the half-light throwing his bone structure into relief so he looked tragic. Every so often, he shuddered. It was cold in the Portakabin, but Olivia knew his shivers came from withdrawal. Colder even than Kiran was Dixie. Her face was turned into the shadows.

'I tried to call it off, Dixie,' Olivia whispered. Everyone froze. 'Earlier today, I got cold feet. Changed my mind. Tried to get my phone from Mr Sadler to call and cancel the plan, but he was in a mood and the phones had gone on the earlier bus. Then I thought I could stop us going to the services, so I kicked Kiran's swim bag out of the bus . . . I thought we'd have to go back for his EpiPen, didn't realise it would be in his other bag, but luckily for me he remembered his jammers anyway and got in a flap.'

He protested. 'They're worth three hundred pounds. We're not all as excessive as you seem to think, Olivia!'

'I know, Kiran, I was relying on you to want to go back for your stuff. And you did, we turned back. Didn't stop at the services. I thought then it was over. But they followed us. And then Dixie . . .'

'I *what*?' Dixie hissed. 'I tried to help you. I only wanted that ransom money to pay them off for you!'

Olivia felt hot tears behind her eyes.

'Wouldn't have made any difference.' Jones startled them into silence. 'It won't be over until you're no further use to them, and that's when you'd really be in trouble. That's when they'd decide to shut you up once and for all, stop you taking *dossiers* to the police station. You know, it's always the daft kids or the smart kids who get dragged into county lines – daft ones because they're vulnerable and smart ones because they think they know better.'

As he was speaking, Jones inched away from the door, towards Olivia. She could see Alix eyeing up the escape route, moving the weight between his feet, like he might need them. Temi was rapt by Jones, caught in the man's spell. And Kiran, of course, was doing exactly what he was told. But Alix started to sidle towards the door.

Jones went on, 'Teenagers always think they know it all, but you lot, Christ, you're another level. I reckon that school has told you you're the crust on the custard so many times that you've started to believe it. But you have to realise you can't beat the gang. I've been trying to get out myself, but they don't let you walk away.'

Alix bolted for the door. Jones spun into his path and caught the boy with one hand clamped around his throat. Alix was tall and fit, but there was no weight to him, not enough heft to barrel past Jones. The man barely moved his arm and Alix sprawled back onto the floor.

Jones tugged down the sleeves of his waxed jacket. 'Don't take advantage of my kindly nature. I try to help you and it's like each one of you in turn is determined to make my job harder. Olivia, frankly, I expected more from you.'

She scoffed, 'Sorry, *Dad*!'

This, it seemed, was a sass too far.

Jones grabbed her by the lapel of her coat and dragged her into night air that was as white cold as the moonlight.

Chapter Thirty-Seven

6.30 p.m.

I gulp down night air like it's cold water. It clears my head. I need to tell DS Slocombe about the ransom. If Mariah isn't going to do the right thing, and if Kash is going to be a doormat, then I'll have to. Akin has gone to call his private security guy with the new information; suits me, I'd rather speak to the detective alone, given there are things I don't intend to share with Akin, especially as we're over. Over over.

I head to the Great Hall. It's a mess: floor littered with cardboard cups and biscuit wrappers, a map spreadeagled, even a couple of overturned chairs. It's like a tornado has passed through, which I suppose it has, metaphorically speaking.

I find the DS in the lobby. She's on the phone but holds up one finger. I wait. She glances at me as she listens. She makes notes in a palm-sized pad. Behind her, the golden names of scholarship pupils scroll across the walls. O. Smith is there on the newest wooden panel. A few boards to the left take me back in time to J. Kent, the edges of his gilt letters rubbed off. Back through the decades, I reach those who must be dead now. A knot of grief tightens my chest. They were the brightest stars once, now faded. It doesn't take long.

'Ms Smith?' Slocombe is off the phone.

I'm about to launch into the ransom when she holds up a picture of Olivia on her device. I lean in to see. It's a still from a CCTV camera. Grainy, with that up-high perspective that makes everyone look like blocky characters on a video game. Olivia at the bus stop across the road.

'Here's another one.' Slocombe swipes her screen.

Olivia, same uniform, same place. The light is different, the weather. Another day.

'And again.' Slocombe swipes.

'What is this?'

'We ran facial recognition software to check the kids' movements around school—'

'Why are you checking up on them?'

'To see if they might be in contact with anyone of interest. Do you know this young man Olivia is talking to?'

She shows me the CCTV picture again. It's Olivia and, yes, there is a lad too. In a hoodie. Waiting for the bus. I raise my hands and let them drop.

'From the way they're angled together, we think they're talking,' she says.

'Who is he?' I ask. Slocombe must know him, know of him, or she wouldn't be asking.

'A scrote.'

'In a gang?' I ask.

'Course.'

'There's a lot of scrotes around here, the school isn't in the best part of town, I guess they didn't have urban issues when they built Saints in eighteen-something . . .'

'Does Olivia know this boy?'

'Never mentioned him. Looks to me like they're just waiting at the bus stop.'

Slocombe holds up another picture. Olivia again. Different bus stop. I recognise it, it's about a mile from the school, on the same road. She's partially hidden by an advertising billboard.

'She jumps off the bus here but gets back on the next one,' Slocombe says. 'Why do you think she's doing that?'

'To meet a friend?'

'Why? She only gets off for a couple of minutes. She's done it quite a few times. Always stands behind this billboard. It happens to block the view of the camera. Then she jumps straight back on the next bus.'

'Who knows the mind of a teenager?' I try for an ironic tone that fails me. My heart is skittering. 'What's your line of enquiry?'

'I'm curious about this contact—'

'It's not a contact, it's two people waiting at a bus stop. That lad isn't even at the second bus stop, is he? So they're not travelling together . . .'

'Is it possible that Olivia has got caught up in something she shouldn't?'

'Like what?'

'We both know drug dealers target naive young people . . .'

Injustice fizzes through me. 'I think you don't have any leads and you're getting desperate. Do you have any idea where our kids are? Any clue if they're even alive?' There's a catch in my voice but it only makes her narrow her eyes. 'Olivia isn't naive, she's a scholarship student, bright as a button, hates drugs, volunteers in a clinic . . . When you've found my daughter and her schoolmates, I'll ask her about this boy, but until then, DS Slocombe, maybe we can focus on finding the kids, not blaming them?'

Slocombe says nothing, watches my face. She's letting me rant until I give something away. And I can hear myself falling into the trap, like most people do, of going on the offensive. Offensive is a high-risk strategy. Better to tread water . . . Wait it out.

I take a breath. 'If I knew anything that might tell us where they are, *anything*, I'd share it. I'd do anything for her.'

'I'd do anything for my kids too.' She steps closer. A bitter whiff of coffee on her breath. 'The difference is, I'd do it above board, whereas you . . . I wonder who you have on speed dial, who's your phone-a-friend?'

'I'm a full-time worker and a single mum, I don't have time for anyone else. All these parents have friends in high places . . . Ayesha with her secret service, Jack Kent with his fan club, Akin and his private security. But I'm not in their league. We just scrape by.'

'Maybe you've got friends in low places?'

'I don't know what you're talking about.'

'Why did you leave the police?'

'You've been fixated on my history since you got here. It's ancient—'

'It's not, though, is it?' Slocombe steps back and niggles the space between her front teeth with a thumbnail. 'What about the lost years . . . You're a young plod on the beat and then you're a personal trainer with a teenage daughter. Where did you go in between? Why is there no record for a PC Emily Smith?'

My teeth screech when I clench them.

'I know who you are, *Emily Smith*. So what are we dealing with here?' Slocombe leans in too close. 'Like mother, like daughter, is that it?'

Chapter Thirty-Eight

6.35 p.m.

Outside the Portakabin, Olivia's hair lashed her face. She staggered to a halt on her tiptoes when Jones released her. He interlaced his fingers on the back of his head and turned a full circle, sending a volcanic breath into the sky, a groaning noise like he regretted something he hadn't even done yet.

'Kids, these days. Always want a shortcut; instant fame, instant riches, like they're entitled to be special. When did everyone need to be special? God, I sound old . . .' He shook his head. 'I came for you as soon as I heard about this minibus plan. These corner boys do not understand how this country works – you stay in your lane. Lowlifes can do what they like to other lowlifes, drug deals on the Abandon Hope Estate . . . But we can't rob the likes of Saints kids, you lot have someone who cares. That's what makes you special. The police care, the papers care, even the Twitter cares.' He swiped his phone and showed Olivia that #SaveSaintsKids was trending. 'And now one of ours is dead and the other one is in a state. You lot've seen faces and vehicles. And the last thing I want to do is hurt five kids, even if a couple of them are pricks . . .'

'Only Alix is a prick,' said Olivia. 'Couldn't you put Crowbar in the BMW and take it to wherever you dumped the other one? It would look like they attacked each other.'

'This isn't a Sunday night TV show, Olivia, it has to make sense. And you don't seem to realise that people like me . . . I'm known to the police. Worse, I'm known to the gangs. I don't get a slap on the wrist when things go wrong. I came here to clear up a mess before it dirties the shoes of my boss and if I don't deliver, I will be dead.'

'Run away, then, just go,' Olivia insisted. 'You said before you wanted to leave. You must have money, savings, you're old—'

He bobbed his head to one side.

'—older than me. Go now. Change your name. Go wherever criminals disappear to, the Costa del Crime. What have you got to stay for? A wife, kids?'

He shrugged in the negative.

'You could have someone in your life if you weren't such a— Go to Spain. Go to Brazil, open a bar.'

'Alright, alright. Christ, you have so many ideas, all at once. I couldn't cope with this over breakfast. How does your mother manage?'

He massaged his forehead.

In a low voice, he went on. 'I need to know what I'm dealing with here. Who did that idiot, Crowbar, speak to on the phone?'

Olivia explained about Dixie's dad. 'They reckon he does dodgy deals. He's a property developer. A suspiciously successful one.'

'What's his name?'

'Keith Ashworth. They call him Kash.'

Jones pulled his mouth upside down.

'His company is called Haven, after his wife, Mariah Haven. Dixie's mum.'

'The Haven Group?'

'Kash is her dad. He builds massive stuff, whole blocks of flats, that new marina . . . He can't be dodgy, can he, if they're so well-known? And Dixie's mum, Mariah, is my mum's best friend.' Olivia thought about it for a moment. 'My mum's only friend.'

Jones walked around in a circle, his hands clutching his head like he had a migraine, the gun pointing up into the sky.

'What?' Olivia demanded.

'That absolute *goldfish* demanded money from—Fuck me!' He indicated the barn where Crowbar lay bleeding. 'I've cleaned up some messes in my time, but that phone call puts this out of my league.'

Chapter Thirty-Nine

6.40 p.m.

'PC Emma Smiles.' DS Chantale Slocombe brandishes the name like a trump card. 'Took me a while – it was on the tip of my tongue – but I only got there with a little help from DC Singh, who tells me there was never a PC Emily Smith in Sussex Police. But then another name came to me' – she taps her forehead – 'PC Emma Smiles. Distinctive, memorable. Emma to Emily. Smiles to Smith. Then I placed you. We didn't meet at Hendon, it was that training course. I remember a joke our trainer made during roll-call; *PC Emma Smiles – does she, though?* He was right, you were very serious back then.'

She has no idea.

I come over all *Emma Smiles* and simper. 'Seems like a long time ago.'

She doesn't return any smiles.

'We looked up PC Emma Smiles.' She pinches her fingers together in front of my face. 'No dabs. Your fingerprints have been wiped from the database. That gave me pause . . .' She waits and when I don't offer an explanation she provides her own. 'Only reason the fingerprints of a police officer might be wiped from the system is if they've been removed to protect a legend.'

It's true that a legend, a secret identity, needs to be watertight.

'You got me.' I shrug. 'Emily Smiles, legend in her own lifetime.'

To her credit, she doesn't look smug.

'So you were undercover? Inside an OCG, I presume?'

Organised Crime Gang.

She's not far wrong.

I first met PC Chantale Slocombe, as she was back then, on the Undercover Foundation course. It's designed to find police officers suited to covert work. They tend to recruit young ones because criminals can smell a copper a mile off, so better to have UCOs who don't stink of the nick. I was only twenty-two, she must have been about the same.

I recognised her as soon as I saw her this afternoon. She hasn't changed much in twenty years. Just looks more tired.

She sniffs loudly. 'Don't understand why you got selected and I didn't.' She gently kisses her teeth to show she's being ironic. 'At the time, I thought perhaps they didn't have as much covert work for Black girls. Then I came to realise they saw that I was better suited elsewhere.'

'Sounds like it,' I say. 'You're a DS now. Very impressive.'

She ignores the flattery. 'Once I remembered you, I really *remembered* you, you know? I knew you'd get through that course. You were . . .' She waves her hand.

'Unremarkable? A nonentity? An outsider?' It's not very complimentary, is it, when someone tells you you're suited to living a lie?'

'You were a blank slate. And, like I say, serious. You've changed a lot, your hair . . .'

I cut it off. Along with the crook of my nose and the Zeppelin tits that made my back ache. I don't go into that. Instead, I ask if she wants to know why she didn't pass the UCF course.

She does.

'Do you remember the role play?' I ask.

It was twenty years ago but she nods like, *Hell yeah*. I'm the same, I recall those formative years better than I remember last week. She says, 'We had to pose as a buyer and secure drugs from a cop posing as a dealer. I bought them without any problem. Thought I'd cracked it.'

That's not quite how it was. First of all, Slocombe looked too good to pass as a junkie. We'd been told to scruff up. She didn't remove her braids, which looked expensive, obvious even to me, an ignorant white girl. It wasn't fair that she had to lose a costly hairdo when all I had to do was not wash for a week in order to look like a junkie, but I guess the course leaders were blokes who didn't know about women's hair, especially the demands of Black women's hair. But braids aside, it was the role play that was the real problem. She sidled up to the officer playing the dealer and asked if she could buy a wrap. Used all the lingo. Couldn't fault her acting, she looked properly nervous. Maybe she was. Then he asked who the drugs were for. She went on the offensive, came over aggressive like a desperate junkie, forcing the deal through to get the evidence she needed . . .

And that was the problem.

I tell her: 'He said you could have a wrap for free if you blew him—'

She clicks her fingers and points one at me like a tiny gun. 'That's right, he did. That was a test. But I got out of it.'

'You shouldn't have done that—'

'They didn't expect me to actually blow him!'

'You shouldn't have given him the chance to ask for sex. You made yourself vulnerable. Any real addict would save themselves the tenner. As soon as you refused, he knew you weren't desperate . . . he knew you weren't really a junkie . . . he knew you were a cop. If that had been the real world, he'd have kicked the shit out of you.'

Slocombe purses her lips and grunts, *huh*.

That had been the last time I saw PC Slocombe. Until this afternoon. So maybe she has changed, not much gets past her now.

The DS shuffles on her stool. 'So what did you say? When he asked you?'

'I said the wrap was for a friend, who was sick. He tried the same offer, free wrap for a blow job, but I gave him a dirty look and he took the money. Would you give a blow job to save your friend a tenner? No. So it was convincing.'

'You passed.'

'And then I passed the UCA and the advanced course.'

'Nice.'

'But you're the DS,' I say.

'I am . . .' It's like she comes back to the present. 'I won't break your cover, but if you think the OCG has taken your kid to get to you, I need to know. These lot' – she jabs her thumb to indicate everyone in the school – 'can go on believing you're a PT.'

'I am a PT. That's not a legend, it's my job. I left the force years ago. I'm *out*.'

'Why did you leave?'

'Covert work and single parenting? I don't think so . . .'

She digs out her notepad and flips the pages. I know the trick. A moment to think. She flips it shut again.

'But you did infiltrate an OCG?'

'For two years. If you look up a Gemma Smith, birthdate 1980, you'll find an extensive criminal record.'

'So birth name is Emma Smiles, Gemma Smith was your UCO identity, and Emily Smith is a third name.'

'Like you say, you chose names close to your own. Makes you feel like you've hung on to a bit of yourself. Although . . .' I stop because I don't know how this sentence ends.

'Although . . .?'

'How can you not lose yourself?'

Slocombe shakes her head.

There's a bark of a voice outside. Slocombe is distracted but pulls her attention back to me.

'If you're no longer a UCO, why didn't you tell me about your links to a gang? I've had to waste time establishing if you were still undercover, if your covert work could be related to this kidnapping, if someone had come after you via your daughter. I thought perhaps you were being coerced and that's why you hadn't said anything.'

'I'm being coerced by you.'

'Surely you want—'

'Don't tell me that I want to save my daughter. Everything I do is for her.'

'Emily—Emma—'

'Emily. It's been a lifetime since I was Emma.'

'Could the disappearance of the kids have anything to do with your OCG work?'

I'm not telling her about Kershaw. I can't risk it . . . not yet.

'I left years ago.'

'That's not an answer.'

'They've not cared enough to find me in the past, so why now?'

She flips that notebook again. Leaves it open.

'Why did you get out of UCO work when you were good at it?'

'Told you.' I grimace. 'I got pregnant.'

'How?'

'How do you think?'

Shadow of a smile.

'I mean, if you got pregnant while undercover, was it . . .?'

'What?'

Slocombe's voice drops. 'Were you raped?'

'No.'

'Oh.'

'Is that worse, that I wasn't raped?'

'God, no, I didn't mean—'

'I had a relationship. I was under for a long time. It just happened. I can pick locks, break into cars, cook up heroin, put a street price on anything from weed to handguns, but turns out I can't take my pill on time. As soon as I realised, I got out. Ran. Changed my name. Changed my face . . .'

'And was the father . . .?'

'A criminal?' I ask.

She nods.

'I was undercover in an OCG. I didn't meet many nice chaps with good prospects.'

'Was he dangerous?'

'Not to me.'

'Did he know about the baby?'

'No. Or he might not have let me go. Look, male UCOs have relationships all the time. There are babies born into the crime world and left in there . . . I wasn't having that for my baby. So I got away and gave us the most generic names I could think of.

Emily Grace for me, Olivia Ruby for my daughter – literally the four most common names in the year she was born. I'd had the good sense to use a common surname when I went undercover, so I stuck with Smith. And here we are. We've managed. Thrived. These silver-spoons at Saints don't think so, they think I'm a failure, but I look at where I came from, what I've been through, what I got away from, and I'm quite proud. Olivia's going to have a great life. She'll do medicine. She'll save lives, like you do, like I did before I made the best mistake of my life.'

Slocombe folds her arms over her chest. She reminds me of my headmistress, who could wither you with her disappointment.

'But that's not the end of it, is it?' she says. 'I got a call from the NCA ...'

'National Crime Agency?'

'... asking about one of the parents here.'

'That will be Keith Ashworth,' I say. 'Known as Kash. Dixie's dad.'

Now she looks smug. 'And how do you know he's on the NCA's radar?'

'Because I'm their snout.'

Her face remains as still as the wall behind her.

'Informant,' I clarify. 'Not a UCO. I'm civilian now. Unpaid.'

'I thought it was a bit much to place a kid in a school so that her mum could go undercover.'

'That's not what happened. Olivia got here on her own merit, I'm not having you take that away from her. And what kind of parent would use their child to infiltrate a target? It was the other way around ... Olivia and Dixie became friends, then Mariah and I became friends, then I realised she was *Mariah Haven*, a way in to the Haven Group, the one that everyone says must be a front because how else do they finance these luxury developments? So I realised I could use Mariah to get to Kash, to get inside their home.'

'Listen to yourself – an informant working in your daughter's school. You asked what parent would do that – you're doing it! You can't leave it alone.'

That hits me like a slap. Because it's true. When I was under, I always felt I could get closer, delve deeper, linger a little longer. Find out more. I thought it was dedication. Maybe I was as addicted as the losers buying the drugs?

'Why put yourself in danger?' Slocombe presses.

'It's the *same gang*, Chantale. Kash is money laundering for the gang I was embedded with years ago. They were a London outfit then. Now they're everywhere. They're expanding faster than bloody Aldi.'

Slocombe smiles and purses her lips at the same time. It falters as I tell her about the National Crime Agency's case, how they suspect Keith Ashworth is a 'clean skin', a legitimate businessman with no convictions who can siphon illegal earnings through his company. The NCA needs me to gather evidence that proves a link between him and the OCG. They can then apply for an Unexplained Wealth Order against him. It's a fairly new law that forces private companies to reveal their accounts to the police. And that, in turn, allows the NCA to seize assets that belong to the gang and gather further evidence for a criminal case against the OCG. I'm only one link in the long chain of a complex investigation. The NCA needs me to get close to Mariah, to get close to Kash, to link Haven Group to the OCG. Simple.

'And I want to bring them down, DS Slocombe. I've lived for seventeen years with one eye over my shoulder, wondering if the

OCG might catch up with me. I'd like that to stop. I'm not being paid, I'm not a UCO, I'm doing this for me and Olivia. All I want is for us to be free.'

Slocombe hums in agreement. But she knows I'm holding something back.

Maybe it's not just Kash? I heard the way Mariah spoke to him. *You could have finished him off.*

Meaning Mr Sadler. She was inciting her husband to kill one of the teachers.

And she had Kash, literally, by the throat.

Mariah Haven. The Haven Group. Maybe it's not named for her . . .

Maybe it *is* her?

Chapter Forty

'Mariah fucking Haven.' Jones was *shook*. 'The woman's a legend.'

'She's just Dixie's mum.' Olivia shrugged it off. 'She drives us to school because she doesn't work. She gets her nails done a different colour every Friday. Tootles around in her Tesla.'

'"Tootles around"?' Jones had a good laugh at that. 'Do you think perhaps you've underestimated her? You know, they call her the Gold Digger . . .'

'Rude.'

'They call her the Gold Digger because she moves money like a JCB. By the bulk load. She is the kingpin – or queenpin, is that a word? – of a multi-million-pound crime syndicate. Without Mariah Haven, the Haven Group, there would be no drug trade in this city.'

Olivia frowned into the distant darkness as though the hilly horizon might tilt and tip her world back up the right way again. 'But we're friends with them. Me and Dixie. Mum and Mariah . . .'

'How close?'

'Close close. We virtually live at their house because ours is shit. We stay at theirs when Kash is away, which is half the time because he has developments all over the country, and they have a house in Spain, a ski place, a villa in Florida . . .'

'Then I'd say there are two possibilities. Your mother . . .?' He hesitated for her name.

Olivia resisted for a beat, but couldn't see any reason not to tell him. 'Emily.'

'Emily? One possibility is that she knows what Mariah Haven does and your mum is in deep trouble. Or, two, she has no idea what Mariah Haven does and your mum is in deep trouble.'

Olivia rolled her eyes. He sounded like a teacher trying to be clever.

'So?'

'If your mum is in cahoots with Mariah Haven, then she's in league with some dangerous people. If your mum tries to *get in the way* of Mariah Haven, then she's pissing off some dangerous people. Either way . . .' He shrugged.

Either way, Olivia needed to contact her mother, now. And Dixie needed to warn hers, too.

She asked to go back inside the Portakabin.

He used the key to let her inside, hanging in the doorway behind her. The others had found a blocky torch and it stood in between them, pointing at the ceiling. The pool of mottled light looked like a small moon. They huddled together for warmth under a strip of carpet they must have ripped off the floor. Olivia sat herself down a little way apart from them, away from Dixie, which made it easier to say out loud what she'd just learnt about her mother.

'Queenpin?' Dixie said eventually.

'If that's a word,' said Olivia.

'Head honcho,' said Alix. 'Big cheese. Top banana. The Godmother!'

'Like *Ozark*?' said Kiran.

Olivia hadn't watched that show so instead she said: 'We wondered what your mum did all day. Turns out, this.'

'Is she going to prison?' Dixie asked.

'Not necessarily,' said Kiran. 'She will have overseas accounts and shell companies and a Byzantine paper trail that means the money from illegal activities can't be traced to their legitimate business.'

'But because of us, the police are going to look more closely at their accounts,' said Dixie. 'It'll be my fault?'

'Technically, Olivia's fault,' said Kiran. 'She started it with the highway robbery thing.'

'You have to let us go now,' Dixie said to Jones as she staggered to her feet. 'I need to warn her. Let me use your phone.'

'Sorry, sweetheart, can't have a call linking my phone to hers.' Jones moved to leave the Portakabin, get out of the heat.

'Let us use the other phone.' Dixie kept on. 'Or drive us to a payphone.'

Jones pulled a face. Like that was going to happen.

'What's wrong with you?' Dixie shouted. 'You're a psycho.'

He turned in the doorway. 'Let's hope you don't have to meet any real psychos today, like the boss, for example.' He slammed the door behind him.

'Right!' Temi was on his feet in a flash, dragging the chair behind him across the office. 'Hold it steady.'

Alix held the back of the seat while Temi climbed up.

'What are you doing?' Olivia asked.

'Didn't know if we could trust you,' Alix said. 'So we kept our plan to ourselves.'

'Don't blame you,' Olivia said, 'after what I did.' No one reassured her.

Temi pushed up a ceiling tile and swung like a gymnast into the pitch-dark crawl space.

'There *is* a hatch,' said Kiran. 'Temi reckons he can smash it open.'

'Isn't that going to make a noise?' Olivia asked.

'What else do you suggest?' Alix muttered. 'The Stockholm syndrome approach isn't proving very effective – you're still locked in here with us, aren't you?'

'If Temi's going to make a racket, you need a distraction,' Olivia said. 'I'll keep Jones busy, while you get out and go for help.'

'We're not leaving anyone behind,' said Alix.

'Don't play the hero again,' Olivia muttered. 'Let me distract him while you get away.' After what she'd done – attempting to rob her own friends – she deserved to take one for the team. Deserved to be left.

She raised her hand to bang on the door.

'Wait!' said Kiran. He replaced the ceiling tile, shutting Temi into the crawl space. 'Huddle under the carpet, everyone. He might not notice that someone is missing.'

While the others got under the carpet, Olivia pounded the door until her fist stung.

It opened a few inches and nearly hit her in the face.

'What now?' Jones asked.

Olivia flashed her eyes over her shoulder. 'They're angry, I think they might hurt me.'

Jones made a small hand gesture that meant, *come on.*

She followed him across the concrete, resisting the urge to glance back and see if Temi was on the roof. Jones led her to the Range Rover and they got in the front seats.

'Heated seat?' asked Jones.

'Please. Is Crowbar alright? Should we go and check on him?'

Jones dismissed the idea with a curl of the lip. They sat in silence while heated needles prickled through her. She'd hoped to come up with something to say on the way to the car, but her thoughts were bouncing too high to catch. This was why she overprepped for exams. She wasn't one of those who could wing it—

'What does your mum do for a living?' He filled the silence.

'Personal trainer.'

'You on a scholarship or something?'

'Bursary.'

'Second-class citizen?'

Everyone assumed her school was snobby. But Saints were more judgemental about grades than money.

'It's not their fault I'm a pauper,' she said.

'Seems like you're the boss of this group, anyway.'

'That's a low bar.'

He allowed himself a slow smile.

'So what have your mum and Mariah fucking Haven got in common?'

'Prosecco?'

He laughed.

'They're outsiders, I suppose. We're a charity case and Dixie's family have got money but they're . . .' She looked away.

'Chavvy?' he supplied.

'I was going to say *arriviste*.'

He flourished his hands.

'*Parvenu*,' she said.

'Hark at you, with all your learning,' he said.

'You see, you're the snobby one. Why shouldn't I know all the words?'

He humphed. 'Do you really think your mum doesn't know what Mariah Haven does?'

'She knows Kash is up to something. People tell her the gossip when they're working out; endorphins make you chatty.'

'She must be a smart woman, your mum—'

Patronising.

'—because she raised you and you're smart. Unless you were adopted, were you adopted?'

'No.'

'Well, then.'

'Why are you asking? Do you know something?'

'Have you ever asked yourself why your mum wants to be in someone else's house so much?'

'Because Mariah's got a gorgeous and functioning kitchen and we've got a glorified campsite.'

'I think your mum is gathering evidence.'

A bat glitched the headlight beam.

'What?' Olivia turned to face him. 'What evidence, what for?'

'She's undercover.'

'She is not!'

He shifted round to face her.

'She got you into that school so she could get close to Mariah Haven.'

'No, I got in by passing a test, actually. Dixie was right, you are a psycho!' Olivia wrestled with the door handle and flung it open. She spun out of the seat onto broken concrete. 'What kind of mother would put their child in danger for the sake of an investigation? She's not police, I'd know if she was—'

'You didn't know about Mariah Haven either. Some police officers live undercover for years.'

'She's a personal trainer, bad with money, good at being a mum, and that's all there is to her.'

Olivia put her hand on the door to slam it in his face, but something made her wait for his reply.

'Mariah fucking Haven.' Jones held her eye contact. 'We underestimated her, didn't we?'

A beat. Olivia felt hot and it wasn't the heated car seat.

'Do you think you might be underestimating your mum too?'

Chapter Forty-One

6.50 p.m.

When you're undercover, no one – not your family or friends or even other cops – can ever know. Secrecy is so much a part of the culture, the institution, the training, that it doesn't feel dishonest. As impossible as it might seem, you learn how to live with deceit until it becomes as inconspicuous as blinking, instinctive as sweating, a seamless flow of lies like circular breathing on a didgeridoo. You didgeridoo what you have to do because you might fucking die if you didgeridon't.

And now DS Slocombe knows I'm a snitch. Which interrupts my flow.

I'm not telling her about the ransom, not yet. I need to be the first to speak to Mariah. I need to contain this situation. She is the only one with any information on the whereabouts of our kids. I need her. But I've been spying on her in her own home. What do they say? Keep your friends close and your enemies closer? I've certainly been doing that – two birds with one stone – and I don't think she'll like it much.

I find my frenemy in the Great Hall.

'Where is everyone?' I say. 'Looks like the aftermath of a toddler's party in here.'

She doesn't move. Her head is thrown back and she watches me along the length of her nose like she's balancing something precarious on the end of it. The artificial light picks out her bone structure and reminds me of how bloody beautiful she'd be if she didn't fuck up her face. She knows. About me. I can tell. God knows how she knows, but she does. Her glossy lips are dripping venom.

I keep breathing. Loosen my jaw. 'What's the matter?' My voice falls out of my mouth.

'Oh, babes,' Mariah sighs. 'How could you?'

A folding chair stands between us. She bends at the waist and puts the fingernail of one index finger under the seat and whips it high into the air. It slams shut and slaps the parquet in front of my feet. The sound of a double-barrelled shotgun. She's on me in that moment, nose to nose so I can smell the perfume from her cleavage. It's a masculine scent, pissy and territorial.

'Kash is unhappy,' she says, 'because I brought someone into our home who wasn't family. He's always said it's only family we can trust. But I insisted. I let you in. But you came to spy.' She spits the last word so hard it lifts the hair off my face.

I barely have time to part my lips—

'Don't even speak.' She steps back, lifts her phone and taps the screen. There's a photo. A still. A badly framed shot of someone approaching a car. The image is taken from inside, a wing mirror is in the shot and the background bulges like it's been taken with a fish-eye lens. There's a long brick wall . . .

'Who's this?' she asks.

I recognise the location. It's right outside Mariah's house. Her wide driveway.

'That's me.' I'm in sportswear, as usual, and I'm wearing the Saints beanie. 'I'm walking past your car on your driveway. Probably going home, why—?'

She taps the screen. It's not a still, it's a video. On screen, I don't walk past, I walk right up to the car, coming so close that my body from hip to tit is all that's in frame. Then I bend down, my face a pale flash, and straighten up before walking off. The video stops.

'Right?' I say.

'Footage from the Tesla. Sentry mode. Do you know what that is? Security feature. The Tesla has got cameras that monitor its surroundings, in case some bastard reverses into it or keys the door. If the car is alerted, for example, by someone touching the vehicle, then the cameras record the feed onto a hard drive. Kash only just thought about checking it. He had a lot of time to think while he was out looking for Dixie and your daughter.'

He'd waited out there for an hour to hand over the ransom. He wasn't doing nothing all that time.

'He decided to check our security cameras at home, see if anyone had been snooping about in recent days, maybe watching Dixie, planning to take her. But there was nothing suspicious at the house. And then, just now, he remembers sentry mode. Goes outside to get the feed off my car. But this is all he found, one saved clip from months ago – look at the date.'

I squint at her phone but I'm not seeing any detail. Blood is strobing through my head.

'November something,' she says. 'Long before you spent Christmas around our dining table, you and Olivia.'

I straighten up. She has a tendency to get mawkish.

'I'm always at yours, so what's the fuss about me walking past your car on your driveway?'

'That's what Kash thought. He tried to convince himself that you weren't doing anything untoward. Cos why would you?

But then he went out to check the sentry mode on *his* Tesla and he found another saved video. Guess what? Same thing . . . You, fiddling with his car. And so he felt about under the wheel arch, and he found this . . .' She twists my wrist with the talons of one hand so that my palm faces up. She squashes a heavy black button onto my grip. It's greasy with oil and road muck.

I don't have time to act out a response.

'Then he went to my car and checked the same wheel arch.'

She grabs my chin, the movement as fast as a snake-strike so I can only clamp my fingers around her forearm. I'm not quick enough to prevent her from squeezing my mouth open and pushing inside a second gritty, bitter button that lands on my tongue. She releases me and I instinctively spit it out into my palm with the first tracker. She snatches them both out of my hand while I use the other sleeve to rub grime from my mouth.

Two trackers that I placed on their vehicles. One of them spent the best part of two months tracing Kash's every move, from home to office to remote meeting points, which I fed back to the National Crime Agency, who have been cross referencing ANPR or CCTV to establish if he was meeting with vehicles belonging to the gang. Spoiler alert, he has. Mariah hasn't. I guess you don't have a dog and bark yourself.

Mariah inspects her right hand. My face broke one of her nails. She rips it off and flicks it away. It lands under a radiator like an iridescent beetle.

I pick up the fallen chair, open it out, and fold myself onto it. It makes me feel small and prim, but I stay there. After a moment, she drags a chair closer and sits with a crunch of wood. Her Lycra-ed legs grate as they cross.

'Why is Kash so sure the kidnappers want Dixie?' I ask.

She narrows her eyes. 'Don't kid yourself that every parent here isn't thinking about their own child first and foremost.'

'Kash thought someone might have been watching you, following Dixie, trying to get to her. Why would he think that? Unless . . .'

Mariah tilts her head like she's indulging me.

I open my mouth to deliver some line that will lure her into confessing about the ransom demand, but I close it again. I'm so tired. Tired of hiding. I want to talk without chewing every word that leaves my mouth to make it easier for someone else to swallow. 'I know about the ransom. I heard you talking to Kash. You lied to me.'

'You think that's the headline? You. Have been spying. On me. In my home. For months!'

I shift my weight so my knees are planted wider. 'And you think *that's* the headline? Our girls are missing, Mariah. You knew where they were hours ago and didn't tell me, didn't tell the police, didn't tell anyone who could have found them, and now that chance has slipped away and you let me go on wondering if they were alive or dead. We cried together—'

'We cry together every fucking Friday night when I put on my Big Ballsy Ballads playlist and crack open the Bolly. And all the time, you were spying on me!'

'Who cares?' Now I'm on my feet and she follows suit. 'Who cares about me and you? Tell me where Kash went to deliver that ransom. Or tell the police, I don't care. But give our girls a chance.'

Mariah lunges for my face again, but this time I'm cat-quick. I slap her hand away. Another nail comes free and we both glance as it lands. I use the advantage to flip a chair up into two hands, the only weapon within grasp. I honestly don't know what she's capable of anymore. She's a head taller than me and furious. But, in the end, she's a money launderer and a bag of Botox, and I'm a trained cop and a triathlete. I fancy my chances. I could pop her inflated fucking face if I had to.

'One word from me' – Mariah hisses over her pointed finger – 'and I could have Olivia killed.'

'So you know where they are?' I pant.

She grins, showing a sheen of Turkish teeth. 'If you've been spying on me all this time, you know who we're dealing with.'

I let the chair slide through my grip until its weight rests on the floor. I don't tell her that I know exactly who we're dealing with. I've known them half my life.

Instead, I take a step forward. I come up to her chin. But I lift my bare face and whisper into her painted one.

'If you hurt my daughter, I'll finish you, Mariah. Kash too. I won't rest until you both go to prison and never see Dixie grow up. If you touch a hair on my daughter's head, I'll fucking orphan yours.'

Chapter Forty-Two

6.50 p.m.

'Literally the only badass thing my mum ever does is cold water swimming.' Olivia kept one hand on the passenger door as she leant down to shout into the vehicle at Jones. 'And then she needs a hot water bottle down her trousers.'

'I'm not saying she's badass, I'm saying she's a cop,' Jones said. Olivia slammed the car door in his face. The window slid down. 'If anything happens to her, you'll have no one!'

She marched towards the cabin, stumbling gracelessly on rubble. The cabin would be cold and dark – and hopefully it would be empty because the others had got away – but she'd rather be in there, alone, than out here with someone bad-mouthing her mother. With a few thudding footsteps, Jones caught up.

'People who work undercover maintain different lives as easily as you manage different social media accounts.'

'You seem to know an awful lot about it. Maybe you're the spy? Maybe you're trying to recruit me for the gang? Is this to do with the money I owe?'

'That's pin money. No one cares. They said you have to pay it back to scare you, to keep you working for them. But you look so much like someone I knew in the early days, someone who worked undercover in the gang, the best snout I ever met. She never raised a red flag, then brought the whole lot down.'

'And?'

'And I'm telling you this because if she's snouting on Mariah Haven then she's in trouble,' he said.

'What do you care?'

'You're a kid. I have standards.'

Olivia scoffed. 'You're tired and emotional.' She took the last few steps to the Portakabin and slapped her hand on the door. 'Let me in, please. I'm cold.'

He patted his pockets for the key. It gave her an excuse to dramatically press the bridge of her nose. Which stopped the threatening tears from coming.

'What sort of trouble?' she asked in a small voice. 'Are you saying Mariah will hurt her?'

Jones put the key in the lock but stopped, staring at it.

'The gang will stop them both from talking to the police.'

'What, like, kill them?'

'Like torture them to find out what they've told the coppers already, then kill them so they can't give evidence.'

'Oh, right.'

The shock of it stalled her mind. Thoughts twisted out of reach like falling feathers. She shook her head, once, hard. It was like the moment she turned over an exam paper and fear triggered her lizard brain – she always got the freeze response: shallow breath, cold sweat, head void. It was physiological, so she could control it. She closed her eyes and made her lungs push out her ribs, then drew them back in.

Okay.

She opened her eyes to see Jones frowning at her.

'Alright?'

She'd started a chain of events that might lead to her mother being tortured. That was not alright. But the only person who could stop it now was her, so she needed to think straight, not panic.

The cabin window was dark. No torch inside. The others must be gone. It would be better if Jones didn't realise that just yet . . . She had to buy them more time to get away.

'Why don't you just leave?' she asked.

'I need to deal with Crowbar first.'

'I mean from the gang. Get away from this . . . life of crime. You don't seem all that into it.'

He gave a single hard laugh.

'I'm not sure it's something you're *into* . . .'

'You said yourself your boss is a psycho.'

'He is that. Look, if I ever get away, I'll send you a postcard. Deal?'

'How will you know where to send it?'

'Oh, I'll find you.'

She managed a small, uncertain laugh, which was interrupted by a crash.

Over by the barn.

Adrenaline shot up Olivia's spine and she clutched his arm, which he'd flung in front of her.

Another metallic clang.

'Crowbar?' Olivia asked.

'Stay close.'

She marched behind him across the concrete. In the darkness beyond the barn, a scuffling, gasping, animalistic noise was getting louder, moving this way.

'Stay back,' hissed Jones.

He leapt forward to grab at a hunched shape that burst around the corner.

Clatter of metal. A crowbar twirled across the concrete, lit up by headlights.

Someone bucked and fought in Jones's arms, the pair casting impossibly long shadows that ran up the barn to loom over them. As soon as Jones realised he was holding a girl, Dixie, he released her. Then disappeared around the corner to find the real threat.

Olivia grabbed her friend by the biceps and spun her into the shadows against the barn.

'What is it?'

'Crowbar,' Dixie said. 'I fell over his body. I think the boys have killed him.'

Chapter Forty-Three

6.55 p.m.

Mariah leaves me standing under the scholarship boards. I always thought she was oblivious to what people say – how their admiration for her *ballsiness* hides a sense of superiority at her *brassiness* – but in fact she knew it all along, she played with it, used everyone's prejudice against them. She's clever. But that only makes her behaviour worse. She's closed that clever mind to the damage she's doing.

Maybe I'm the same? I don't want to see the truth.

Like Olivia on that CCTV at the bus stop . . . If it was anyone else's kid, I'd have no doubt – they were doing a drop. I grab my phone and go to WhatsApp to open the ongoing chat between me and my daughter. Reams of it. We're in contact all day long.

I'm hungry. Unless it's cottage pie
How does the post office work?
Don't wear lipstick, it's so embarrassing
Do we do God?
Pick me up later. If you can be normal
How much do teeth cost?
My friends have so much mental health

Her lovely nonsense.
I scroll back in time.

Everyone is going to see Taylor Swift, can I?

Request denied – too expensive.

Skiing?

Request denied.

Bedroom glow up?

Denied.

Our daily interactions do involve a lot of talk about money. Always wanting for something. Don't we all? But Olivia isn't someone who takes *no* for an answer. She gets what she wants. She went to Tay Tay in the end ... We must have found the money somewhere. I open my banking app. I know she never went skiing – I would have noticed that – but we did end up refreshing her bedroom. I scroll through my bank statements until I find a payment to B&Q. A lick of paint with materials that cost less than a hundred quid. But just above that outgoing payment, an incoming amount catches my eye.

Refund – £100.

Refund from what? It doesn't say.

I look back at other dates when she asked for something and find that most of them are followed by an incoming payment marked 'refund' or 'rebate'.

Only this morning, she asked about her birthday meal ...

I zoom up to today's date.

And there it is ...

Bursary Honorarium – £250.

I click to see 'more details' of the payment. It's not from school. It's a transfer from her account. My stomach zips up tight. I navigate to her personal account.

So many transfers from her to my account, labelled *Refund, Rebate, Bursary Honorarium*.

And there are incoming payments to her account: fifty pounds. Another fifty. And then £1,000.

Who would pay Olivia so much money?

A day later – cash withdrawal of £900.

I scroll back in time.

This is repeated over and over. Money coming in, cash taken out.

I clutch the phone to my belly. I'm so hot it's like my whole menopause has come at once. Questions pour out of me like sweat.

Who is paying her?

For what?

And why does she take out so much in cash?

The door to the hall bursts open. Ayesha and Jack brush past me. It seems they've bonded after the run-in with Maunder. A common enemy uniting them. I have to get out of here. I put my other hand to my face and realise I'm crying. Akin catches my wrist as I walk past.

'Don't,' I hiss. 'They'll see us.'

'But they already know.' He moves to touch my face. I shake him off and storm out to the quad, my arm still heavy with his touch. The gravel path leads to the car park. I'm surrounded by stone buildings whose pointed gables shank the sky. Mariah's Tesla gives out a glow, as though lit by candlelight. She's with Kash in their little cocoon. I reach them and jab my thumb on the silly sunken handle to open the back door. Then fall into the seat and let the door slam. Kash turns in the passenger seat. Mariah adjusts the rear-view mirror to see me.

I still have my phone in my hand with the banking app showing.

I go on the offensive. 'I don't care what you've done or how angry you are, I need to talk to you.'

I can only see a slice of her face. She's reapplied her eyelashes.

'Do you know about this money Olivia has been getting?'

Kash puts his hand out for my phone. I let him take it and scroll through my bank statements. Soft light covers the tired circles under his eyes so that he looks model-handsome. That was my initial impression when I first met him: he was gigglishly hot. I was sitting alone in his kitchen, at his island, holding a flute of his booze. Mariah was in the house somewhere, flitting about after our girls – although, in hindsight, knowing what I know now, she may have been taking calls she didn't want me to hear. Kash strolled in and cheek-kissed me without breaking stride, as though a stranger appeared in his home every day, and I thought how cool it was for this hot man to accept me with no reservations, *mi casa es su casa*, any friend of my wife is a friend of mine, no comment beyond, 'More fizz?' to which the right answer in that house was always, *Yes, more fizz*.

Now I wonder if he was toeing the line. Mariah's line.

Kash hands back the phone.

'That's a lot of money for a teenager' is all he says.

'The police have CCTV of her getting off the bus at a strange stop. Looked like she was doing a drop.'

He grinds the heel of his hand into his eye sockets.

'She's been cuckooed,' he says. 'Sorry.'

'Sorry, what? Sorry, as in commiserations? Or sorry, as in you knew?'

'Of course we didn't know,' Mariah butts in. 'What do you take us for?'

'A money laundering front for an organised crime group, that's what I take you for.'

Mariah says nothing but picks up my trackers from the console and closes them in her fist. I have a crazy vision of her crushing them to dust and letting black sand pour out like an hourglass marking time. But of course she doesn't do that, she just grinds them against her palm while she's thinking.

'It's not even your betrayal that pisses me off the most,' she says. 'It's the time I wasted on you. Hours spent praising your child – and by extension, you – even when it made Dixie feel second rate by comparison. Olivia's scholarship, her grades, her PBs. We had to tiptoe around your hard-luck story, fluff up your feathers with your *perfect daughter* because she's the only thing that makes up for the fact that you've done nothing with your life, achieved *nothing*, not even a functioning fucking kitchen, just a child you conceived on some one-night stand, and now you have to fatten yourself up on her achievements like crumbs from the table—'

'Mariah,' Kash whispers. It's the first time I've ever heard him pull her up.

'Get out,' she says in a dull voice.

I hesitate. Who is she talking to, me or him?

Kash turns to see me.

'You have to get out. We're going.'

'Where?' I ask.

'The people we work for—' His eyes dart crazily. It's probably the first time he's spoken openly about the gang and it's about as comfortable as wetting his pants. 'You know what they're like.'

I nod.

'They called us. We've got to meet them. Outside.'

'Do they have the girls?' I corrected myself. 'The kids?'

'They don't like us being in here with the police. I think—' His voice chokes.

'We think they'll hurt Dixie unless I meet them,' Mariah says. 'So get the fuck out of the car or you're coming too.'

Chapter Forty-Four

6.55 p.m.

In the hazy beam of headlights, Jones stood stock-still with both arms rigid by his sides, like an avatar waiting to join a game in *Fortnite*. He held in one hand half a hockey stick. The business end. At his feet was a dark pile of something, presumably Crowbar.

Olivia dragged Dixie away by her sleeve around the corner of the barn.

'Why didn't you go with the boys?' Olivia whispered.

'Didn't want to leave you. But we should run now while he's distracted.'

'It's freezing,' Olivia said. 'If we end up wandering the woods all night . . . It won't help our mums, will it? We'd do better to stay. He said he'll drive us back.'

'You don't trust him? Especially now the others have gone. He'll be cross. He might kill us.'

'I don't think—'

'I'm not going to kill anyone.' Jones stepped around the corner.

'Jesus!' Dixie. 'You move like a ghost.'

He held the bloodied hockey stick in gloved hands.

'I take it the boys have gone? Where do they think they're going? We're miles from anywhere . . .'

'We're in the south of England, not the Outback,' Dixie said.

'This is like *Lord of the* fucking *Flies*.' Jones threw the hockey stick into a pile of rubble, where it bounced and disappeared. 'Which one of them did that to him?'

'I don't know, I didn't see. The boys ran ahead of me.'

Olivia glanced at Dixie, wondering if she was remembering Kiran on the bus. The sound of a dropped egg . . .

'We need to dispose of that hockey stick properly,' Dixie said. 'The police might work out that one of the boys hit Crowbar, and Kiran hit the other one . . .'

She ran over to the rubble, stumbling onto the pile, looking for the bloody hook.

'Don't touch it!' said Olivia. 'It'll look like the two dealers got in a fight. Attacked each other with the hockey stick. They both handled it, it must have both their fingerprints on. It would look like Crowbar died here, which he did. Then Cole drove off with a head injury. Then he crashed the minibus and went through the windscreen, which finished him off.'

Dixie stood up on the mound of rubble, a hunched shape in the dark. 'But the other one died before Crowbar. Can't they work out what time someone died?'

Olivia scrunched up her face to consider it. Her knowledge was based more on *Silent Witness* than A-level biology. 'Not *that* accurately.'

Dixie hobbled off the rubble. 'So it might look like it had nothing to do with Kiran? Or any of us?'

Jones chipped in: 'In this theory of yours, why didn't Cole take the BMW? If it was me, I'd take a BMW as a getaway car, not a conspicuous minibus the police are looking for.'

'Good catch,' said Dixie sagely.

'Because . . . the BMW has a flat tyre,' said Olivia.

'Has it?' Dixie asked.

'It will if we give it a flat tyre,' said Olivia. 'Maybe that's why they started arguing, Crowbar and Cole? Blaming each other for wrecking the getaway vehicle by driving onto this rough ground.'

Dixie added, 'We were locked inside the Portakabin, so all we could hear was raised voices, engines revving, the sound of fighting. We were terrified.'

'And cold. In a huddle under a piece of carpet for warmth.'

The girls nodded at each other with pursed lips like they'd got a good grade for a joint piece of coursework.

Jones gave a long whistle that suggested he was impressed, and somewhat horrified.

Olivia dropped her head back and saw a gash of moon through the black ceiling of clouds. The start of a new cycle. Her birthday month. 'Cole was only a year older than me. He was the one I met at the bus stop. Who looked like Keanu Reeves. I suspect he had a shit life. No dad, like me, but a shit mum, too, so that made a difference. He didn't get any breaks. When I was with him, I got a glimpse of how my life could have turned out, you know, if things had been different. He felt like a warning, the Ghost of Christmas Past, an alternative version of what might have been. Almost like I'd dodged fate, and I was about to get rumbled . . .'

The other two stayed quiet.

Olivia's shoulder twinged and she put one hand up to take the weight of her elbow.

'Now he's dead,' she said.

'But he got you into all this,' said Dixie. 'Aren't you a bit annoyed?'

'I am, yeah. Mostly with myself.'

Jones sniffed. 'If it's any consolation, the gang would have killed these boys for what they did today, and they would have done it a lot more slowly. These kids were loose canons who exposed the boss to unwanted attention from the police. There's no coming back from that. Corner boys with ideas. The boss would have made an example of them. Hurt them first, to find out if they'd been shouting their mouths off to you kids or your parents. Fancy phoning Mariah Haven!' Jones ran his hands through his hair. 'Silly little sods!'

Dixie kicked a stone that bounced across the concrete and hit some metal object that sent a lone toll into the darkness. Her voice sounded just as hollow. 'Is it like in the films? Do they tie you to a chair and snap your fingers?'

Jones frowned at the macabre question. When he realised she was serious, she wanted an answer, he shifted his weight onto both legs. 'He's into drills, the boss. It's got a lot more blood-thirsty than it used to be.'

'Compared to the good old days?' Olivia muttered.

Jones shot her a look.

'And that's what they'll do to our mums, is it? Drills?'

Jones rubbed a hand over his face.

'If they think your mums are snitching to the police in the hope of getting their missing daughters back ... Then, yes, my boss will grab them the moment they step outside that school gate.'

There was a long pause in which the trees wavered in the wind.

'And then drills,' said Olivia.

Chapter Forty-Five

7.00 p.m.

I'm half-in and half-out of the Tesla when an angry *twink-twonk* and an amber flash from the car next door makes us startle.

'My nerves.' Mariah slaps her hand on her chest.

Now that it's after school hours, the car park lighting has gone to energy-saving low-level mode, so I recognise Jack Kent from his boots and trouser legs. He's almost running to his vehicle. I stand up to intercept him as he rounds his car.

'Fuck me, Olivia's mum!' he says and staggers back as though I'd swung at him. While it is always tempting, I did not actually pose him any danger.

'Emily,' I say. 'Again.'

Kash gets out on the opposite side of the Tesla.

'What's going on, mate?' he says. 'What's the hurry?'

'What's going on is that hashtag-save-our-saints has come up trumps. One of my followers has been out there tirelessly combing the countryside for any sign of the kids and—'

'You're not live-streaming now,' I say. 'Just tell us what happened in as few words as possible.'

'I've got a location. For the kids.' He holds out his phone and Kash reaches over the bonnet to snatch it. We're on opposite sides of the vehicle so I can't see.

'Some guy on Twitter . . .' Kash pinches the screen, zooming in on a picture or a map. 'That's a different road to where the bus crashed.'

Jack doesn't question – or doesn't notice – why Kash knows that. Kent is careering ahead, oiled by his own brilliance.

'Show me,' I say, and Kash hands over the phone.

The photo shows a lane closed by a strip of blue and white tape, police vehicles in the distance, a sign for a farm shop in the foreground. Easy to find with a two-second Google Maps search.

Kent says, 'I showed this to DS Slow Coach and she confirmed the vehicles are police dog handlers. They're putting sniffer dogs in a different location to before, widening the search area.'

'So the kids aren't there now?'

'Thing is, I know this area. I've filmed there. Alix was with me. There's an old bunch of barns near the reservoir that we used as a base. I reckon Alix might make for there. Slow Coach fobbed me off, says they'll get to the site, but it's outside the search area based on proximity to the crashed bus. Won't listen to reason. So I'm going there now. It's less than half an hour away, she can't stop us. It's been too long, it's getting too cold. The kids have only got a couple more hours at this temperature.'

He bounces his keys on his palm. I wonder if he's taken something. Kash glances at the jumping hand too. I don't rate Jack's ability to drive safely right now.

'Maybe someone should check out this farm,' I say. 'Maybe you can drive him, Kash?'

He cocks his head at me. Eyes narrow. I've forgotten the script.

'I think you'll find Mariah needs me here.'

'Nah,' Mariah says from inside the Tesla. 'You go with Jack to this farm. We can sort out any business here, can't we, *Olivia's mum*?' She unfolds from the passenger seat, looming behind me in the narrow aisle between vehicles.

Jack's eyes dart between us. He knows something is off and is deciding if it's important or just women's business. Whatever he thinks, he decides to stay out of it and turns to Kash, bouncing his keys as a question.

'Right, then,' says Kash. 'But I'm driving. You're wired.'

Mariah puts both hands on my biceps and steers me away from his car.

'Too much coffee,' says Jack as he gets in.

'I believe you,' says Kash, 'though millions wouldn't,' and slams the door.

His Tesla makes a spacey thrum as it slopes away.

'And then there were two,' says Mariah.

'Where do you have to meet these contacts, then?' I say.

'Not far. I'll drive.'

'I need to be here for Olivia.' I don't say that I can't come in case someone recognises me.

'What happened to' – she puts on a whiny voice – '*I'll do anything for my Olivia*? They might know where she is.'

'I'd do anything smart, yes. They just want you – as their banker – away from the police.'

'I don't really care if you come, I only said it to get rid of Kash. He'd have stayed if he thought I was going alone. I reckon he thinks they're more likely to kill you than me, so it's better we go together.' She shrugs and walks away towards her Tesla.

Her lime-green outfit mixes with the orangey hue of night lights to give her the queasy colour of a mannequin that matches no human flesh.

'I'll come with you,' I say. 'But we can't take your car. If we drive out of here, someone will see us. There are loads of journalists, someone might follow.'

'I ain't fucking walking. Not in platform trainers.'

'We'll take my car. It's parked outside.'

Side by side, we walk to the school gate.

Chapter Forty-Six

7.00 p.m.

'When can we phone our mums?' Olivia asked Jones as they drove over the broken concrete. The cabin retreated into the dark. She never wanted to see a Portakabin again.

'Soon as we see a payphone,' he said.

'They're extinct, Grandad,' said Dixie.

Jones didn't reply but bristled in a way that made Olivia think of her furious cat when he saw birds through the window.

'What if they leave the school?' Dixie pressed. She didn't have a cat, couldn't read the signs.

'They'll stay at school, if they know what's good for them,' muttered Jones.

He raced along country lanes as though trying to catch his own headlights. It could have been soporific except every jolt made Olivia's left arm throb. She was in the passenger seat and the belt pressed her sore shoulder.

'The problem is the boys,' she said.

'Isn't it always?' muttered Dixie.

'We should have tried to find them,' Olivia said. 'What if they get back first and speak to the police before us? Give a different version of events? The real story.' She looked hopefully at Jones. 'Or will it be okay once we're all back safe – the police will drop it?'

Jones scoffed. 'You think all those parents are going to let it lie? The MP and the doctor? The other one – TikTok Jock?'

'They might drop it when they hear that one son smashed someone's ear with a hockey stick, another son said there was a gun when there wasn't and a third said the phone didn't work so he could be a hero.'

They fell silent. Soon, they pulled onto the dual carriageway and the Range Rover pitched like a boat as they crossed the turbulent Downs and descended towards the city. Street lights marked a false horizon along the coastline. Beyond, the red lights of wind turbines winked in the void of the sea. They could keep going. Run away from the mess they'd made. Maybe that was what Jones intended to do, drive straight through town onto a ferry—

'It's a coincidence, though, isn't it?' Dixie interrupted Olivia's spiral of thoughts. She didn't reply. It wasn't the first time Dixie had mentioned this *coincidence*. She kept circling, nipping the soft underbelly of the topic. 'Fancy, you working for the same gang as my mum? And your mum investigating them all those years ago. What are the chances?'

'It's not a coincidence,' said Jones. 'It's the biggest gang in the country.'

His phone pinged. It sat in a bracket stuck to the windscreen. He wouldn't let either of the girls hold it, in case they did something silly. But his screen was busy with social media notifications. #SaveOurSaints.

'Can I?' Olivia waved a finger up and down, making a scrolling motion.

'Go on, then. Best know what's happening . . .'

She scrolled up through the feed.

They were big news.

'There are reporters outside school,' Olivia said.

'I thought you said the gang would grab our mums?' said Dixie. 'How are they going to do that with all these cameras there?'

'They won't do it in front of the cameras,' Jones said. 'They'll grab them somewhere nice and quiet. A side street or car park.'

A new post pinged.

Minister's son 'missing' in school bus mystery

Olivia said, 'So the boys aren't back yet—'

Dixie launched herself between the seats and grabbed at the phone. Jones swung a paw and knocked her backwards into her seat.

'Don't make me dump you on the kerb,' he said.

Dixie huffed back in her seat. Olivia was more interested in the phone. Dixie had only managed to jab the screen so that the feed rolled backwards in time. Olivia squinted at it. It was now showing posts from previous days, weeks, months. Olivia tapped a fingertip on the Saints logo at the top of the screen.

'Leave it!' Jones said.

A pop-up box said *Following since 2019*. The year she'd joined Saints.

'You didn't start following Saints because of the kidnapping today,' Olivia said.

She wanted to snap her fingers and pause the world so she could think. She'd known the truth in her bones the whole afternoon. Why was Jones taking such an interest in her? Why did he keep asking questions about her mum? Why was he bothering to take them home?

Street lamps soared overhead as they reached the city limits. She glanced at his profile, lights strobing his face like an identity scanner, peeling back layers, tearing away years. She chewed her cheeks, tasting old blood.

'When you were in the gang, back in the day . . .' she asked, 'how well did you know my mum?'

Chapter Forty-Seven

7.10 p.m.

We cut across the dark quad, the gristle of frozen grass under our feet. I lead Mariah to a side gate, hitting the green button to pop the lock and let us onto a street. A bus bustles to a halt and opens its doors to release late commuters onto the pavement in peevish knots. We fall in step behind men in suits who don't acknowledge each other but herd towards the nice terraced houses opposite the school. The fastest suit presses a button at the traffic lights and the green man appears. I tug Mariah's sleeve to keep pace across the main road. Another suit gets a call and presses a phone to his ear.

'Yeah, nearly home.' Then, 'Yeah, reporters are outside, there's a BBC van.' And then, 'Yeah, absolute worst nightmare, poor kids. Pour me a negroni.'

We reach the far pavement and peel away. The journalists are gathered around the main entrance to the school. I direct Mariah down the side street where I parked, what seems like a lifetime ago. My car is squeezed into a space a dozen or so vehicles along. This road is narrow with low mews-style houses on both sides, two rows of parked cars leaving a single lane in between. Local residents avoid this street because it gets clogged. The houses are mostly Airbnbs, occupied in summer by beachgoers, but shuttered in January. So there's not a soul, only parked cars. I take out my keys and press the fob, making my lights flash an amber warning.

Over my shoulder, a seagull is raiding a wheelie bin.

'Slow down,' I say to Mariah. 'I've got a stitch.'

'Thought you were fit?' Mariah doesn't slow down.

'It's the stress, breathing too shallow . . .' I glance back again. 'And I want to make sure none of the journos follow us.'

'They're not going to spot us here, are they? It's dark.'

I beep the car again, lights flash, locks thunk. A car engine revs as though a driver has missed a gear. I glance back, but it's at the top of the road, driving past the junction. We reach my car and I open the boot to put my bag inside. Mariah gets into the passenger seat and immediately spins around to order me to hurry up. I ignore her and slam the boot. But my keys are in there. I open the boot again and rummage through my Mary Poppins bag's bottomless depths.

'You just had them in your hand!' says Mariah.

I tell myself to slow down, more haste, less speed. The keys have slipped down amid my clutter. I take each item out of my tote bag.

In the rear-view mirror, I see Mariah's eyes. If I'm not mistaken, they look moist. She's human, after all.

'You didn't tell me about Akin Abiola,' she says.

I stop rummaging and hold her stare. After all that's happened today, the revelation that's brought her close to tears is me keeping my love life a secret.

'He's married,' I say. 'I had to be careful.'

'I was your best mate.' Her eyes are huge and luminous, so much like Dixie's.

'In fairness, there's a lot you haven't told me.'

'That's just business. This is matters of the heart.'

A cackle makes me startle, but it's only the seagull.

'I wasn't proud of it. Maybe I thought you'd disapprove, tell me to stop . . . You're quite old-fashioned at heart, a stickler for manners, right and wrong.'

'Not gonna lie, banging a married man is not feminist, babes. But he is scorchio and his wife is a show-off, so . . . You should have trusted me. End of.' She adjusts the rear-view mirror to check her lashes. 'There was this guy up north who got done for money laundering for one of the Balkan gangs. Do you know how they caught him?'

I do know. I studied the case. It involved an Unexplained Wealth Order, too, like the one the NCA will apply for on the basis of the evidence I've provided – a link between Haven and the OCG. But I let her tell it.

'They tracked him on Instagram. He couldn't stop show-ing off. Las Vegas, hobnobbing with stars. Photos of himself backstage, red carpets, all that. He courted attention and got it – mainly from the National Crime Agency. But we keep our head down, me and Kash.'

'Kash owns half a dozen holiday homes.'

'He's a property developer. And . . .' Her lashes flick. 'And it's hard to stop.'

I take a few more items out of my bag. Tiny torch. Jiggler keys. Lighter. All my tricks of the trade.

'It's the same undercover,' I say. 'Hard to stop. I always thought I could get closer, find the smoking gun, get *more*.'

'You got close enough to us. In our home. In our heads. This has cut me up, babes.'

'Me too. You're my friend—'

'How can you say that when you ratted on me? I feel stuff, you know.'

'You weren't my friend when I started. Just a mark. Then we became friends. It was unexpected because, in case you haven't noticed, I don't have many. It's like one of those films you like, a rom-com, enemies-to-lovers, only I don't suppose we'll get a happy-ever-after, will we? But I do love you, you and Dixie.'

'Don't know if I believe a word you say anymore.'

'Do you know what I wish? I wish I'd come into your house and found nothing. No link to the OCG. I wish you were clean. Or just a little bit mucky. Fiddling the books, maybe, a bit of tax fraud, nothing more than that. I wish you weren't money launderers for a criminal gang who specialise in extreme violence and guns and drugs and trafficking girls and everything that is fucking up our society and threatening our kids. Because if you hadn't been doing all that, then I could have taken a look at myself in the mirror and thought, *You're a bad person, Emily, ratting on your friend*, but instead I look in the mirror and think, *Someone's got to stop this nasty fucking business and if it's not you, then who?*'

I hear a rough engine. Hesitant brakes. I grab my keys and slide a couple of items into the hidden waistband pocket of my leggings, then step into the road to open my driver's door.

There's a sudden roar of acceleration.

I watch a van coming down the street.

Here we go, I think.

I drop my backside onto the driver's seat with my feet still on the road.

'Friends of yours?' I say to Mariah.

Chapter Forty-Eight

7.10 p.m.

Jones traversed the city using residential roads, crawling at the twenty mph limit, dodging speed bumps in the rat-run between cars parked outside terraced houses. The route was slow-going, but avoided cameras, and it would only be a few more minutes before they reached their mums. The pain in Olivia's shoulder was forgotten, a fresh shot of adrenaline numbing her body and focusing her mind to a pinpoint. His eyes flitted between the road and her face as though he didn't know which would be the first to throw an obstacle in his path.

'How can you be sure I'm yours?' she asked.

'Timing. And just— She wasn't a cheat. Unless you were adopted, you were mine.'

'But she lied to you the whole time she was undercover.'

'She had to do what she had to do. That's different to doing something you don't have to do. Like falling in love. And a pregnancy explained why she upped and left so suddenly. Who did she say was your father?'

'Someone she couldn't contact. When I was little, I assumed it must be Doctor Who, obviously. Made sense. But as I got older and wiser, I figured it was a holiday romance, a one-nighter . . . She said she only knew his nickname, not his real name, so that was that.'

'It's not a lie. I'm not exactly on Facebook. And we are cagey about real names. I only knew your mum as Gemma at first. She was a regular user when I started with the gang – an addict, I thought. I didn't touch users—'

'You'd sell to them, though?' Dixie fired a shot from the back seat.

Olivia shushed her. Jones ignored her.

'Gemma seemed to have control over her habit. She'd come off the gear every now and then, take a break so she didn't get a tolerance, and she didn't suffer too bad with the rattling, so I didn't think of her as a junkie.'

'Rattling?'

'Withdrawal symptoms, shaking and chattering, all that . . .'

Exactly what she'd seen Kiran doing earlier.

'Of course, *now* I know your mum didn't rattle because she wasn't really on drugs in the first place. It was all an act. I just thought she was smart enough to start dealing in exchange for freebies, and had got clean as she worked her way up the ladder.'

'You make it sound like an office job.'

'Wouldn't know, never had one . . . Once she started earning real money, she stopped using and didn't even drink. She'd grown up on a rough estate – at least that was her story – and she said she had no intention of going back to that life, she'd rather conduct the music than dance to someone else's tune – I never forgot that. We got together, both working for the gang. There were a lot of hotheads, a lot of hardmen, but Gemma was a diplomat. And she made no bones about looking after herself. She sacked off wasters, ordered beatings for dealers she caught skimming, didn't let anyone off light when they deserved it. Zero tolerance for abusing the girls. That sort of thing has got much worse now ... She knew the price of everything and everyone, kept the lads calm and stopped any beef. But, looking back, she was filing it all away, gathering information, putting names to faces. Spying, basically.' Jones stopped talking and just drove for a moment, circling a mini roundabout at the top of the park.

'How come you didn't realise she was a cop?' Dixie asked.

'Love-blind, I suppose. Thinking with my—' His eyes dodged Olivia and fixed on the road. 'Let's just say I wasn't thinking straight. And she was bloody good at calling our bluff. More balls than the National Lottery. Do you know what she'd do? She'd say the police pay through the nose for informants, so they'd better keep on her good side. If you think you're sassy, young Olivia, you get that from your mum.' He gave her a grin that was quick to fade.

They were past the park and on the downhill stretch towards school. She was running out of time.

'Can I know your name?' Olivia sounded more meek than she intended.

They stopped at a red traffic light and waited while no one used the crossing.

On the first amber flash, Jones accelerated.

'They call me Kershaw,' he said.

'Is that your real name?'

He didn't answer.

Kershaw. Didn't suit him. And if it wasn't his real name, then she might as well stick to Jones.

'Why haven't I heard from you before now?' she asked.

'You were never supposed to hear from me at all. I mean, this can never work, can it? We're never going to be Papa and Nicole.'

'Who?'

'Old telly advert. See, I'm not used to dealing with kids. What I'm saying is, I never intended to approach you. It's only because of today . . . You pair have made quite a nuisance of yourselves.'

'If Mum ran away from the gang, how do you even know about me?' Olivia asked.

'Gemma disappeared out of the blue. One night she just didn't come home. Left her stuff, her passport, vanished. Obviously, people like us don't call the police. I went driving around all the places she might be. But a few days later there was a raid at our lock-up and I only missed getting arrested because I was out of town looking for her. Everyone concluded she was the snout and she ran because she knew about the sting. I got heat from people who thought she'd tipped me off and that's why I was out of harm's way. I couldn't believe it, though. She must've been undercover for *two years,* man. It meant our whole relationship had been cover, but I *knew* her. We were real. I didn't want the gang sending heavies after her so I convinced them I needed to find her myself, *teach my woman a lesson*, all that Alpha shit. Took me another two years to find her. She was bloody good at covering her tracks. And when I did, she had a toddler. You. That's when I realised she'd left because she was pregnant and wanted to get the baby away from that life. Which was absolutely the right call. She didn't know if she could trust me or not – I was, after all, a wrong'un – and she decided not to take the chance.'

'What happened after you found her?' Olivia asked.

'Kept my distance, kept my eye on her.'

'You've been stalking her?' said Dixie.

'I'm not saying it's healthy . . .' Jones huffed. 'In my defence, I made sure the gang never found her.'

'You don't need to protect her.' Now Olivia huffed. 'Not when you've already said she was the best undercover officer you'd ever seen.'

'Oh, she's the most devious person I've ever encountered. Fair play, the only one who's ever got clean away from the gang. I'm not saying I protected *her*, only that I protected her trail, if you see what I mean. I found her so they didn't have to. Told them I dealt with her. Acid.'

'Fuck.' Dixie put her hand to her face.

'Acid was all the rage for a while . . .' Jones mused. 'Once they lost interest, I watched you both from afar. I could never approach because it might risk you being found by the gang. They'd have killed the lot of us. But I've watched you grow up . . .'

'Creepy,' Dixie said.

'Hence the social media alert on Saints?'

He blew out a sharp breath. 'Your school doesn't half show off. I know about your swimming. Your chemistry prize. The straight run of grade nines at GCSE – that was in the paper. I knew you were at a swimming trial today. Did you make the nationals, by the way?'

'We bombed,' Olivia said. 'Were you there?'

'I never get that close. Although if I had, I could have shut this can of worms before it opened up. As soon as I got the call about one of our idiot fucking corner boys taking a Saints minibus, I knew it must be you. And I wasn't having that.'

'This is heart-warming,' said Dixie.

He shot her another of his bristling looks and Olivia wondered if Dixie had overstepped. He had a temper like her cat, quick to swipe. But he got distracted by his phone ringing. He snatched up an AirPod case from the console and fumbled the buds into his ears. Hit the green button. She couldn't hear the call. But from the way he kept his eyes fixed dead ahead without straying even once to her, she deduced the call was about them. And from the fact that he took his foot off the accelerator so that the vehicle coasted almost to a stop, that it was serious. He grunted, pulled out the ear buds and dropped them in the drinks holder, still avoiding her eye. After a beat, Olivia picked up the AirPods and stowed them safely in the case.

'We're nearly at school,' she said.

'Change of plan.'

He swung the vehicle into the maw of a side road, tyres squealing through a semicircle to turn back on themselves.

'What about my mum?'

'They have her.' Jones's face shut down into that fish-eyed look. 'And now they want you too.'

Chapter Forty-Nine

7.25 p.m.

The van stops beside my car. No screech of tyres. Nothing to draw attention.

Mariah scrambles for her door handle, but a massive belly blocks her window. Hands grab my arm and I'm out of the car, on the ground, then up again and through the double doors of the van. No point fighting, not yet. I slide over the ridged metal floor, out of control, until I stop myself with a grinding knee. My heart seems determined to climb out of my body, so I put a hand on my chest to comfort it. Outside, Mariah is needing the full effort of two men. They deposit her, with a little more respect than they showed me, onto one of the wooden benches that lines the side of the van. The doors whoomp shut and we're done.

The van kangaroos away. Mariah almost sprawls on the floor but stops herself. I let the motion throw me onto my hands and knees, and from there onto the bench opposite her.

'Hold onto the side,' I say as we pick up speed.

My mouth is bleeding, but the thugs were quick and clean, I'll give them that. One split lip isn't bad for a double snatch that took seconds. My leggings have a hole in the knee, though, which pisses off some irrelevant part of my mind.

Mariah straightens her hair in a strangely housewife-y way.

I can almost see her cogs whirring.

'Did you do that on purpose?' she says. 'You were stalling, you knew they were coming.'

'You want the girls back, don't you? So we'll let them take us to them. And work it out from there. I know gangs. I knew they'd come for you, in case you did a runner. But they needed to grab you somewhere quiet, a nice side street. They don't want it live-streamed on Twitter by one of those sharks outside school.'

'Cold,' Mariah says.

That makes me laugh. *I'm cold?* 'This whole show is for you, Mariah Haven of the Haven Group. This is your welcoming committee.'

'It's fine. They know where Dixie is. I know where their money is. It's quid pro quo. I don't know what you've got to offer them, mind . . .'

'I've been lying to these arseholes all my life. It's not like I've forgotten how.'

'True that,' Mariah concedes. 'You are dishonest *as fuck.*'

I nod. 'I own that. Everyone's got their *thing*. Talking of *things*, it would be a bad thing for you to tell them I'm an informant, you know that, don't you? A bad thing for me and for you.'

'It might get them off my back.'

'Only for the five minutes it'll take them to put a bullet in my face. Then they'll want to know how much you've told me during our boozy nights together, what access I've had to the information you hold, because I'll be sure to inform them before they shut me up that I spend most Friday evenings in your home. I am, after all, an informant. As soon as they know you're BFFs with a snout, you'll be joining me in the old acid bath—'

Our chat is cut short by a swerve that has us planting our legs wide, undignified, like kids on the potty. We're going uphill.

Sharply uphill. That means we're going to the Hope Estate. Otherwise known as the Abandon Hope Estate.

The van levels off and then the ride gets smoother, the driver more relaxed now they're in home territory. We cruise to a halt. In barely a heartbeat, the doors fly open. Cold night air jumps us. The same two thugs signal Mariah to come forward, and when she tries to step down, they bury their hands in her armpits and lift her onto the pavement. There's a beat where she pulls herself to her full height, as tall as both of them, and flicks her hair into place. But then they grab her biceps again and frogmarch her towards a grey pebble-dashed house with metal sheets over the windows.

Another two come for me.

'I'm with her,' I say.

They twist my arms and push me towards a different, but equally grim, house. This makes the ground slide out from under me more rapidly than their manhandling. They're splitting us up.

That's a red flag.

It means one thing. There's no quid pro quo here. They're going to interrogate us.

I'm bundled through a front door that's been knocked off its hinges one too many times. Down a hallway, through a rancid kitchen, into a back room. It contains a single mattress in the corner, no sheets or pillow. The door slams and I don't bother to check if it's locked because I know there will be someone standing guard outside. From my leggings pocket, I pull out a stubby tube that might pass for lipstick, but conceals a short, sharp blade. I'm not stupid enough to think I can fight anyone with it. I'm not a corner boy armed with a zombie knife, but it might help me get out of here if I can use it to jimmy one of these windows. There are two, one looking into a tip of a back garden and another to the street outside. I start feeling around that frame for a latch. I need to be quick.

The fact is, they'll start with Mariah. She's the one they want. Their money man. Woman. They'll want to know how much she told the police today. Did she cave and give them up?

My stomach shrinks at the thought of what they might do to her. I saw 'interrogations' in the past and know that the level of violence has only got worse. I take a good look around for anything that might be useful to me. The ceiling is covered in water stains the colour of big yellow bruises. She doesn't deserve that, Mariah, no one does. But, at the same time, I know that the longer they spend with her, the longer I have to get away. And I will get away. Because Olivia needs me. And the clock is ticking for me because, sooner or later, Mariah will tell them I'm an informant. Even if it buys her no more than five minutes respite, she'll take it. I've only got as long as she can hold out.

Chapter Fifty

7.25 p.m.

Jones drove past the bus stop where Olivia had once got off the number 29 to pass an envelope of cash to a lad who took it into the Hope Estate on an electric scooter. Now, the Range Rover swept up the hill on the same route, past tired-looking houses that turned into exhausted-looking houses and then terminally ill-looking houses. They parked behind a van. Two beefy guys with the air of bouncers milled about in the road, clapping dinner-plate hands in the cold air. They were both buzz-cut bald and their skin looked red raw in the wind.

Behind them, the windows of two semi-detached houses were boarded up with metal panels. The front doors hung off and there were graffiti tags all over the brickwork.

'Do people live here?' she asked Jones.

'Not if they can help it. It serves as a doss house, I suppose, for the corner boys.'

'What's your house like?'

'Country cottage,' he said. 'Roses round the door.'

Down the hill, back the way they came, she could see the copper rooftop of her school. *Stranger Things* needn't have invented the terrors of the Upside Down. If they'd wanted opposite worlds in close proximity, one dark and one light, they could have used down there in the town and up here in the Abandon Hope estate.

'Stay here,' said Jones.

'Wait—'

He didn't. He slammed the door without looking back. One of the bouncers followed him and the other one stayed by the Range Rover, fingers drumming the roof. Jones disappeared inside a house.

Olivia took off her seatbelt and clambered into the back to sit with her friend.

'Do you think they've got guns?'

'Yes.' Dixie nodded once. 'This whole set-up feels . . . gunny.'

'Imagine living here.' Some of the houses looked wrecked but inhabited. Only the two across the road were actually boarded up. 'I thought my house was bad. It's actually quite nice.'

Dixie shifted forward in her seat, peering intently through the windscreen.

'Look in the back of that van,' she said. 'Do you see what's on the floor?'

Olivia saw at once what she meant. An incongruous, lime-green pompom. The sort that middle-aged women have hanging from their handbags.

'That's my mum's,' said Dixie, unnecessarily, because who else would have a lime-green one?

'They're here.'

'I don't like this . . .' Dixie said. 'He's delivered us to them. I knew we couldn't trust him.'

'Maybe your mum brought the ransom and they're going to do an exchange?'

'Why would she come in the back of their van? Why has her tassel thing been pulled off her bag? Why—' Dixie chewed her fingers. 'We have to find her. Your mum might be here too.'

She was right. None of this was good. And Jones . . . maybe Olivia did have Stockholm syndrome? Because who was he, really?

'Do you think he's even my real father? He could be lying.'

'But he knows stuff.'

'Or he made up stuff?'

'Shiiit,' said Dixie, making the word take a while. 'He could have done.'

'Okay, we need to go now. Same as before, yeah? I'll cause a distraction—'

'It's my turn.' Dixie pulled her glove half off her hand. 'Ready?'

'Not really.'

Dixie cracked her door and slid silently onto the pavement. She stood up and slammed the door, hard. Then howled. A banshee cry. Wordless. Primal. A prey animal giving its last. The bouncer trotted round to her side of the vehicle to see what was happening.

Olivia heard the low rumble of his voice between Dixie's gasps.

'My hand!' Dixie screamed again. 'It's shut in the door!'

Olivia looked at the fingertips of Dixie's glove poking through the closed door.

'Open it, open the door!' She made eye contact through the window. Olivia spun onto her bottom so her feet were on the seat. Bent her knees. The bouncer leant forward to lift the handle. As it opened, she slammed her feet against the door and it crashed into the front of his skull. He folded onto the pavement like a collapsed deckchair. Dixie followed up with a stomp. He didn't stand up.

Olivia slid out through the same door and stepped over him. Dixie pulled her glove back on.

'So long as no one comes out to see what all that fuss was about, we're golden,' said Olivia.

The wind carried a drumroll of waves from a mile away. No sound of movement nearby. They waited a few moments to be sure. There was nothing more that needed to be said, so they set off in silence.

Chapter Fifty-One

7.35 p.m.

I start working on a metal panel that's bent away from the corner of the window as though someone else has already had a good go at it. There's a shrill cry outside. It makes me pause, but only for a moment. Must be a fox, it's so wild. There it is again. The tip of my blade catches hold of a screw head and, with a pressure that makes my wrist complain, grinds it around in the flaking concrete. I keep turning until the screw drops into foliage outside the window that smells like an overgrown box hedge or the place that everyone comes to piss. The cry wasn't Olivia, couldn't be. I know her noises. When she was little, she'd try to trick me into thinking she was injured. She was bloody convincing, but I could always tell. When she was really hurt, I could pick out her cry across a busy playground like a penguin in an Antarctic huddle.

I hear another sound that makes me stop.

A man's voice. Inside the house. He speaks again and I know. Kershaw.

When I heard that name earlier, as the previous owner of the red BMW seen on the motorway, I hoped it was a coincidence. Feared the implications if it wasn't. He's the only other person who knows who I am.

And he's here. He's found me. Found Olivia. And knows that the best way to me is through her.

My head spins as though I stood up too fast.

Can't let him see me.

I jam my blade into the next screw head and twist—The tip breaks. I push the flat bit against the head, but it's too wide now, won't catch. It skids off and scores the steel. *Fuck!*

Kershaw will recognise me despite my new nose and tits. We were so close he could name the constellations of my moles. He must know I'm undercover, or an informant, or *something*. Chances are, he hates me, he's been stewing all this time, *waiting*, and he'll identify me to the others. They'll kill me. Or he'll kill me. And they'll torture Mariah for being friends with me. Because of the gang's money launderer being best friends with an undercover cop . . .? They're not going to let that go. And what will they do to our girls? I dread to think . . .

I shove the metal panel, but it's no good, it won't budge.

I retreat behind the door. I've got nothing except a lipstick-sized blade, and the element of surprise.

A knock. It's him. It's been eighteen years, but I even remember his fucking knock.

I press against the wall. I want to shriek like that fox outside. But I stay in the moment. Steady breath. Still hands. A breeze through the open window brings a waft of sweet vanilla. That pops my focus. *Sweet vanilla.* Superdrug's finest body spray. One that Olivia loves.

A shadow passes outside, only visible by a fleeting darkening of the tiny holes in the metal panel. Blink and it's gone, wouldn't have noticed it but for the sweet vanilla tugging my attention to the window.

She's here.

Coming round the back of the house. A creak snaps my focus back to the door. An arm's length from my belly, the handle turns. My thoughts whirl and settle on one idea that takes the air from my lungs. If they want to know what Mariah has told the police – or told me – they'll torture her. But how will they torture her? By making her watch them hurt her daughter. And once they know who I am . . .? Olivia.

I almost run to the window, call out to her, but that's not the right move. I have one chance to make the right move. It needs to be a checkmate. I shift the remains of the blade into a fist, the better to jab it sideways into an exposed neck. Even if it does belong to the only man I've ever loved. It's about the best I can hope for, as the door swings open.

Chapter Fifty-Two

7.36 p.m.

The girls scuttled past the smashed-up front door into the relative safety of the shadows at the side of the house. It was abandoned and overgrown, but there was a narrow path, maybe just a flat drain, between what was once a flower bed and the wall. It reeked of foxes and nettles.

Olivia tried not to let anything touch her. They passed metal-shuttered windows. Garden gate long gone. The kitchen bulged out at the back, its lights pricking the metal panels, almost star-like, but not pretty.

'Where are they?' A brutish shout from inside the house. 'Fucking kids!'

'Quick!' Olivia hissed, but Dixie was already heading away from the house into the garden. She plunged into the darkness, merging with a shape that might be an old child's swing. Upstairs, a window creaked open. Beneath it, Olivia pressed back against the wall. A cigarette butt landed near her feet in a shower of sparks and the window closed again. She slid along the back wall, stamping on the cigarette, and squeezed herself through a broken fence slat into the neighbouring garden. This one didn't feel any more hospitable. Nor did it allow any better access. This house was also boarded up, both semi-detached homes condemned. Here, one metal panel had been torn off the window and dumped on the patio, leaving a graffitied pane exposed. No curtain, no net. Nothing inside, except a wall with torn-off shiny paper and a man shouting at someone out of sight. Double glazing prevented her from hearing the details. She crept closer to see more of the room.

Dixie's mum.

That's who he was shouting at.

The absence of sound made it seem like she was on television. Familiar but unreachable.

And her body language. The tension in her imposing frame was matched by a coolly murderous expression trained on the man with the flying spittle. The look of an animal, an apex predator. What came to Olivia's mind was an owl. She had held one once at a petting zoo and it had claws like Wolverine. She half expected Mariah to swoop. Instead, she pointed one talon at the door and said – easy to lip-read – *I want my daughter, now!* Clearly, the bloke recognised the same predatory look in her eye because he pulled a gun on her.

A scuff of footsteps from behind made Olivia shrink down, but it was Dixie. She wasn't even crouching out of sight. Just standing in plain view, staring into the window. Her whimper made Olivia grab her hands before she could do anything rash.

'Dixie—'

The girl spun out of her grasp and snatched up an empty beer bottle that lay on the ground. She threw it against the glass. It bounced off and smashed on the patio stones. Olivia grabbed Dixie's arm and pulled her down to cower under the wall.

'He had a gun pointed at her!'

'But—'

Olivia was interrupted by a scream, loud enough to be heard even through double glazing. It was a man's scream, and he kept on screaming. Dixie craned her neck to see the glass.

'Blood!' she said.

Olivia looked too. It was all over the glass.

Beside them, the back door bulged once, twice, then burst open. Mariah staggered into the garden, shouting for Dixie. The girl ran into her mother's arms. The guy with the gun came soon after, crouched and clawing at his face, which seemed to be weeping blood. He tried to wipe it away with his big paws, one still holding the gun. Mariah shoved Dixie behind her and backed away onto the grass. But the man cleared his vision enough to see her and advance with the gun held out.

A second man emerged.

'Oi, oi, oi! Boss wants her alive.'

'She clawed my fucking eyes out!' said the bloodied man.

His mate grabbed his chin to look at his face.

'They're still there, mate.'

'She tried to blind me. With her fingernails. Fucking psycho. I won't kill her, I'll just beat the living shit out of the jumped-up b—'

'Don't call me a bitch,' said Mariah. 'Or I'll finish the job and keep your eyeballs.'

The second guy pushed his mate aside. He had a crowbar in one hand. Another one.

Mariah took half-steps into the garden, each foot testing the ground beneath the unkempt grass and detritus. Dixie pressed into her back, their legs jumbling like a pantomime horse.

'Where you off to, Mrs Haven? Boss wants you. Bring your daughter. Lovely-looking girl . . .'

'Leave her out of this,' Mariah said.

'And where's the other one?'

'Not my problem,' said Mariah. 'I came here for my daughter and I've got her now, so I'll be on my way, thanks very much. I'll call the boss and set up a meet. We can talk in a more civilised environment.'

They edged further away, leaving Olivia in shadow under the window.

A voice from inside the house snatched both men's attention.

In that moment, Dixie's mum turned as quick as an owl, her gaze falling like a beam on Olivia. Mariah flicked her chin towards the fence. The broken slat where Olivia had squeezed through. She mouthed, *Go!*

Mariah barged Dixie across the grass in the opposite direction, keeping the girl out of shot behind her bulk, drawing the two blokes away from Olivia like fish on a hook. As the men's backs turned her way, Olivia stayed low and crept across the patio. At the fence, she cast one last look at the crowbar in the man's hand. It flashed up into the air. Mariah flung her arms wide to shield her daughter and Olivia ducked through the fence.

Chapter Fifty-Three

7.38 p.m.

A man steps into the room. I push myself away from the wall and embrace him from behind, one hand scooping his arm up behind his back, my other hand pressing a makeshift weapon against his jugular. The vein rises to meet my fingertips. The only part of him that moves. He has a dab of grey in his sideburn, a pale scar that's also new to me.

'Hello, Gemma,' he says over his shoulder. 'You're looking well.'

The curve of his backside imprints my belly. His left hand flexes where it's trapped between my breasts. I either have to cut him while I have the chance or face the fact that I won't hold him for much longer. I hope he can't feel my heart giving high fives to his palm.

'Did you take my daughter to get to me?' I whisper.

'This isn't my doing.'

'Coincidence, is it?'

'Not really, your girl's been working for the gang in secret. Like mother, like daughter.'

I give his arm a warning tug. He winces, showing teeth.

Maybe I should tell him he's Olivia's father? Would he get his head around that news quickly enough to want to protect her rather than hurt her? Or would it make him even more vengeful? Do I have any clue how he might react after eighteen years?

'She's outside,' he says. 'You might want me to get to her before the others do.'

'Why did you bring her here?'

'Thought it was about time we had a family reunion.'

My grip slackens and he doesn't waste the moment. He twists and backhands the weapon onto the floor, then pins me to the wall with my wrists by my hips, his body full-length against mine, knees embedded in my thighs. He gives the stumpy knife on the floor a look of disgust.

'I've seen more dangerous blades of grass.'

'I don't recall being all that impressed by the size of your weapon.'

His smile rises and falls at the sound of a door crashing open outside.

'Shame we haven't got time for this.' His eyes flit between mine, seeking a way inside my mind. 'You could've told me, you know. About her.'

'Be realistic.'

'You could've trusted me.'

'It's not a question of trust. You don't *hope for the best* in this game. You make sure. I made sure. Sorry, but that was my call, and it was the right one.'

'Yeah, well . . .' An inch-wide gap appears between us as he drops the eye contact. The closest I'll get to an admission that I'm right.

'Does Olivia know?' I ask.

'She wheedled it out of me. She's like a very pretty and intelligent pitbull.'

I don't smile. I couldn't even if I wanted to. My lips are stiff with the fear of what Olivia is thinking right now, about her father, about me. 'You had no right. What if she hates me—'

'She doesn't. But I've carried this for years. Told no one. Not even my old man. He died thinking he had no grandchildren. I kept it in here.' He releases my wrist in order to slap his chest.

'How long have you known?'

'Since I first saw her. She was a toddler, but I knew she had to be mine. I stayed away because you'd made clear that was what you wanted. And even I could see that was what you needed. I didn't want to drag you back to this life, so I said nothing. Until today, when I started to talk to her, it just came pouring out.'

'Well, thank you very much, Oprah, for sharing your truth.'

So this is how he will dismantle my life. First, he dragged me into the darkness, now into the light. I should have been the one to tell her. I should have—

But I didn't, did I? I kept living the lie, a different lie, a better lie, but still a lie.

He blows out a long breath. 'I know it's not been easy, Gemma—'

'Emily.'

He sneers. 'Doesn't suit you. Too frilly. But, yeah, I suppose I can understand why you did it. What were you supposed to tell her? *Your dad's an ageing reprobate destined for prison or the wrong end of a zombie knife*? She'd hardly have wanted to get to know me, would she?'

'Depends if you were offering her a step onto the property ladder, like a real dad. She's very pragmatic, my daughter.'

He laughs once. 'With that kind of moral ambiguity, she's a chip off the old block.'

'Me or you?'

'Both of us.'

He lets go and I rub my wrists where he's given me burns.

'What happens now?' I ask.

'The boss is coming. He'll want to know what she's told the police, your mate Mariah fucking Haven. He doesn't know you're here.'

'You going to tell him?'

'He's going to recognise you. You haven't aged a bloody day, the more fool you. And you can't even distract him with your tits anymore.'

Men yell inside the house. He glances away. Something's happening. He bats the door aside and strides out towards the front door. I'm about to slink off in the opposite direction when he heads back.

'They've done a runner, the girls, Olivia and the other one. They brained one of our lads and legged it. They're on the warpath.'

'We have to find them.'

That's when we hear glass smash in the garden. And voices I know – Mariah and, worse, Dixie. They're both screaming.

Chapter Fifty-Four

7.40 p.m.

Olivia pressed her hands over her ears when the screaming started. First Dixie's howl of shock, then Mariah's roar of pain. Crouched behind a wheelie bin on the other side of the wooden fence, Olivia moved around on the spot as though chained there. A dull thud – a boot, maybe, or the crowbar – made the screaming stop. That was even worse. She felt herself whimper and splayed her hands over her mouth instead.

If anyone should be screaming, it should be her. Yes, Mariah was involved in something illegal to do with money, and Dixie had tried to play the kidnappers at their own game, but it was Olivia who tipped the first domino of the day. Everything that has happened, every wobble and fall, was her fault. And now she was cowering, hiding, whimpering in fear.

She crawled onto the grass, feeling around in the dark for anything to defend herself with; she didn't know what. She touched and discarded empty bottles, chunks of brick, a mug without a handle. Under the swing set, her hands found a metal bar about the length of a golf club. She ripped it free of grass that wanted to keep it and gripped it by one end. Cold seared her palms.

Over the fence, she heard muted voices, scuffling, pants of pain. That big bloke hurting Mariah. God knows what Dixie was doing. Knowing her, not hiding and whimpering, but something bold. Earlier, out at the barns, Dixie had come back for her when she could have run away with the boys. Olivia stood up and swung the rod two-handed like a baseball bat.

She walked off the grass, around the wheelie bin, to the gap in the fence. The loose slat hung to one side. The garden beyond was lit by spillage from the kitchen window. Mariah sat atop tangled legs, her torso held up by a hand around her throat. She looked broken. The crowbar swung at the man's side. Olivia tried to calculate the number of steps to cross the garden and whack him. Would he hear her coming? Would Mariah look up and give her away? She had to take the chance. She held the rod high in her right hand—

And it whipped out of her grasp.

She spun round to see Jones. And her mum. Olivia was hit by a tsunami of her mother. It hurt, the tight grip around her sore shoulder, but she let herself be held while Emily made noises into her neck, hardly discernible words, and part of her wanted to curl into her body like a baby kangaroo. But it was too late for that. She pushed her mum away.

'Mariah and Dixie,' she whispered. 'He's got them.'

On cue, over the fence, a thump and a gasp of pain.

Dixie found her voice again, screaming for it to stop.

It wouldn't be long before the guy turned on her too.

Olivia locked eyes with her mother.

'Mum, I have to—'

Emily took three strides backwards, steadied her stance, then bounded forward and launched herself at the six-foot fence, grabbing the top and propelling herself with one kick clean over. The whole row of panels swayed violently but she landed with a gentle thud on the other side.

'Fucking hell,' said Jones. 'Don't expect me to do parkour.'

'Well, you'd better do something,' said Olivia. 'Or give me back my stick.'

He shifted the rod into the other hand, lowered his shoulder and took a run at the gap in the fence. He ploughed right through the wood. Olivia pushed aside the splintered slats and followed her parents into the other garden. They stood side by side on the grass.

Emily must have already done something to the thug with the crowbar because he was sprawled on the patio. Jones pulled a gun and the bloke stayed down, clutching the ground. Mariah didn't get up but lay on the grass. Dixie didn't try to help her mother but ran instead to Olivia, who pulled her into her side.

The kitchen door swung back, releasing more light and another man. Olivia hadn't seen him before. Had no idea who he was. But clearly everyone else was only too aware. The atmosphere thickened like it did when the headmaster sidled unexpectedly into class.

Unlike the reptilian Dr Sam Maunder, though, this one was more of a turtle. He had a bald head, mottled by a too-dark tan. A crushed boxer's nose flattened his face. And his squat frame was swamped by a shapeless wool coat like a shell. He moved across the patio with a severe limp.

Jones kept the gun on the thug.

'Whatcha doing that for?' Turtle guy said without looking at him.

'Thought you'd want her alive?' Jones nodded at Mariah. 'Meathead here was beating the shit out of her.'

Turtle guy tipped his chin in agreement.

'Fuck off, you,' he said to the thug on the floor. 'Learn to control yourself.'

The guy scrambled to his feet and lumbered into the house. Jones returned the gun to the back of his waistband.

'Sorry, love,' Turtle called to Mariah. Then, to Jones, 'Help her up. She'll catch her death on that wet grass.'

Mariah waved them both away and pushed herself onto her feet, cradling her left elbow with her right hand.

'He hit me with a fucking crowbar,' she complained.

'Then you should've done as you was told, you silly moo,' said Turtle.

'I assume you've met the boss before?' Jones asked Mariah.

She shook her head. 'I keep my distance. Plausible deniability.'

'Not willing to get your hands dirty, more like,' said the boss.

'Mariah Haven meet Hugo Boswell. Boss meet Mariah Haven of Haven Group.'

The boss ignored her. He walked past Jones and went right up to Olivia's mum, toe to toe, nose to nose. A tug in Olivia's belly made her want to go to her mother's side, but she resisted. Why was he more interested in Mum than in Mariah? They were about the same height, but he was twice the width. Emily averted her eyes, submissive, shrinking. He frowned and took his time to look her over. Then grabbed her jaw and turned her face side to side. Now, her eyes flicked up and held his gaze, a shade of a smile on her face, a cocky look unfamiliar to Olivia. Who was this woman?

'Hello, Gemma Smith,' he said. 'Haven't seen you since you put me in prison.'

Chapter Fifty-Five

7.45 p.m.

'Nothing to do with me,' I say. 'It wasn't me who put you inside.'

And it's true. That raid on the gang, a week after I made a run for it, didn't come directly from my intel. Yes, I contributed to the overall operation, but there must have been another UCO on the inside because the drug squad knew things I didn't. They hit a warehouse I hadn't managed to recce yet. But I know how it must have looked to Hugo 'Boss' Boswell.

I've spent the last eighteen years terrified that my old life would catch up and take away my new one. Names and faces from that time have grown in magnitude, leaving me afraid of shadows that loom larger than whatever casts them. Well, now the boogieman has appeared. I'm waiting for a jump-scare.

The boss didn't get any prettier in prison. After all the good work I did under his broken nose, he only went down for some bullshit lesser charge that fell far short of the reality of his offences. The murders, the trafficking, the drugs. He wriggled out of all that by launching his own kind of defence – most likely, a campaign of intimidation against witnesses and victims. Was it worth my two years undercover to send him down for five, out in three for good behaviour? If it wasn't for Olivia, I'd say not. But at least I got her out of it.

The boss left prison a decade ago, I read about it in the paper. Went right back to what he did before. But he's old-school, in a gangland that's only getting more global, technological, violent. Looks like it's taken its toll. He's a shrivelled old tortoise.

'You had your snout in my trough,' he announces.

'I was an undercover officer, yes,' I say. 'For two years.'

He nods. 'Well, fuck you very much.'

'That raid wasn't down to me. I left because I was pregnant.'

He spins on his heel. To Kershaw.

'What you got to say for yourself?'

Kershaw mutters, 'It's news to me.'

'You said you'd taken care of your woman,' the boss indicates me, 'but this one is still pretty. Look at her – hair's a bloody mess, but if she scrubbed up . . . Gorgeous!' He drags me in front of him, showing me off to Kershaw. It reminds me of all the times I saw him grab some young girl, trafficked from abroad, handling her like livestock. How I wanted to shoot him dead on the spot. Now, my fingers itch to shake him off, or worse. I was angry non-stop for years after his half-arsed trial. All those girls . . . and he got away with it.

I give myself a mental shake. Get into the moment. I feel his scaly fingers on my elbow. I see Olivia's halo of hair backlit by the kitchen lights. I smell her vanilla scent. I take it all in, a trick I used when I was undercover, to hold back panic, to stay in character, like an actor. *I will get out of here. I will get her out of here.*

The boss leans on my shoulder while he shifts his weight, favouring a good leg. It's an old injury that must have got worse with age. My head whiplashes as he shoves me towards Kershaw. I stagger and stop a metre from him. Olivia yelps and I hold out a hand to silence her.

'Do it now,' says the boss to Kershaw. He steps behind my left shoulder, his bad knee behind mine. 'So I can watch you do it.'

Mariah crosses the patio and pulls both girls behind her.

'What do you think you're doing?' the boss says.

'Look, old man,' says Mariah. 'You ain't doing this in front of my girl. This is not what I signed up for. Now, I've got my hand on your purse strings, which is much the same as him having his finger on that trigger.' She glances up and I realise Kershaw has his gun drawn, arm straight, not a metre from my face. Mariah goes on, 'I don't want to get this close to the action. That's the whole point of me. I'm your "clean skin" and without me, your money's going straight into their hands.' She nods at me. Big thanks, Mariah. 'So, you clean up your mess, but I'm taking my daughter. This is no place for the likes of us.'

Behind my shoulder, the boss smacks his lips. Then he must nod or something because Mariah shoves Dixie towards the side of the house and tows Olivia behind her. As they round the corner, Olivia twists her shoulders to see me and I nod, telling her to go on. When I look back to Kershaw, I see one black eyeball of a gun barrel.

'Do it,' says the boss. He releases my elbow. 'Or is there some reason you don't want to, Kershaw? I had my doubts about you two. Bit too close, lovey-dovey, and now there's this girl. How old is she?'

'Too young to be mine. Get on your knees,' he says to me. 'Kneel now. Knees!'

Alright, alright. I drop to my knees.

The gun is so close I can't get it into focus.

'Stay on your knees. You always were best on your knees.'

'Get on with it, pervert,' says the boss. 'Haven't got all—'

I hook my arm around his good leg so that the knee bends. Instantly, his bad knee collapses under his full weight and he topples. I roll the other way and scramble towards the broken fence. My ears explode. A gunshot. I slip-slide over wooden slats, winded by shock, and crash down behind the wheelie bins in the other garden. It takes a second to realise I'm not hit. Dragging myself onto all fours, I look back to see the boss's head turned awkwardly in the grass, facing my way. A third beady eye weeps in the middle of his forehead. When I get to my feet, ears still ringing from the blast, Kershaw is gone.

Chapter Fifty-Six

7.50 p.m.

A gunshot. Olivia had never heard one before, not in real life, but there was no doubting it. She turned on her heel, pushed past Mariah and ran back the way they came, down the side of the house towards the garden. She staggered as a man barrelled around the corner into her path. Jones barely broke stride but scooped her up by the waist with one arm, knocking the air from her lungs and carrying her unceremoniously back to the street.

'My mum,' Olivia coughed into his shoulder.

'She's coming,' he said. 'We need to move.'

Olivia was dumped on her feet beside the vehicle that had brought them there. The van in which they'd spotted Mariah's lime-green pompom was still there, too, doors gaping. She stepped over and plucked up the keyring, thinking it better to leave no trace. Jones pointed one arm down the road and fired his key fob. The Range Rover flashed in response.

'Get in, if you want to live,' he said to Mariah and Dixie.

But what about her mum?

'You have to go back for her—' Olivia said.

Jones flicked up his chin to direct her attention to the far side of the houses.

Emily was running full pelt in their direction.

Now they scrambled towards his vehicle. Mariah and Dixie piled into the back, Jones gunned the engine and Olivia left a back door open for her mum, while she jumped in the front. The vehicle was already rolling as Emily landed heavily inside, half on top of Dixie, and shouted for them to go before her door even slammed.

The Range Rover roared away.

In her wing mirror, Olivia saw two guards run into the street, stopping with their arms flopping, but neither of them did anything. No weapons raised. They were lost without their boss. One corner and they were out of sight.

Jones wound through the concrete landscape until the vehicle accelerated through a traffic light turning amber. They passed – as though through a looking glass – out of the Hope Estate and into the gracious terrace-lined avenues of the old town. He swung onto a wide road, where he slowed to the speed limit, checking his rear-view mirror until he was apparently content that no one had followed him.

'I can drop you close to school then I need to move.'

'How do I get hold of you?' Olivia asked. 'If I have . . . questions.'

'You don't need me.'

They passed a takeaway and the smell of hot fat made her stomach mewl.

'What if *you* need *me*?' she asked.

He clicked the radio on and music filled the cabin.

'Do you know what I realised today?' he said just loud enough for her to hear.

'That stalking your daughter is a poor lifestyle choice?'

'No— Well, I did realise that I thought I was doing it to protect you, but I've actually been doing it for myself. When I drive by your house—'

'You know where we live?' she said.

He sighed like, *Of course*, but went on. 'What I realised today is that I'd like to have normal things to worry about.'

'The cost of living crisis. Whether your daughter will ever be a homeowner. Climate change.'

'It's better than who's going to get shanked or go to prison.'

'It's not glamorous, you know, a life of crime. Doesn't make you special. Grow up, man-baby.'

He smiled at the telling-off.

The copper roof of her school came into view. Her insides lurched like someone had pulled a rip cord.

'I'm in trouble, aren't I? It's going to come out. What I've done. I'll never be a doctor.'

'Your mum won't let that happen.'

'Can I have your phone number? I won't put it in my phone, I'll remember it.'

'What for? I can't stay here now.'

'But if I get expelled, we can start a family business? Like *Breaking Bad*? I'm good at chemistry.'

'Not funny. I bought my ticket out of here when I pulled that trigger.'

'We're ten minutes from the ferry port. Dump the car, go as a foot passenger. Do you have a passport?'

'Several.'

'Do you have one here?' When he nodded, Olivia grabbed his sleeve. 'Send us a postcard?'

In reply, he glanced at the rear-view mirror to see Emily. She must have been watching them because he gave her a slight smile and turned down the music.

'That was a bit like old times, eh?' he said. 'The thing with the knee . . .'

Olivia scrunched around in her seat to see her mum. She looked the same, but . . .

Her mum shrugged one shoulder. 'Thought it might give me a chance to get away before *someone*' – she wide-eyed at Jones – 'put a bullet in my head.'

'Wait, what? I told *you* about the knee. What did you think all that "kneel, get down on your knees, just kneel on your knees" was about? I'm not the Hot Priest from *Fleabag*.'

'That was supposed to be a message? That I would understand? Just saying "knees" repeatedly until I worked it out? Why didn't you shoot the fucker without me collapsing his knee? He was right there! You made it harder by shooting him when he was falling.'

'I didn't want to shoot you, did I?'

'I was on one side. I could have shot him with a blindfold on.'

Olivia made eye contact with Dixie, who pulled the expression that meant she shipped people. Gross. Olivia faced the front. Literally one minute of their bickering and she was grateful to be the child of a single mother. Thank God Jones would have to go on the run.

Chapter Fifty-Seven

7.55 p.m.

Kershaw stops going on about the boss's knees and turns the music up again. He always did take credit for stuff that wasn't his idea. I let him get away with it out of guilt at being under-cover, but it might have annoyed me if we'd been in the real world. Ah, who am I kidding? I let it go because I was silly for him. I could only walk away because I was taking a part of him with me.

My thoughts are spiralling, hands shaking, I'm in delayed shock. We could have died. Should have died. The OCG world is even darker than when I was under. It's Darwinian – only the ruthless survive to pass on their skills, resulting in a race-to-the-bottom contest to be the hardest, the sickest, the bloodiest. I'm not up to it anymore; my skin has thinned, living up here in the light. And that's why I'll do anything to stop Olivia getting sucked down. Too many kids slip in and get mired. I won't let her sink.

I lean over to Mariah.

'You're in over your head,' I say.

She purses her lips.

'Our girls are children. Incredibly smart children, but they still need us. They've worked so hard. They're full of potential. Full of hope.'

'What are you saying, Emily?'

'I'm saying that whatever our girls have done – whatever we've done – I don't want them to be the ones that suffer. If the school finds out what they did today . . .'

I let the threat hang. Mariah tugs her bottom lip.

'Think of the sacrifices we've made to give them a better life. The scholarships, the bursaries, the homework, the tutoring, support every single day for the last seventeen years. Have we really come this far just for a criminal record to ruin their lives before they've even begun? All because some lowlife got them to drop a few packages off the bus.'

'That was Olivia, not Dixie.'

'But Dixie gave them your number. And the NCA know you're a money launderer. Who are they going to believe?'

'Fuck you.'

'No, Mariah, *fuck you* if you think you can perform this high-wire act without putting Dixie at risk. We've both made bad decisions, our girls have followed suit, but why should we let them take the blame? I remember you saying that life is like Formula One – some people always start in pole position. This school was their chance to get a head start.'

'Fucking true.'

'Well, don't you see? If our girls take the blame for what's happened today, it'll put them back to whatever is the opposite of pole position.'

'Back of the grid.'

'Back of the grid. And they'll never catch up . . . all because of one little mistake.'

Mariah slides around in her seat.

'Why would I trust you?' She chews a craggy fingernail that's been revealed by the fake one that fell off.

'Because we're as bad as each other.'

The music stops abruptly. I wonder if they heard that last comment, but Olivia is too busy giving directions to Kershaw. They have the exact same profile.

'Drop us at Asthma Corner.' She points down a side street that runs along the back of the school's playing field.

'Asthma . . . what?'

'It's where the young kids go to vape,' says Dixie, sitting up from in between us and rubbing her eyes like she just woke up even though we've only been in the car a few minutes. 'Look, there's Dad!'

The Range Rover pulls up and Dixie scrambles over her mum to get out and run to Kash. He's standing on the pavement below the branches of a tree overhanging the cast-iron railings that fence in the school. He holds her to his chest, talking urgently into her ear.

'Is he doing a runner?' I ask Mariah. 'It will only make him look guilty.'

'Exactly,' she says.

Mariah is the fist, Kash is the velvet glove.

He glances over at us. I buzz down the window and call out, 'Did you find the boys?'

'Police had the lane closed. Turned us back.'

At least it kept Jack Kent busy for a while. Kash gives Dixie a kiss on the forehead and then flips up his collar. He sets off around the corner of the railings on foot. We watch him walk away behind iron bars.

Someone's got to take the blame.

I get out of the vehicle, sliding on a rink of rotten leaves. The plan is for the girls to slip in through a gap in the fence, a missing railing, and cross the rugby pitch to the school. As though they'd made their way home on foot. Not sure how else we could explain us arriving together.

I nod at Kershaw. He doffs an imaginary cap.

And that's how we put the matter of us to bed.

Mariah and I set off along the pavement to circumnavigate the school and go in by the – very conspicuous – main entrance. It's cold, the wind has cat claws. For the first time in what feels like hours, I think of the boys, hoping they're somewhere safe.

'Your criminal,' she says. 'He's hot.'

We pass the big white H of a rugby post.

'He's not mine.'

'Still fancies you.'

'Moot point,' I say. But my heart trills like a bird in a cage. We move on. Soon, we approach the dumpsters at the end of the street where I met the journalist. 'So is everything you and Kash own held in his name?' I never managed to get my hands on the Haven Group financial records. That holy grail eluded me. It'll be a treat for the NCA once Haven is forced by the Unexplained Wealth Order to open their account books.

'Kash and I agreed that we can't both go down. Dixie would be on her own. So we made contingencies. Everything is in his name.'

'You're not as daft as you look,' I say.

'Took you long enough to notice.'

'I assume you'll go abroad, just in case. Where you going to go?'

'Leave it out, Emily, like I'm going to tell you. Is that even your real name?'

'I've used it for eighteen years. It's on my passport. I bet Mariah Haven isn't on yours.'

'Too right.' She sounds smug. Pleased with herself. That ignites me again.

'How can you justify yourself? These people, they're the lowest of the low.'

'Have I ever told you about my mum?' She says it in the perky voice that means she's annoyed.

'Never mentioned her. I thought she must have passed?'

'We don't speak. I cut her out of my life. She's why I'm in this mess. Because of her brothers, twins, a good bit younger than her, my uncles. Their dad, my grandad, was a rough drunk. My uncles waited until they were big enough and then kicked the shit out of him until he left them alone. But for all their bluster, my uncles were a chip off the old block and they took advantage of my mum just like their dad had. Bled her dry. She bailed them out of debt and when the loan sharks came back again, she had nothing left to give. They broke her nose, busted her eardrum, put her in A&E. That's how I found out. Of course, it turned out my sister knew all along but did nothing, didn't even come to the hospital. But my uncles still owed money and my mum begged me to help them, said they'd be killed. And by then I was married and the business was doing well so we did one job for this gang . . . But I didn't realise how big they were, a network, like a corporation. I thought the scam would be a one-off, bounce their black money through a renovation to give them legitimate invoices and in return they'd leave my mum alone. I got her out of London, gave her a fresh start, new flat . . . and the gang did leave her alone, but only because they latched onto us. One more job, and another, each one getting bigger. I thought I could bail my mum out, but she ended up sucking us in. And she still serves my fucking uncles a roast every Sunday. Waiting on them like a subservient bitch.'

'Is that why you won't serve the other parents so much as a cup of tea?'

She curls a snarky lip in response.

'You did alright out of the gang,' I say. 'Must have half a dozen houses your mum could stay in.'

'Well, she'll end up on the street if the assets get seized, won't she? Her brothers will soon disappear if she doesn't have anywhere for them to kip.'

What a sob story. My silence is a sympathy void.

She smacks her lips. 'I'll never end up like my mum. The only real insurance is money. And power. I wanted both of those things. And I got them.'

'Don't the gang take advantage of you just like your grandad and your uncles did? You and Kash could have built a legit business, given your mum something to be proud of.'

'Don't fucking talk about my mum!'

'Then don't use her to justify your bullshit,' I say.

'Alright, maybe I'm psycho. Or a basic bitch. Or stuck-up like my uncles say. Maybe I just wanted a nice fucking kitchen and saw a way to get it. We all want to see our kids have a better life than us.'

'You don't better yourself by siphoning money for a drug gang.'

'Don't be pious, *Gemma*. You must have done your fair share when you worked for a gang. Don't tell me you spent two years undercover, got pregnant with the hot criminal and didn't enjoy it? Christ, you had a licence to kill, an excuse to get away with anything.'

'That's not exactly how it was . . .'

'And then going undercover in my house consisted of drinking Bolly while swiping Tinder.'

'I didn't think I was investigating you, Mariah, I thought it was Kash.'

'You thought I was too stupid to know what he was up to?'

'I thought you'd closed your mind to it. All the evidence pointed to him.'

'What evidence?' she asks.

I scoff. 'Can't tell you that, can I?'

'Weren't you scared undercover?' she says.

'All the time. Aren't you scared?'

'Never.' But she speeds up, Lycra scraping. We round the corner and head for the porter's lodge. My phone pings – a text from Akin. I read it.

'The girls are back,' I say.

'Right, we're on. I want the full Gwyneth Paltrow from you. If you're so good at pretending, you do it now. Tears, snot, ugly crying.'

This is it. One more mission until we're finally free.

Chapter Fifty-Eight

8.10 p.m.

As soon as someone spotted the girls crossing the quad, the highbrow hush of Saints was broken.

'We got this,' Olivia muttered.

'Stay on script,' Dixie agreed.

A woman raced up who seemed very pleased. She introduced herself as Detective Sergeant Chantale Slocombe. Temi's dad also appeared, but the police officer swooped the girls out of his way and into a room. Outside, they heard another detective in a long woollen coat saying that Dr Abiola could ask questions once the girls had been checked over. Then Kiran's mum arrived and was loud and scary. Alix's dad was just loud.

Dixie and Olivia sat perfectly still like that bit in *Toy Story* where all the toys have to wait for the humans to leave before they can relax. Detective Slocombe explained that they were trying to locate their mums. Did they need anything? Water? Blankets? A doctor?

Temi's dad was a doctor, but she seemed to want to keep them apart, and that suited Olivia because she didn't know what to say about the missing boys—

The officer's phone pinged.

'Oh, thank God,' she muttered and spun off her chair to leave.

As the door closed behind her, there was a muted cheer outside.

'The boys?' Olivia asked Dixie.

'I reckon.'

Someone brought in hot chocolate, biscuits, blankets that they put around themselves as though they were chilled to the bone. Yes, they'd heard from the boys and they were not hurt. Finally, their mums burst in and put on a show that was so over-acted, Olivia thought they'd blown it, but in the background, she saw one of the porters – the grumpy one – wipe away tears. Even the detective, who looked tough enough to give the boss a run for his money, allowed herself a smile and a nod at her sidekick, who pushed his hands deep into the pockets of his long coat so that it flapped open like a cape.

The girls asked for a minute alone with their mothers and closed the door.

Mum and Mariah plumped down, dropped the smiles and got to business.

'So are we clear? You two are not taking the rap,' said Mariah.

'None of this is your fault,' Emily agreed.

'Just stick to the story,' said Mariah.

Olivia's eyes stung as tears rose.

'But what about the boys? They know what happened. They'll tell the police.'

'There's always a way to get people onside,' Emily said.

'They messed up too,' offered Dixie.

'Kiran attacked the minibus driver with a hockey stick. Temi told us there was a gun when there wasn't. Alix could have called for help but didn't because he wanted to be a hero. Nobody covered themselves in glory. One thing this school teaches us is the importance of reputation. I don't think those boys want universities and future employers to know what they did today.'

'Then that's how we get them on our team,' said Mariah.

'Can we do this?' Olivia asked.

Mariah sniffed. 'People do it all the time. Criminals. Politicians. Undercover police. Tell the story you want them to hear. It's like putting your makeup on in the morning, give yourself the face people want to see.'

'Undercover, it's called a legend,' Emily said. 'Your life is a narrative.'

A few minutes later, a police car swept through the gate and stopped beside the Great Hall. Its blue lights roamed the stone walls. They went outside in time to see the other parents rush the car. Its doors were barely open before they hauled their boys out and grappled them into embraces. It struck Olivia that parenting was a brutal form of love. Three couples – Akin and Temi, Ayesha and Kiran, Jack and Alix – expressed their feelings with a primal dance.

'I need to get them alone,' Olivia whispered.

'Get in there now,' her mum said, 'take control . . .'

Olivia felt herself propelled by a shove in the back. She reached Temi and Alix. They swept her into a mass hug. Even Kiran joined in.

Olivia pulled back and said very loudly, 'Where are our phones? I bet we've got loads of messages.'

The boys' heads popped up. Someone said the bags are outside the Great Hall. They left at a half-run, Olivia checking over her shoulder that Dixie was with them.

As soon as they reached the deserted corridor, Olivia hissed to the boys that they should shut up and listen. They were alone for now, but they didn't have long.

'We need to tell the same story,' Olivia said. 'So that no one gets in trouble.'

'Why can't we just say what really happened?' Kiran. 'It wasn't our fault.'

'Do you want them to know you killed the driver with a hockey stick?'

Kiran narrowed his eyes. 'Are you, like, making us feel guilty so we say what you want?'

'Emotional blackmail,' Alix said. 'But she's right. We need to get our story straight.'

'I wasn't the only one swinging a hockey stick, Kent,' said Kiran.

'That guy crawled out of the barn looking like something from a horror movie. What else was I supposed to do—?'

Temi cleared his throat. 'We all did our bit. I kicked a guy in the face. I had to make sure we were safe, but . . .' His voice collapsed.

'It's alright,' Olivia soothed. 'We set off this morning as a team. Team Saints. And we're still a team. Only the game has changed. We're basically Spartans now. *Hold the line!*'

'That was *Gladiator*,' said Kiran.

'Whatever. Musketeers, one for all and all for one.'

Silence.

'Right?'

Everyone agreed.

Olivia told them exactly what had happened and, crucially, what hadn't.

Chapter Fifty-Nine

8.25 p.m.

The kids file into the Great Hall like a reluctant boyband. We break into a smattering of applause, which has them rolling their eyes. A patrol picked the boys up after they found a house and called the police. Slocombe wants them to answer some basic questions right now. But Ayesha is displeased.

'These *children* are tired and hungry. The emergency is over. It is no longer a fast-time inquiry. If these children are put through any more of an ordeal, I will be having words with the Chief Constable. All that's left is an investigation into the assault on Mr Sadler and it seems clear the two dead men found at the scene were embroiled in inter-gang violence. We will gladly help the police with enquiries – tomorrow.'

'It's up to the police to decide what investigation—' DS Slocombe tries to stand her ground despite the threat about the Chief.

'And while you're getting those ducks into a line, we'll take our children home.' To drive home her point, Ayesha punches her arms into a coat and slings a handbag over her elbow. She may be a Labour MP, but she has Maggie-grade iron in her blood.

The other parents cold-shoulder Slocombe, too, averting their gaze and concentrating on packing up their belongings as though she's a beggar making her way through a train carriage. She'll get nothing off this lot tonight. Which is good for us.

I find myself next to Ayesha, who looks me in the eye but chews her lip.

I let a tempting gap of silence open up.

'I need to tell him,' she says quietly.

'About his father? It sounds like it's the right time.'

'But how?'

I think of Kershaw. A name I hoped Olivia would never hear. I always told myself I couldn't trust him, but maybe I didn't trust myself. Instead, I need to trust my daughter; she's an intelligent girl, wiser than I was at her age. I think of that adage about delivering our kids onto the shore and retreating with the tide, but I don't say it out loud because I don't want to sound like a coffee mug. Instead, I say, 'It's about time they realise adults don't always colour between the lines.'

Ayesha treats me to a rare smile. 'I'm going to have to woman up, aren't I?'

'We both are, they need us, they've seen too much of the world today. Maybe we should form a support group? Or just get a coffee?'

I half expect her to flinch, but she grips my wrist. 'I'd actually like that.' She sounds a little surprised by the notion, but I decide to take it at face value and offer her my number, which she takes and pings me hers. Kiran comes over with his Space-Age bag on his shoulder. Ayesha puts her hand to his forehead.

'You're clammy,' she says. 'Are you feeling okay? Have you got your EpiPen?'

'I need to tell you about something important.' His eyes flick to mine and away. I wonder what he's got to hide. 'Can we go home now and talk?'

Ayesha responds like there are jump leads on her heart, pushing her son ahead of her at arm's length, one hand steering his shoulder. Whatever it is, she'll make it right.

Akin also directs Temi towards the door and they pass close to me. Akin pauses and lets Temi go on ahead. My eyes skitter over his and he inclines his head.

'Shona is frantic,' he says. 'I need to get home.'

'She'll be glad to have you back.'

Temi looks round for his dad, a little shell-shocked.

Akin whispers, 'He's so quiet. It's not like him.'

'They're exhausted,' I say. 'He'll be fine.'

Akin grips my bicep. 'I feel like there's something you're not telling me.'

There's plenty he never told me either. I guess we all present the best version of ourselves. And maybe, if we're allowed to, we live up to it. I won't tell him what I did, what the girls did, what Temi did.

'Let's just take our kids home, Akin, and be grateful for what we've got.'

Akin releases me and leaves.

I glance around the hall. Jack and Alix seem reduced. I hope they'll get past this, rebuild themselves better and stronger. They're alright, really, despite being pricks.

Maunder excuses himself to go to his office and phone the school governors to give them the update. I wonder if they'll be updating him on the status of his employment. If Ayesha has anything to do with it . . .

Singh goes outside to stand down the uniforms, flipping up the collar of his Luther-style coat as he strides away. Living his best life, that one.

Slocombe asks if she can speak to our girls before we leave. Mariah and I share a look that says, *Let's do this.*

Chapter Sixty

8.35 p.m.

DS Chantale Slocombe perched on a fuchsia-pink sofa. Olivia sat on her fingers to hide their shaking. Her mum was out of sight on a seat in the back of the room, but she could feel her presence like an open door.

'When did you first realise something was wrong?' The detective asked.

Olivia explained about a man she thought she recognised in the viewing gallery at the pool. His distinctive Stüssy hoodie.

'You didn't say anything to a teacher?'

'I wasn't sure if it was him or not. And it's kind of embarrassing . . .'

Slocombe nodded as though she had heard this so many times. It was shocking what people, especially people-pleasing young women, will do to avoid awkwardness.

Olivia told her about the BMW with the same lad in the passenger seat and another man – who they would come to call Crowbar – driving.

'Was it this vehicle?' Slocombe held up a photo. Olivia's heart lurched to see it again. The image was from ANPR, the red vehicle captured on a nondescript stretch of road.

Olivia nodded.

'How did you know this man? The one in the hoodie?'

Olivia told her about meeting him at the bus stop outside school.

'What was his name?'

'Cole.'

'That's all you knew?'

'He might have told me his last name but I forgot and didn't like to ask again. He could be weird, oversensitive. Everything I said seemed to come out the wrong way and offend him. He wouldn't have liked it if I'd forgotten his name. So I only know Cole.'

'Some people do that on purpose to make you try harder to please them. It's a form of control.'

'God, yeah, that's so true, that's what he did. Put me on the back foot. Most days he was there after school and he'd talk to me. It was getting a bit much, actually, so one day I came out later than usual, hoping to miss him, but he'd waited for me. Said he was worried how I'd get home safely otherwise. He was getting . . . possessive, you know?'

Slocombe nodded. She did know.

'A couple of times he got on my bus even though that wasn't the bus he needed. I was frightened he was going to follow me home, so I got off a couple of stops along, said I had to meet my mum and got on the next bus instead.'

'To shake him off?'

Olivia gave a tight nod.

'So he was pestering you?' Slocombe asked.

'He was just . . . Boys, you know? They think you're there for their entertainment.'

Slocombe sighed.

'He didn't actually *do* anything, so I didn't tell anyone. I might have mentioned it to Dixie. She's my best friend.'

'Not your mum? The school?' Slocombe pressed.

'I thought he'd given up. Until today at the woods.'

'Back up a bit. What happened at the service station?'

Olivia frowned like she was confused. 'We didn't go to the service station. Not today. We always stop in the same place to buy snacks. It's a ritual we have. But then Kiran Reid lost his jammers, so we—'

'Jammers?'

'Fancy trunks. Olympic swimmers use them. Honestly, Kiran isn't that good, like saving one second isn't going to make all that much difference, but he has all the gear, so . . . They cost about three hundred quid, he left them at the pool and was going into a panic attack over it. Fair enough, I wouldn't want to tell his mum that I'd lost my kit. So, we turned back for them. Mr Sadler is nice like that—Mr Sadler!'

'He's okay,' Slocombe was quick to reassure her. 'He's in hospital.'

Olivia's eyes stung. She let tears fall and it helped, releasing some pressure. She whispered: 'I thought he was dead. He was crumpled in a heap. He looked like something dumped by the side of the road, a pile of bin bags. It was horrible to see him like that. He's a really nice teacher.'

Slocombe squeezed Olivia's fist.

'This was in the woods? Can you tell me what happened there?'

Olivia explained how Dixie had to stop for a bad tummy. Then the BMW pulled up and the two lads went into the trees after her, so Mr Sadler went after them.

'The whole thing was my fault, revenge because I rejected Cole, and I feel so guilty . . .'

Olivia was crying in earnest, fat drops like summer rain falling on her cold hands, and it almost felt true, what she'd said, about Cole being a sex pest as well as a corner boy. Her voice wavered as she soldiered on, describing how they left the woods and reached the Portakabin.

'And Dixie was there. They locked us inside with her and' – Olivia pulled her sleeve over her hand and wiped her eyes definitively – 'that was the last we saw of them, Cole and the one we called Crowbar.'

Behind her, Olivia heard the shushing sound of her mother recrossing her legs.

Slocombe had to lift herself up with both hands in order to sit further back because she'd slid to the edge of the sofa. She looked over the few notes she'd taken. Took her time to gather her thoughts.

'They put you in the Portakabin and left you there?'

'They locked the door,' Olivia repeated.

'And what did you do?'

'Freaked out. I was convinced they'd assaulted Dixie, you know, and that's why she was being so quiet.'

'Did they assault her? That would have been the one you called Crowbar, who also attacked Mr Sadler?'

'Dixie said not. But she was kind of spaced.'

'Spaced, how?'

'Shocked. Shut down. Didn't want to talk. And she *always* talks. The boys were set on escaping. They tried to smash the window and Temi found a hatch in the crawl space. And then we heard shouting outside so we shut up to listen. But it was too far away to hear what they said. And then the minibus drove off and it all went quiet.'

'Did the minibus drive away before or after it got dark?'

363

A hot hand of panic around her throat. Like forgetting her lines on stage. They hadn't rehearsed this part of the script. She had to improvise . . . 'Under those big trees, it felt dark even when it was light, you know? It was so cold too. Like the sun never reaches that place. Even in the office, we were freezing, so we huddled down under a piece of carpet. And after they drove off in the minibus, Temi got the hatch open and we climbed out and just ran for our lives. We got split up and lost the boys, so we walked over a field to the road and a car happened to pass, so we got a lift and— Here we are.'

Slocombe made notes.

'What about the car you got into?'

'Didn't really see it. It came along the lane with its headlights bright, blinding us. But it stopped and we got in. I said we were lost and needed to go to town and he drove off. Hardly spoke. I felt panicky then, paranoid, I thought maybe he was with *them*. But he turned onto the main road towards town so we kept quiet. Dixie was shaking, holding my hand. When we got out, he just drove off.'

'I'm surprised this man didn't put two and two together and realise you were the missing kids.'

Olivia shrugged. 'He didn't have a radio on. Maybe he didn't know?'

'What kind of car?'

'An old one? It smelled.'

'Of what?'

'Just . . . of man.'

'It was old like a vintage car?'

'No, a family car, what do you call it, a saloon? It could have been any car, we just jumped in, we were so scared.'

Slocombe pressed her lips together for a moment.

'And then you came to school?'

'Not all the way to school. I asked him to stop as soon as I saw a payphone and so he dropped us off, but it was a defibrillator. We realised we weren't far away. It's easy to find your way around town because all the roads go downhill to the sea.'

'That's true,' said Slocombe. 'Do you remember your route?'

'Yes, we walked past terraced houses.'

The police officer sighed. Apart from the Hope Estate, a post-war experiment, it was a town of terraced houses.

Olivia fought the urge to say more, to be teacher's pet, to impress this important woman with detailed knowledge. But details could be her undoing today. The less said the better.

'Anything else?' DS Slocombe asked.

'Only that I'm sorry.'

'For what?'

'For talking to that boy, Cole, and making this happen.'

Slocombe shook her head at the notes in her lap.

'Don't blame yourself. No one else is going to.'

The police officer looked up and nodded.

'Why don't you go home? We can talk again if there are any more questions.'

Olivia got up on wobbly legs. The tears in the back of her nose tasted like that morning's rain, the tick of the clock like the dripping forest trees, the cold creep of air when Slocombe threw open the door like the yew fingers stroking her face. She pulled herself up and felt her knees lock, taking her weight. Her mother fell into step beside her and squeezed her hand as they passed the golden scholarship boards with her name on.

Chapter Sixty-One

8.55 p.m.

Outside, Mariah offers us a lift home. She lowers her voice and speaks in a flat tone that I now realise she uses all the time on Kash, like he's a member of staff.

'We're in this together now, Emily. Or whatever your name is.'

'Are you going to drag Dixie to some non-extradition country?'

Mariah scoffs. 'I'm not going anywhere I can't get a cup of Earl fucking Grey. This is nothing a new passport can't sort out. I have no intention of going dark . . .'

'Are you really going to let Kash take the flak?'

'He wouldn't want Dixie to be motherless.' Mariah leans in. 'You wouldn't want Olivia to be motherless either, would you?'

I stop in my tracks.

Mariah keeps moving. 'Walk, Emily. Make it look normal for Detective Slow Coach.'

I follow her to the car park. She moves like she was born to this. Not this school. Few people are born to that. The rest of us are just privileged imposters. No, Mariah moves like she was born to rule the world. She'd do it one way or another. The absence of any remorse annoys me more than her criminality.

I speed up and grab Olivia's arm, pulling her back to my side. Mariah turns, says my name in her warning voice.

I'm not interested. 'I don't need a lift, my car's outside.'

'The reporters will photograph you.'

'Let them. I've got nothing to hide. We'll see you around.'

I drag Olivia towards the iron gate. It swings open as we approach and then we're on the street. The journalists descend in a pack, a wake of vape-smoke behind them, but we catch a lucky break in the traffic and skip across the road before a line of buses arrives to block us. Olivia stops but I grab her sleeve.

'Come on.'

She crab-walks as she glances over her shoulder at her school. In the brake lights of the buses, the façade of Saints College glows red. The colour of vitality, ripeness and the kind of carpet that this school rolls out before you. I also think of red flags, being caught red-handed and warning signs. A car rolls up, making that inhuman sound of a Tesla. Its window whispers open.

'Take care, Mariah Haven,' I say without breaking stride, without looking at her.

'Take care yourself, Emily Smith. Come and visit.'

'Where you going to be?' Always one more question. Always thinking I can get *more*.

'Somewhere warm. I'll get Dixie to snap Olivia. Don't be a stranger.'

The Tesla slips away.

I let her go. I will let her go. Because we're all the same, aren't we, mothers?

In it together. Doing our level best for our precious kids. Whatever it takes.

Epilogue

15th August

8.00 a.m.

I'm in the kitchen when an alarm sounds. It jolts my body like voltage. The dreaded day has arrived. I swipe my phone screen to silence it. Then take a swig of coffee which I have to hold in my mouth because I can't swallow and have to skip across the newly oiled floor to spit into my pristine sink. Rinse the mess, dry the stainless steel so it doesn't stain, press the damp tea towel to my hot face. Fear is burning me up. But we need to get it done, can't avoid the inevitable.

I go to the hall and persuade my throat to work.

'Olivia!' My voice sounds like someone trod on the cat's toy. 'It's time!'

The front door rattles and that startles me, too, but it's just the mail. A postcard lands on the mat. It can wait. Olivia comes down the stairs in three big jumps and snatches up the post without looking at it. She barrels into the kitchen where we've left her laptop open on the counter. Her urgency is so optimistic it makes me well up. My phone pings a WhatsApp notification from another mum. They must have logged on at lightning speed to see their A-level results, the emails drop at eight o'clock. And you'd only be on the chat this fast if you were smug, crowing. I wish Mariah was around to slate the other parents, in case this is an awful disappointment and I need to let off steam.

But when Olivia taps her keyboard to open the email, and leans in to read the results, I see at once that she's fine. Her shoulder blades melt down her back. She turns and I clutch her small frame to my chest, her face tilted under my chin the way it did when she was a baby and would only sleep like this, and I stroke her hair aside to read the results on the screen over her shoulder. Exactly what she needs for medicine. So that's it, then, she's leaving me.

It's a gut punch.

My congratulation comes out as a sob and she says something about *happy tears* and I don't like to say that these are tears of sheer relief. For mothers, relief trumps happiness every time. Relief that her hard work paid off. That a dream she's had since childhood will come true. That life hasn't disappointed her yet. That she's here and safe and officially innocent. That I didn't fuck her up any more than is forgivable.

She pushes me away and picks up the postcard.

We check the stamp and postmark. Somewhere I'll have to look up later.

The front shows a beach the shape and colour of a croissant. 'What's this?'

We both know. But I need a beat.

Olivia turns it over.

Miss Smith,
What's up, doc?
Good luck with the results today.
Jones
PS Do you like snorkelling?

How did he manage to get it here on exactly the right day? Show-off.

I select a magnet and pop the card next to the others on the new American-style fridge.

'Did you know sea snakes can't bite?' she says. 'Their mouths are too small.'

'That's reassuring if we're going snorkelling.'

In fairness, she's earned a break. I don't want to remind her that she's eighteen now and can do whatever she wants. Let her consult me as long as she needs me.

'Let's think about it.'

Olivia thunders upstairs to call her friends. I squeeze my eyes and find there's a little more relief left in me. My girl. Ready to fly.

Acknowledgements

First, as always, Lydia and Frank. You slayed at advising on teenage lingo – thanks, rizzlers, you eat. And Mark, you are the goat.

As ever, the Criminals Minds chat is my water-cooler. Pincers up! A special shout-out to Rachael Blok for wading through a first draft of *Guilt Trip*, back when it had the catchy title of 'minibus book'. Plus Louisa Scarr, Kate Simants, Heather Critchlow, Niki Mackay, Fliss Chester, Harriet Tyce and Clare Leslie Hall for helping me come up with a better title than 'minibus book'.

Everyone at Hove Writing Group who read early chapters – cheers, Monday night crew!

I couldn't have written this novel without Graham Bartlett, aka GB Police Advisor. Well, I could have done, but the police would have been in the wrong place doing the wrong thing.

Kelly Smith at Bonnier Books makes crime (writing) painless! Thanks also to Jon Appleton for copy-editing, Jane Donovan for proofreading, Beth Whitelaw in publicity, Sophie Raoufi in marketing and Jake Cook in design.

High fives to my agents Hattie Grünewald and Jordan Lees at The Blair Partnership, the foreign rights team led by Liane-Louise Smith, and the vital payments people, especially Alex Ford – one day, we'll crack Germany. Thanks to Luke Speed for envisioning my book on screen.

Finally, big thanks to you, the reader, for picking up this story when there are so many other fabulous books on your list – this is for you!

Don't miss the ingenious locked-room mystery from
Jo Furniss

THE TRAFFIC IS BLOODY MURDER

DEAD MILE

'A smart new take on the
"locked room" mystery. I loved it!'
T.M. Logan

JO FURNISS

Friday afternoon, and the traffic is bloody murder.

Sergeant Belinda 'Billy' Kidd is driving home from the airport,
jet-lagged and ready to resign from a career that has left her
traumatised. Menopause has robbed her confidence too –
now she's a traffic cop who's afraid to drive. When brake lights
haemorrhage up the motorway, the cars grind to a halt.
Moments later she finds a dead driver in a black sedan.

He has a metal skewer in his neck. But how? The killer can't have left
the scene without being spotted by the dozens of witnesses – so
he must still be there, among them. If the traffic jam stays put,
they're all in danger; if the traffic clears, she'll lose her suspect.
The clock is ticking, but she doesn't know how fast.

Available now

Chapter One

5.00 p.m.

Friday afternoon, and the traffic was bloody murder. Belinda 'Billy' Kidd should have known better than to take the motorway at rush hour. Plus she wasn't feeling tip-top after a long-haul flight from Australia. As a police sergeant – soon to be *former* police sergeant – she was well aware that 'a can of Red Bull and I'll be fine' could lead to 'but I only rested my eyes for a moment' and carnage.

But what choice did she have? There was no welcoming party at Arrivals. No public transport to her village. So here she was in a hire car. Aircon set to Arctic. Black coffee in the centre console. White knuckles on the steering wheel.

It should only take an hour to drive home. One little hour. An easy drive she'd done a million times. A road she'd patrolled back in the day, though it had been upgraded since then to a three-lane 'express' route that clogged up every Friday into a joyless conga, plodding towards the weekend. Billy hovered in the middle lane even though it wasn't moving any faster than the others. She'd like to put the radio on but couldn't bring herself to glance away from the road long enough to work the unfamiliar stereo. The only sound was the drumroll of wheels.

Wheels skidding, tyres bursting—
Stop it, Belinda.

On cue, red crosses lit up the overhead signs. Brake lights haemorrhaged down the carriageway. She rolled to a standstill. The engine put itself to sleep.

Silence revealed her ragged breath.

Over thirty years behind the wheel. Advanced police driver qualifications. One horrible incident. Now this; heart thumping like a windscreen wiper on full pelt.

She'd had a proper panic attack the first time she drove on a freeway in Australia. Her sister told her it's the menopause. Lots of women lose their confidence in mid-life. *Get on the HRT*, Mel said, *you'll be back to your old self, Sergeant Billy Kidd, scourge of scamps and scoundrels and scumbags.* But she didn't drive again on Aussie asphalt. And even now, back on British tarmac, she was at a standstill on a Friday afternoon and thoroughly relieved about it.

How can you be a police officer if you can't drive?

Oh, give it a rest, Belinda.

If someone spoke to her the way she spoke to herself, she'd tell them to stick it up their exhaust pipe.

In the outside lane to her right, a silver fox in a BMW hammered his steering wheel. In the inside lane to her left, two women stared ahead with identical profiles. Mother and grown-up daughter. Thirty years difference made them look like a before-and-after advert. She followed their gaze up the carriageway. Stationary as far as the eye could see.

Billy broke the other-worldly silence by clicking on the radio.

'Scores dead in a series of coordinated attacks—' The presenter's voice sounded both grave and gleeful. 'Following a car bomb explosion outside the train station at 4.30 this afternoon, gunmen opened fire inside the concourse. Transport hubs across the city are being evacuated. Police have barricaded roads leading to and from the city centre, which is effectively locked down—'

The roar of a motorbike engine outside on the carriageway threatened to drown out the news. She cranked up the volume on the radio.

'—and reports are coming in now of a second car bomb. There was an explosion in the Deadwall Tunnel at 5 p.m. precisely. This is looking to be the most deadly incident on British soil since the London bombings on the seventh of July 2005—'

No wonder the motorway was at a standstill. The Deadwall Tunnel was the main route into the city from the east. Billy wasn't sure exactly where they were – there was a high barrier on both sides of the motorway so she couldn't look for landmarks – but the tunnel could only be a mile ahead. She dropped her face into her hands. Outside, a door clunked and Billy's head snapped straight back up.

In her mirrors, she watched drivers emerge from their vehicles to peel sweat-darkened shirts from their backs, make phone calls, turn forlorn circles like lost tourists.